VIRTUES OF WAR

VIRTUES OF WAR

BENNETT R. COLES

TITAN BOOKS

Virtues of War
Print edition ISBN: 9781783294206
Electronic edition ISBN: 9781783294220

Published by Titan Books
A division of Titan Publishing Group Ltd
144 Southwark Street, London SE1 0UP

First Titan Books edition: June 2015
2 4 6 8 10 9 7 5 3 1

Visit our website: www.titanbooks.com

A CIP catalogue record for this title is available from the British Library.

Printed and bound in the United States.

TO MY FATHER

DRAMATIS PERSONAE

Lieutenant Katja Emmes (operations officer of *Rapier*)
Lieutenant Charity Brisebois (navigation officer of *Rapier*, known as "Breeze")
Lieutenant Commander Thomas Kane (commanding officer of *Rapier*)
Sublieutenant Jack Mallory (pilot of a Hawk anti-stealth warfare craft)

RAPIER STRIKE TEAM

Lieutenant Katja Emmes (Alpha-One)
Squad Leader Assad (Alpha-Two)
Trooper Hernandez (Alpha-Three)
Trooper Jackson (Alpha-Four)
Trooper Cohen (Alpha-Five) strike pod pilot

Sergeant Suleiman Chang (Bravo-One)
Squad Leader Lu Chen (Bravo-Two)
Squad Leader McKevitt (Bravo-Three)
Trooper Sakiyama (Bravo-Four)
Trooper Alayan (Bravo-Five) strike pod pilot

KRISTIANSAND CREW MEMBERS

Commander Kristine Avernell (commanding officer)
Lieutenant Sean Duncan (executive officer)
Lieutenant Dan "Stripes" Trifunov (pilot)
Lieutenant Carmen Hathaway (supply officer)
Lieutenant Makatiani (ASW director)

OTHER TERRAN MILITARY PERSONNEL

Captain Eric Chandler (commanding officer of *Normandy*)
Colonel Alexander Korolev (commander of the Levantine
    Regiment)
Commander Cassandra Vici (commander of the Saracen troop)
Saracen platoon commanders   Lieutenant Scott Lahko
                                Sublieutenant Wei Hu
                                Lieutenant Serge Wicki
                                Lieutenant Sven Pletsers
                                First Lieutenant Gopal Sung
Warrant Ali al-Jamil (Astral Intelligence)
Sergeant Rao (Saracens, Fifth Platoon)

GLOSSARY

AAR	anti-armor robot
AAW	anti-attack warfare
AF	Astral Force
AG	artificial gravity
APR	anti-personnel robot
ASW	anti-stealth warfare
AVW	anti-vessel warfare
CO	commanding officer (or captain)
DR	dead reckoning
EF	expeditionary force
EF 15	Expeditionary Force 15
EM	electromagnetic
FAC	fast-attack craft
NavO	navigating officer (or navigator)
OOW	officer of the watch
OpsO	operations officer
SOA	speed of advance
SF	special forces
SupplyO	supply officer
TLA	three-letter abbreviation
UNREP	underway replenishment
VOI	vessel of interest
XO	executive officer

OFFICER TRADES

Line officer in charge of the general operations of the Astral Force warships, this trade is exclusive to the Fleet

Strike officer commanding AF ground operations, this trade is exclusive to the Corps

Pilot officer operators of the Astral Force small craft, this trade exists in both Fleet and Corps depending on the craft being piloted

Support officer divided into three distinct sub-trades—Supply, Engineering and Intelligence—this trade fulfills the Astral Force non-combat roles for both Fleet and Corps

EXTRA-DIMENSIONAL

Brane a region of spacetime which consists of three spatial dimensions and one time dimension; humans exist in one of several known branes

Bulk an area of spacetime which consists of four spatial dimensions and one time dimension

Ctholian Deep a region of the Bulk more than 16 peets away from the brane in which humans exist

Peet the unit of measurement to describe how far into the fourth dimension something is, in relation to the brane in which humans exist

Tenebral implosion a specific effect inside the Ctholian Deep

Weakbrane another three-dimensional region of spacetime displaced from humans within the Bulk

SHIPBOARD

Aft	toward the back of the ship
Bow	front of the ship
Bridge	the command center of the ship
Bulkhead	wall
Deck	floor
Deckhead	ceiling
Forward	toward the front of the ship
Flats	corridor
Frame	an air-tight bulkhead which divides one section of the ship from another
Galley	kitchen
Hatch	a permanent access point built into a deck (as opposed to a door which is built into a bulkhead)
Hardpoint	a small mounting on the outer hull which holds a weapon until the weapon is launched
Heads	toilet
Ladder	a steep stairway leading from one deck to another
Main cave	main cafeteria
Passageway	corridor
Port	left
Rack	bed; also a verb meaning to sleep
Starboard	right
Stern	back of the ship
Washplace	sink, shower

1

Size doesn't matter in zero-g. But if in doubt, carry an automatic weapon.

Lieutenant Katja Emmes reached down her armored spacesuit, suddenly wanting the reassurance of the assault rifle tethered to her waist. The suit bulked out her petite frame, but without gravity she glided unencumbered along the hexagonally shaped central passageway.

Most of *Rapier*'s crew were already in position for the strike, hunkered down in their turrets and damage control stations. Katja confirmed that her troopers were ready in the two strike pods and made her way forward for the descent.

Rapier was tiny by Terran warship standards, barely thirty meters from stem to stern. In her short time as a strike leader, however, Katja had come to admire the formidable little craft and her crew. Say what she might about the Fleet in general, the fast-attack crews were well chosen.

Alone in the passageway, Katja paused, suddenly feeling the weight of responsibility on her shoulders. Today was the real thing, not a simulation. She was leading nine troopers into a hot zone with no Corps backup. Once they were on the ground, there was no higher authority to help her—she was all the authority they'd have.

She pulled up her helmet and looked at her reflection in the faceplate. Was that a suitable war face? Would it inspire her troopers and intimidate her enemy? She absently ran a gloved hand through her close-cropped blonde hair and stared into her own dark eyes. There could be no hesitation, no uncertainty. She'd always wanted the chance to prove herself.

This was it.

The six-sided passageway ended at a heavy hatch. Katja hooked one foot into a nearby handhold, turned the lock on the hatch, and swung it open. Dazzling light flooded outward. She closed her eyes and continued blind, releasing her foot, swinging through the opening, and then pulling the hatch shut behind her. As she heard it clamp she opened her eyes slowly and spun around.

The glare streaming through the windows was painfully bright, but her eyes adjusted enough to make out the world of Cerberus, looming huge before her. The white clouds and small blue seas were particularly brilliant, but even the ruddy land masses shone vividly under the scorching glare of Sirius. It was little wonder most of the people who lived under the light of the Dog Star went mad.

Katja strapped into her seat and secured her rifle.

Rapier's bridge was just large enough for two pairs of seats and accompanying control panels. In the lower front pair sat the ship's cox'n, Chief Petty Officer Rishi Tamma, and the navigator, Lieutenant Charity "call me Breeze" Brisebois. All eyes and hands were busy—neither looked back at Katja's arrival.

On her right, *Rapier*'s commanding officer, Lieutenant Commander Thomas Kane, glanced at her with brows raised in query. The military-issue spacesuit he wore was no different from those of the other crew members. Although still young, he possessed the eyes of a man who had experienced much.

"Troopers ready," she said without ceremony.

Thomas nodded, his eyes hard as he stared out at the looming planet. Even after five hundred years of space travel, atmosphere penetration was still a risky maneuver.

In the front row, Chief Tamma keyed his speaker to ship-wide broadcast.

"*Rapier* is go for strike, Captain."

"*Rapier* is go for strike," Thomas repeated on the broadcast. Then, "Pilot, start descent."

"Yes, sir," Tamma replied.

The ship had already completed two orbits, both to reconnoiter the site and to bleed off velocity, and was "hovering" in a near-geosynchronous perch. Lost among the scatter of satellites and orbital dhows, *Rapier*'s presence hadn't yet incurred any interest from the local warlords.

That was about to change.

The looming edge of Cerberus's visible horizon slid out of view to the left as Tamma banked the fast-attack craft into her sharp dive, and the planet's massive, reddish surface filled the bridge windows. Faint shifts in her seat's local artificial gravity field confirmed to Katja that they were descending. Nose down in the still tenuous atmosphere, *Rapier* saved her fuel and let the planet's gravity well do the work.

The first moments of the fall were uneventful, the tapestry of land, lakes, and cloud far below, virtually unchanging. Then the first flickers of super-heated air wisped past *Rapier*'s nose, and Katja felt her harness pressing uncomfortably against her chest.

The pressure increased as an orange cone of gas shrouded the craft's nose. Katja labored to keep her breathing steady, forcing air into her flattened lungs.

It was Thomas who spotted trouble first. "Viper, three-one-five mark zero-four-zero, two hundred-k, archons one-five-zero. Desig Tango-One."

Katja strained to read her 3-D display, picking out the craft off their relative port bow, already one hundred kilometers up and climbing to intercept. *Rapier* was plunging past the two hundred kilometer mark, and was at her most vulnerable. This was not a good place to get caught.

Thomas's voice carried firmly over the roar of re-entry. "Full power dive."

The constriction in Katja's chest immediately eased as *Rapier* accelerated downward. Unease kept her breathing tight, however—they would need to slow down before rendezvousing with the surface. She flicked a glance at Thomas, who appeared unfazed.

"Unknown spacecraft." A scratchy, heavily accented voice, speaking in English, came over the civilian frequency. *"This is*

Cerberan Orbital Authority. Terminate your approach and move to low orbit."

Katja watched the symbol on her display as the warlord patrol ship closed rapidly, highlighted with a red diamond indicating Breeze's weapons-lock.

"Authority!" Thomas screamed into the radio, in his best imitation of panic. "Mayday! Mayday! We're going down! We've lost thruster control—we're trying to air brake! Keep clear! Keep clear!"

Instantly the symbol on Katja's display changed vector as the patrol craft altered course. It was close enough now to have a visual on *Rapier*, streaking through the sky like a meteor. Most likely the Cerberans were saying prayers already for this doomed interloper.

It was a brilliant maneuver.

At sixty kilometers altitude, Thomas ordered the engines reversed. It was like deploying a parachute, and *Rapier* shuddered with the strain of deceleration. Katja heard a groan escape her own lips as her vision faded to red. The roar of the atmosphere was drowned out by the screech of the engines. The orange gas on the nose faded, replaced by a larger cone of tortured air that was instantly superheated by the forward exhaust of *Rapier*'s accretion-thrust drive. The entire ship was enshrouded in a massive fireball.

"Ready morningstar, salvo size one," Thomas ordered. "Target surface, dead ahead."

Breeze's fingers fumbled across the weapons console. "Ready!"

Rapier's speed faded fast as the engines countered the ship's suicidal dive, but the orange-hot canopy grew even larger, fueled now by *Rapier*'s own reverse-thrust. To the eyes on the patrol craft, she still appeared to be plummeting to her doom. Detailed tracking analysis would reveal her speed as well below safe atmospheric levels—but it was doubtful the Cerberans were paying such close attention.

Katja's system still showed the patrol craft loitering more than a hundred kilometers from the surface.

"Stand by to fire," Thomas ordered. "And stand by to cut engines on my mark."

Rapier dropped through thirty kilometers. Twenty… Ten…

"Mark!"

Katja lurched in her seat as the engines died. The flare of superheated air faded instantly, to be replaced by a dazzling sunburst that rocketed ahead from the starboard wing. The morningstar missile took its name from the fiery nature of its fusion makeup, and for a few shining moments it burned as a second sun in the Cerberan sky.

Rapier rolled into inverted flight as the morningstar struck the surface. The explosion tore out a small chunk of the planet and hurled it into the sky in an impressive cloud of smoke and debris. Katja, looking "up" through the bridge windows, watched the explosion with no small amount of professional respect.

Another glance at her 3-D display confirmed that the ruse had fooled the Cerberan craft, which continued its patrol high above.

The ruddy landscape seemed to close in over their heads as *Rapier* descended. The inverted flight plan allowed the bridge crew a good visual appreciation of the terrain. Tamma maintained the hypersonic flight path with the ground almost close enough to touch.

Thomas keyed commands into the console between their seats, and brought up a real-time image of the strike site. Katja peered intently at the cluster of buildings and the long, low greenhouses that stretched away in all directions. It was a large farming complex, remarkably industrialized for this part of Cerberus. The Doppler-shift of the image reduced clarity, but nothing seemed out of the ordinary.

The site certainly wasn't expecting visitors.

"Commencing circle," Tamma said.

Rapier banked into a long, circular path around the site, maintaining five kilometers distance.

"No comms traffic," Breeze reported. "No fire-control radars."

Katja nodded.

Thomas keyed the ship's intercom. "Prepare for insertion."

At his order, Tamma flipped *Rapier* into an upright bank, maintaining her circular path.

Katja unstrapped and clambered out of her seat. As she retrieved her rifle, Thomas put a firm, gloved hand on her wrist.

"Good luck."

Flushed with adrenaline, she nodded curtly and made for the hatch.

Rapier's main passageway was hexagonal for strength. And thanks to its configuration, Katja was able to walk swiftly down one of the angled bulkheads, despite the banking maneuver. The interior was dim after the brilliant sunlight of the cockpit, but she moved confidently through the shadows and quickly reached the port-side hatch.

It was open, and she climbed into the small strike pod.

Four troopers were strapped into their seats in the pod, armored spacesuits locked down and ready. Katja took a few seconds to visually inspect their gear before settling into the left front seat, next to the pilot. The engine's rumble was barely audible through the ship's frame. Gazing out through the windshield, past the bulk of *Rapier*'s lean, dark fuselage, she saw the broad port wing where the mighty cylinder of the port engine perched impossibly on its tip. As she watched, the red and blue landscape of rural Cerberus flashed silently past.

Looking past the pilot, she peered through the windshield of the starboard strike pod.

"Bravo-One, Alpha-One," she said across the strike team frequency, "confirm status."

In the other pod, Sergeant Suleiman Chang glanced her way and lifted a closed fist. *"Bravo Team ready."*

"Alpha Team ready." She switched to the ship's frequency. "Mother, Alpha-One. Strike team go for insertion."

Thomas's voice was in her ear. *"Mother, roger. Go for insertion."*

A heartbeat later, Katja felt the g-forces as *Rapier* banked hard and accelerated toward the strike site. A digital countdown appeared on the console.

Three... two... one.

The strike pod catapulted clear of *Rapier*'s hull. Katja grunted as she was compressed in her seat. The retro-rockets fired immediately, robbing the pod of both its hypersonic speed and altitude. Tears welled up in her eyes as the deceleration forced her forward against her straps, but through the blur she saw the starboard pod mimicking her maneuver, just a second behind.

Then the pressure eased, and the craft landed with a jarring bump.

Katja slammed the control to swivel her chair around as the pod's doors flew open and disgorged the first three troopers. A second later she was unstrapped and charging behind them.

2

Her helmet's visor damped the glare of Sirius overhead as she ran down the ramp. Dust swirled on the rough ground from the pod's vents bleeding off heat, but Katja easily recognized the off-white buildings of the farm's central square. Residences and workshops, she recalled from the briefing, where most of the people would be at this time of day.

She saw three possible targets even before she reached the ground. Weapon raised automatically, she marched forward.

"Get down!" she commanded. "Get down on the ground!"

The first target—a man in his thirties, deeply tanned and powerfully built—raised his hands and dropped quickly to his knees, hooded eyes frozen in shock. Katja swung her weapon to take in two more targets—a pair of middle-aged women carrying plastic boxes—and repeated her order. They dropped their boxes and dove for the ground. Katja registered their screams, but focused on the snap as the second pod's doors opened.

Four more troopers emerged.

She sidestepped the kneeling man, keeping her rifle trained on him as she scanned the narrow street between the buildings. A glance at her left forearm display confirmed that her troopers were fanning out into a perimeter around the strike pods. There were no other targets visible.

Slowly and deliberately winking her left eye, she brought up infrared in her visor, but it wasn't much use in this heat. A longer left-wink deactivated the sensor. A right-wink brought up quantum-flux, which was more precise but shorter-ranged. It revealed the telltale outlines of organisms huddled in most of the nearby buildings, but nothing that appeared threatening.

There was no time to lose. If their objective was here, he wouldn't be waiting around long enough to be found.

"This is Alpha-One—clear," she said. "Sound off."

The troopers reported clear in sequence. For now, the landing site was secure.

"This is Alpha-One," she said. "Round up."

She approached the kneeling man closest to her, rifle aimed at his chest. "Move there," she ordered, gesturing with her rifle toward the strike pods.

He stared in shock.

She shuffled a step closer, staying beyond his reach and watching for any movement from the two women beyond him. She raised her weapon to point it at his face.

"Get up," she said slowly, "or I blow your head off."

He scrambled to his feet. Katja pointed toward the strike pods, where both pilots were organizing the various locals, having them lay facedown in rows. He nodded, holding up both palms as he stumbled away and dutifully lay down with the others.

The women needed no further convincing. Katja tracked them as they joined their comrades, then scanned the entire square. Within one hundred seconds of touchdown, the landing zone was secure.

"Mother, Alpha-One. Touchdown, ops green. Commencing search."

"Mother, roger."

It was reassuring to have Thomas's voice in her ear, even if he was airborne at a thousand meters and travelling just under twice the speed of sound. *Rapier*, she knew, was circling back to maintain close air cover.

A quick count revealed seventeen detainees, yet there were supposed to be thirty people at the farm. That left thirteen unaccounted for.

"This is Alpha-One. Pair up and commence search." She glanced down at her forearm display to confirm the designation of the building to her right, where quantum-flux revealed at least two targets. "Alpha-One takes building seven."

"Bravo-One takes building two," came the immediate response from Sergeant Chang.

Alpha-Three joined Katja. He was a big trooper named Hernandez, an experienced fast-attack striker whose main job was to make sure the officer didn't get killed.

Building seven was a laboratory. It had no windows on this side and a single door. Katja confirmed her quantum-flux sighting, then hand-signaled to Hernandez.

I see. Two targets. Inside, left, down.

He nodded, watching for her attack instructions.

Buttonhook, I lead, she signaled.

His hand rose slightly, as if to protest, but he thought better of it and nodded. They closed in at the half-crouch, weapons up. Katja kept her quantum-flux on until they were at the door, then deactivated it. Multiple-sensory input could be disorienting in close combat.

She chopped downward with her fist, motioning the attack.

Hernandez reversed his rifle and slammed the butt into the door, blowing the thin plastic wide open. Katja wrapped around the left doorframe and swung her rifle through the room to fix upon two new targets—one man, one woman, stocky, tanned, middle-aged, lab coats—who cowered on their knees in the corner, half-hidden by an observation table. Hernandez was in behind her, covering the rest of the room.

The woman screamed as Katja closed in. Katja raised her rifle to eye level, barrel down to give her a clear line of sight. She wasn't going to be fooled by the appearance of panic.

"Show me your hands!"

The man complied, raising one quivering hand, but the woman gripped his other one and sobbed. Still on the floor, they cowered back as Katja stepped closer.

Doubt struck her. During exercises back home, simulated targets either cooperated or fought immediately. It was hard to tell which way these targets were leaning. She was getting very hot in her suit, and she could sense Hernandez watching from behind.

"Show me your fucking hands!"

The man tried to comply, holding up his free hand higher, but his companion buried her face in his shoulder and gripped even tighter.

Katja activated her comms. "Alpha-One: warning shot."

Her weapon snapped up to point at the wall above their heads. She squeezed the trigger. A single, teardrop-shaped explosive round raced down the electromagnetic rail inside the barrel. The wall exploded in a deafening shower of charred plastic and titanium.

She dropped the barrel back onto target. "Show me your hands. Last warning!"

With some effort, the man pulled his left hand free and held it up. The woman, still huddled against him, revealed her palms.

"Stand up!"

Both of them slid their backs up the buckled wall until they were more or less upright. Katja assessed their eyes, and did a fast inventory of any bulges in their pockets or objects on the ground.

A door hissed open behind her. She snapped into a crouch.

Another man in a lab coat stood in the doorway with a jar of liquid gripped in his hand. His eyes flicked between the two troopers, and she raised her rifle.

He threw the jar and tried to run.

His chest exploded. Blood and shattered bone sprayed through the doorway.

Katja realized then that her finger had depressed the trigger of her rifle. She stared at the carnage, at her first real kill.

She saw a flicker of movement in her peripheral, and smashed the butt of her rifle into the man's face. Her backswing smacked down the woman with a sickening crunch. Both targets collapsed in bloody heaps. Katja winked in quantum-flux and scanned through the walls.

"Quantum clear."

Hernandez was also scanning. "Quantum clear."

She activated comms. "This is Alpha-One. Shots fired, three targets neutralized. No threat. Bravo-One, over."

"*Bravo-One, roger.*"

Katja looked down at her unconscious targets. There was blood everywhere. Her stomach tightened painfully as she fought down the urge to vomit. She forced herself to breathe deeply through her nose. It took a few moments, but her stomach settled and she was able to speak.

"Alpha-Three, DNA-check deceased target."

"Roger."

As Hernandez took a DNA sample of the bloody remains, Katja knelt down and did the same to the unconscious figures, her gloved hands struggling to hold the delicate instrument steady. A prick of skin from each was enough to reveal that neither of these was the individual she sought. Frowning, she quickly searched them for anything of interest.

Hernandez loomed behind her. "It isn't our guy."

"Neither are these two." She stood, and motioned toward the inside door which had revealed the newcomer. "Continue clearing."

It took four minutes to clear the rest of building seven, plus another three to clear building four—the medical clinic. Within ten minutes of touchdown, Katja and her troopers had reassembled at the strike pods. Twenty-seven detainees lay facedown on the ground.

Sergeant Chang and his search partner, Squad Leader McKevitt, had found a teacher and nine children in the school. Chang approached Katja as she surveyed the detainees.

"Including your three, that's everybody, ma'am," he announced. "We're ready to DNA-check."

Katja looked up at her second-in-command. He was tall and heavy-set, with thick, powerful limbs, a flat face and square jaw. Although his eyes were hidden behind his darkened visor, Katja knew that they were peering at her with bright, penetrating intelligence.

"Do the checks—but not on the children."

"Yes, ma'am."

Chang barked instructions and under the cover of pointed rifles, three troopers began moving slowly along the lines of prone detainees. Each DNA check was quick and only briefly painful, and in just over a minute revealed the bad news.

Their target of interest—a Centauri spy who was selling weapons to the Cerberans—wasn't among this crowd. Every

DNA check revealed its subject as a descendant of the original ark ships that had colonized the system, two centuries ago.

Her mind raced as she tried to decide what to do next. Doubt led to frustration, which gnawed at her. She should have anticipated this, and already been thinking ahead.

Chang watched her. "Shall we do the children, too, ma'am?"

"Yes," she replied. "Gently."

She was thankful to Chang for providing her with a moment to think. No one actually thought that the spy was a child, but she needed to consider her options without appearing indecisive.

Intel had suggested where the weapons were hidden, but her main priority was to capture the Centauri agent. There were plenty of buildings to hide in, but with so few troopers it would take hours to search them, and leave too many opportunities for escape. Questioning the locals might provide information, but if these people were actively cooperating with the Centauris, they would lie through their teeth—unless properly motivated.

Pushing aside her uncertainty, she issued her orders.

"Bravo-One, we'll start interrogating the detainees. Alpha-Two team, Bravo-Two team, start searching the greenhouses. Alpha-Three and Bravo-Three team up and give them a hand. Alpha-Two, you coordinate."

The troopers moved to comply. Katja and Chang circled the detainees for a moment, then Katja pointed wordlessly at an older man. According to the briefing Cerberans revered their elders, and she figured this would have maximum impact. Chang grabbed him by the collar, hauled him to his feet, and gripped him tightly.

The man's tanned skin was weathered and his posture stooped. His lean face sagged under a halo of white hair. Blue eyes of surprising brilliance stared up in fear. On Earth, Katja would have guessed him to be over a hundred, but life under Sirius was known to be hard. For all she knew, this wretch might not even be old enough to be her father.

She leaned in close. With her black, armored suit and visored helmet, the only human part of her that was visible was the bottom half of her face. She forced her lips into a smile—an alarming display of humanity in the midst of overwhelming technology.

"You understand me, don't you?"

The man nodded.

"What's your name?"

"Thapa, ma'am."

"Now we're friends," she said. "And friends help each other, don't they Thapa?"

He stared at the ground.

"Don't they, Thapa?"

He nodded.

"There's a person on your farm that we need to talk to. I don't know his or her name, but maybe you do. This person is from a place called Centauria. Do you know who I'm talking about?"

A voice sounded in Katja's ear.

"This is Alpha-Three, suspect, greenhouse four."

Chang answered immediately. *"Bravo-One, roger. Interrogate."*

There was already someone present at the farm beyond what they'd expected. Excitement fluttered in her gut, but outwardly Katja's expression and tone didn't change. She leaned in toward her prisoner.

"Do you know who I'm talking about, Thapa?"

Thapa shook his head.

"I'm disappointed, Thapa," she said. "I thought we were friends."

"This is Alpha-Three, negative suspect." False alarm. *"Continuing search."*

"Bravo-One, roger."

Katja's excitement slid into frustration at the report of the false alarm. Time was short before news of the raid reached the local warlords; she needed to speed this up.

Her armored fist smashed into Thapa's jaw, sending him staggering backward against Chang's bulk. She grabbed the long strands of his hair and turned him so he could see the lines of prone detainees.

"Point at one of these people, Thapa," she instructed him. "Any one will do."

With a hand visibly shaking, Thapa indicated a man three people away.

Katja hefted her rifle, fighting down the inner qualms that threatened her conscience. "Tell me about the person from Centauria, Thapa, or I'll shoot the man you just pointed at."

Thapa swallowed, and spoke with a hoarse voice. "There is no one."

Katja sighed, stirring up anger to gain strength. These people were rebelling against Terran authority, she reminded herself fiercely.

She motioned for Chang to bring Thapa closer. The trooper lifted him like a rag doll and carried him over, slamming him down next to Katja.

She moved in to whisper in his ear. "Don't doubt me. You talk to me about the person from Centauria, or I start killing people." She was close enough to smell his sweat, to feel his terror.

"This is Bravo-Two, suspect greenhouse one."

"Bravo-One, roger. Interrogate."

Katja stepped away from the old man, raising her voice for everyone to hear.

"There's no point in protecting this criminal, Thapa. We will find him sooner or later, with or without your help. So the choice is yours, Thapa. Either you're my friend—" She dropped her rifle to rest its muzzle against the head of the person Thapa had selected. "—or you're this man's executioner."

Muffled sobs squeaked out from various detainees.

Thapa shook his head desperately. "Please, we are simple people. We know nothing!"

She felt the pressure of the trigger, heard the wet explosion at her feet, felt the blood and shards of skull bounce off her armored legs. Heard the screams all around her. Saw Thapa's horror and rage.

"This is Bravo-Two! Target mobile, northbound from greenhouse one, high speed."

"Bravo-One, roger. Prosecute."

The distant zings of weapons firing pierced the air, followed very shortly by the thumps of exploding rounds.

"He's in a damn speeder! Northbound and out of range."

Katja stepped back from the prone locals, mind racing. She glanced down once at the dark, bloody crater where a man's head used to be, and the terrified detainees on all sides.

She had to get out of there—she fought down both tears and nausea. Chasing the moving target offered the perfect excuse.

"All units, Alpha-One: break away, break away."

Chang threw Thapa to the ground and moved to the ramp of his ship. Both pilots retreated into the pods and fired up the engines.

Katja switched freqs.

"Mother, Alpha-One. Target northbound from greenhouse one at high speed, request you prosecute. Strike team breaking away."

"Mother, roger. Tally-ho."

The first of the search teams sprinted into the drop zone just as the black shape of *Rapier* flashed by overhead. Seconds later, the air shook with a deafening sonic boom that rattled walls and toppled chairs. The detainees scrambled to cover their ears and protect their heads. Within moments Katja's Alpha Team was assembled and climbing into the strike pod.

"We'll pick him up," she barked to Chang. "You return to Mother!"

Chang nodded. He stood at the bottom of the ramp, covering the detainees as his last two troopers hustled back from their pursuit.

Katja ran up into the pod and threw herself into her seat. The doors were closed and the ship lifting off even before she'd strapped in and spun her seat forward.

Airborne to clear the rooftops, the strike pod rocketed over the farm. Katja scanned ahead and immediately saw a plume of smoke from the road, not two kilometers distant. *Rapier* was already in her turn to conduct a follow-on attack, if necessary.

"Mother, Alpha-One. Tally-ho. Break engage."

"Mother, break engage."

Rapier eased her turn to swing wide of the target, but Katja's attention was focused on the rising column of smoke that was fast approaching.

"Alpha Team, Alpha-One: standard sweep upon landing."

Seconds later, the strike pod thumped down on the road. Katja flew from her seat and raced down to the ground.

The air speeder was a charred, twisted wreck. A trail of debris was scattered back down the roadway. Katja swept her rifle over fields of red grass, looking for unusual movement, then focused in on the smoking remains of the speeder. Alpha-Two indicated a single immobile target inside the speeder. Katja closed in while the others maintained perimeter.

The man was dead. She wasn't surprised—*Rapier*'s weapons were designed to take out aircraft and ground batteries. But she was disappointed. A dead prisoner offered little in the way of intelligence.

"Alpha-One, Mother. We've detected an emergency transmission from the strike sight. Stand by for pickup in three-zero seconds."

Katja's frown deepened. Her eyes scanned over the broken remains of the speeder's passenger compartment, in the ridiculous hope that perhaps some vital bit of damning evidence might be lying on the seat. Part of her wanted to stay and search, but the local warlords were now alerted, and her team could not be officially sighted on Cerberus.

She pulled out her DNA scanner and reached toward the corpse, even as she gave her order. "Alpha Team, breakaway."

The troopers retreated to the strike pod, Hernandez hanging back to make sure the officer didn't get herself killed. She took the DNA sample from the corpse, and then hurried inside the pod.

They were airborne seconds later, climbing vertically to meet *Rapier* as the fast-attack craft swooped in for pickup. Within moments the strike pod was secure alongside its twin, and *Rapier* was climbing spaceward at inhuman speed.

3

The red landscape of Cerberus tipped as *Rapier* banked hard to port. Thomas Kane gripped both armrests tightly against the strain, watching his display as one of the strike pods maneuvered for pickup. The other was vectoring to the smoking wreck of the Cerberan speeder.

If Breeze had possessed any skill with the weapons, the speeder could have been saved. As it was, they'd be lucky to find anything in that charred mess. He angled the strike camera back toward the central square of the farm, and saw the last of the locals scrambling indoors for cover.

Sure enough, moments later he heard a frantic distress call broadcast from the farm. The game was up.

"Pilot," he ordered, "bring us around to collect the second pod. Prepare for deep space."

"Yes, sir," Chief Tamma said, even as he turned *Rapier* again and throttled back. The black column of smoke on the road ahead came into view, and Thomas could just make out Katja Emmes's strike pod beside it. He activated strike comms.

"Alpha-One, Mother. We've detected an emergency transmission from the strike site. Stand by for pickup in three-zero seconds."

Thomas heard the distant thump astern as the first strike pod docked with his ship. He scanned his 3-D display for any suspicious movement from Cerberan vessels in the atmosphere. High above, the warlord patrol craft they'd previously fooled had altered course and was descending from orbit.

Emmes was still on the ground—what was she waiting for?

"I think we should go back to the farm," Breeze said suddenly. "There's lots of time before any of the warlords respond."

Thomas bit down his sharp retort, reminding himself that she was just an intelligence officer, and had little appreciation for real tactics. He momentarily considered pointing out the patrol craft that was already en route, but knew he didn't have time to waste.

"No," he said simply. He was the captain, and didn't have to explain himself to her.

"Second pod is inbound," Chief Tamma reported.

Thomas looked out through the bridge window and saw a squat form sail over *Rapier*'s hull. Tamma had slowed their flight to a crawl for quick docking, and Thomas cringed at how exposed they were. One shoulder-launched missile hiding in those tall crops, and his ship was finished.

"Set AA weapons to auto," he said, not trusting Breeze to respond quickly enough, and anything coming fast would be an enemy. He checked the 3-D display again. The warlord patrol craft was descending steadily, but was still high enough that it wouldn't be able to properly scan the site yet.

No other activity.

"Both pods secure," Tamma said.

Immediately Thomas tapped in a course that led away from the patrol craft, and pointed them spaceward. He forwarded it to the pilot.

"Steer this course, attack speed."

Rapier lurched upward. Thomas was pressed back in his seat as they accelerated to escape velocity and beyond. Within seconds the pale blue sky began to darken, and the first stars became visible. He tried to watch the 3-D display as *Rapier* rocketed toward the orbital traffic zone, but things were happening too fast for him to track.

"Evasive maneuvers," he ordered.

Tamma was a star fighter pilot by trade, and Thomas trusted that a pilot's instincts would serve them better than his own as they closed on the crowded space.

"*Intruder vessel.*" The voice came from the warlord patrol

craft. *"This is Cerberan Orbital Authority. Stop your ascent and stand by to be boarded."* The patrol craft was ascending quickly, no doubt on full burn as it struggled to escape Cerberus's gravity.

Rapier jinked right as Tamma maneuvered. Thomas saw a glint of metal flash by to port—some unknown Cerberan dhow. The 3-D display was glittering with contacts ahead, vectors pointing in every direction.

"It's getting crowded, sir," Tamma said as he eased them to port and up to keep clear of a hulking merchant tanker.

Thomas didn't reply, watching as the patrol craft labored to catch them. If *Rapier* could just clear the traffic zone, he could get them to real speed and clear the area. If no one could prove that they'd been on Cerberus, nothing could be tracked back to Terra.

The top turret suddenly blazed to life. Tracer rounds shot forward into the blackness. Something exploded ahead.

"AA to manual!" he shouted. "Breeze, get control of your weapons!"

"You told me to put them to auto!" she shouted back.

Rapier lurched again to avoid the cloud of debris sweeping past them. It might have been a ship, a satellite or a cargo pod, but whatever it was it had come too close and too fast for *Rapier*'s self-defense computers.

Thomas cursed inwardly. A trail of wreckage wouldn't help them hide. On his display, he could see the patrol craft entering the orbital zone, slowly gaining on them. Barked orders sounded over the public channel, instructing all craft to steer clear. He watched the vectors begin to change as civilians moved to avoid the patrol craft. Some of them, however, turned directly into *Rapier*'s intended path.

One of the symbols on the outer edge of the orbital zone suddenly flashed, and switched from neutral yellow to hostile red. Thomas stared at the readout—that "neutral" had just activated fire-control radars.

"Viper, three-four-zero mark zero-one-zero," he said, "two thousand-k. Desig Tango-Two." There was another warlord patrol craft waiting for them.

Breeze's missile lock appeared on the target.

Thomas gripped his chair as *Rapier* swerved again, considering his options. It was hard even to maintain tracking on the two hostiles amidst the sea of clutter—and if it was hard for *Rapier*, it would be nearly impossible for the Cerberans.

He looked up through the bridge windows at a mass of civilian craft all within visible range. Several were clearly pointed spacebound. He dropped a waypoint right in the middle of the cluster of contacts.

"On my mark, go emission silent and steer for waypoint zero-one."

"Roger," said Tamma.

Breeze fiddled with her controls. "Roger."

"Mark."

The 3-D display altered color, indicating that the contacts were no longer held live as *Rapier*'s sensors went silent. All vectors were maintained as dead-reckoning from the last information. The star field ahead swung to port as *Rapier* turned toward the waypoint, revealing the fast-approaching muddle of civilian ships.

"Slow ahead both engines," Thomas ordered.

Tamma repeated the order even as he throttled back to something actually approaching a safe speed. Thomas leaned forward, studying the vessels ahead by eye. One of the contacts climbing toward deep space was a tug with a fat barge behind it.

Perfect.

"Pilot, get us in behind that tug and tow, high off the port bow."

"Yes, sir."

Rapier approached the busy space lane and angled up away from Cerberus, easing over toward the plodding tug and barge. Cerberan civilian ships carried only the most rudimentary tracking systems, and *Rapier*'s black hull made her very difficult to spot visually with only the stars as backdrop.

The barge loomed ahead. *Rapier* nudged forward and down, coming alongside at barely a wingspan's distance, and matched velocities. To any Cerberan sensors, she and the barge would show as a single, massive contact.

Thomas sat back, feeling the sweat in his spacesuit.

"Pilot, maintain position on the barge until we're free of the orbital zone, then plot a safe course for a flank speed run."

"Yes, sir."

There was a long moment of silence on the dark bridge.

Breeze turned in her seat.

"So that's it? We're not going back?"

Thomas's reply was cut off by the sound of the hatch opening behind him. In the reflection from the bridge windows he saw Katja Emmes enter. She squeezed her armored bulk into the seat next to him, glanced at the view outside, at the 3-D display, then faced him.

"Strike team secure, sir," she said. "No casualties."

He nodded. "Very good, OpsO."

"No, it *isn't* good!" Breeze protested. "We have to go back."

Thomas could see in her pale features that his OpsO had no interest in going back to Cerberus. And while he had no qualms about continuing the raid, he knew that it was an impossibility.

"Our presence is known to the Cerberans, Lieutenant Brisebois. We can't go back today." He looked straight into her eyes. "This discussion is over."

She glared at him, then at Emmes, then swung back to face forward.

He understood her frustration. This was *Rapier*'s first operational strike since their deployment to Sirius two months earlier, and the first high-profile mission of his command. This six-month deployment might be the only chance he had to prove his abilities as a combat commander.

He couldn't afford to waste opportunities.

The barge and tug were continuing their steady course—ten minutes or more until they cleared the traffic zone. With all sensors at standby, there was no way to track any approaching warlord ships, but the chatter on the civilian radio circuits suggested that the warlords were still clearing traffic out of their way as they climbed to pursue their quarry. It seemed as if his little hiding trick had worked.

He glanced at the tiny image he kept taped to his console. He and Soma stood on the observation deck at Olympus Mons. It had been taken the day after he proposed, and the smiles on both their faces were almost stupidly broad. It had been an exciting, romantic adventure, that trip to Mars, and the perfect, symbolic place for their engagement, sitting between his Earth and her Jupiter.

Well, Ganymede, actually, but Jovians didn't like to distinguish between the moons these days, especially when it came to voting blocks in the Terran Parliament.

He figured he should send her a message—it had been a while. Not while *Rapier* was on patrol, of course, but when they returned to *Normandy*. If nothing else, he needed to confirm the date for the wedding, so he could invite his fellow officers. It was all going to happen pretty fast, when they got home from this deployment.

He sighed. Battle stress, command stress, and now wedding stress. Some days were definitely better than others, and now he had to write a post-mission report that wasn't going to help his career.

"Lieutenant Brisebois," he said suddenly, "do a quick walk-around of the ship. Assess any damage and check with all stations."

She noisily unbuckled from her seat and pushed past him. He ignored her, turning his attention to his other officer.

Katja Emmes had been a last-minute replacement when *Rapier*'s previous OpsO had been sent home for a family emergency. She had joined the ship in-theater, and was still learning all the nuances of being shipborne. But he could see potential in her. She was young and full of intensity, and there were some real smarts behind her butchy façade.

She stared back at him, and let out a long sigh.

"I'm sorry, sir. I made a mistake."

Her open admission caught him off-guard. A part of him admired her honesty. Another part immediately began assessing how much of the blame could be shifted to her. He studied her as he replied.

"First time in the shit is always tough. Things get messy."

She shook her head, frowning deeply. "But it's my job to keep things clean, sir."

He understood her pain. "Katja—"

Her eyes snapped up.

He caught himself. "May I call you Katja?"

"Yes, sir." Traces of amusement welled up from the depths of her eyes, and a smile tugged at her lips.

He felt a tiny smile shape his own lips.

"Katja, I've been on the ground, in the shit. I may be Fleet but I also did four years as a platoon leader in the Corps. On the ground we never have the whole picture, and we're usually dealing with some very immediate threat to our health. We process the info we can, and we act on it. A strike officer never makes mistakes, she makes judgment calls."

Katja pursed her lips. "What if her judgment isn't good?"

"Then she learns. If she isn't dead."

She smiled, and focused on him with the full intensity of her gaze. She was actually quite pretty, he noticed suddenly.

"Thank you, sir. I'll learn from this. I won't let you down again."

He glanced out at the looming tug and barge, and again at the display. "Go check on your team, OpsO. I expect we'll be clear of Cerberus and sprinting for home in the next ten minutes."

"Yes, sir."

She gathered her rifle and pushed aft to exit the bridge. He watched her go, once again thinking about the post-mission report he had to write.

He might ultimately be responsible for everything on his ship, but that didn't mean that one of his subordinates shouldn't share some of that responsibility. She was young, and would have plenty more opportunities to prove herself.

A twinge of guilt gnawed at him, but he pushed down the feeling. He couldn't afford to look bad. She could.

4

Finding an object the size of a boulder in the vastness of space was no easy task.

This, Sublieutenant Jack Mallory concluded as he eased his control stick to the left and moved his little ship into another slow turn, was probably why micro-asteroid mining had never really taken off, despite all the Gaian propaganda over the years. He'd like to see one of those crazies suit up and try to even find—let alone rendezvous with—an actual space rock.

Jack centered his control stick and settled into his new course. Training automatically drew his eyes up to sweep the starry sky, then down to check his flight and hunt controls. Everything was clear. His new course had put Sirius astern of his Hawk, and it was a relief to not have the sun's glare in his eyes. No sign of his quarry yet, but with a bit of luck that was about to change.

"Viking-Two ready for dip," he said over the circuit.

"*Rog, Two, go for dip.*"

The other Hawk, flown by Lieutenant Dan "Stripes" Trifunov, was holding position at the edge of the search sector. Today he was just an observer, though. Jack needed to prove himself if he was to earn his anti-stealth wings. And today his target was a boulder-sized, automatic device that would simulate the movements of an enemy stealth ship. His job was to find it before it could launch a simulated assault.

"Deploying big dipper."

Jack turned his attention to the multidimensional picture that was beginning to form on his hunt controls. Despite its innocuous name, the big dipper was one of the most sophisticated pieces of equipment in the entire Terran arsenal. It had already phased into the Bulk, and was relaying gravimetric information via its brane-straddling relay system. Jack did one last sweep of the controls, then focused in on the hunt.

Anti-stealth warfare hadn't been Jack's first choice in flight school, but once the choice had been imposed upon him, he'd learned to appreciate the wonder of it all. Perched in the three-dimensional brane that made up humankind's perceived existence, Jack could look deep into the Bulk, where gravity ruled and the laws of physics displayed their true nature.

Humanity had known of the Bulk's existence for centuries, but it was only in the last fifty years that men and women had begun to venture forth into it. Stealth ships risked their very existence every time they dove into the Bulk, but since it made them utterly invisible in the normal three dimensions, it made them powerful military weapons.

Terra had been the first to develop such ships, but some of the more advanced and ambitious colonies had been close behind. With the ships had come a whole new arena of warfare—one with which Jack had become fully engaged.

Studying his 3-D readout, Jack identified the knuckles in spacetime that indicated gravity wells. Viking-One was too small to have much of an impact, but because Jack had a recent radar fix he was able to pinpoint the minute knuckle she created. A larger one was moving slowly across the brane on a bearing low off the bow—*Kristiansand*, the Terran destroyer to which both Vikings belonged.

Irregularities down one bearing suggested recent activity at the jump gate back to Terra. The dark energy used to hold open that extra-dimensional portal emitted weak but very specific waves in the Bulk when a ship passed through. A shallow bending to starboard gave evidence of the large terrestrial planet Cerberus, detectable even at this distance, and the entire region was warped slightly by the background gravity wells of both Sirius and its tiny-yet-massive white dwarf companion.

Jack paused the dipper at seven peets—the ideal depth for this particular place in the Bulk. In general, the deeper the probe moved, the clearer the spacetime curvature became, but Jack had to tread carefully. Targets on the brane were best tracked between five or ten peets, but stealth ships could move above or below a second brane in the Bulk—the "weakbrane." By doing so they could mask their movements.

The weakbrane varied in opacity at different locations, and could exist anywhere from eight to thirteen peets. Jack didn't know where his target was resting, and standard procedure was to go shallow at first. Things started to get weird at sixteen peets, and only a very brave, desperate, or foolhardy stealth captain went even close to that far in.

"Dipper steady at seven, confirm that you have my picture."

"Affirm picture. Report."

Jack studied his hunt controls carefully. His Hawk had uplinked its info to Stripes, and the senior pilot was looking at exactly the same information as he was. There would be no blaming the equipment if Jack missed something that Stripes could see.

"Initial sweep is nominal—only contacts are Viking One and Longboat," Jack reported.

Mentioning *Kristiansand*'s call sign suddenly reminded him that the destroyer's anti-stealth team was observing the exercise, as well. He breathed deeply. No pressure.

He studied the curvature lines that traced across his 3-D display, and compared his own intuition to the hunt control info. Nothing obvious leapt out at him. There was a slight irregularity on a bearing low off his starboard quarter—perhaps an indication of stealth ship movement. He tapped in a series of quick commands and a red line stretched away from the center of his display along the bearing in question.

"Viking-Two fishing true one-four mark one-two."

To navigate, all ships worked in a coordinate system based on two imaginary, perpendicular 360-degree circles fixed in space. Jack's bearing line was 140 degrees clockwise in the horizontal by 120 degrees clockwise in the vertical. The coordinate system was anchored to the main star—in this case, Sirius—and gave all spaceships a common frame of reference. It was invaluable to navigation, and just as useful to anti-stealth warfare.

No military term ever survived long without being reduced to a TLA—three-letter abbreviation—and anti-stealth warfare was no exception. Over the last two generations ASW, as it was called in official documentation, had grown from being a curious and confusing peripheral of Fleet doctrine to being the premier arena of space combat. Or at least, Jack thought wryly, that's what the instructors at the ASW school on Pluto had preached.

While no one doubted the deadly effectiveness of stealth ships, the pace of the hunt left most Astral Force members yawning and reaching for coffee. Fleet-wide, ASW was known as "awfully slow warfare," and Jack often wondered if his surprise assignment had been due to his laid-back nature. As he started lowering the big dipper for a sub-weakbrane sweep, he wondered—and not for the first time—whether during his tests he should have adopted the arrogance expected of a fighter pilot.

The dipper was just passing eleven peets when Jack noticed something. He halted the probe and let the picture sharpen.

A shallow but unusually elongated knuckle was warping spacetime along a bearing 09-mark-10. It was moving fast enough for Jack to see the relative bearing as it shifted before his eyes, which meant that it was very close or moving very, very fast.

His eyes darted to his flight controls, then up through the cockpit windows for a visual sighting. Nothing but stars.

"This is Viking-Two. One fast-mover, zero-eight mark one-zero, drawing left. Investigating."

"*Viking-One, rog.*"

Jack shifted in his seat, suddenly interested. Stealth hunting was based entirely on bearings. Distance was impossible to judge if based on one observation only. And while most normal contacts moved slowly enough to enable multiple bearings, this contact was tearing across spacetime.

He locked in the last thirty seconds' worth of readings, then pushed forward both his control stick and throttle. The Hawk shuddered with the sudden acceleration, and Jack grinned. He sprinted forward for twenty seconds, then reversed thrust to kill his speed and stabilize on a new course.

Within moments he was able to re-establish his spacetime picture. The fast-mover was still blazing across his scope, and his computer quickly compared his new readings with those from his previous position. The triangulation was rough at best, but Jack estimated the contact's distance at somewhere between two and three million kilometers.

His eyes went wide.

5

Even before he read the computer's calculation, Jack knew what to expect. His hunt controls confirmed it—the contact was moving at one-tenth the speed of light.

There weren't any natural objects that moved that fast, and very few civilian ones, especially out in this neck of the woods. Jack immediately began comparing the gravimetric signature— allowing for the warping caused by its high speed—to known military contacts. The computer narrowed the search to less than a dozen, and Jack carefully scanned each "spacetime fingerprint."

"This is Viking-Two. Identify fast-mover as one Terran fast-attack craft, *Blade*-class. Speed point-one-c, distance between two and three million. She's going somewhere in a big hurry."

"*Viking-One, affirm—one* Blade *FAC. Longboat and I triangulate to make her distance three million,*" Stripes confirmed. Then he added, "*Not bad, Jack. I'm sure you appreciate us tossing a little bit of reality into today's exercise.*"

Jack grinned. He watched as the fast-attack craft bent spacetime across his display, marveling at its speed. Normally such a small ship would barely register, and certainly not at three million kilometers, but her speed was high enough to affect her mass so that she exhibited the spacetime cross-section of a Martian mining platform.

A new, female voice came onto the circuit. "*This is Longboat. Based on spacetime signature, that FAC is* Rapier. *EM suggests that she stirred up quite a hornet's nest on Cerberus. Longboat silent."*

Jack wondered for a moment what kind of mission *Rapier* had been conducting on Cerberus. He'd only seen pictures of the Fleet's fast-attack craft, but he'd heard that they were wickedly fun to fly. And they snagged some of the coolest missions around, getting into the thick of it while the rest of the Fleet conducted exercises and sovereignty patrols.

He made a mental note to find out how to request a transfer.

"Viking-Two, we still doing ASW here?"

Stripes' voice shook Jack loose from his thoughts. He did a quick sweep of the visual, of his flight controls, and then focused again on his hunt controls—looking for the faint disturbance he'd marked before *Rapier's* sudden appearance. It was gone. Then Jack reminded himself that he had changed his own vantage point considerably since his first bearing line, and he shifted his focus.

Sure enough, the disturbance was still visible down a new relative bearing. He typed in a second line. The red bearing popped into view on his display, intersecting the old bearing from his previous position.

"Viking-Two fishing true one-four mark zero-niner."

He now had two lines on his possible contact, but there was still far too much uncertainty to start drawing conclusions. Despite the claims of the Fleet promotional material, his instruments were only accurate to within fifteen degrees either side of the bearing.

Some contacts, such as attacking gravi-torpedoes—or fast-attack craft on full burn—were easy to pinpoint, but ships in general were too small and too slow to nail down unless they were very close. It would take multiple bearing lines and a whole lot of time to prosecute a stealth contact.

Since he couldn't expect help from Viking-One or Longboat today, he was on his own.

Loaded aft in the Hawk were fifty devices known as barbells. Like the big dipper, these barbells could reach into the Bulk to search for gravimetric readings while still maintaining a link to the brane. Disposable items, Jack could drop them at intervals behind his Hawk and leave them to listen at whatever depth he programmed into them. They could last for days before their batteries finally died, but he only had a limited number of them, so he had to pick carefully where he dropped them.

"This is Viking-Two, I'm going to sow a barbell line to investigate bearing crossover two."

"*Roger.*"

He set off on a course perpendicular to the bearing of interest where his two red lines intersected on his display. He dropped a barbell every two thousand kilometers on a dead-straight run. This cautious approach took thirty agonizing minutes, but as the fifth barbell deployed Jack was able to come hard right and increase speed to separate his own sensors from those of the drones. If he'd calculated right, his five barbells would offer a good radial cross-section of the target.

After a short sprint to remove himself from the barbell line, Jack slowed his Hawk to give the big dipper maximum clarity.

At first, the signals were unclear. His hunt controls gave a separate readout for each drone, and it took time for Jack to interpret the slight fluctuations. He lifted his helmet an inch and ran his fingers through short, sweaty hair, breathing deeply. It took about a minute per barbell, and when he finally looked up at his 3-D display, he sighed in frustration.

The "crossfix" was a mass of red lines, all pointing in vaguely the same direction.

He checked his big dipper, focusing the search down a bearing that went through what best approximated the crossfix of barbell bearings. There was something out there, but whether it was natural or man-made, on the brane or in the Bulk, there just wasn't enough information to tell.

"*Viking-Two, what's your status?*"

Jack seated his helmet properly again and stared out through his windows at the stars beyond.

"This is Viking-Two..." He struggled to think of a suitable report to give, considering he'd probably just wasted an hour of his time.

Then a star blinked.

Jack froze, any words dying in his throat. Something had passed between him and the star. Something had passed *close* enough to actually eclipse a fiery ball of gas bright enough to be visible thousands of light years away. Every space pilot appreciated the inconceivable distances involved in space travel, and every military space pilot knew this one simple rule.

Stars don't blink.

Jack kept his eyes frozen in place, dropped his visor, and tapped the visual lock button on the side of his helmet. A red square appeared on the inside of his visor, marking the bearing and relaying the information to the vessel's computer. He transferred the image to one of the hunt screens, replacing the barbell data.

Then he activated the Hawk's long-range camera and pointed it down the bearing. The live image just showed the usual starry background. He switched to infrared. The picture became even more confused as the residual heat from thousands of suns mixed together in the cosmic background. He started shifting the viewer through the EM spectrum, looking for something that might stand out.

"Uhh, Viking-Two... Say again your status?"

"Viking-One, stand by. I think I've got something."

The view revealed nothing in the ultraviolet. It was only when it reached microwaves that the mystery object emerged. Everywhere in the universe there is a background murmur of microwave radiation—a remnant of the Big Bang visible in all directions. Stars and other celestial objects outshine this backdrop, but only two things actually make the microwaves dim: the coldest of deep space debris, and spaceships trying to hide.

"Uhh, Viking-Two, roger... Jack, we're getting a little low on time here. I suggest you start your search again down a bearing from you of one-seven mark zero-eight."

Ignoring Stripes, Jack recorded the microwave image.

"This is Viking-Two, tally-ho, one viper bearing three-five mark zero-eight. No duff."

"Say again?"

Jack repeated his report of a visual sighting, and forwarded the image to Stripes and *Kristiansand*.

Several moments of silence followed on the circuit, but Jack was already rushing to gather more information on this mysterious ship he had spotted. He had little doubt that it was a ship. Although the microwave silhouette was fuzzy, there was no mistaking the symmetry of form found in man-made objects.

More than likely this man-made object was up to no good, considering how hard it was trying to hide itself. No EM emissions, no artificial gravity, no speed of note. This ship was moving in the brane, but it might as well have been a stealth ship, for its lack of signature. Civilian ships routinely blared across the full EM spectrum, and those with artificial gravity dug huge wells in spacetime. Even military ships maintained an ID beacon during peacetime.

Jack grinned.

Those Gaians could hunt their asteroids all they wanted. He'd just bagged himself a bad guy.

6

It took an hour to ensure that the strike pods were re-powered and serviced, and to confirm that each of her troopers had stowed the gear properly, secured their weapons, and made the appropriate ammo-free declarations.

Katja took direct control of the evolution, carefully inspecting half of the assault rifles before they were locked up. She personally surveyed each pod for damage that might compromise its hull integrity. She even double-checked the emergency supplies.

Eventually, however, there was nothing left to check. Her troopers and their ships were ready for the next strike. Finally, she ordered Chang to get himself cleaned up.

He floated ahead of her in the passageway, the other troopers already dismissed. His broad, dark face was unreadable as usual, but she saw that he was looking at her with an expression she hadn't seen before.

"Ma'am, do you want to do a debrief?"

The very thought made her stomach turn. "Not yet, Sergeant. Give the troopers some time to unwind."

"Yes, ma'am. But do *you* want to do a debrief?"

She suddenly felt like punching him. Her suit was very hot, and she was close to throwing up.

"What the fuck did I just say, Sergeant!"

Chang nodded, but continued to look at her in that odd way. "Yes, ma'am."

She turned herself awkwardly, then pushed off down the passageway to her own cabin.

The door slid open. Breeze was still in her spacesuit, helmet floating within arm's reach. She was just beginning to strip down to her coveralls, and looked up as Katja entered, her face severe.

"Hey, Ops," she said. "Congratulations on avoiding friendly casualties."

If this was Breeze trying to be nice, Katja wasn't in the mood. "Thanks."

She floated past her cabin mate, fiddling with her suit controls. Breeze was squeezing her spacesuit down to fit it back into the warbag clipped to her belt. She seemed to notice Katja's trouble.

"Do you want me to get someone to help you with that?"

Katja waved her away, and tapped again at her controls. Finally, the uncouple command took. With a soft hiss her suit cracked open and she began to worm herself out. Breeze said something while Katja still had her head inside the suit. When she emerged she looked into the hard eyes of her cabin mate.

"Did you say something?"

"Yeah," Breeze said, her glare scathing. "I asked if you had a good interrogation."

Katja felt her temperature rising again. "Not really, no. I don't have any additional intelligence to report."

"I hope not, considering you didn't do anything with the intelligence you had."

"What?"

Breeze crossed her arms, her anger clear.

"I don't appreciate risking my life—or the lives of our field operatives—for a complete waste of time." Before Katja could respond, she continued. "Do you have any idea how much effort it takes to gather intelligence on Cerberus? Do you have any idea how long it took us to find leads like we had today?"

"And I suppose you just expected us to waltz in and find the Centauri sitting at a picnic table cleaning the weapons?" Katja grabbed the edge of the bunk to steady herself, squeezing hard. "If you don't like how we conduct strikes, then pick up a rifle and join us on the ground next time."

Breeze rolled her eyes.

"Any monkey can go down and start shooting up the place," she replied. "We actually had a location for a fucking Centauri agent! And you couldn't be bothered to search the place before you started shooting the locals."

"This isn't training, Breeze," Katja gritted. "Real shit goes down. It gets messy."

"Not as messy as it's going to get for our operatives. They're going to have to go underground, and we'll have to start all over again!" Breeze collected her helmet and attached it to her belt, along with her other warbags.

Nor as messy, Katja knew, as her punching Breeze in the face, either, which was perilously close to happening. The last thing she needed right now was a lecture from a staff weenie.

"Next time," Breeze said, "I'll have to give you more precise orders before you go down."

"I don't work for you." Katja's fists clenched.

Breeze stopped and stared.

"Actually, you do," she said flatly. "I decide our missions based on Astral Intelligence. You carry them out according to my instructions."

Katja felt her cheeks burn. "No. I decide our mission based on your reports. How I carry them out is between me and the captain."

"Listen," Breeze said, "when you've been working this star system as long as I have, we can discuss a sharing of responsibility."

Katja gripped the bunk frame even tighter.

"When you have as much time in rank as I do, we can discuss your attitude."

"Don't confuse your seniority with my authority." Breeze turned and floated toward the door, indicating that the conversation was at an end. "I have to get back on watch."

Then Katja was alone in the cabin.

She looked down at the dark coveralls plastered against her body, and felt a new wave of nausea wash over her. She swallowed hard, pushed into the heads, peeled her clothes off as quickly as she could, and climbed into the narrow wash stall. A hot sponge was ready, as always, and she scrubbed furiously.

A few moments later, she looked down at her pink skin. It was scrubbed raw. Tiny water droplets floated around her in a thin mist. A vision of her target's body, exploding through the doorframe, filled her mind. Then the blood that splashed against her armored leg as she executed that man on the ground.

Her guts contracted in white pain as bile burned up her throat and shot across the wash stall. It splattered against the smooth surface and ricocheted around her head. She hunched down under her hands, pulling her legs up as high as she could. Her stomach heaved again, but she curled tightly into a ball and controlled herself, taking deep, gasping breaths.

She floated in her tight ball for a while, resting. She might have cried, but not consciously. When she uncurled, she saw that the wash stall was filled with puke, and she sighed as she reached for the vacuum. Designed to scoop up any stray water droplets, it worked just as well for bodily fluids.

Taking some deep, calming breaths, she grabbed a fresh sponge and quickly patted herself down again. She toweled off and grabbed a new set of clothes.

It took a few minutes to stow her armored suit so that it would be easily accessible for the next time. This routine activity was soothing and she took her time, putting on some music to help free her mind.

She hooked in at her desk, and randomly picked up the framed image she always carried with her. It had been taken just a few months ago, when the whole family had gathered in Santa Fe for Mom's birthday. Her niece and nephew had probably already changed since then. Her two brothers and her sister looked as they always did, and Mom had looked especially pretty that day.

Father, of course, never changed. Even though he was smiling in the image, Katja could see his dark, penetrating stare. He always looked at her that way, with that same mixture of disgust and curiosity. And, she hoped, some hidden pride.

She wondered what Storm Banner Leader Emmes would think of his daughter's first operational strike on foreign soil. She frowned, because she already knew. He would lecture her again, using one of the many examples from his long career in the Terran Army, on how important it was to think under pressure, and not react on instinct, as she was so prone to do.

She felt a tear well up and quickly brushed it away. No doubt he would side with Breeze, and tell Katja what a fuck-up she was.

She could see her own reflection in the framed glass and almost laughed for having thought that it was a war face. That wasn't the expression of a warrior, she told herself. It was the face of a scared little girl who was in over her head.

She put the photo back and pressed her fists against her forehead, trying to stop the flood of tears that were welling up. Sergeant Chang's expression had probably been his way of hiding the disgust he felt for his new officer—but at least he'd had the courtesy to say nothing. Katja could only imagine what the rest of her troopers thought.

And what did Lieutenant Commander Kane think? Their quick exchange had revealed little of him, other than that he too had more experience as a warrior than she did.

She wiped her eyes. Allowing herself to be weak was not the answer. She hadn't endured so many years of training and hardship just to crumple after her first mission.

Her fists clenched, focusing her anger. Fuck them all.

7

Jack didn't really understand why the line officers were always in such a foul mood. They outnumbered the other officers aboard *Kristiansand*, and had a complete monopoly on the chain of command. Fleet regulations required that everybody had to do what they said.

Nobody ever made movies about support officers—not that Jack blamed them. Supply and engineering really weren't that sexy—and most of the Astral Force recruiting posters featured proud, noble line officers.

Jack just couldn't figure out why they were so grouchy all the time.

As he lay in his rack in Club Sub, enjoying the last few moments of his rest period, he wondered if maybe they all just wished deep down that they were pilots. Everybody knew that pilot officer was the most difficult of the four trades to qualify for. Half the Astral Force were failed pilots, and the other half were wannabe-pilots.

At least that's what he'd heard.

The soft hiss of the door caught his attention, and he heard one of his cabin mates step inside. Glancing at his chronometer, he realized that the morning watch was already over, and if he didn't hurry he'd miss breakfast. Pushing aside his privacy panel, he slid off the rack and stepped down to the deck.

The air in the four-man cabin was stale—Club Sub, where

the sublieutenants bunked down, wasn't known for its high standard of cleanliness—and Jack wrinkled his nose slightly. The lights were still dim from the night routine, but as Jack reached for his washing kit, someone switched on the day lights, and he was blinded.

From behind his shielding hand, he shot a look at the other subbie who had just entered the cabin.

"A little warning, please," he said.

"Oh, sorry, Jack," came the sharp reply, "did I disturb your beauty sleep?" It was Ethan Kubrac.

"No, no. I was getting up anyway. It's just easier on the eyes."

Towel and wash kit in hand, Jack squinted in the harsh light. Ethan had seemed like a really nice guy at the start of the deployment, but like all line officers, he just seemed to get more pissy with each passing day.

Ethan sagged on his feet as he opened his locker, eyes heavy with dark bags. He didn't even look at Jack, and started to go through the motions of slowly stripping off his gear. He looked terrible—Jack couldn't remember seeing anyone look so bad since the mandatory summer of strike officer training he'd done after his first year at the College.

"Ethan, I gotta say—you look like crap."

"Well, try standing a one-in-three watch routine for a few weeks, and see how you look, Jackass." Ethan didn't even look up as he spoke.

Jack frowned. He didn't like that nickname. As he moved past Ethan and toward the heads and washplace, he recalled the expression he'd heard many times. *Line officers eat their young.* The few times he'd seen Ethan or Vijay being grilled on watch certainly backed up the expression.

As he turned on the water and climbed into the shower, Jack wondered if Ethan had come under particularly heavy fire from one of the senior line officers. As he showered and dressed, he thanked God that his aptitude tests hadn't recommended him for the line. Suddenly, being ASW instead of a fighter pilot didn't seem so bad.

* * *

The wardroom was a small but pleasant compartment forward in the ship. It was the social space for *Kristiansand*'s officers, with a conversational grouping of couches flanked by a dining table on one side and a bar on the other.

The bulkheads were dressed up with real wood paneling and both the bar and dining table sported a high polish, but there was only so much that could be done to disguise the fact that this was a spaceship compartment, when the deckhead was open to reveal cabling and piping. The furniture was comfortable but had that indefinable "government" look to it, and the carpet looked to be made from the same indestructible material that was used to coat stellar research probes.

Jack walked up to the galley window and peered in to where the cooks were serving up the last of breakfast. On the far bulkhead of the bright, clean space he could see the long window where the crew were served their food, and just to his left was another window through which the chiefs and petty officers were served.

Considering *Kristiansand* had a total complement of eighty-five souls, it seemed overkill to have three separate social and eating areas. Four, when you considered that the captain always dined by herself. Apparently this practice was steeped in a thousand years of naval tradition, but Jack just didn't see the sense of it.

He waved in a friendly way to catch the attention of one of the cooks.

"Morning, sir," the man said. "Cutting it pretty close, even for you, this morning."

Jack smiled. "I just want to make sure everyone's properly fed before I chow down. You know how much I like to eat."

"That I do. The usual, sir?"

"Yeah, thanks."

Within moments Jack was handed a plate piled high with bacon, sausage, eggs, and French toast dripping in syrup. His stomach grumbled as he took in the blissful aroma and made his way back to the dining table. Most of the officers had already finished, but he still had the supply officer for company.

Lieutenant Carmen Hathaway was one of the nicer people on

board. Despite being a lot older than Jack—he guessed she was probably late thirties—they seemed to have a lot in common, particularly their amusement at the follies of line officers. She had spent most of her career in the Research division of Support, and had apparently been encouraged to cross-train into Logistics to help her career along.

Carmen didn't strike Jack as a woman hell-bent on climbing the Astral ladder, but he admitted privately that maybe when he got to her age he might be hungry for a promotion, too.

She was a very slender woman, with small features and a pale complexion. Her graying, reddish-blonde hair was pulled back into a severe ponytail and her eyes were bright as she glanced up at the chronometer on the bulkhead.

"I think this is a new record, Jack. You know, I'm not going to keep my cooks on the line just to wait for you."

He knew that her words were nothing more than gentle needling. It seemed to be how almost everyone on board spoke to him.

"I have it down to an exact science," he protested. "They'll never have to work an extra second on my behalf."

"I'm more worried that, with the work day starting at 0800 and all, you might not have the chance to properly enjoy your morning feast."

He shrugged. "I don't have a patrol today. Stripes is going up at 1600, but otherwise we're just on standby. Trust me, I've got plenty of time."

The handset on the bulkhead buzzed, and as Carmen reached to answer it Jack tucked into his breakfast. He listened idly even as he shoveled food into his mouth.

"Wardroom, supply officer... And good morning to you." Carmen's eyes turned back to Jack. "Yes, as a matter of fact he's right here." A smile spread across her features. "We'll be right there."

She downed the last of her tea.

"I hope you don't get spacesick with a stomach that full."

He sighed, dropping his utensils to the plate.

"Are they turning off the gravity again?"

"No, but unless your Hawk has been fitted with AG, you're in for quite a few hours of floating."

"What do you mean? I don't have a patrol today."

"Well, we have a little mission for you."

"What? What sort of mission?"

"We'll just have to go to the bridge to find out."

"When?" He took another mouthful.

"Now." She glanced at his plate. "So you better inhale that pile, because I don't want to see wastage."

Jack took a gulp of water and shoveled the remainder of his eggs into his mouth. As he rose to clear his plate he took the sausages in hand, and chewed them down quickly as he followed Carmen into the passageway and forward.

He was still licking his fingers clean as they stepped through the door into *Kristiansand*'s command center.

The bridge never ceased to amaze him. A perfect sphere ten meters in diameter, its entire inner surface was an exact projection of the view of space outside the ship. The crew was stationed on a transparent platform that cut the sphere in half at the equator, their consoles small and dim so as not to impede the overall view. Stepping onto the bridge was like stepping into outer space, and if it was allowed Jack would have loved to spend hours just hanging out here.

He followed Carmen carefully through the dimly lit space, weaving past consoles dedicated to ASW, fighting the odd sensation of the abyss beneath him. The bridge team members were positioned at their consoles in a circular pattern around the central command chair, the personal 3-D displays casting a ghostly light on the intent faces of the operators.

Anti-vessel warfare, or AVW, and anti-attack warfare, AAW, each had their fiefdoms around the rest of the circle, and in the normal watch routine *Kristiansand*'s three warfare directors took the general duty of officer of the watch. The OOW usually sat in one of the two raised chairs at the center of the bridge, where he could tie the visual information on the sphere's surface to the details being supplied by his three warfare teams.

Right now the OOW was Lieutenant Makatiani, who also happened to be the ASW director. He wasn't seated in his chair, and although it was difficult to tell in the darkness, Jack thought he saw the commanding officer and the executive officer on the bridge, as well.

Jack forced himself to not stop at one of the ASW consoles to see how the tracking of his mystery ship was going. He stayed with Carmen as she greeted Makatiani, who greeted her with a nod, then stepped back to let her view the captain and XO.

Jack didn't cross paths with Commander Kristine Avernell very often, but he knew to keep his mouth shut in her presence. She was a short, somewhat plump woman whom Jack had never seen lose her temper, but who carried herself with such an air of unshakeable authority that she never needed to. Her large eyes revealed a keen interest in everything around her, while her weathered face and graying brown hair hinted at years of experience in space.

He reckoned she was even older than his mom, and probably as strict. She was definitely an enigma, but as the master of this vessel a certain mystique seemed appropriate.

Lieutenant Sean Duncan, however, was no mystery at all. The XO was a charismatic figure fifteen years younger than the captain. Ethan had told Jack early in the deployment that Duncan was tipped to get his own ship soon, and was apparently one of the rising stars in the Fleet.

The captain spoke first.

"Morning, SupplyO. Morning, Mr. Mallory. We've had to change our plans a little. This mystery ship is proving tough to track, and I doubt we'd find her again if we broke off to rendezvous with *Normandy*, as scheduled."

Jack was pleased that his mystery ship was such a high priority for *Kristiansand*, although he was a little disappointed that the captain didn't give him credit for finding it.

"SupplyO," Duncan said, "my understanding is that the medical supplies we're delivering to Cerberus are fully contained in four standard, sealed crates."

Carmen nodded. "That's right. It's all medicine, so it packs down well. I'd hoped to get some blankets and bandages from *Normandy*, but that's extra to what was promised to the Cerberan government."

"Four crates will fit into a single Hawk, won't they?"

No one answered for a moment. Then Jack realized that the question had been directed at him. Four crates? He had no idea how big four crates were.

Carmen answered quickly. "Yes, they'll fit. No problem."

Avernell and Duncan exchanged a glance. The captain nodded.

"Mr. Mallory," she said, "we'll be going to launch stations in thirty minutes. You'll fly the supply officer and the XO to *Normandy*. Lieutenant Hathaway will organize the loading of the humanitarian supplies, and the XO will report to EF Command via line-of-sight comms our tactical situation here. Officer of the watch…"

Makatiani responded to her quiet summons immediately. "Ma'am?"

"Inform *Normandy* that we are remaining on station, and that we are sending one of the Hawks to pick up the supplies and to deliver a full tactical report."

"Yes, ma'am."

"XO, stress to Command that if we break our tracking of this contact, it will be lost. Either they have to put another ship on tracking duties, or have someone else deliver the supplies." She revealed the glimmer of a smile. "I recommend someone else deliver the supplies."

Duncan nodded. "Yes, ma'am."

Avernell cast her gaze over them all. "That's all, thank you."

Duncan immediately stepped down from his chair and headed for the door. Carmen gently brushed past Jack and headed after him. Jack stepped away so that he was no longer in the Captain's gaze, and stopped.

What just happened? He had to fly to *Normandy*? In thirty minutes? For a long moment he stood in the darkness of the bridge, idly aware of the quiet activity around him.

"Jack." A firm hand pressed down on his shoulder.

He looked up to see Makatiani next to him. The OOW led him to the nearest 3-D tactical display. It was zoomed out to show the majority of the inner Sirian solar system. He pointed at the display.

"We're here, straddling the Cerberan orbit at Z-plus forty million. *Normandy* is here, inside the Argusan orbit at Z-plus two hundred million."

Jack stared at the display. "That's over a billion kilometers away!"

"And to make it there and back in time for us to make our scheduled delivery to Cerberus, you'll be balls to the wall the entire way. So make sure your reserve tanks are full."

"Yeah…" Jack was having real trouble focusing on what to do next—things were happening fast. "But, I still have to get the Hawk ready."

"Then get your crew going—they know your bird is on standby right now."

"But…"

Makatiani's dark features hardened with impatience. "Jack, are you a qualified pilot or not?"

"Yes!"

"Then do your fucking job, and get your bird ready to fly. I don't have time for this." The OOW turned away abruptly.

Jack left the bridge, mind racing. He wasn't paying attention to where he was walking, but habit steered him straight to the hangar. It was the largest open space in *Kristiansand*, although it looked full right now with both Hawks parked side by side.

The bulkheads were cluttered with a mixture of fire-fighting and mechanical equipment, everything squeezed to the edges of the hangar to make room. The deckhead above supported a network of heavy lifting equipment and the deck was anti-skid to give better grip in case of spills.

One of the birds had panels off as the techs did routine maintenance, and the other was being attended by the ground crew. He approached the crew chief.

"Hey, Chief, I just got word that I have to fly in thirty minutes."

The petty officer nodded, and didn't pause in his slow walk around of the Hawk.

"Yes, sir—bridge just called down. It's actually twenty-two minutes from now. We're topping up your reserve tanks, getting some food loaded for you and your passengers, and starting flash-up. She'll be ready for your checks in ten."

"Great."

The petty officer finished his walk around and turned to face Jack. "Sir, your flight suit is being prepped and will be ready in five. Looks like you'll be gone for at least a day, so I suggest you go and pack a change of clothes."

Jack nodded. He hadn't thought of that. He left the hangar and headed back for Club Sub. Hopefully he could collect up his stuff without disturbing Ethan or Vijay. But he was getting off the ship for a day or so, and going to one of the huge invasion ships. A change of scenery was always nice, and flying there himself made it that much sweeter.

8

Instruments reported otherwise, but Lieutenant Charity Brisebois was sure that *Rapier*'s bridge was colder than the rest of the ship.

Breeze never liked to show weakness, but as she pulled the hatch shut behind her and turned to take in the familiar view, she wished again that she had thought to bring along her combat jacket. She almost hoped they would go to a higher state of alert, because then she could live in her cozy, heated spacesuit.

Katja Emmes was in her usual seat, with the full suite of control panels lit up around her. The other three seats were powered down to standby, and the general darkness gave a good view of the stars outside.

"Evening, Katja."

The OpsO didn't look up from her display. "Evening."

Even though the four stations were identical, interchangeable in their functions, the captain's rule was that each of the four watchkeepers stick to the designated seat. So Breeze pulled herself along the port bulkhead to keep clear of Katja and descend to her own seat. As NavO she had the port seat in the lower, forward row, while as OpsO Katja got the port seat in the upper, aft row.

It was inconvenient and undignified, having to sit practically at Katja's feet during each turnover.

She unclipped her warbags and hooked the belt to the side

of her chair. She flashed up her own control consoles in the full officer of the watch configuration. From standby it only took seconds for Breeze's displays to come on line, and she carefully scanned the 3-D navigation display and the ship systems display.

At a glance, everything appeared normal. As she always did, she looked over her shoulder and smiled. "Ready when you are."

Katja didn't smile back, the fatigue heavy in her eyes. *Rapier* had been out for five days now—her mission had been extended a day by a boarding they'd finished three hours earlier—and by the time they returned to *Normandy* she would be dangerously close to the seven-day max. This limit was imposed by fuel and supply restrictions, but human endurance had to be factored in, as well.

Katja robotically recited the OOW turnover report.

"In position Sirius one-seven-three million, sub-Cerberus one-zero million, bearing true three-four-niner mark four-one. En route to land in *Normandy*, ETA 0900 in fifteen hours.

"Primary contact of interest is Centauri frigate desig suspect one-eight, bearing true zero-four-zero mark one-zero-five," she continued. "She's inbound from the jump gate, destination unknown. We've had no contact with her, but if you use the strike camera you can get a visual. Orders are to observe her, but not interact unless provoked.

"Other contacts of interest include merchant ship one-seven, the *White Star*—" She pointed at the contact on the 3-D display, "—maintaining her course and speed en route to Laika, and *Kristiansand*, who is remaining on station to track her mystery ship. She dispatched one of her Hawks, Viking-Two, about eleven hours ago, and it's due to land in *Normandy* in thirty minutes."

"Lucky bastards," Breeze said. "That was just about our time slot, wasn't it?"

Katja frowned. "Yeah. But I think it was best that we did the boarding—Hawks are a little under-equipped."

"Fair enough."

"No evolutions are scheduled for your watch," Katja continued. "When you read through the messages, take note of *Kristiansand*'s summary of her hunt so far. I think their mystery ship might be connected to what we were looking for on Cerberus. All ship systems are nominal, although fuel, food, and oxygen are all below thirty percent. Our anticipated levels upon return to *Normandy* are all below twenty percent, and the captain has advised Command that we are not capable of doing another unscheduled operation. *Rapier* is on a course of one-niner-eight mark three-one-five, speed five-zero-zero."

Breeze repeated the course and speed back as a formal acknowledgement of the handover. "On a course of one-niner-eight mark three-one-five, speed five-zero-zero, I have the watch."

"NavO has the watch. OpsO has a date with her rack."

Was that a joke? Wow. Katja must be tired. Throughout their entire fast-attack training course together, Breeze had only ever seen her smile when she was punch-drunk with fatigue. Tired people did lots of strange things, but Katja's thing had been to make un-funny jokes. It hadn't endeared her to anyone.

Katja put her console to standby, gathered up her warbags and released from her straps. "I've organized the recordings from our boarding, just in case you want to review them for anything I missed."

The thought hadn't even occurred to Breeze. But considering Katja's record for ignoring important details, it was probably a good idea. "Thanks. I'll skim it tonight and take a more thorough look again tomorrow when my eyes aren't glazing over."

"I'm pretty confident we got everything. At least we didn't pull out early this time."

Breeze refrained from comment. Frustration still gnawed at her regarding the botched Cerberan strike. It would have been her first big bust, and she had been pleased with how well all her research had come together to point at that particular farm on Cerberus. To see it wrecked by a trigger-happy butch who couldn't follow the simplest instructions was almost too much to take.

"Agreed," she said finally.

To be fair, though, it wasn't Katja who had ended the strike early. As *Rapier* circled low for another pass over the farm, the panicked voice of one of the locals sending out a distress call came through loud and clear while the strike team had been chasing down the suspect. Thomas immediately ordered the withdrawal—prematurely, in her opinion. There had still been plenty of time to send the strike pods back to the farm.

She'd read his final report, and had been surprised at how much blame he had placed upon Katja's actions. Not that Breeze disagreed, but she hadn't expected such an obvious example of covering his own ass.

She heard Katja push herself out of her seat and move aft. "Have a good watch."

"Thanks," she said. "Sleep well."

The hatch opened and closed behind her, and she was alone.

It was still a novelty to her, having charge of a Fleet warship. It certainly wasn't something she'd sought out, nor was it something that particularly interested her in the long term.

She had done her stint of line officer training during the year-long selection phase, but that had been more of an introduction to the basics of space travel. Never had one of the cadets been given anything close to real responsibility. The entire summer had been a fire hose of astrophysics and relativistic theory combined with ancient traditions and stratified codes of conduct. It had been preferable to the brutality of strike officer introductory training, but even so it had solidified her decision to go into Intelligence.

And yet, here she was, with charge of a Fleet warship. Alone on the little bridge, with no one at hand but herself to fly the ship, conduct communications and, in an emergency, fire the weapons. It was very different from being a support operative, and even after two months Breeze failed to understand the appeal.

She scanned her displays again. Fuel and oxygen were as low as Katja had reported, and approaching critical levels. If *Normandy* needed another fast-attack mission, she would have to scramble one of *Rapier*'s sister ships, *Sabre* or *Cutlass*.

Yesterday the ship had been en route back to *Normandy* when Breeze had noticed a merchant ship in the space lanes, headed for Laika. The Centauri-flagged *White Star* was in fact on the vessel-of-interest list. When she had reported it, to her dismay, Command had responded with orders for *Rapier* to board the vessel.

Thomas had immediately redirected them along an intercept course, and sixteen hours later the strike team had conducted an unopposed boarding. Four hours of searching had revealed nothing of interest, and *White Star* had been cleared to continue on her way.

An extra twenty-four hours in space and nothing to report. Combined with the fruitless strike against the Cerberan farm, it had rankled her all the more.

Breeze pulled up the message file and read through the Fleet traffic that *Rapier* had received in the eight hours since her last bridge watch. Most of it was routine logistics and intelligence— nothing that concerned *Rapier* directly. She paid closer attention to the report from *Kristiansand*. A civilian ship outside the space lanes, running silent and near-invisible.

Most interesting.

This could be evidence of Centauri meddling in Sirian affairs. After the Sirian Wars—known throughout the Astral Force as the Dog Watch—Terra had issued a decree instructing the colonies to stop selling arms to any of the Sirian factions. And yet, somehow, the warlords still seemed to find a way to rearm, often with Centauri-designed, robotic weapons.

Astral Intelligence had long suspected the Centauri government of weapons running, but evidence was difficult to find. Years of patrolling the space lanes within both Centauria and Sirius hadn't provided any proof of direct involvement, despite a huge increase in commercial shipping between the two systems every year.

Until now. Possibly.

Individual ships were nearly impossible to find in the vastness of space, except for the fact that ninety-nine percent of all civilian craft *wanted* to be easy to locate, and carried standard beacons. A wide range of electromagnetic transmissions helped to pinpoint them, as did energy signatures from propulsion drives. Besides military vessels, the only ships who actively tried to hide in the depths of space were pirates and other criminals.

Breeze tried to keep her mind objective, but a growing excitement welled inside her as she realized that she might just have stumbled across proof of Centauri arms smuggling. Provided the Centauris didn't interfere.

What was that Katja had said about a Centauri warship?

She studied her 3-D display and located the yellow "suspect," called up the standard information on the contact and realized that it was actually going to pass fairly close. Leaning forward in her chair she peered out through the bridge windows, curious if she could see it unaided. There was nothing obvious, but a single bright star caught her eye.

She activated the strike camera and locked it into the coordinates of the Centauri frigate. The camera searched the depths of space for several moments, then centered on a tiny, brilliant point of light. A quick manipulation revealed this particular star to be a sleek, gleaming spaceship. Unlike the dull, charcoal-colored Terran warships, Centauri warships reflected the light of Sirius off their silvery hulls.

Breeze zoomed in as far as her camera allowed, and studied the unfamiliar curves of the foreign frigate. She was suddenly very aware of her ignorance of the Centauri fleet. Terra's oldest and largest colony had ships of varying sizes, and they were referred to generically as cutters, frigates, and battle cruisers.

She recognized this one as a frigate only because the report identified it as one. It was an attractive design, all smooth curves, again quite unlike the imposing, brutish shapes of Terran ships. Even in their instruments of destruction, the Centauris had style.

Breeze remembered seeing the first "Centauri-style" buildings being constructed in Lorient when she was a child, and even though fashions had moved on the Centauri architecture had a timelessness to it that kept the buildings popular. Centauria had long been admired for its harmony with nature.

During her two years in the diplomatic corps, Breeze had met a fair number of Centauris, and despite their government's strange obstinacy against Terran diplomatic initiatives she had considered most of them quite impressive as individuals. Of all the colonies, Centauria was the only one truly competent to sit at a table with Terra as a respected partner—it was their insistence on being treated as a sovereign equal that caused the problems.

Breeze tried to zoom the camera in further, but the magnification was maxed. It was frustrating to be so close to an actual Centauri warship and not be able to get a better look. She recorded a few images, but knew even as she did that they would be practically worthless to Intelligence.

Relaxed in her seat, floating loosely against the straps, she ran her hands down her long braid and glanced idly at the various readouts on her console. There were no evolutions scheduled for her watch, nothing to keep her busy for the next four hours. She thought about reviewing the boarding, as Katja had suggested, but she couldn't muster the enthusiasm.

Her thoughts clouded over with the fact that she had just spent the better part of a week on this crappy little ship, enduring the way-too-intense Katja and condescending Thomas. Risking her life to make the intelligence find of the year, and they were coming home with nothing.

She stared at the fuzzy picture of the Centauri frigate again. It looked like one of the brand-new class, first spotted by Terra only this year. A good close-up look would definitely be of value.

That, at least, would help redeem a crappy week.

She studied *Rapier*'s intended flight path, and realized that if she altered course to port she could significantly reduce the closest point of approach. Maybe bring them close enough to get some good images and an EM signature recording.

The captain's standing orders gave her, as OOW, the freedom to adjust course by fifteen degrees either side of the intended flight path, generally for contact avoidance. She did a quick projection.

That would be enough.

So she took the ship out of autopilot and slipped her hand over the control stick. Ever so gently, so as not to create an obvious acceleration, she turned *Rapier*'s nose to port. The starscape beyond the windows drifted right and the single bright star moved toward the center of her view. Her fifteen-degree limit prevented her from pointing right at it, but it became clearly visible up ahead.

Locking the camera onto the frigate, she began digging through her control screens to figure out how to start recording on *Rapier*'s limited EM sensors. By the time she'd figured out how to capture and record emissions from the frigate, the image in the camera had grown considerably.

She puzzled over the EM sensors for a few minutes, trying to make sense of the readings. At first there were only a few standard emissions—a beacon, an anti-collision radar, a coded transmission. The transmission was a lucky catch—the super-computers in *Normandy* might be able to break it down.

Breeze smiled. This was gold.

Then another emission lit up her sensors. It was strong, and focused in a tight beam. She glanced at the monitor, and was surprised to see the Centauri ship filling the screen. She zoomed out further. Its aspect had shifted again as it got closer.

Flashing on the 3-D display caught her eye. A glance revealed that the Centauri frigate was now on an intercept course with *Rapier*. Peering through the bridge windows, she could clearly see the tiny, bright object shining in the blackness. She looked back at the monitor in time to see a pair of shining orbs separate from the frigate and disappear from the camera's view.

Her stomach knotted in sudden fear. Had that ship just launched something?

Two new objects lit up on the 3-D display, the computer taking several seconds to assess them as suspect.

They were closing on *Rapier* fast.

"Oh, shit."

9

She fumbled for her warbags, tearing open the emergency spacesuit as she unstrapped from her seat. As she floated free in the bridge, she pulled herself into the suit, yanking herself back down as she sealed it around her neck.

Then she grabbed her helmet and keyed the general alarm.

The jarring *bong-bong-bong* sounded throughout the ship for eight seconds, enough time for Breeze to snap her helmet in place and strap into her seat again. Then she hooked her helmet into the ship's broadcast.

"Battle stations! Battle stations!"

The two fast-moving objects were almost upon her. As panic welled up she opened the throttles and pulled hard to starboard on the stick, grimacing as the g-forces pulled her to the left. She reversed her turn and reached for the automatic weapons setting, having lost sight of the attackers.

The bridge door flew open behind her. In the reflection of the windows she saw Thomas diving into his chair, helmet still in his hand. He flashed up his console even as Katja fumbled through the airlock and found her station.

"Report!" The captain's voice was loud, but steady.

She reversed her turn again, straining against the acceleration.

"Centauri frigate bearing zero-four-zero mark one-zero-zero, closing fast. Two missiles launched, inbound."

"Confirm missile launch?"

"Yes."

Breeze felt a faint buzz in her seat. Her console indicated that the tail turret had opened fire. One of the inbound targets disappeared from her 3-D display.

The other veered off dramatically.

Chief Tamma finally reached the bridge, scrambling along the starboard bulkhead to his seat.

"Weapons to manual," Thomas said, strain appearing in his voice.

Tamma flashed up his console and within seconds had taken the conn.

A silvery object sailed past *Rapier*'s bow.

"Target crossing!"

Breeze tried to lock on, designating the top turret to engage.

"Hold fire!" Thomas ordered. "Hold fire!"

Breeze saw the red veto light ignite on her console, as Thomas locked out the weapons.

Katja spoke up. "Centauri frigate one-eight is closing, shining with fire-control radar. They've got us locked up."

Breeze switched her console from OOW to NavO, which gave her clearer access to the weapons. Top turret was still trying to lock onto the small object that was buzzing around *Rapier*. She designated all three remaining morningstars to the frigate. Why were the Centauris being so openly aggressive?

"Break engage!"

The command from Thomas was clear, if incomprehensible. Breeze de-assigned the morningstars and top turret. She felt heavy as Tamma pulled the ship away from the adversary.

"Goddammit, sit tight!" Thomas shouted. "That wasn't a missile—it was a robotic sentry."

A what? Breeze forced air into her constricted lungs. Everything around her had gone wrong so fast that she didn't even know what to think. She barely registered the next thing Thomas said, speaking on the external radio.

"Centauri warship, Centauri warship, this is Terran warship off your port bow. Withdraw your sentry. Withdraw your sentry. Over."

The 3-D display revealed four more small objects moving

around the frigate. The lone sentry near *Rapier* seemed to hesitate in the space between the ships. Finally, a response in a crisp, Centauri accent sounded over the circuit.

"Terran warship, you have conducted a hostile act against my vessel. Over."

Breeze looked back at Thomas, ready to explain that it was the Centauris that had fired first. He didn't meet her eye, instead glaring at his 3-D display. He swore under his breath.

"Centauri warship, there has been a terrible mistake. Your sentry approached my vessel too quickly, and was misidentified as a missile," he said. "We want to de-escalate this situation, and have turned away from you. Withdraw your deployed sentry. Over."

After a moment, the single robot sentry began to move back toward its mother ship.

"Terran warship, I… am also de-escalating." There was a pause, then, *"This incident will be reported to my government. Over."*

Thomas let out a long breath. "Centauri warship, roger. I am steering well clear of you and will continue to monitor this circuit. Terran warship out."

The camera showed the frigate make an obvious gesture of turning away and its vector began to point away from *Rapier*.

Breeze watched it go. She felt her teeth chattering inside her helmet, and she kept her hands firmly on her console.

"Wow," Chief Tamma said finally, "you don't see that every day."

"Sir," Katja said, "all sections report at battle stations. Shall we stay closed up?"

In reply, Thomas activated the ship-wide intercom.

"This is the captain. We have just avoided an incident with a Centauri frigate. Through… diplomacy, the incident was halted before it became actual combat. The danger has passed and we will revert to regular cruising watch. That is all."

Katja followed this with the standard call to secure battle stations and for Bravo Watch—Breeze's watch—to close up. All through the ship, Breeze knew, the crew members were stowing the emergency equipment they had just pulled out, and muttering about getting back to their racks.

Around her on the bridge, no one moved.

She unsealed her helmet and lifted it off, feeling the cool air against her sweaty hair. Chief Tamma and Katja both pretended to study their consoles.

Thomas was looking right at her. "NavO, what happened?"

She took a couple of breaths, fighting down the awful feeling in her gut. She replayed the sequence of events in her mind, recalling that their orders were to observe the frigate, but not interact.

"Sir, I was conducting passive observations of the Centauri ship when I noticed that it was closing us. I... altered fifteen degrees to port to maintain our distance but it changed course again to close. I saw two objects release from its hull and come at us at high speed. I wasn't sure what they were, so I brought the ship to battle stations."

His gaze was unsettling. She couldn't tell how much he believed her.

"Lieutenant Brisebois, all Centauri ships carry robot sentries with them." His slow, careful tone was insulting. But she forced herself to keep quiet and listen. "These are small, unmanned craft with basic sensors and weapons. They act as scouts and as defense—they are not used for attack."

"Well, I couldn't tell what they were!" She felt humiliated, especially with Tamma and Katja watching.

Thomas nodded. "Chalk it up to experience. Centauri missiles have active seekers that'll light up your EM alarms like Christmas. Did you see any alarms like that?"

"There was some alarm. I didn't have time to tell what it was."

"Probably the fire-control radar," Katja offered.

Oh, and now the jar-head is an expert at space combat. Breeze could feel herself getting hot in the spacesuit. "There wasn't time," she said, forcing her tightened lips to form the words.

Katja's smug reaction deserved a smack.

Thomas, however, seemed to relent.

"For the safety of the ship, NavO, you did the right thing... under the circumstances. But I want all three of you to study up on Centauri tactics and equipment. They seem to be sending more and more ships to Sirius, and we'll probably bump shoulders with them again."

"Yes, sir," Katja said immediately.

"Yes, sir," Tamma echoed.

Breeze bit down what she really wanted to say.

"Yes, sir," was what escaped her mouth.

"OpsO, Pilot, that'll be all."

The others took their cue, powered down, and left the bridge. Breeze fumed silently as she waited for the airlock door to close behind them. Arguing with Thomas wasn't the way to go, she knew, and she forced her anger down. This was a moment for deep regret and humility.

"Captain," she said, looking up at him with her eyes wide, "you have to understand—"

"You stupid fuck."

She stopped dead, her apology forgotten. She blinked as she tried to find her voice.

Thomas continued. "Do you have any idea what nearly just happened there? You opened fire on a Centauri fucking warship. We are not at war, Brisebois, but a few more incidents like that, and we will be."

"It was a drone!"

"They don't make that distinction. Do you think we'd just laugh it off if they shot one of our strike pods?"

I'd laugh it off, she thought, *if Katja was on board.*

"No, sir," she said aloud.

"You nearly got us killed, Breeze," he persisted. "And you could have started a war."

She found the idea almost incomprehensible. And as embarrassed as she was, she found herself largely worried about what he would include in his report. She didn't want a black mark against her.

"I understand, sir," she said, shooting for contrite. "I'm very sorry and it won't happen again. I'm happy to arrange recognition testing for myself before every mission, until you're confident in my abilities again."

Thomas sighed, and rubbed his eyes.

"That won't be necessary. Now, for the report, is there any reason why the Centauri ship might have considered *Rapier*'s actions aggressive? Is there anything you did that differed from our flight plan?"

Turning fifteen degrees toward the frigate occurred to her, but she'd already reported that it was the Centauris who had turned first. This wouldn't be a good time to contradict herself.

"No, sir. I was observing passively with the strike camera and the EM sensors. I didn't shine anything at them."

Thomas nodded, obviously deep in thought. He unstrapped from his seat and floated for the airlock.

"Okay, NavO." His voice softened. "Have a good watch. And call me if that Centauri does anything unusual. And if you have any doubts."

She gave him a humble smile.

"Yes, sir."

He disappeared behind the airlock door, and she was alone again.

There was no way anyone could have known whether those were missiles or sentries. She'd acted to protect the ship—no one could fault her for that.

She hooked down her helmet, but decided to stay in her spacesuit. It was cold on this bridge.

Now more than ever.

10

The main hangar was just over three hundred meters long and seventy-five meters wide. It housed one hundred strike fighters, parked in two opposing rows facing outward, their wings folded for storage.

A complete repair facility filled the forward end of the space, and the after end was set aside for visiting ships, as well as the three fast-attack craft maintained under the invasion ship's control. Two of them sat at rest—*Cutlass* and *Sabre*—with a space being readied for the third.

Upon arrival, Jack barely had a chance to glance at the hangar. His attention was focused on the directions of *Normandy*'s ground crew, and making certain he didn't clip one of the fighters with his Hawk's stabilizers as he taxied to his own parking spot.

Now the XO and SupplyO were off making arrangements for the packaging and loading of the humanitarian supplies, and Jack had been given some time to explore the monstrous ship.

Jack's boots thudded softly on the deck as he strolled down the line of fighters, his eyes taking in the sleek, black machines.

The strike fighter was a remarkable piece of engineering, he mused. Designed to be equally at home in the cold depths of space and the hot soup of atmosphere, it carried the smallest fusion drive ever built and a revolutionary camouflage skin that blended with whatever background it encountered. The variable-sweep wings had razor-sharp leading edges and a flexible, trailing membrane that provided maximum aerial maneuverability, but stowed away for high-speed space flight. Two cannons and an assortment of missiles and bombs gave the fighter its teeth.

Jack wandered off the taxiway and strolled alongside one of the fighters. He ran his fingers along the cold, smooth surface of the fuselage, tracing along to the open cockpit. His eyes ran over the stenciled name: *Lt. Lo "Hunger" Pang.*

As lame as the call sign was, Jack couldn't push down his envy. This fighter belonged to that pilot. Jack enjoyed no such pride of ownership for the Hawks he flew. The Hawks were the property of *Kristiansand*, extensions of their mother ship, and had no identity of their own. Stripes had once been a star fighter pilot—hence his call sign—and he would always retain that honor, even though advancing age had forced him to switch to Hawks.

Jack was just Jack, destined to "drive the bus." No doubt the flight school had had a good reason to direct him into ASW, and if he couldn't have faith in the Astral Force's personnel selection, he was in the wrong business.

A short warning klaxon caught his attention, and he looked up toward the ceiling—or deckhead, he reminded himself—of the hangar, high above. A pair of wide panels slid open, revealing a large platform that slowly lowered on its invisible, electromagnetic lifts. Jack watched with interest as a great black bird came into view. The stubby nose tapered back into a long, cylindrical body and wide, delicate wings. A low, round turret sprouted behind the bridge, another hung below the fuselage, and two strike pods nestled organically into the tail end of the craft.

The wingtip engines still glowed from their long run—massive pods that seemed impossibly heavy on the wafer-thin wings. Looking closer, Jack noticed that each wing had a pair of bulges midway between the fuselage and engine pods, and as the platform touched down on the hangar's main deck, he saw that one of the bulges seemed to have experienced a controlled explosion.

Dwarfing the fighters lined up on either side of its path, the fast-attack craft rolled off the platform with a gentle whine of its engines. The startlingly black quality of her outer skin, Jack understood, was a combination of space camouflage and heat-resistance to protect it against super-high-speed drops. As the big plane—*no, small ship*—moved past him, he saw that the entire leading edge of the hull was scorched. The burst bulge on the wing showed clear signs of blast damage. The name and hull number were barely visible in deep red letters on the side of the fuselage.

RAPIER TFA 09

He took an involuntary step back as the throbbing engine passed. There was considerable heat radiating forth, forcing him to shield his face. Then the stern of the ship came into view and the heat faded. Jack took a good look at the strike pods as they hugged *Rapier*'s quarters, and wondered idly how without wings they flew in an atmosphere.

At the very stern of the ship was a spherical pod from which protruded two thin barrels, and Jack realized he was looking at a tail turret.

The fast-attack craft cleared the twin rows of fighters, and pulled in between her two sister ships, *Cutlass* and *Sabre*. With surprising grace, she pivoted around and rolled gently backward into her parking space. The engines hummed for a moment longer, then began to wind down.

Curious to get a closer look at the ship that had caused such a disturbance during his ASW exercise in the Bulk, Jack strolled along the fighter line toward *Rapier*. A ramp lowered from the ship's belly and several crewmembers emerged. As Jack approached they began setting up connections between the ship and the deck.

Reaching up to touch the black skin, he was surprised at how cold it was. Whenever he returned from a surface run in the Hawk his fuselage would be simmering with residual friction. Considering the punishment *Rapier* seemed to have endured, he'd almost expected her to be too hot to touch.

An indistinct announcement sounded inside the ship's hull, and within moments additional crewmembers began trooping down the ramp, carrying bags over their shoulders. Jack saw their tired faces and realized that they must have been gone for days.

Jack's missions rarely lasted more than four hours, including flight time. He couldn't imagine spending days in the Hawk. Intrigued, he stood to the side of the ramp and peered upward into the dark interior.

Three troopers descended in silence, eyeing Jack warily as they passed.

He smiled automatically. "Hey guys. Good mission?"

"Yes, sir."

There was no change in expression, no slackening of pace. He'd heard that troopers could be a bit unfriendly, so he didn't try to further the conversation. Instead he turned to the next blue jumpsuit that came walking down.

And his attention was immediately refocused. The woman had long, wavy brown hair that fell past her shoulders, and brilliant blue eyes that sparked with curiosity when they set upon Jack. Her easy smile made his blood rush, and he felt his own grin broaden. Jack guessed she was probably ten years older than him, but in really good shape for her age.

She reached the deck and turned to face him, looking him almost eye to eye.

"Hi," she said. "Are you the homecoming guard?"

He laughed. "No, I was just admiring your ship and thought I'd come over and say hello." He extended his hand. "Jack Mallory. I'm a pilot."

"Oooh, a pilot—wow…" She took his hand softly in hers, making a show of being impressed. "You like saying that, don't you?"

He felt himself redden, his thoughts tumbling over themselves under her gaze. "Sorry—I'm still getting used to saying it. Umm, I didn't catch your name."

She glanced at the rank on his shoulders. "To you, Subbie, my name's ma'am."

He winced. "Right, sorry, ma'am." Was there any way he could screw this up more?

She suddenly laughed and touched his arm. "I'm just messing with you. Relax, Jack. My name's Charity Brisebois, but everyone calls me Breeze."

She resumed her walk toward the nearest exit from the hangar. Jack kept pace.

"You work on board, ma'am?" He gestured back into the ship.

Breeze rolled her eyes. "Oh, spare me. 'Ma'am' makes me sound like a schoolteacher. Call me Breeze, *please*."

"Sure, Breeze. You'll have to give me a tour one day."

"Of *Rapier*? Why?"

He shrugged. "It looks cool."

She gave him a strange look, but seemed amused.

That was good enough for him. "Any chance we could chat over a drink?"

Her amusement deepened as she suddenly re-appraised him.

"Well, I am starving. Let me get the smell of ship off me and I'll take you somewhere nice. It'll be good to talk to someone who isn't fast-attack qualified."

Jack glanced back at *Rapier* as they exited the hangar.

"Is it stressful on board?" he asked.

"Typical stuff. It doesn't matter how good the intelligence is before a mission—troopers always find a way to screw things up." Her gaze was distant for a moment, but then she smiled and refocused on him. "Day to day, it's like any small unit. When you live in really close quarters, you run out of things to talk about, pretty quick. Don't you get bored hanging out with pilots all the time?"

He considered. "Well, there's only two of us on board. The rest are all line officers."

She smiled. "And we know just how charming they tend to be."

"You're not a line officer?"

"Intelligence," she said. "What do you mean when you say there's only two pilots on board?" She gestured back toward the hangar. "You guys must wear out planes pretty fast."

Jack felt a moment of unexpected regret, then realized that he had been secretly hoping Breeze would think he was a strike fighter pilot.

"No, I'm just visiting from *Kristiansand*," he said. "I fly a Hawk."

"Oh, so you're doing the medical supply run." She seemed to take this information with interest. "Nice."

"How did you know that?"

She smiled playfully. "Intelligence."

They strolled down one of the many broad, reinforced passageways that tunneled through *Normandy*'s bulk. The decks were bustling with activity as the afternoon watchmen came off shift. Jack still hadn't learned all the rank insignia, but he knew that if the coveralls had markings on their sleeves, it was an enlisted rank, and bars on the epaulettes meant officer. In the pilot world ranks didn't mean much—everybody just did their job.

"So, have you been in the Fleet long?" he asked.

"Five years—I joined a little late. I did my subbie tour here in Cerberus as an analyst, and then did a couple of years in the diplomatic corps as a flag lieutenant."

"Wow, that must have been cool."

"Oh, yeah. The cocktail parties sometimes went to four in the morning."

Jack glanced at her, and saw a sparkle in her eyes. "And now you're fast-attack. I thought that was only for the intense. The Fleet guys who wished they were Corps."

"Mostly," she agreed. "But it's also for the Fleet guys who don't want to waste their lives as anonymous staff officers scrambling to try and outdo each other with pettiness. I've seen what old Fleet guys become—bitter, bored, and fat—and I don't want to be that way. Fast-attack is a ticket on the express train."

She fell silent for a moment, her last statement hanging in the air. Jack could hear an edge in her voice which was at odds with her casual demeanor.

They reached officer country. Breeze stopped at a particular door and tapped in her entry code. The door slid open.

"Home sweet home," she said with a smile.

He glanced through the opening, and saw a typical single cabin—oversized, fold-down bunk, comfy chair and bulkhead-mounted entertainment unit, desk with foldout chair and a door that presumably led to the ensuite.

"I think the best thing about getting promoted one day," he said, "will be getting my own cabin."

She entered and tossed her bag on the comfy chair.

"I never would have gone fast-attack if they hadn't provided us proper quarters on the invasion ship. You think your cabin is small? You should see the shoe box I squeeze into on *Rapier*."

"Basically a shelf to sleep in?"

Breeze glanced over her shoulder. "A shelf for *two* of us to sleep in."

The lift of her eyebrow got his attention. "Another charming intelligence officer?"

She laughed. "A butchy Corps officer, actually. We get separate bunks, but I'm sure she wouldn't mind a little snuggle."

"Nice."

Breeze sat down on her bunk and pulled off her boots. "Oh, that feels good."

She slipped off her socks and stood, wriggling her toes on the rug. With her boots off she was short enough to have to look up at Jack, and she did so now with playful eyes.

"Honey, I gotta have a shower. These lieutenant cabins may be big, but they're not that big. And we've just met. How 'bout you head on down to the star lounge and get a drink? I'll be there in about twenty."

"Sure. Take your time."

He stepped back out into the passageway and heard the door shut behind him. Movement drew his attention to the right.

Turning, he saw a compact woman striding down the passageway, a green bag over her shoulder. She had very short, blonde hair and pale skin that made her big, dark brown eyes even more prominent. Her gaze bore through him, her expression not welcoming.

But Jack was riding a wave of confidence, and his smile burst forth unassisted. The bag over her shoulder gave him a cue.

"Hi there," he said. "You from the fast-attack craft?"

She slowed, and looked surprised by his greeting. "I'm Lieutenant Emmes, *Rapier*'s strike officer. Can I help you?"

He thrust out his hand. "I'm Jack Mallory. Can you tell me where the star lounge is?"

She nodded down the passageway. "Two frames up, one deck down."

"Thanks. Hey, I just met your shipmate, Breeze. We were going to rendezvous at the star lounge in about twenty minutes—you want to join us?"

If the woman's expression changed at all, it became even harder. "No thanks."

The glint of gold off her left chest caught his eye. It was the strike officer qualification badge. "You're Astral Corps. That's interesting. Maybe I could ask you a few questions about what you do?"

"Is this how you introduce yourself to everyone?" she asked.

"No, not everyone." He laughed. "At least I didn't tell you I was a pilot right away."

She dropped her gaze with a scornful sniff. "Oh, well, *now* I'm impressed."

She walked off without further comment.

Jack found himself standing alone in the passageway again, a frown on his face. After a moment he started off for the lounge.

11

As soon as the door shut behind her, Katja threw her bag down on the chair as hard as she could. The burst of rage felt good, and some of the tension eased from her stiff body.

Strikes and boardings she could handle. Days fighting space sickness in zero-g she could handle. Even sharing a cabin with Charity Brisebois she could handle. But being chatted up by one of Breeze's little boy toys—

That was too much.

She stood in the middle of her cabin for a long moment, relishing the quiet and the gravity. A few long, slow breaths, and the last of her anger subsided. Kicking off her boots and activating some Mozart, she reached over her desk and accessed the queue of incoming mail flashing on the screen. Mostly routine administration messages from the regiment—she skimmed the subject lines and deleted as appropriate.

There was a personal message from her sister-in-law, and another from her mother, both reminding her that it was her niece's birthday in a couple of days. She made a note to write some suitably auntie-like greeting tomorrow.

The last message in the queue was from an official Corps address, but she smiled at the subject line: *Levantine Jihad*.

It was a colorful note from Lieutenant Scott Lahko, her oldest friend in the regiment. He dispensed the usual hacks about her spending too much time with the Fleet, then invited her to the monthly trooper social gathering, known affectionately as the Jihad. She glanced at her watch and saw that it had already started.

The fatigue that had weighed her down upon leaving *Rapier* suddenly lifted. Having a few drinks with people she understood might be just the thing to relax.

A hot shower helped work out the knots of tension in her shoulders. She lingered a few moments in the steamy water and let the music caress her ears. Every basic space course taught the importance of conserving air and water—and a career in the Corps had drilled the same principles into her—but it didn't take anyone long to figure out that a ship the size of *Normandy* didn't operate under the same rules.

Every ship recycled about ninety-nine percent of its air and water, but that one percent lost was critical when the nearest resupply was several billion kilometers away. In an invasion ship, however, the sheer volume of water and air it carried meant that nearly half could be lost before rationing took effect.

Katja had long since outgrown any sort of heroic notion that military service should always be hard. Like soldiers since the time of Troy, she'd learned very young to grab ahold of good times when they came, because there was no guarantee they'd come again.

Fresh clothes felt soft on her skin, and the green Corps jumpsuit was a welcome change from Fleet blue. When she emerged from her cabin she felt a new skip in her stride, and smiled easily at the people she passed on the way to the star lounge.

She heard the low murmur as soon as she descended the steep staircase the Fleet called a "ladder." Ahead, the wide opening to her destination beckoned.

The star lounge was the largest communal space where officers could socialize. Taking its name from the broad, deck-high windows that offered a magnificent view of the cosmos, it offered a full bar and café at the forward end, an area of comfortable chairs and couches at the other, and an open central area that was used for events as diverse as dances, military parades, and fancy-dress mini-golf tournaments. The lights were dimmed in the bar and café area, but even as her eyes adjusted Katja could easily make out the group she sought.

The Levantine Regiment was *Normandy*'s reason for existence—at least for this deployment, as the regiment rarely used the same invasion ship twice—and had been Katja's professional home since graduating from the Astral College. It boasted six infantry troops, including Katja's own Saracens, as well as a pair of armored troops and another pair of engineers. Like all regiments it had a strong tradition and identity, and it was the fundamental unit to which all troopers felt their allegiance.

Katja was proud to call herself a Saracen, but if ever she saw trouble approaching a Crusader, an Ottoman, a Spartan, or a man from any of the other troops, she would quickly make that trouble her own. Back on Earth the troops were scattered by distance and different routines, but on deployments they always drew together.

Her eyes passed right over the various couples and groups seated at the café tables, and focused immediately on the sprawling collection of men and women wearing green coveralls. She was immediately struck by how fit they all looked—not a flabby belly or large butt among them. Lean faces and tight haircuts abounded, with laughter as the order of the day.

It didn't take long to spot Scott Lahko. Tall, thick, and brutish, he was a butt-ugly ape with a loud voice and even louder laugh. If his olive skin and black hair were any guide, he traced his heritage from the Levant, making him the ideal choice for the occasional public relations maneuver—as long as he wore his helmet with the visor down.

He spotted Katja as soon as she approached, breaking off his conversation to greet her.

"Big K! Back from the wars." He reached out and punched at her shoulder, but she swatted his hand away.

"Keeping you safe, Scotty." Her eyes were barely level with his chest, but she stared up at him fearlessly. She took in the small group of officers around her, all men and all at least a head taller than her. "How you doing, boys?"

None of them were Saracens, but they greeted her amiably. Scott picked up the thread of his story again. It was an old tale from the Dog Watch, and Katja had heard it many times before, so she slipped into the context without much effort, adding her own comments when Scott got just a little too far from the truth. The story concluded with a roar of laughter.

"Lieutenant Emmes," came a female voice from behind, "you look thirsty."

Katja turned and saw her troop leader, Commander Cassandra Vici, holding a mug of beer in each hand. Vici was tall and lean, with a thin, angular face that had hints of white, faded scarring, and black hair that hung straight to her shoulders. She wasn't smiling, but Katja had learned to recognize the intensity in her dark eyes as good humor.

She took the proffered beer.

"Thanks, skipper." She peered around the room. "Looks like a good crowd tonight."

"The past few days have been busy with section training, so it's time to blow off some steam."

"I bet the troopers are partying hard down below."

"How was your mission?"

One thing was always certain about Commander Vici—she wasted little time on small talk. Katja knew the question wasn't just a polite inquiry, either. Vici wanted an informal report.

She quickly summarized the mission. Facts only—no interpretation. She knew well that her own opinion would hardly make the mission look like a success.

Vici nodded, then grabbed Scott's elbow. "Lahko, since Emmes is here I want to speak to all the Saracens. Find the others and meet me by the windows in ten."

"Yes, ma'am."

The troop commander moved away through the crowd with a determined stride.

Scott looked down at Katja. "Hey, I read up a bit on your FAC. You never said you worked with Thomas Kane."

Katja shrugged. "You never asked. It didn't seem important, but I just found out a few days ago that he did a stint in the Corps."

"No shit. Who do you think recommended this little trooper for his commission?"

She was surprised. "You know Kane?"

Scott laughed. "That story I was just telling about the Dog Watch? Who do you think the lieutenant was who busted us?"

"I had no idea." She felt a smile growing on her lips. "I can see him busting you, too. But I also understand why you were never charged."

"He was no-nonsense in the field, but, man, did he have a good sense of humor in barracks. Hey! You should invite him here this evening. He wasn't Levantine, but once a trooper, always a trooper."

A flurry of emotions swarmed through Katja's chest. "Oh, no, I'm sure—"

"Yeah! Give him a call," Scott persisted. "Just see if he wants to come down for a drink. It'll be good to see him."

"Scott, I'm sure he's still busy writing his mission report—"

"All the more reason to get him out for a friendly drink."

"He's your friend—*you* call him."

Scott grabbed her shoulders and gently but firmly turned her and pushed her away from the bar. "You call him, and tell him to be here in twenty minutes. I have to go round up the other Saracens. I'll see you at the windows."

Propelled clear of the crowd, Katja stopped for a moment, feeling exposed and stupid. Professionally, there was nothing wrong with inviting her CO out for a drink, especially since he was a former trooper. But something was making her feel guilty, and she was embarrassed at her own guilt.

She forced herself to take a step forward, then another.

There was a bank of comms stations near the entrance, and Katja sidled into one of the half-booths. She searched out the cabin number for "Kane, Thomas, Lt(C)." When the five-digit number appeared before her, she felt a knot in her stomach. Procrastinating for a moment, she took a pull of her beer and gazed around the room. Maybe he was already there...

Frowning, she put down her glass and tapped in the number before she had a chance to think.

The sound of ringing warbled in the headset. Once. Twice.

Maybe he wasn't home—

"Lieutenant Commander Kane."

"Uhh, hi, sir. It's Lieutenant Emmes."

"Hi, Ops. What can I do for you?" His tone suggested mild surprise.

"I'm not disturbing you, am I, sir?"

"Not really. I was just thinking about getting something to eat before I finish off the mission report."

"Oh. Well, umm, there's a Levantine Jihad going on down in the star lounge, and, since you used to be a trooper yourself, I was—that is, we were wondering... hey, do you know Scott Lahko?"

There was a pause, and Katja felt her stomach contracting to one tenth its normal size. Could she sound more like an idiot?

"Scott Lahko..." Thomas mused. "Oh, yeah, one of my troopers. Good kid."

"Well, he's here, and when he heard that you were the CO, he said you should come down and have a drink with us."

"That's nice he remembers me."

"And not just him, sir. I mean, it'd be nice—for me—to spend, to have a drink with you." Katja closed her eyes and rested her head against the bulkhead. Her cheeks were burning.

"I'll come on one condition, Katja."

"What's that, sir?"

"That you stop calling me sir. At least for an evening."

She laughed nervously. "I'll try my best, sir. Ah! Shit. Okay, now I'll try my best." His warm laughter eased the knot in her stomach. A bit. "We're just having a snakepit with our troop commander. We should be done in about twenty minutes."

"Great. Have you eaten?"

"Me? Uhh, no. Just beer so far."

"Do you and Lahko want to eat with me at the star lounge? I'm starving."

"I'll ask him. If not, I'm sure he'd be happy to just drink at the table."

More laughter. "Then he hasn't changed much."

"See you soon, sir."

"Katja..."

Her cheeks flushed anew.

"Thomas."

"See you."

She heard the line click off, but she stood with the headset to her ear for a long moment, forehead against the bulkhead.

12

On the far side of the lounge, the officers of Saracen Troop were gathering around their commander. Katja moved quickly through the tables and up to join them. Besides Vici and Lahko, she recognized Sublieutenant Wei Hu, Lieutenants Serge Wicki and Sven Pletsers, and First Lieutenant Gopal Sung.

Wei had taken over Katja's old platoon when she was transferred to *Rapier*, but she barely knew him. His lack of experience and smooth, youthful features made him seem even greener than he was. Wicki and Pletsers were both tall North Europeans, and Gopal was a short, wiry Himalayan. The first lieutenant was a platoon leader like other junior officers, but had the additional responsibility of being the troop's second-in-command.

Katja had worked with these men for years before going on her fast-attack course, and she slipped into the group effortlessly. Feeling immediately at home, she very much appreciated Vici's gesture to include her, even though she no longer had an official role in the regiment.

"Troops, it's been a good couple of days," the commander began. "I'm pleased with the maneuvers, especially because we beat the Spartans at their own game." This comment drew chuckles, but Katja could only guess at the meaning. "Gopal, you did well as commander when they took me out."

"Thank you, ma'am," Gopal said.

"I'm not going to keep you long—and I figure Lahko's already too drunk to remember anything important—but I'm going to be in planning meetings tomorrow, so I won't have time to brief you then. Here's the situation.

"The cease-fire on Cerberus is holding, but Intelligence reports a lot of unrest, particularly in the Lhasan region. It seems, Emmes, that your little raid drew more attention than we expected—it's probably a good thing that you got out as fast as you did. Fleet's going to try and soothe everybody by delivering humanitarian supplies to Free Lhasa in a few days. Our regiment has had no official change of orders, but I wouldn't be surprised if we pay the Cerberans a visit within the next month. So schedule some heavy-grav training over the next couple of weeks."

"Yes, ma'am," Gopal said, speaking for them all.

"The official Laikan government has been making some friendly overtures to Terra recently, and the Expeditionary Force is scheduled to conduct some military operations in Laika's vicinity as a gesture of goodwill—and to put on a show for the insurgents. My understanding is that the entire EF will rendezvous in the Anubian system, do some exercises near Laika, and then split off again. This shouldn't affect us.

"Otherwise, Centauri military presence is light, and reported piracy incidents are down. We're coming up on the mid-deployment leave period, so have your plans for personnel rotation on my screen by the end of the week. Any questions?"

There were none.

"Then have a good evening."

The six junior officers instinctively straightened to attention and waited as Vici departed. Then, as if a switch had been thrown, they all relaxed and took long pulls of their drinks.

Gopal wrapped a strong arm around Katja's shoulders.

"Good to see you, Big K," he said. "It's nice to feel tall for once."

Katja's eyes were nearly level to those of the first lieutenant, and she met his gaze while trying to suppress a smirk.

"If you keep touching me, I guarantee you'll feel weak and broken pretty soon."

He backed away with a great show of trepidation.

"How was your mission?" Wicki asked. "Sounds like you're just making more work for us."

Katja shrugged, and quickly described the events of the strike. The other platoon leaders listened with interest, asking pointed questions when relevant. None of them seemed to think that the incident in building seven was anything noteworthy, and while they all agreed with Katja that a continuation of the search would have been best, no one questioned the outcome of the mission.

"Sounds like the Cerberans were on to you," Gopal concluded. "Not much you can do at that point but bug out."

Katja sighed, feeling better for having discussed the mission with her colleagues.

"It's frustrating, though," she said. "And it means we have to go back again when there's new intelligence."

"I'd rather that, than for us have to mount a rescue mission to bust your ass out of there."

"Fair enough."

"Yeah, forget about it." Lahko stepped into the middle of the circle. "Everybody made it back, and we'll sort it out later. Tonight we drink, because it's jihad." He hefted his beer and shouted in his full combat voice. "Jihad!"

Echoes of "jihad" were cried out from the Corps crowd across the star lounge, as well as the inevitable ululations. Katja always wondered if any Muslims in the regiment were offended by this, and she cast her eye over the crowd to watch for reactions. She saw a mix of disinterest and disbelief, but no apparent outrage.

She also saw the familiar form of Charity Brisebois, all smiles as she sat down at a table with that young pilot of hers. Katja took another gulp of beer and wondered when Breeze had found the time to troll the Astral College for a boyfriend. Katja was almost thirty, and Breeze was at least a few years older—what in the world was she doing with that kid?

And then she saw Thomas wandering in from the passageway. Without thinking she waved her arm. He spotted the motion and smiled as he waved back. She weaved her way through the tables to greet him.

They met about halfway. He looked fresher, and more relaxed. The deep fatigue was still haunting his eyes, but he was doing his best to hide it behind a friendly smile.

"Hi, Katja."

"Hi, Thomas."

He looked at her for a moment, then cast his gaze around the room.

"Pretty good crowd tonight. Troopers were always better at partying, as I recall."

"And getting into trouble," she replied, "if my sources are correct."

"Oh, really? What do you hear?" He cocked an eyebrow.

Katja felt herself going red, and quickly relayed the tale Scott had been telling earlier. At first Thomas looked puzzled, and Katja wondered if Scott hadn't invented the whole thing. But then the slow dawn of realization broke across his features.

"Ahh, *that* time." He rolled his eyes. "Yeah, I thought he was going to get busted down to trooper again. Lucky for him, Headquarters was hit by a suicide bomber that same morning and we had to scramble. Lahko earned a medal of bravery that day, so his little indiscretion was forgotten." Thomas smiled and shook his head. "Quite a guy." He looked around. "Where is he, anyway?"

Katja quickly looked over her shoulder to where the Saracen officers were still standing by the windows, all watching her with interest. Again she felt her cheeks burning, but she ignored the feeling and motioned for Scott to join her. He made some parting comment to the other officers and worked his way over, grinning broadly.

"Lieutenant Kane," he said enthusiastically. "I can't believe I'm seeing you here."

Thomas stepped beside Katja, his arm brushing against hers.

"Lieutenant Lahko, I can't believe you're still alive."

Scott bellowed his laughter and shook Thomas's hand. "Me, too—and still so pretty!"

"That was going to be the next thing out of my mouth."

"Never out of mine," Katja interjected.

"Yeah, yeah, you're just jealous," Scott said without missing a beat. "Hey, you guys grab a table. Thomas, you eaten?"

He shook his head. "I'm starving."

"Great, I'll get drinks. You guys look at menus."

Scott pushed away between the seated patrons, leaving Katja

and Thomas alone again. There were several tables on the edge of the dining section, next to the open dance floor. She quickly noticed that the only ones available were right next to Breeze and her boy. Thomas had already spotted the opening and he motioned her forward.

"I see Breeze and her date," Katja said as they moved through the tables. "Maybe we should give them some space."

Thomas nodded. "Makes sense."

Breeze spotted them as they approached, and greeted them with a friendly wave. Katja hoped that would be it, but Thomas steered over to her table.

"Hi, NavO," he said. "Good to get some R&R after a long mission."

She leaned back in her chair and offered a warm smile. Under the relaxed charm, there was something in her look as she glanced between Katja and Thomas.

"Absolutely. You two should have told me you were coming down—we could have made it a *Rapier* night out."

"Oh, we didn't plan this," Katja said quickly. "I just came down for the Levantine Jihad."

"Yeah," Thomas added more leisurely. "Turns out one of OpsO's fellow troopers is a guy I used to serve with. They invited me down to talk about old times in the mud."

"Sounds like fun," Breeze said. "The intelligence folk sit around and spin tales about the reports we wrote. And sometimes, when we get really crazy, we relive the best briefings we ever gave. Good times."

The pilot laughed appreciatively.

Breeze gestured at him. "This is my friend Jack—he's a pilot. And I'm discovering that he knows a hell of a lot about multidimensional physics, too."

Jack grinned and extended his hand to Thomas.

"Hi, how you doing?" he said enthusiastically. "I didn't catch your name."

"Thomas Kane. You fly strike fighters?"

Jack's enthusiasm dimmed for a second, Katja thought, but he rebounded quickly.

"No, I'm a Hawk pilot. I'm with *Kristiansand*. I was just

telling Breeze how I spotted that mystery ship."

"Oh, *you're* the one." Thomas nodded. "Sharp eyes."

"Thanks. The real trick is—"

"Jack," Thomas interrupted, laying a hand on the pilot's shoulder. "The existence of that ship is top secret. Now, Breeze is cleared to that level, and as it turns out so are Ms. Emmes and I. But I'm pretty damn sure that doesn't apply to everybody in here. So stop talking now."

Jack looked surprised by the rebuke.

Breeze leaned in to coax Thomas's hand off him.

"Don't worry—Jack wasn't discussing any details. He was just talking about how hard it is to spot something like that in space."

Katja's attention was suddenly drawn by the looming form of Scott Lahko, balancing his own full mug in one hand and a full pitcher of beer in the other. With surprising skill, he set everything down on the table next to Breeze and Jack.

"Hey, you guys talking or drinking?"

"I'm drinking." Katja sat down across from him. As he topped up her glass, she appreciated once again the simple pleasures of being in the Corps. Good friends, no games. The way military life was supposed to be.

13

Thomas had never really suffered from space sickness, but he still appreciated artificial gravity when it was on offer. He enjoyed the feeling of power as he strode down one of *Normandy*'s wide passageways, pushing himself along with a firm, heel-to-toe action. To most people, it was walking. To a veteran of zero-g, it was freedom.

Lieutenant Sean Duncan didn't seem so enamored with the whole walking thing. He was almost as tall as Thomas, but he was struggling to keep pace.

"Thomas, we're not late," he said. "And if anything, I'm the one who's supposed to be nervous."

Thomas slowed, smiling. "Just stretching the legs. Sorry."

There was no hurry, but both officers had long ago developed the very useful habit of getting to briefings well in advance. They had each suffered their share of embarrassments at the Astral College, either by giving poorly prepared presentations or by conducting oh-so-stealthy sneaking into the back of a room when the briefing had already begun.

Today in particular there was reason to be early. Sean was scheduled to present to *Normandy*'s command team the analysis of the mystery ship. There was nothing like a room full of line officers to strike fear into the heart of a presenter, but as the second-in-command of a destroyer, Sean spoke with an authority unusual for his rank.

Thomas had often wondered why executive officers didn't get the appointment to lieutenant commander. He privately considered Sean's role to be more worthy of appointment than his own, even if he would never admit it. The Fleet, though, had a romantic attachment to the position of ship captain, no matter how small the vessel might be, and as a captain Thomas was automatically honored above his peers.

So, for now, Thomas was winning the race with his old friend. But both FAC captain and destroyer XO were stepping-stones to promotion, so there was no telling who would climb the next rung first.

"That was a pretty wild party in the end," Sean said. "Those troopers are crazy."

Thomas nodded, remembering the later hours of the Jihad. "Ten years ago I could have kept up."

"Ten years ago, Thomas, you'd have been leading the charge. You remember that little incident of the 'Moon Over Busan'?"

"I don't know if my thirty-eight-year-old moon would be as welcome on display as it was back then."

"Well, what about that friend of yours? The big guy—what was his name? He seemed pretty eager to show some skin."

"Scott Lahko? Yeah, he's commissioned from the ranks, so he parties on a whole different level. He's our age, but you'd never believe it."

"He did in our young Jack Mallory pretty good."

Thomas laughed. "That kid isn't even old enough to drink, let alone make an ass out of himself."

"Well, they *both* made asses of themselves—and left me free to chat up Breeze."

"Ever the predator, Sean." He shot his friend a look. "I thought you'd slowed down, skin hound."

"You gotta admit, Breeze is hot. I'm surprised you haven't taken a shot at her."

"She's one of my officers. I don't fish off the company pier."

Sean scoffed loudly. "Since when? Are you telling me it's St. Thomas, now?"

"That, and the fact that I'm engaged."

"Oh, right. I keep forgetting." He paused, then added, "When do I get an invite to the wedding?"

"As soon as I'm given the clearance from the boss. You don't actually think I have any say in the matter, do you?"

"Mmm-hmm. I only met Soma that one time, but I can tell she's the type who knows what she wants. And with all that money to spend, I'm sure it'll be the wedding of the century. Will it be on Earth or Ganymede?"

"Earth, for sure—somewhere by the sea. Jovians love open skies and pounding surf."

"Maybe I'll bring Breeze as my date."

"Be my guest. But I think Jack might have beaten you to it."

"Not a chance. He was passed out by midnight."

Thomas laughed. "If not Breeze, you could always take Katja."

"Who?"

"The little blonde one. My OpsO."

Sean frowned. "What fun would that be?"

"Seemed to me she's kinda cute."

"Yeah, but Breeze said she was gay."

"Who, Katja?"

"Yeah."

This came as news to Thomas. He'd thought she was giving him a bit more than just professional attention at the star lounge—although it had been a little awkward. Maybe she was just sucking up to her boss.

Normandy's main briefing room was aft of the bridge and forward of the Intelligence cell. As they entered the dimly lit space, Thomas guessed that the compartment probably displaced the same volume as *Rapier*'s entire interior. Three giant screens commanded the forward bulkhead, looming over a semicircular briefing platform that faced a theater of comfortable chairs. Each chair in turn had a console that could be fed detailed information.

They were alone in the room, but Sean wasted no time. As Thomas found the appropriate lights to switch on, Sean started uploading his information on the mystery merchant. *Normandy*'s intelligence gurus had been examining the data continuously, but *Kristiansand* had sent a burst transmission with updates.

"It was pretty slick of the captain," Sean said as he brought up the information he wanted. "As soon as she read my message, saying we'd be delayed to give this brief, she radioed the Hawk and changed its patrol pattern, just to get these shots. It approached on low power, so the target probably thought it was just space clutter."

Two of the screens lit up behind him, each showing a different visual of the mystery ship. One was a microwave representation, and the other was dark and unclear—taken with visible light.

"These are about three hours old."

Thomas whistled in appreciation.

The grainy image of the long, gray ship didn't reveal fine details, but the telltale bulges of snap-on cargo bays spoke volumes. This was a large, deep-space carrier—not at all the sort of ship usually used for clandestine activities. Someone with very deep pockets—someone like the Centauri government—had to be bankrolling this operation. The third screen then lit up with a projected path of the ship, based on the recorded course and speed, and the details revealed there only added to the mystery.

Sean switched the screens to standby and forwarded data to the audience consoles.

Thomas took a seat on the far side of the theater, far enough away from the center to ensure that he didn't ruffle any feathers. Although he didn't know the *Normandy* staff, he guessed there would be egos involved.

In fact, Thomas only knew one member of *Normandy*'s senior staff—the commanding officer himself. Captain Eric Chandler had been *Victoria*'s XO when Thomas and Sean had joined their first ship, just in time for what had been scheduled as a routine deployment to Sirius. What followed was a full-blown civil war that had exploded across this, the third most populated of all human colonies, and the history books had many names for it. The End of the Laikan Hegemony. The War of Religious Freedom. The Splintering of Sirius.

In the Astral Force, those nasty years were known as the Dog Watch, and Thomas had grown up very quickly as a junior subbie in an old destroyer on the front lines. Eric Chandler, as XO, had taken it upon himself to get young Sublieutenants Kane and Duncan up to scratch.

Chandler was the ideal after whom Thomas had always

wanted to model himself. He would never have his old XO's raw charisma, but if he could even come close to emulating him, that would be better than most.

Sean occupied the exact position Chandler had filled so well. Watching him prepare his notes for the brief, Thomas suddenly worried that he wasn't going to win the promotion race.

In the long term, however, he had a subtle advantage. Sean was smart, and bold, but not very polished when away from the bridge. His drunken antics during the Jihad had been pretty typical—and contrary to their earlier conversation, Thomas doubted that Sean had scored any points with Breeze.

Maybe it was Sean's upbringing on Mercury. Even though his accent had faded, his rough-and-tumble approach to life gave strong evidence of his heritage. Thomas hardly came from a privileged background, but being from Earth conveyed an automatic advantage.

Soma came from a good family and had an excellent education. The fact that she was Captain Chandler's goddaughter didn't hurt either. It had been Chandler himself who had made certain Thomas and Soma would meet, and with this new connection, Thomas found himself once again under the watchful eye of his old mentor.

So while it was fun to reminisce about the wild days of youth, if he really wanted to achieve his ambitions, Thomas had to change his ways. Being engaged to Soma had helped put a stop to his wandering eye, but cleaning up his act wouldn't be enough. Moving forward, he had to find a way to stand out.

He had to find a way to shine.

Normandy's officers began drifting into the briefing room. They glanced curiously at Thomas and Sean, but other than a few nods offered no welcome as they filled up the second row of seats. They were a mix of lieutenants and commanders, and Thomas guessed they were a mix of Line and Intelligence.

One Corps officer slipped in quietly and took a seat in the front row, and Thomas had to strain to make out the single star of colonel on his collar. Surprisingly, no one called the room to attention, but the colonel didn't seem to mind. It took a moment, but then Thomas recognized the Levantine commander.

Soft-spoken and sharp-witted, Colonel Alexander Korolev was an enigma in the Astral Force. His name was becoming well known, yet with his brown hair and brown eyes, he had the most unremarkable features—the sort of man you wouldn't look at twice. Thomas had heard rumors that Korolev had been with Special Forces, and it made sense. Such a man would blend into the scenery.

"Ladies and gentlemen!"

Normandy's XO stepped through the door from the passageway. Everyone sat to attention, and the XO stepped aside. Captain Eric Chandler entered the briefing room. His thick brown hair was sprinkled with just enough silver to add distinction to his charm. He scanned the room as he crossed to his central seat. His eyes lingered on Thomas for a second, then he turned to acknowledge Korolev.

"Relax, please everyone." The assembled officers eased into their seats. "Good to see you, Colonel."

"Likewise, Captain."

Chandler turned to address Sean, a faint smile on his face.

"When I heard that a destroyer XO was briefing me today, I couldn't bring myself to think it might be you, Mr. Duncan. You realize I'm feeling very old right now." He turned to take in Thomas, as well. "And you just had to drag Mr. Kane along with you—what, for old times' sake?"

"I can't shake him, sir, no matter how hard I try. It's a pleasure to see you again, sir."

"It is," Chandler agreed. "But now tell me about this mystery ship of yours."

Thomas listened with interest as Sean briefed the small audience on how *Kristiansand* had stumbled across this mystery merchant. Damn good eyes on that young pilot, Jack. And from what Sean reported, it was no mean feat for *Kristiansand* to maintain a track even now.

The photos Sean projected on the screens had been taken by the destroyer's lone remaining Hawk from just over one million kilometers.

"Her track doesn't lead back directly to the jump gate," Sean noted, "so we can safely assume that her course kept her off the regular space lanes for most of her journey. We can only hypothesize as to why, but most scenarios suggest illegal activity. *Kristiansand* is maintaining her mark, and we should be able to track her to within about a million kilometers of Anubis."

The mystery merchant was moving in the general direction of the gas giant Anubis, and most likely headed for the terrestrial moon Laika—one of the most populated worlds in the Sirian system.

"At that distance, the Anubian gravity well will be too deep for us to track the ship gravimetrically, and we'll probably want to either board her or close for visual tracking. Either way, *Kristiansand* recommends that we prosecute the contact directly, due to the risk of early detection. No doubt this mystery vessel is watching its surroundings closely. If we try and hand off to another ship, they'll probably be suspicious about seeing two Terran warships nearby.

"Thus, I recommend our humanitarian mission to Laika be assigned to another unit."

Thomas heard amusement in Captain Chandler's response. "Sean, I'd be appalled if Commander Avernell recommended anything else," he said. "If she thought a humanitarian mission was a better use of her ship than hunting bad guys, I think I'd recommend that she transfer to the Home Guard."

Kristiansand's XO smiled in return. "Delivering humanitarian supplies is important, certainly," Sean said, "but unfortunately our ship is the key player here." His eyes danced over to Thomas. "Perhaps one of the FACs could deliver the supplies."

Chandler laughed before Thomas could blurt out a reply. Other line officers joined in.

All eyes went to Thomas.

"Lieutenant Duncan," Thomas said after a moment, "the task of picking up after your unfinished business is hardly new to me, but in this case, I think I'll have to decline."

"That's what I like to see in a line officer," Chandler said. "Hunger. And the instinct to blade your peers. I trained you both very well, I think."

Again laughter rippled around the room.

"Might I bring the discussion back to the mystery ship?" Colonel Korolev said. The quiet words cut through the mood.

"Before any ship approaches the target," he continued, "we need to learn a little bit more about it."

"What more do we need to know?" Chandler asked. "We've found our smoking gun."

Korolev's eyebrow lifted slightly. "We might have found a gun, but I'm not sure we can say it's smoking just yet."

His tone was light, but his words hit home. Impatience flashed across Chandler's features.

"Respectfully, Colonel, merchants with nothing to hide don't skulk around in deep space at atmospheric speeds." He pointed at the projected picture. "Time is money for these guys, unless they have money invested in something a little less legal than shipping."

"Oh, I want to have a look at this ship just as much as you do, Captain Chandler," Korolev countered. "I'm just cautioning against jumping to conclusions."

Chandler smiled. "Nobody's jumping to conclusions, Colonel. But we have to act quickly. The situation on Laika is tense right now, despite what their government says, and if this ship is transporting weapons, it might be just the extra firepower one of the factions would need to stir things up again. If that happens," he added pointedly, "we'll have to deliver a lot more humanitarian supplies."

"Then let Astral Intelligence have a look. Perhaps one of our ships closer to the jump gate can discern how this target broke away from the space lanes."

Thomas silently agreed with Korolev. This ship *was* suspicious, but if the Fleet played its hand too soon, any evidence might disappear out an airlock. Careful surveillance, however, might confirm the ship's guilt, and reveal her contact on the ground.

Chandler shook his head. "At her current speed, she's only a few days away from the Anubian lanes. Once there, she can merge with all the other traffic, and we've lost her. Another Centauri warship came through the jump gate today—that makes it three." He paused, then continued. "I think that's half their fleet they've got in Sirian space now." This drew some laughter from his staff. He continued, serious once again.

"Clearly Centauria is taking a big interest in Sirian affairs—who knows how long they've been smuggling weapons to their factions? We can't wait to find out via the twenty-four-hour news networks." He turned to Thomas. "Get *Rapier* ready for immediate deployment."

"We'll be spaceborne in two hours," Thomas replied, suppressing a smile of excitement. "At low speed we can pick her up in a day, and trail her all the way to Laika."

Chandler shook his head.

"No, board the suspect and search it for contraband."

"Perhaps we should wait to see if the ship makes a rendezvous," Korolev suggested. Again Thomas agreed.

Chandler clearly did not.

"No, *Rapier* will board before she reaches Anubian space." His tone indicated that there was to be no discussion. "That ship knows we're here, and is probably getting info fed to her by those Centauri warships. She might already know about *Kristiansand*, so I don't want Avernell making any sudden moves. This merchant is nervous, and ready to dump her cargo at the first sign of trouble. *Rapier* will close on low power to within ten million, then strike at max speed and board without warning."

Sean leaned his hands on the podium. "Sir, orders for *Kristiansand*?"

"Tell Captain Avernell to provide support for *Rapier*'s boarding. Maintain an ASW posture, and keep an eye out for Centauri stealth ships that might be shadowing their smuggler."

"Yes, sir."

"Oh, and after the boarding, take your medical supplies to Cerberus, as intended. The admiral has ordered the EF to Anubis as a show of support to the Laikan government, so if things blow up at Laika, we'll be there to deal with it. If this mystery ship winds up to be nothing, you'll still be best positioned out between the orbits to deliver the supplies. And if *Rapier* does find something, your humanitarian mission will give you a good reason to get in close to Cerberus, just in case we have some punishment to deal out."

"Yes, sir."

Chandler stood. "That's it, gentlemen. Let's move." Thomas rose with the others, and couldn't help but cast a smile of triumph at his friend. The captain's orders were rash, but this was a chance to make a name for *Rapier*, and for himself. He might win the race after all.

Sean was frowning, but his expression suggested that he wasn't worried about their friendly rivalry.

14

Katja relaxed and took deep breaths. Twenty hours out from *Normandy*, after creeping through space in low-power mode, this last sprint to the target had been a deafening, blinding, crushing shock. The serenity that came after was invigorating.

Thomas turned his head inside the helmet. Their visors were open, so he didn't bother with his mic. "Based on the last burst from *Kristiansand*, our target is right where we expected her to be. She's activated her lights and gravity—I think they're trying to look innocent."

Katja glanced down at the 3-D display. "Still no reaction to our presence?"

"Hard to say. I haven't picked her up on sensors, probably due to Cooperan smear. If they're running silent, like Duncan said, they might not even see us coming."

"How much time until intercept?"

"We'll start decelerating in four minutes. We're going to swing wide and bleed off as much energy as we can in the turn, match velocities and come up on their starboard quarter for boarding."

"When will you start the hails?"

"As soon as we begin the turn. It'll take forty-five seconds, so be ready to deploy as soon as we take station."

"Yes, sir."

"Good luck."

Did he hold her gaze for an extra second? Katja wasn't sure.

Then she realized that she was staring, and abruptly pushed herself out of the chair and left the bridge.

She had less than thirty seconds to move aft through *Rapier* and take her seat in the strike pod. She made it in twenty, gave a quick sitrep to her team, then strapped in.

"*All personnel,*" came Thomas's voice, "*stand by for deceleration.*"

The force came quickly, pulling Katja down in her seat. The roar of the engines shifted to a screech, and she felt the breastplate of her armored spacesuit begin to constrict. The artificial gravity built into her seat protected against sudden acceleration, as did the ship-wide inertial dampening system, but no AG system yet designed could compensate fast enough to completely eliminate the stresses imposed by a fast-attack craft on full burn.

The stars outside began to slowly shift, rotating and then falling from view. Training kicked in, and she focused on drawing air deep into her lungs, ensuring that the full capacity was used. Exhaling was even harder, as she had to force herself to resist the crushing pressure. Looking down at the console, she saw the red digits passing through thirty and counting down.

At twenty seconds the pressure began to ease. At fifteen, the dull, gray shape of the target rose over *Rapier*'s hull as the fast-attack craft settled into a steady course and speed.

At ten seconds, Katja glanced at the pilot, Trooper Cohen, who nodded in return.

"All units, Alpha-One," she said, "stand by for insertion."

Trusting Cohen to launch on the mark, Katja focused her attention on the target. It was a large freighter, with a long central spine supporting crew quarters forward and engineering spaces aft. Modular cargo sections were attached along both sides of the spine, designed for easy removal and transfer to orbital elevators. She recognized the body style as Centauri, though it was the first such vessel she had seen with her own eyes.

The strike pod lifted off from *Rapier* with a jolt, then pushed forward at speed toward the target. Katja locked down her helmet visor and leaned forward to ensure that Chang's pod was moving with hers. As with any standard boarding, she would board with Alpha Team from one side and he would board with

Bravo from the other. Both teams would fan out and clear the area, with the intent of meeting up in the middle.

She scanned the hull as it swept past beneath the pod, noting the heavy layer of dust that obscured any markings. The structure beneath looked intact, with no obvious signs of age.

Chang's strike pod disappeared behind the freighter. Katja scanned for a hatch. She and Cohen spotted the dusty entrance at the same time. The pod rolled to present its belly to the ship, and with the help of cameras Cohen slipped over the waiting hatch. Katja felt a slight thump of contact, then another as the automatic seal grabbed hold of the freighter's hull and latched the pod down.

She spun her seat around and motioned sharply downward with her hand. The troopers unstrapped and opened the pod's deck hatch. The first trooper, Squad Leader Assad, descended through the seal. A few moments later a light cloud of dust billowed up through the opening, indicating his success at overriding the freighter's locks. Trooper Jackson went down; Hernandez followed. Katja moved up the pod's bulkhead and then pushed off, passing through the faint dust cloud in the seal, and through the thick outer airlock of the freighter.

As soon as she was through she felt herself begin to sink—there was gravity inside. Swinging her legs under her she landed with as much grace as was possible in an armored spacesuit.

With hand signals she directed the troopers forward, taking third position down the dimly lit, narrow passageway. Assad was on point. There was nothing to see except the huge bulk of Jackson's armored form in front of her, so she brought up Assad's helmet cam on her forearm display. The quantum-filtered view jerked and bounced as he moved forward.

Her team met Chang's without incident, facing each other at a crossroads on the ship's main longitudinal passageway. Alpha Team took up position looking forward, Bravo aft.

As she lifted her rifle, Katja felt a wave of nausea deep in her gut. She forced it down, ignoring the familiar self-doubt, as she looked up at her massive second-in-command.

"No reception party," he said. "Either they're hiding, or they're busy. Neither option is good. Take the engine room as planned, but if you see anyone on the way, immobilize them immediately—don't wait for the sweep."

Chang nodded, and looked at his watch. "Sixty seconds?"

Katja checked her own. "Sixty seconds. Move."

Bravo Team went down the passageway, swift and silent as shadows. Katja looked forward, past her crouching troopers. The passageway was eerily quiet. She called up the interior plan for this class of ship.

"Alpha Team, we take the bridge, but we neutralize anybody along the way. Move."

Assad, followed by Jackson, rose and advanced, rifle up and ready. Katja was close behind, scanning the bulkheads on either side with quantum-view and IR. Hernandez, her bodyguard, brought up the rear. Fifty yards along, a ladder led up to the next deck. They were up in seconds and moving forward again, door to the bridge in sight.

There was movement in her scopes. Human forms, two, in a compartment to their left. Quick taps up to Assad halted the group. She gestured.

I see. Two targets. There. She pointed ahead and to the left. *Alpha-Two, Alpha-Four, buttonhook. Alpha-Two lead.*

Nods all around. The door to the compartment was manually activated. With Hernandez covering the passageway, she grabbed the handle and flung the door open. Assad was inside in a heartbeat, Jackson right behind. Katja heard a gasp, a thump, and a grunt. She looked through the door and saw a man and a woman, in civilian clothes, facedown on the deck. Her troopers crouched over them like giant, mechanical apes, applying restraining ties to arms and legs.

She glanced at her watch: forty-five seconds. They had fifteen more to get to the bridge. She motioned her team out of the space.

With her augmented vision she could see four people through the last bulkhead. She signaled to her troopers, and ordered a fast assault. Assad tried the airtight hatch.

Locked.

She motioned him clear, raised her rifle and reached for the trigger of the grenade launcher that was slung under the barrel.

The thick hatch exploded as the grenade detonated on

impact, filling the passageway with smoke. The troopers kicked the remains of the twisted metal aside and charged through the opening. Katja followed.

The bridge was clouded with dust, but Katja identified the four merchant crewmembers instantly. Her troopers barked orders for the targets to drop to their knees.

Through the smoke emerged a middle-aged man in nondescript civilian clothes. He was covering his face. His skin was pale and soft, his belly obvious even under the loose cloth. Katja grabbed him with an armored grip and threw him to the deck. She placed a foot on his back and her rifle to his head. The weight of her spacesuit—the little she allowed to actually lean on him—made him gasp in pain.

Glancing around the bridge, she saw that the other three targets were subdued.

"This is the Terran Astral Force," she declared. "If you cooperate you will not be harmed. If you resist, you will die."

She stepped off the prone target. He rolled onto his side and groaned. Circulation units were clearing the smoke, and through the haze Katja got her first good look at the other targets. All were dressed in civilian clothes, and none looked threatening.

"Bravo-One, Alpha-One—bridge secure. No casualties."

Chang's response was immediate.

"Bravo-One. Engine room secure. No casualties. Two targets, three others detained en route."

"Four targets here," she replied. "Two others detained en route." She switched to inter-ship freq. "Mother, Alpha-One. Touchdown, ops green. Commencing search."

"Mother, roger." Thomas's voice echoed in her ear.

Back to strike freq. "Bravo-One, Alpha-One—commence search."

"Bravo-One."

All the targets were watching her with wide eyes. The bridge was bright and modern, with soft, beige bulkheads and ergonomic consoles that wrapped around large, comfortable seats. The blackened remains of the hatch littered the deck, but it was obvious that this was a well-maintained ship. She studied the navigation projection on the starboard bulkhead, noting what appeared to be a straight run from a mining facility in Sirius's Kuiper belt.

The recorded route of the freighter didn't tie in with what *Kristiansand* had reported, but Katja didn't worry about the details. All was not as it seemed.

The troopers were watching the targets with leveled weapons. All remained in place and waited for her word. Behind her visor she once again steeled herself.

Jack shifted in his seat, looking closely at his display to see if *Rapier* was still producing even a glimmer of spacetime distortion. The fast-attack craft had dug a gravimetric trough during her high-speed assault on the mystery freighter, but now that she had dropped her speed and taken station she had all but vanished.

Kristiansand was drifting in her patrol box and was equally invisible across the dimensions, although her homing beacon gave Jack a continuous bearing on his mother ship. At first, the idea of flying support had sounded exciting to Jack, but now that the initial action was over he realized that this might be a bit of a yawner.

Looking at the spot on his scope where dead reckoning told him *Rapier* was, he imagined what Breeze was doing. He pictured her sitting behind her console, long hair falling past her shoulders as she carefully surveyed the situation. Most likely she wore a spacesuit for such an operation, but in Jack's mind she was just in her coveralls, zero-g holding up those great tits. Of course, zero-g wouldn't let her hair fall past her shoulders... Jack briefly debated whether his image should include falling hair or floating tits.

A quick re-imagining placed Breeze's hair under a hat and brought his image in line with the laws of physics.

He'd have to check *Kristiansand*'s schedule after this run, and find out if the ship planned to rendezvous with *Normandy* anytime soon. Better yet, if he could do more shuttling to the invasion ship. Or maybe, when this boarding was over, *Rapier* could dock with *Kristiansand* for a post-mission briefing...

After two months in space, Jack found his mind wandering often to the possibility of entertaining Breeze in his rack. No doubt a hot cougar like that could teach him a thing or two.

But she was more than just sexy. She was smart, and fun. Jack had seen clearly how the XO had been ogling her. That big strike officer, Scott or something, had been trying pretty hard, too. Watching Breeze toy with them had been great fun, especially since she dropped everything whenever Jack spoke.

He had played it cool that evening, but it was pretty clear which guy Breeze had been thinking about going home with. Shame she'd been so tired from the mission.

Jack couldn't wait for their next meeting.

An alert from his console pulled him back to reality. He blinked, did a sweep of the visual, of his flight controls, and then focused again on his hunt controls. Before he could figure out what had caused the alert, a red line appeared across his display.

"*Viking-Two, Longboat.*" It was Lieutenant Makatiani from *Kristiansand*. "*Fishing true one-six mark one-zero.*"

Jack spotted the disturbance on his display. How long had that been there? He tapped in the commands to drop in his own bearing line. There was something out there.

"Viking-Two, uhh, fishing true," he said. "Zero-four mark zero-eight."

The red line from his position intersected that from *Kristiansand*, some twenty-five thousand kilometers from Jack's Hawk. Not too close, but not that far, either. And, Jack suddenly realized, not too far from *Rapier* and the mystery merchant ship.

He steered his Hawk to point at *Rapier*, then pushed open the throttle. Doctrine demanded that, once an initial fix on an extra-dimensional contact had been established, he was to relocate at best speed to continue triangulating. This could be in any direction—ideally perpendicular to the bearing, but a feeling at the back of Jack's brain told him that it would be wise to get a little closer to the boarding.

15

Katja pocketed the data crystal that contained the merchant vessel's entire flight log. It would take hours—or days—to go through it all, but even glancing at the information as it downloaded, Katja had noticed a few suspicious items. The real question now was, was this merchant crew part of the smuggling operation, or were they just mules for an unknown agent?

On an impulse, she raised her rifle to point at the face of one of the kneeling targets. His face blanched, terror filling his eyes. She watched him carefully—his fear was pure, with no sign of detached calculation or tactical awareness. The other targets looked equally terrified, and she decided they were probably legitimate merchants.

She lowered her weapon.

"Who is the captain of this vessel?" she demanded.

Frantic glances passed between the targets. Then, the man whom Katja had taken down raised his hand.

"I am," he said. "Daragh Wu. This is the Centauri Merchant Ship *Astrid* on a routine commercial run from Kuiper Base Charlie to Laika."

"What's your cargo, Mr. Wu?"

"Iridium ore."

"Do you have all of your documentation?"

"Of course."

Katja smiled. "So you won't mind a bit if we have a look around."

"Just please, don't hurt my crew." He stared at the deck, defeated.

"That depends entirely on them." She looked up at her troopers. "Alpha-Two Team, collect Targets One and Two and bring them here." Assad and Jackson moved to obey. As they reached the door Katja spoke again. "Oh, and at the request of their captain, don't hurt them."

Assad couldn't suppress his smile. "Yes, ma'am."

Hernandez shepherded all four members of the bridge crew into a corner, where he could cover them solo and free up Katja to inspect the bridge. She pretended to ignore the activity, even attaching her rifle to her belt and turning away completely, as if lost in thought. Her ears, however, tracked every sound the targets made—little more than short breaths and shuffled movement. To them, she was in complete control of the situation, and she was beginning to believe it herself.

As the other two targets were brought in and placed on the deck next to their colleagues, Katja examined the various engine settings displayed on the consoles. All systems appeared fully operational, but nothing was running at higher than a minimum.

"Mr. Wu, how are you keeping to your schedule?" She looked over at him, her expression light and disarming. "I know how it is for space traders—time is money."

He raised his eyes to meet hers, but only for a moment. "We're actually... a little ahead of schedule."

"How much?"

"Excuse me?"

"How much ahead of schedule."

"Uhh, I don't have the exact figure." He began to rise. "I can show you—"

"Stay down." Both troopers raised their rifles in augmentation of Katja's gentle words. "Give me an estimate. Humor me."

"Maybe twelve hours."

She nodded. "This looks like a pretty nice ship, although I admit I've never seen the class before. What's your top speed?"

"Point-zero-nine-c."

"Not bad. I bet you have to use that sometimes, to make up for lost time when the loaders are slow."

"We manage," he replied.

"The loaders must have been really fast at your last stop. Do they have modern facilities at Kuiper Base Charlie?"

He stared stupidly at her.

"I said…" she repeated slowly, "do they have modern facilities at Kuiper Base Charlie?"

He swallowed. "Umm, not bad. The crews are hard-working."

"They must be, since you're so far ahead of schedule that you're drifting through extra-solar space at less than six kilometers per second. That must be one hell of a low SOA, to let you loiter for so long."

He was beginning to sweat. Certainly no spy, here.

"There was… a delay at the port on Laika," he said. "We've been told to hold off."

"Really? You were asked to hold off at three hundred million kilometers? That must be some stack of freighters waiting to get down to Laika."

"Alpha-One, Bravo-One. Poss suspect, deck two frame niner-alpha. Investigating."

Katja keyed her mike. "Alpha-One." She glanced at the bulkhead chronometer. The strike team had been on board less than seven minutes, and already they'd found something. Chang was good. She looked back at the merchant captain, who watched her like a rabbit, nervous and eager to bolt.

"Mr. Wu, I'm a patient woman, but I don't like being lied to. Do you understand that?"

"Yes."

"So you're going to tell me the truth from now on?"

"Yes."

"Why are you traveling so slowly?"

He hesitated, but clearly didn't have the stomach for this. "So that your ships wouldn't detect us."

"Why are you so far out of the space lanes?"

"So that we wouldn't be seen."

"What was your last port of call?"

"It really was Kuiper Base Charlie, but that was nine weeks ago."

"Did you rendezvous with any ships since then?"

"Yes."

"Who?"

"A trader named Cobb. I don't know where he was coming from."

"Did you take on cargo from him?"

"Yes. Ten sealed crates."

"What's in them?"

"I don't know."

Katja hardened her expression. Time to get nasty.

"If you lie to me I'll have one of your crew executed. There are five of them in here, so I guess that gives you five lies before you die."

One of the prone targets squirmed. Another whimpered. Wu was sweating freely, and he wiped his eyes.

"I'm not lying!" There was real panic in his voice.

"Where are the crates?"

"In a small hold under the deck in the number two generator room."

She keyed her mike. "Bravo-One, Alpha-One, new info. Space under the deck in number two generator room."

"Bravo-One. Tally-ho."

Katja frowned. Chang had already found the crates. Apparently his search procedures were faster than her interrogation methods.

"Mother, Alpha-One. Sitrep."

"Mother, go."

"Suspect cargo discovered. Bravo-One Team on location, Alpha-One Team en route with Target Zero-Zero."

"Mother, roger. Kristiansand's Hawk has reported possible stealth activity. Checking now, but I recommend you expedite."

She looked back at the merchant captain. "Get up, Mr. Wu."

The merchant hesitated. Hernandez stepped in, hauled him to his feet and threw him forward. He would normally have been taller than Katja, but was hunched over so much that he actually had to look up to meet her eyes.

"You're going to show me these crates."

He nodded.

She switched to strike freq. "All units, Alpha-One. Alpha-One Team en route to suspect cargo with Target Zero-Zero. Mother says expedite. Bravo-One, get those crates open. Over."

"*Bravo-One.*"

Katja grabbed Wu by the collar and propelled him forward through the smashed bridge hatch. Hernandez was close behind. She hustled down the passageways of the ship, practically dragging the gasping civilian along with her. Stealth was no longer important, and her armor whirred softly to move at her desired speed. Hernandez' heavy footfalls naturally fell into rhythm with her own, and the metallic thump of their steps formed a beat for Wu's labored breathing.

Jack eased off the throttles again, finishing his third sprint in six minutes. *Kristiansand* was maneuvering as well, and between them they had managed to build enough of a cross-section to rough-in the location of their stealth contact.

It was hard to pinpoint, however, because it was moving too fast. Jack waited impatiently for his hunt controls to clear after the sprint, then studied his readouts. His big dipper and the three barbells he'd dropped before each sprint all began to tie in, and Jack suddenly felt very hot in his suit.

"Longboat, Viking-Two—assess probable shadow bearing zero-eight mark zero-niner, shallow!"

The stealth ship was closing on *Rapier* and the merchant ship at cruising speed—probably the fastest it could go and still maintain the spacetime picture. Its intentions seemed pretty clear.

"*Longboat, roger. I am maneuvering to cover your attack. Prepare to engage.*"

Jack felt his throat tighten. Engage? As in attack for real? Holy shit.

He swung the Hawk to an intercept course and pushed open the throttles. His spacetime picture began to smear, but the computer adjusted to keep the symbology accurate. His fingers fumbled with the safety switch, but within moments he had armed all four of his gravi-torpedoes. He confirmed that they were set for a shallow run into the Bulk.

Alarms suddenly blared on his hunt controls. His eyes shot to the display where three bright red symbols had detached themselves from the stealth ship. One headed to *Rapier* and the merchant ship, while the other two turned and sped toward *Kristiansand*.

"Flash! Torpedo, torpedo, torpedo!"

Number two generator room was a small space, perhaps thirteen cubic meters, filled almost entirely by heavy machinery. As Katja arrived with Wu and Hernandez, Chang glanced up from where he crouched on the deck, then returned his gaze to the open space below him. Trooper Sakiyama was below, working to break the seal on the top crate.

"The crates are protected by an encrypted EM barrier," Chang said without preamble. "The lock will take at least fifteen minutes to pick, but if we smash the surface we risk a blast. And the contents will probably be destroyed."

Katja turned to Wu, who was huffing and puffing, his face red and slick. "Unlock the crates."

Holding up his hands placatingly, Wu nodded and climbed down into the hold. He typed in a sequence of numbers on a tiny control panel, causing a little red light to turn green. He looked up, nodding again.

Katja gestured at the crate. "Open it."

As Wu was fumbling with the lock, Katja heard Thomas once again in her ear. But it was no soothing murmur she heard.

"Alpha-One, Mother! Stealth attack! Withdraw! Withdraw!"

The lock clicked open, and Wu lifted the lid. It took only a moment for Katja to recognize the cargo inside. The long, silver tubes were unmistakably mountable missile launchers. These weren't just weapons—these were components for Centauri robotic weapons.

Frustration welled up inside her. The first real evidence of Centauri involvement and she was being ordered to withdraw. That awful, familiar feeling crawled up her throat—uncertainty. Disobeying a direct order was unthinkable, but to abandon such a find was equally so.

An idea struck her. "Alpha-One, roger. We're bringing one of the crates with us."

"*Mother, negative. Leave everything behind and get your ass out of there!*"

"Alpha-One, roger." Switch to strike freq. "All units, Alpha-One. Break away."

The two younger troopers beside her turned in surprise. Katja ignored them, staring impotently at the cached weapons before her.

Then the deck heaved with such violence that Katja hit the opposite bulkhead before she even knew what was happening. But instead of falling, she gasped as some invisible force slowly but powerfully tugged her sideways across the compartment. All around her, the bulkheads of the ship groaned under the stress. Her vision began to fade, and she couldn't breathe.

Then, slowly, the pressure eased, and she sank gently to the deck. All around her, troopers were struggling to pick themselves up, eyes wide.

Chang was the first to recover. He rose and pushed Sakiyama toward the door. "You heard her! Move!"

Katja jumped down onto the opened crate. "Wu, get out."

The merchant, his ears bleeding, stared at her blankly. She pointed her rifle at him.

"Out!"

He scrambled up out of the hold, limbs wobbling. Katja lifted her gaze. Chang and both troopers were at the door, staring at her with concern.

"Ma'am, break away?" Chang said.

"Bravo-One, put Target Zero-Zero in the engine room and then break away. Alpha-Three and I will leave in a moment."

There was no comprehension in Chang's eyes, but neither was there any hesitation. "Yes, ma'am."

He and Sakiyama hustled Wu from the room. Katja crouched down on the crate, looking closely at the weapons. The faint click of her camera recorded still images to back up the live feed that her helmet always provided. If she couldn't take the weapons, then at least she could take evidence.

Click. Click. Click.

"Ma'am," Hernandez said, "what the fuck was that?"

Katja turned to him and reached up her hand. He yanked her

out of the hold and together they ran for the strike pod.

That, Katja thought to herself, was a gravi-torpedo.

Jack slammed his fist down on the hunt controls.

The stealth ship was gone. His big dipper was deployed all the way to fourteen peets, but it still couldn't detect any ripples in the Bulk. He impotently fired off another barbell, not caring what depth it was set at.

They had been lucky. The torpedo fired at *Rapier* had exploded harmlessly at three kilometers distance. The two fired at *Kristiansand* had both been easily seduced by decoys. Jack shook his head—it looked as if the stealth ship didn't want to destroy either Terran vessel.

It had trumpeted its presence with a high-speed approach, then fired off weapons programmed not to use their curvature detection gear. But Centauri stealth captains were neither ill equipped nor stupid. That ship had just sent a very clear message: *I know where you are, and I don't like what you're doing.*

And then it had vanished into the Bulk.

Jack hadn't even had a chance to get a shot off before he lost contact. Even *Kristiansand*, with her far more capable sensor array, was coming up blank.

Commander Avernell had ordered her ship to clear away from the merchant, and for *Rapier* to do likewise. Stripes was launching to join the hunt, but they would find nothing. Jack rubbed his eyes, and realized that his spacesuit was soaked with sweat.

Suddenly, everything wasn't so much fun anymore.

16

Had she been sitting safely in her office back home, or even aboard one of the well-defended Astral bases, Breeze would have thought that things were getting interesting in Sirius.

But because she was stuck aboard this tiny, vulnerable fast-attack craft right in the middle of the action, she was having a lot of trouble being so objective. From this perspective, things were just getting *dangerous*.

At least this time there was a backup plan. She was still aching, and her ears were still ringing two days after the near miss. Thank God they'd been able to maneuver the ship to place the merchant between themselves and the explosion.

Unable to sleep, Breeze had been on her way to the main cave to find a friendly crewmember. But when she'd emerged from her cabin she'd seen Thomas floating in the center of the flats, staring up at the top turret. Quickly abandoning her plan, she'd smiled and explained to him that she was just looking for a snack in the galley.

Katja stuck her head down from the hatch. To Breeze's surprise, she was grinning.

"Top turret checks out, Captain. No leaks."

He laughed. "I'm glad you enjoy your work."

She pulled herself out of the turret and curled in the air to right herself.

"I've been aboard five weeks, and I've never actually been up there." She shrugged. "I'm a girl who likes big guns." A moment later her eyes widened slightly and she blushed. She half-covered her eyes with one hand. "Scratch that from the record, please, sir."

Breeze rolled her eyes. Katja really needed to work on her flirting.

Thomas laughed again. "Scratched. But I think for the record I have to say that *Rapier* is a tough little ship."

"Correct me if I'm wrong," Katja said, recovering nicely, "because I don't want to tell my troopers a lie, but doesn't a gravi-torpedo make a tiny black hole?"

Thomas considered for a moment.

"Well, sort of. When it activates it releases a flurry of gravitons, which bend spacetime into a very small but very deep gravity well. Anything located at the same spot will be 'sucked in' so to speak, and torn apart. A black hole is similar, except a few million times stronger and a lot more permanent."

"So that's why we were pulled sideways in the merchant ship?"

He nodded. "You and the entire ship were being pulled toward the gravity well. The ship's AG messed things up a bit, and probably shielded you, but that torpedo exploded several kilometers away. Had it been a real attack, the weapon would have exploded in the same three-dimensional space as the ship, and you wouldn't have felt a thing."

"Boom."

"Exactly. Gravimetric attacks take microseconds, and it doesn't matter how big the ship is. *Rapier* or *Normandy*—you get torn apart just as fast."

Katja shook her head. "I'd rather stick to big guns, sir."

"Speaking of which, Command is very impressed that you got those pictures. That was quick thinking, Ops."

"I just didn't want to leave empty-handed again."

Breeze was amazed at how much Katja could get away with when speaking to Thomas. She was basically criticizing him for pulling out of the Cerberan strike early. And all he did was laugh. If Breeze had said something like that, she'd probably get a formal warning.

"Well," she said, tired of listening to the two of them prattle on, "from what I hear, our government presented those photos to the Centauri embassy, along with some stern words of warning."

"Good," Katja said. "Maybe Centauria will finally back off and stop fueling the fire."

"Maybe," Thomas said, "but that's none of our business. We just keep doing our job."

"Yes, sir."

The way she looked at him was amazing. Breeze had noticed it in the star lounge—and it seemed to be entirely beyond what he deserved. She had no illusions about what Thomas was. His career was about to take off, or get put into a permanent holding pattern. This tour as an FAC captain was his pivotal moment. He was out for himself—as much as any of them were.

Was she the only one who could see it?

Then again, Katja had developed a crush on their chief instructor on the fast-attack course. It had been fun watching her struggle with puppy love for Commander Maxwell, botching just about every chance she'd had to talk with him socially. Breeze had made a point of charming the pants off Maxwell, especially when Katja was around to see it.

"Max" had been a bit of a stuffed shirt, but her social efforts had helped her to earn top student on the course. Katja could keep her rigid, Corps code of honor. Breeze was going places.

The hull check complete, Thomas excused himself and headed for his cabin. Katja and Breeze were left to stare at each other until Katja muttered something about getting some sleep and pushed past.

Breeze pulled herself down the flats and continued toward the main cave.

The cafeteria was dim, except for the soft glow coming from the forward drink machine. A silhouette against one of the small, starboard windows revealed a second person present—the bulk immediately suggesting *Rapier*'s senior trooper.

"Hi, Sergeant."

Sergeant Chang turned from looking out the window. His broad face seemed unexpressive, but Breeze noticed the slight lift of his eyes.

"Lieutenant. Working late?"

She moved closer, anchoring herself with a hand on one of the tables. "Can't sleep. There's a lot going on."

He grunted non-committally.

"How are your ears?" she asked.

"The ringing's gone, so I guess I'm that much closer to being deaf."

The fact that he didn't use the word "ma'am" suggested one of two things. Either he was incredibly insubordinate for a trooper, or her suspicions were correct.

"You should get checked out when we're back on Earth. I know a good doctor in Tokyo."

His eyes flicked around the otherwise empty room.

"I know him too."

She nodded. It was pretty easy for folks to guess that she was a spook—what, being an intelligence officer and all—but others were harder to spot. While "Suleiman Chang" didn't appear on any highly classified lists that she'd seen for this deployment, he'd clearly had training that didn't show up on his personnel file.

She pushed off from the table and joined him at the outer bulkhead, careful to avoid silhouetting herself in front of the window.

"I'm not pleased with how the Cerberan strike went," she said. "Why didn't you search the buildings I'd designated?"

"It was next on the to-do list. It's always better to get a local to crack and tell us everything, to avoid the risk of exposing our sources. That guy in the speeder was a distraction, but at the time he looked pretty suspicious, and was worth pursuing."

"Even though you knew where to look?"

"What would you be saying right now if he'd been the Centauri spy? What if he'd gotten away while we were following your recommendations?"

"You might have at least started with the designated buildings, rather than searching everywhere *but*."

Chang didn't answer right away, and she thought she could feel his frown in the darkness.

"How many field missions have you done?" he asked.

She hated that question, especially from someone in Chang's position.

"I'm a support operative," she replied. "I get the missions prepped."

"Then leave the execution to us," he said. "If we'd gone straight to the target, anybody with any smarts would have been tipped off that we knew where to search. That would have risked our sources on the ground. That's why we tried to get a local to spill the beans."

She gave up—there was no point in arguing. Instead she switched topics.

"You handled your officer pretty well. Pity she's so green. That little execution will probably cause some problems down the road."

Chang didn't reply. He just looked out the window again.

Loyalty within the Corps always amazed Breeze. She made a show of looking out the window, and chose her words carefully.

"Scary to think that a Centauri stealth ship might be right in front of our eyes, but we'll never see it. I think things are heating up."

Chang nodded, the movement barely visible. Then he pushed away from the bulkhead and headed toward the door.

"That's why you're an intelligence officer," he said, "and I'm just a jar-head... ma'am. I don't have to worry about stuff like that." He moved with surprising grace for such a big man, and disappeared out into the flats without another word.

Breeze sighed and moved to prepare a squeeze-bulb of coffee at the forward drink station. Field operatives didn't like being criticized, she knew, but she didn't think her words had been too damning. Maybe there was a reason Chang wasn't on the highly classified lists.

On an impulse, she made a second bulb of coffee and headed for the bridge.

Chief Tamma had the watch. He was in his usual seat—forward and starboard, next to Breeze's—and surrounded by the small galaxy of readings that made up the OOW console. He smiled in surprise as she pulled herself down into her seat and flicked him the coffee bulb.

"Hey, Breeze. Thanks."

She hefted her own coffee in salute.

"I know how hard it is to stay awake these days. Almost as hard as trying to get some sleep."

He chuckled in appreciation. As the ship's cox'n he was the senior enlisted person on board, but his long career as a pilot made it nearly impossible for him to bark and growl like a cox'n was supposed to. He was a great leader for the troops, though—fit, good-looking, and charismatic.

"Maybe you should try reading one of your intelligence reports," he said. "Those always put me to sleep."

She laughed and kicked him playfully. "If it wasn't for my reports, you'd never get to do anything interesting."

He shrugged. "Sitting here at a dead stop isn't top of my list of interesting things."

"Consider it a stakeout."

"Sure, and we all know how interesting those are." His wry smile robbed the words of any real malice.

"So where's our friend now?"

Tamma pointed at the 3-D display. "Making decent time, but not in a hurry, it seems. I expect her to reach our position in about ten hours."

"Well, we'll be here when she arrives."

Rapier was holding position one thousand kilometers from where the mystery merchant *Astrid* had dumped her cargo, before fleeing noisily back toward the jump gate. The little FAC could become very dark and quiet when she wanted to, hopefully enough so that no Centauri stealth ship could detect her.

And now, according to an intelligence report, a certain Cerberan vessel of interest, or VOI, had left orbit and was on a direct heading for the dumped cargo. *Kristiansand* had given the area a wide berth on her way to deliver humanitarian supplies, but both Terran warships remained very aware of the unfolding operation.

"I have a burst report ready to send to Command," Tamma said.

"No," Breeze said, and she shook her head. "We stay silent for now. I don't want to risk giving away our presence, especially if that stealth ship is still out there. Let the VOI pick up the cargo. Then we've got him red-handed."

"I'm worried, though, that with all the traffic in the Anubian system, our signal might not get through to the EF."

"It's a risk," she said, "but there's nothing Command can do, anyhow. We'll report to them after the pickup." She paused, then added, "Have the EF exercises begun yet?"

Tamma checked the watch notes. "All five battle groups are in the Anubian system, but the first rendezvous isn't for another few hours." He read further. "They've moved the underway replenishment to low orbit over Laika... I guess that stealth attack got everyone's attention."

"What do you mean?"

"Ships are pretty vulnerable in an UNREP. Stealth warfare's a lot harder close to massive bodies, because the spacetime curvatures mask ship movements both on the brane and in the Bulk. Anubis is big even for a gas giant, and with fifty or so moons swirling around it."

Breeze remembered once, as a subbie, being aboard a ship doing a low-orbit UNREP over Mars. The red planet had filled half the sky and she'd felt like they were low enough to bump into one of the high mountains. She'd even been able to make out some of the bigger cities by eye.

"Even so, they'll still be vulnerable if somebody on Laika's surface wants to take a shot at them."

"Not likely. The entire Expeditionary Force will be there— they'd flatten the shooter and turn his whole region into glass."

"True," Breeze admitted. Plus, she thought, the moon of Laika was one of the only civilized places in all of Sirius. She couldn't imagine them wanting to bring down Terra's wrath on their home... not again.

Besides, the Terran space station positioned permanently at the jump gate monitored all traffic in and out of the Sirian system, and had reported a grand total of three Centauri frigates and one stealth ship. A big showing for the Centauris, but hardly anything a Terran expeditionary force needed concern itself with.

"Well, that's it for me," she said, unhooking from her seat. As she left the bridge, Breeze enjoyed an unusual feeling of inner peace. Dangerous though it might have been, the ship had survived the action. Terran forces were asserting their dominance in the Anubian system while the diplomats came down on Centauria with evidence her ship had provided.

If *Rapier* could trail the approaching VOI back to Cerberus with its smuggled weapons, some brutal Cerberan warlords would earn a bruising. And then, finally, she might get some credit for all her hard work.

17

Jack was glad the seat in his Hawk was so comfortable—because he seemed to be spending a lot of time in it. But at least he wasn't bored.

Every mission was different lately, from discovering mystery vessels to tracking Centauri stealth ships. And as Jack ran through his pre-flight checklist, he realized that this latest one was quite different indeed.

Entry into the atmosphere was enough to test any pilot's nerves. So he checked on the status of the Hawk's heat shield, then checked it again. He re-familiarized himself with the operation of the flaps, ailerons, rudders, and all of the other flight surfaces that would affect the ship while planetside.

While he finished up, he could hear the busy murmur of *Kristiansand*'s supply department as they prepared for the delivery. Looking back over his shoulder, he saw the stack of plastic crates being strapped to the deck of the Hawk's after cabin. No less than seven crew members were coming along for the trip, and they were being led by Carmen Hathaway herself.

Just then, the supply officer stepped up through the Hawk's rear cargo door and squeezed past the crates. She—like everyone on the mission—was wearing her undress blues. Since this was a humanitarian mission, it had been decided that everyone should look sharp. One never knew when the local media would be around.

She greeted him with her usual smile.

"Hi Jack," she said. "You're looking smart. I almost feel like a diplomat, having my pilot so well turned out."

Jack returned her smile. "I've never flown in undress blues before. I'm just glad we're not in high-collar whites."

"There are limits," she replied. "They need us to make Terra look good on this mission, but I refuse to turn it into a parade." She scoffed. "Hell, why don't we just pull out an honor guard, to escort the supplies off with six pall-bearers?"

Jack laughed. "Hey, don't moan at me—I'm just the chauffeur."

Carmen gave his shoulder a squeeze. "Get us there and back safe—that's all I ask. Oh, and maybe pose for a photo or two, if the media show up."

She retreated to check on her team, leaving Jack to ponder the idea of being on the front page of the local paper back home. He could just picture himself holding a small Sirian child, with his Hawk in the background and an expression that combined heroic concern with carefree confidence in Terra's actions. That would certainly please the family and friends. Maybe he'd even get a parade...

"Hey, you ready?"

Carmen's words snapped him out of his daydream. He looked back and saw that the Hawk's cargo door was closing. The supply team were belting into their seats. Jack did a quick survey of the visual, the flight controls, and the hunt controls. The ground crew outside gave him the thumbs-up.

He fired up the engines and within thirty seconds his flight controls showed green. Still feeling strange in his uniform, he quickly conducted radio checks with *Kristiansand* flight control, hangar control, and with Carmen on the internal circuit.

Amidst the usual barrage of warning lights, the Hawk rolled forward through the airlock, and Jack waited patiently as the door closed and the air was pumped out. The outer door began to open, and he dropped his visor to shield his eyes from the brilliant light that lay beyond.

Cerberus loomed below, its reddish surface dotted with occasional white clouds. Jack waited until the access light switched to green, then eased his plane forward. He accelerated forward, and the Hawk was flying free.

He took a moment to study his planetary navigation screen and confirmed his intended landing zone. The computer displayed the recommended entry path, and he saw no reason to disagree. So he nudged his controls forward and dipped the Hawk into a gentle dive.

Kristiansand quickly fell astern as the Hawk began its descent on a path that opposed the Cerberan rotational direction. In essence, by flying "backward" Jack was using his own thrust to bleed off the Hawk's geo-stationary speed while getting additional braking from the atmosphere. The reverse-orbit entry was standard for all atmosphere-capable spacecraft, and Jack had no desire to buck the system.

The entry was uneventful as the Hawk shed altitude and slipped across the terminator to the Cerberan night-side. Jack kept a careful eye out for other ships, knowing that orbital dhows were notorious for quickly changing course and speed. On any of the Terran worlds he would have checked in with Orbital Control, but out here in the colonies such organizations rarely existed.

It was every ship for herself.

The first signs of atmospheric braking were subtle—a slight change in the rate of deceleration, and a slow rise in the temperature readings from the heat shield. Jack tightened his grip on the controls.

"Ladies and gentlemen," he said over the internal circuit, "stand by for turbulence."

Then the Hawk started to vibrate. The dark Cerberan horizon far ahead began to glow red, then orange. Temperature readings switched to yellow. The blinding orb of Sirius exploded into view in a sunrise far more dramatic than any back home.

The orange glow of super-heated air began to flicker at the edge of his vision. The sky began to brighten. The Hawk lurched to port, but Jack fought it back to a level descent. Sirius climbed higher in the sky, out of direct view. The orange glow began to fade. The heat shield readings began flashing red. The buffeting increased.

Jack struggled to get the feel of his flight surfaces. The Hawk leaned to port, then lurched to starboard as he overcompensated. Shouts of alarm rose dimly behind him. He leveled the Hawk amidst the steady vibrations. Wisps of cloud flashed by his canopy. He checked his altitude—archons ten. He checked his speed—two thousand kph. He checked his entry path.

Right on target.

He eased back on his throttle and continued his slow descent. The Hawk was an aircraft now. Pale blue sky stretched in all directions, dotted by white wisps of distant vapor. Jack eased his jittery control stick to starboard, still bleeding off speed as he moved into a long, curving descent toward the settlement known as Free Lhasa.

The air was filled with ships, all moving with unique courses and speeds, and all much too close for comfort. He brought a map of the terrain up on one of his hunt displays and peered out through the canopy to get his visual bearings. Everything in the soup of air was close—often too close for sensors that were used to dealing in millions of kilometers. The radar was already a mini-galaxy of blips and symbols, and Jack quickly dismissed it as useless.

He used the map to chart his course, and used his eyes to not smash into anything. Terran rules of flight ordered all craft to move at a safe speed based on the traffic density and prevailing weather conditions. As a military pilot Jack had some license to bend those rules, and he had learned long ago the advantage of speed. At twice the speed of sound, the only way he would run into another craft would be if he purposefully aimed directly at it. Otherwise, everything fell behind him, drawing left and right out of his way.

At that speed, however, Free Lhasa came over the horizon very quickly, and Jack pulled back hard on the throttle as the outskirts flashed past underneath him. He overshot, but used the broad turn to drop altitude. Turbulence over the city was troublesome, but he quite enjoyed the challenge, now that he was getting used to atmo again. A quick glance at his terrain map showed the landing point, approaching quickly, and he further reduced speed and altitude.

No doubt the locals had been impressed by the sonic boom

of his first overflight. Jack intended to match that with a fast, crisp arrival.

The landing point was the center of a large city square, and Jack picked an unpopulated spot between a dry fountain and an empty amphitheater. He came in fast, then swung the Hawk through a tight half-turn right over the landing spot, using his engine thrust to kill the last of his speed. Six or seven g's later, all he had to do was gently lower the craft out of its hover to touch down.

With the gentlest of bumps, Jack Mallory landed on Cerberus.

He looked back over his shoulder, grinning. Carmen was white, and struggling to breathe. Behind her, someone had puked all over the medical supplies. There was silence from the supply team.

Well, he had warned them about turbulence.

"Ladies and gentlemen," he said matter-of-factly, "welcome to Free Lhasa."

As he faced forward again, he heard Carmen unstrap herself and rise from her seat. She spoke quietly but firmly to her team, and there were a few quiet replies in turn. The industrious sounds of straps being removed mixed in with the squish of cleaning fluid being sprayed on the containers. Jack hit the release for the cargo door, and moments later the hiss of hydraulics was accompanied by the waft of pressure change as the door slowly lowered.

Looking out through his cockpit windows, he saw a delegation of locals walking toward the Hawk. He quickly scanned for any good-looking women, and came up disappointed. No children, either.

Around the edge of the square he could see small crowds of other people—maybe that's where the media were being cordoned.

He powered down the Hawk and unstrapped himself, moving aft to see how the unloading was going. Carmen had already disembarked to greet the locals. Members of the supply team were efficiently rolling the crates down the ramp and onto a motorized dolly brought along especially for this trip. Jack held back, giving them their moment of glory as the heroes of the day. Then, once the cargo had been cleared from the ramp, he stepped forward to survey the scene.

There were seven members of the local delegation, all dark

and wiry and short. Jack had trouble distinguishing one from the other, but he guessed they were all at least as old as his grandparents. They looked on with expressionless faces, all eyes on Carmen as she spoke slowly and clearly to them. When one local finally did answer, his voice was too quiet for Jack to hear.

He descended the Hawk's ramp and sidled up to Carmen. She glanced at him, but otherwise kept her attention on the local.

"That is very kind of you," she said. "We would be happy to share a toast with you at the medical center."

The local looked at Jack. He looked at Jack's face, then at his shoulders. "You are very young to be the next-in-command. You must be very skilled."

Jack didn't really know what he was talking about, but he recognized a compliment when he heard one.

"I've worked hard on my skills," he said with great modesty. "Thank you."

"You and your commander will be our honored guests." He turned back to Carmen. "Have your team come with us."

The locals started walking back in the direction from which they had come. Jack guessed that the low building at the edge of the square was the medical center. Carmen instructed one of her team to stay with the Hawk, motioned for the rest to follow her, then took Jack's arm.

"Nice going, Jack," she said, her voice low. "I was going to leave you to guard the Hawk, but how could I not bring along my 'next-in-command' for the ceremonies?"

"Yeah, what was that about?"

"These folks aren't stupid, Jack. They recognized your rank and saw that you're technically senior, after me. It wasn't quite the moment to explain logistics versus pilots. So congratulations, Subbie—if I get killed you're in charge."

"If you get smashed, you mean," he replied. "We're just going for drinks, aren't we?"

"I think so. Maybe they have something arranged at the medical center."

As they walked behind the group of locals—who were pretty spry for their age—Jack glanced around at the square. It was big, but otherwise unremarkable. There were no buildings above four stories, and every structure showed the wear and tear of this windy, dusty land. He noted again the dry fountain, and wondered if Free Lhasa suffered from water shortages. He'd heard stories about people in the colonies struggling to produce all kinds of basic needs, but he'd never suspected water to be one of them.

There were quite a few people making their way past buildings on the far side of the square, and the same groups of onlookers at the edges, but no one seemed to be paying the team much attention. The entire square had the look of faded glory, and Jack abruptly remembered that he and his passengers were bringing humanitarian supplies. This was not a happy place.

The medical center was three stories tall with long rows of rectangular windows embedded in molded plastic walls. Sturdy and functional. There was a group of locals clustered by the open doors ahead of them, each one watching the *Kristiansand* delegation with the same expressionless faces Jack was beginning to believe were standard on this planet. No one spoke as he followed Carmen through the doors, but Jack certainly noticed that all eyes followed the supply officer.

Had they never seen a blonde woman before?

Inside the doors, a broad lobby was filled with locals, all watching without speaking. The supply team were told where to put the medical supplies. In the strange silence, Jack began to feel uncomfortable. There were probably forty locals in the lobby, including those who had followed the procession in from outside. They were all dressed in nondescript civilian clothes, and ranged in age from young to very old. There was, however, what looked like a news camera.

That made him feel better—nothing bad would happen if there was someone to record it.

Carmen stepped to the middle of the room, and offered her most welcoming expression.

"Thank you for receiving us here today," she said loudly enough that all could hear. "It is an honor for the Terran Astral Force to work closely with the people of Cerberus, and to have the opportunity to come to Free Lhasa." She indicated the crates.

"I hope that these supplies will find good use in your city, and I hope that we can work together for many years to come."

A wizened man stepped forward—Jack thought he might be the leader of the delegation who had spoken to him at the Hawk. He stared at Carmen, but did not speak to her.

"Thapa, is this the same woman?"

A new man separated himself from the crowd. Short and grizzled like all the others, he approached Carmen carefully, studying her. He came right up to her face, having to look up quite a bit to meet her eye.

"No," Thapa said finally, "this woman is too tall to be her."

"A shame," the first man said. "It would have been justice."

Thapa stepped away from Carmen, his face growing cold.

"It will still be justice. I find this acceptable."

"Very well."

The leader moved to stand in front of Carmen, turning to face the news camera. The camera operator gave him a thumbs-up.

Jack heard a scuffle behind him, followed by shouts of alarm. Seconds later, he was grabbed by two pairs of impossibly strong hands, and dragged down. Too shocked to resist, he winced as his knees struck the hard floor. He vaguely saw Carmen thrown down beside him.

"Murderers of Terra!" the leader said to the camera. "For too long you have terrorized and butchered the people of Cerberus! You drop from the sky at will, thinking that we have no defense or recourse. You bring your battles to our soils, and it is our people who die!" He motioned back toward Jack and the others. "Now that will change. Now it is time for justice."

Beyond the leader, Jack saw Thapa take a rifle from one of the other men. Fear twisted his stomach and squeezed his lungs. He tried to breathe, but could focus only on the barrel of the gun as it rose to point at him.

Thapa stepped forward.

"For Pradeep."

He turned the rifle and fired three rounds into someone behind Jack. There were screams, and Jack heard a loud, wet thud on the floor behind him.

"For Shamsul."

Another shot. Jack heard what sounded like an egg crack and then another thud behind him.

Thapa stood before Carmen.

"For Anni."

He spun the rifle and smashed its butt into Carmen's stomach. She lurched forward, but was held up by her strong captives. He struck again, and after the reflex lurch Jack saw Carmen slump, a pitiful whimper escaping her lips. A tiny part of Jack's brain screamed at him to fight, but no part of his body dared respond. He was frozen.

Two butt-strokes to the face and head, and Carmen was dropped to the floor, a bloody, mangled heap.

Thapa loomed over Jack. Jack tried to speak, but his throat was seized shut. He faintly heard Thapa say two words:

"For Quan."

Then the rifle butt slammed into his stomach, and all he knew was ringing, stars, and endless pain.

18

Thomas first learned that something was going very wrong in Free Lhasa when *Rapier* received flash traffic from *Kristiansand* that violence had erupted in the square around the Hawk. Orbital footage of the mob jostling the Hawk and pelting it with rubble had sent diplomats system-wide flying to their comms panels.

Then the mob had somehow produced rocket launchers and blasted a hole in the Hawk's side. The lone *Kristiansand* crewmember had been hauled out, beaten, strung behind a truck, and dragged to her death around the square. Hundreds of Cerberans had cheered while others began to loot the craft.

Thomas signaled *Kristiansand*, offering assistance. The two ships were close enough for video communications and he had actually managed to get her on the screen.

"*Kristiansand*," he said, "*Rapier* can be in Free Lhasa in twenty minutes, and my strike team can recover the body."

Avernell's face had been a stone mask of suppressed rage. But her voice had been as calm as ever.

"*Rapier*, this is *Kristiansand*. Maintain your mark on the VOI. There is no need for a recovery." She had then looked off screen and raised her voice slightly. "Fire."

On his other screen, Thomas watched the devastating effect on the central square as *Kristiansand*'s orbital bombardment batteries opened fire. The first shots tore into the truck that was dragging the dead crewmember. It crashed to a flaming stop as doors and wheels were flung into the crowd. The next shots targeted the mangled remains of Avernell's crewmember, immolating the body and saving it from further abuses. The final shots pounded into the Hawk, smashing it across the square and destroying any sensitive information and technology aboard.

Less than a dozen rounds, pinpointed specifically to stop the direct attack on Terran assets. Thomas watched as the Cerberans in the square fled for their lives, but there was no follow-on attack, and he assessed that fewer than twenty had been killed.

On the first screen, Avernell gave him her attention again.

"*Rapier*, the situation is under control. I am not going to escalate this. My top priority is finding out what happened to the rest of my crew. Maintain your mark and stand by. *Kristiansand* out."

That had been five hours ago. Now Thomas could barely pull his eyes away from the screen. The terrified faces of the Astral Force personnel. The manic intensity of the Cerberans. The blood and screams as bullets flew and bones shattered. Thomas knew enough about close-up violence from his days as a platoon commander, but he'd never seen such brutal, premeditated savagery.

Neither, he figured, had most of the Terran population—until today.

The footage of the slaying and torture of Terran troops crossed the light years in hours. It was sent by the Cerberan terrorists to a local office of one of the Terran news majors, immediately transmitted back via the jump gate to head office, broadcast to the entire Terran system, and then released in its entirety to the military.

Since then Thomas had wandered restlessly between his cabin and the bridge, waiting for news or orders. And the entire time his ship had crept silently through space, thirty thousand kilometers astern of the smuggler.

Then, finally, the footage of the terrorist kidnapping had made its way back through the channels. Thomas was the only person in *Rapier* to have seen it so far, and he knew that Avernell was probably seeing it for the first time as well. He rewound the footage, noting that in the initial ambush, two people were shot dead—each time right after the shooter mumbled what sounded like a name. Then the same attacker said another name, and began to savagely beat *Kristiansand*'s supply officer. She crumpled immediately, but was beaten until her graying hair was matted and red.

The attack switched to the young man crouched next to her. He looked familiar, but Thomas couldn't remember from where. The beating was just as brutal, the butt of the rifle striking down long after the man had slumped into unconsciousness.

He shut off the screen, sickened. Pushed away from his desk, feeling his fists clench.

Something had to be done. He was the commander of a Terran fast-attack craft, right at the scene of the action. He doubted he would ever forgive himself if he sat back and did nothing. Action now could save those people, and make his career.

He opened a channel to *Kristiansand* and requested Avernell once again. When she appeared on the screen, her carefully neutral expression was betrayed by her ashen complexion.

"I assume you've seen the footage," she said.

"Yes, ma'am. Do we know where they're being held?"

"Negative. I'm trying to get the local warlord to communicate right now."

A sudden thought struck Thomas. "I have an intelligence officer on board—she might have connections that can help us."

Avernell nodded. "Very well. The Terran ambassador to Laika is also trying to acquire information, as well as any list of demands."

Negotiating with terrorists? Thomas felt his fists tighten again. This was wasting time.

"Ma'am, if we can get a location I can have a strike team down to recover them in fifteen minutes."

She shook her head. "This situation is already teetering on the brink—further bloodshed could tip it out of control. I've used minimum force in order to contain the damage, and I intend to continue on that path."

"But ma'am—"

"Lieutenant Commander Kane," she said, anger finally showing through, "because you are in command of a vessel I will pay you the courtesy of an explanation. This kidnapping, while horrific, is a minor event in the overall astro-political situation in Sirius. It is contained and Terra is working on finding a diplomatic solution. *Kristiansand* and *Rapier* will stand by as deterrents but we will not be distracted from our mission. It is our job to find proof that the Centauris are arming certain warlords on Cerberus. That is the major event in this theater. As commanders we must check our emotions, and stay focused on our goal." She paused, then continued.

"Trust me, I want my people back even more than you do, but I am not going to jeopardize Terra's position in Sirius. Is that clear?"

Thomas couldn't find fault with her words, even though he wanted to disagree.

"Yes, ma'am," he replied. "I'll get my sources looking for information, and continue to mark the VOI."

"Good." Avernell signed off.

Thomas immediately summoned Breeze to his cabin. He explained the situation and asked if she had any lines of communication that might be able to uncover info on the hostages. With a smile she assured him that she did.

He sent her on her way.

And then he fidgeted. He was in a perfect position to strike. This brutal kidnapping was already system-wide news in Terra, and he could only imagine the outrage pouring forth from the worlds. How could the Astral Force be taken seriously, either by the citizens of Terra who funded it, or by the colonists it policed, if this sort of atrocity wasn't dealt with swiftly? How could he go home at the end of this deployment and face his family and friends, knowing he had been there and not acted?

He tapped his desk console.

Captain Chandler wouldn't sit idly by, he knew. Chandler would find a way to convince his superiors that action was required, and that he was the man to take it. Chandler hadn't risen to his current rank by meekly waiting for orders. He had always been bold, and had tried to instill that in others.

Sean Duncan had never lost that assertiveness, had never turned into the political animal Thomas was becoming. Chandler hadn't become a captain by playing it *safe*. And no doubt Sean, as XO of *Kristiansand*, was even now finding a way to place himself in the spotlight.

Thomas slammed his hands down on the console. He commanded a fast-attack craft, and yet he was powerless to act. After the botched raid on the farm, his career needed this more than ever.

His door chimed and Breeze floated in. Her smile was even broader.

"Captain, I have info on the hostages. They're still in the medical center where the attack happened, but there are indications that the terrorists are going to move them soon. I've put the data into the main computer."

He tried to suppress his own smile.

"Damn, Breeze, that was fast."

She winked. "More than just a pretty face."

"Stay on it," he said, buoyed by the intel. "I'll talk to the adults."

Alone once more, he quickly pondered how best to approach his superiors. The last thing he wanted was for the diplomats to take his intelligence and use it to lean on the warlords. Nor did he want another Astral unit to be tasked into action.

Rapier had to be the ship assigned to make the rescue. *He* had to be the one to make the rescue. But how could he convince Command?

Then it struck him, and he felt his chest tighten. He didn't need Chandler's ability to persuade others, when he had Chandler himself.

Strapping down in front of his console, he drafted a message to *Normandy*'s commanding officer. Since *Rapier* herself belonged to *Normandy*, Chandler was in fact Thomas's immediate superior, even if Avernell was the senior commander on scene at Cerberus. Thomas had no choice but to obey Avernell's orders here, but nothing took away his right to confer directly with his boss.

His fingers tapped out the message.

Subject: Update on Cerberan Hostage Situation

Sir,

Rapier is within striking distance of Cerberus and is standing off with *Kristiansand* while the diplomats try to resolve the situation. I have contact with Astral intelligence units in Free Lhasa who have identified the location and impending movement of the hostages (file attached). I assess that the hostages are in grave danger.

I agree with *Kristiansand*'s current intent to avoid escalating the situation. However, it is clear that the Astral Force's enemies are watching very closely and our credibility may be damaged if the crisis continues for too long. The desecration of Astral assets in Free Lhasa is clear proof that rebellious elements of Cerberan society have been emboldened.

Rapier has the capability and forward positioning that enable us to strike immediately. I will continue to hold position with *Kristiansand* and await further orders.

Thomas Kane
Lt(C)
CO *Rapier*

He didn't need to know the mind of the admiral, the ambassador, or any other senior decision-makers, so long as he knew the mind of Captain Chandler. His mentor *despised* diplomatic dithering, he knew, and favored bold action.

Chandler, as a full captain, would think nothing of overruling the destroyer CO's stance. And he would enjoy pushing his opinion forward to his superiors. After all, Captain Chandler wanted to be *Admiral* Chandler one day.

Thomas attached the hostage info, quickly re-read his words, and transmitted the message. At light speed it would take nearly an hour to reach *Normandy* in the vicinity of Anubis. Then

Chandler would need time to make his case, and then another hour for orders to return.

Thomas took a deep breath, calming himself. For the next few hours there was nothing for him to do but trail the Cerberan smuggler, monitor the intelligence updates, and wait for the order to strike.

19

Katja squeezed into her seat on the bridge, her stomach churning. The rusty orb of Cerberus grew large through the bridge windows.

She'd only seen the footage once, watching in stunned horror as meek and feeble Thapa from the farm had transformed into a raging beast. Her surprise had turned to fury when she heard that Terra seemed to want to find a diplomatic solution to the crisis, and when the orders to strike came direct from EF 15, she had been barely able to contain her glee.

On the viewer positioned between her and Thomas was the grim face of *Kristiansand*'s executive officer.

"We'll shut down as much ground traffic as we can out of the city center," Duncan was saying, "but we can't guarantee that the hostages haven't been moved through some underground method."

"We're waiting for an intel update from the ground," Thomas replied. "My navigator has friends in strange places."

Katja noticed Breeze glance backward. She felt her usual distaste bubble up, but pushed it back down. Breeze's contacts on Cerberus would prove invaluable… *if* they could provide the necessary info.

Duncan smiled grimly. "I have no doubt." His face hardened again as the bridge behind him shook visibly. "We're drawing their fire to give you a clear approach."

A light ignited on Breeze's console, and Katja heard her speak quickly into her headset. Data flashed across her viewer, which she brought to the attention of Chief Tamma beside her. The cox'n, fully engaged in piloting *Rapier*, read the data in a moment, made some quick entries into his flight computer, and nodded.

"*Kristiansand*," Breeze interrupted, "I have just received a current report on the location of the hostages, time-late four mikes."

Katja saw Duncan look down at the info being transmitted from *Rapier*. She brought up her own map and saw that the hostages had been moved to the outskirts of the city. Duncan spoke off camera for a moment, then nodded at the response.

"We'll cover your approach," he said, turning back to face them. "And clear a target zone near the central square, to make them think that's where you're headed."

"We'll drop the strike pods just past the square and circle round for another strafing run," Thomas replied. "No one will notice the strike team."

Duncan looked off camera again, and nodded. "From *Kristiansand*, Godspeed, and smash those motherfuckers."

"*Rapier* receives."

Duncan's face disappeared, and the central console lit up again with a map of the city.

Thomas turned his head to look at Katja.

"We're going in very hot. There's no time for emotion once you're on the ground. You get the hostages out—and nothing else. No heroics. No vengeance. Leave the Armageddon to *Kristiansand*."

"Yes, sir."

As usual, Thomas's words were well chosen. She wanted blood. But he was right. Her job—and that of her team—was to be the surgeon's laser of this operation. Get in, get the people, get out.

Rapier was now close enough to Cerberus that Katja could actually see the tiny flashes of light on the planet's left limb that revealed the location of *Kristiansand*. At current speed, that meant *Rapier* would hit atmo in less than two minutes.

Time to go. She pushed out of her seat, swinging in the zero-g toward the hatch.

Thomas looked up at her. His eyes held hers for a moment,

and she thought she saw something different from the usual cool professionalism of her CO.

"No mistakes, OpsO," he said. "Hostages, not heroics."

"Yes, sir."

Because *Rapier* would be under fire from the moment she hit atmo, if not before, there was a very real chance the strike pods would have to separate at high altitude and high speed. Katja and her troopers had to be ready to bail in the vacuum, if necessary.

She was met by grim, silent faces as she climbed up into the pod. Cerberus was noticeably larger through the windows as she strapped into her seat. Flashes from a single spot in orbit continued to rain down just at the edge of the planet's visible disk, and Katja thought she saw similar flashes erupt occasionally just above the surface.

"Bravo-One, Alpha-One—confirm go for strike."

"*Bravo Team go.*"

"Roger." Switch freqs. "Mother, Alpha-One—go for strike."

Over the ship-wide freq, Thomas's voice. "Rapier *is go for strike. All hands, brace for hostile fire.*"

Cerberus loomed before them. Katja looked out over the black surface of *Rapier*'s hull. The top turret moved experimentally in its position astern of the bridge, twin cannons eager to unleash. Her eyes scanned down the ship's curved hull, and out over her broad port wing. The small mounds on the surface revealed the waiting morningstar missiles. At the far edge of the wing, the mighty port engine burned fiercely.

This ship was ready for battle, and so was she.

The top turret blazing to life was her first warning that hostilities had begun. Twin tracers lit up the darkness of space, painting a line to a sudden explosion ahead—an attacking missile, Katja guessed, stunned at the suddenness of it all. Seconds later, a fiery object loosed itself from *Kristiansand* in the distance. The fireball moved at ungodly speed across the sky and met another object dead ahead of *Rapier*. A silent explosion lit up the blackness, and Katja thought she saw charred remains spinning away of what must have been a Cerberan patrol craft.

The entire engagement took less than ten seconds, in absolute silence and with absolutely no warning. Katja allowed herself a glance at Cohen, her pilot. Cohen's eyes were saucers. Katja hoped her own face didn't display the same shock.

"Helmets," she said over the strike frequency.

The sound of faceplates snapping down proved to Katja that her teammates were as new to space combat as she was. She closed her faceplate and locked it down.

Rapier hit the atmosphere at an angle, and at such speed that there was none of the usual build-up of faint, orange glow. Suddenly the world outside vanished in an eruption of fire, and her own vision tinged red.

If their engines were to fail now, *Rapier* would either smash into Cerberus with the force of a gigaton nuclear bomb, or miss the surface and burn a trail of fire behind her thousands of kilometers long before being flung back out into space.

Katja forced herself to breathe deeply, focused all her efforts on that. She didn't even try to read her instruments, and just trusted that Thomas would get them down safely.

The orange fire faded, and Katja looked down again at the ruddy surface of Cerberus. A flash of metal shot past her vision, and before she could raise her hands in futile defense she was thrown in her seat as *Rapier* rolled. Katja groaned, but kept her vision focused "up" at the landscape.

The top turret was firing three-second bursts, moving rapidly from target to target. The targets themselves remained unseen until she saw tiny explosions far ahead. The ship lurched again, and the ground above became much bigger as she dropped altitude.

The artificial gravity in her seat stabilized, and she was able to survey the landscape without blood rushing to her head. The top turret was still firing, and a large ground explosion indicated *Kristiansand*'s cover fire. She called up a visual on the target zone. The image suffered from the usual Doppler shift, and was jittery as *Rapier* dodged left and right on her attack run. But from what she could see, the strike zone was clear.

"Mother, Alpha-One—strike zone clear."

"Mother, concur. Twenty seconds to town square. At T-plus-two we roll and release."

"Alpha-One, roger." Switch freqs. "Twenty seconds to drop. Roll and release. Simultaneous."

"*Bravo-One,*" Chang said.

"*Alpha-Five,*" Cohen said.

"*Bravo-Five,*" Alayan said.

Pod pilots rarely spoke. Cohen and Alayan were scared.

Rapier was still moving at more than one thousand kph. The outskirts of Free Lhasa were a gray blur mixed with the fire of *Kristiansand*'s bombardment.

"Stand by…" Katja said. The top turret exploded to life again. She gritted her teeth as the ship rolled.

"Now!"

Her seat punched her from underneath. Her suit flattened against her chest. Stars danced in her eyes.

The city of Free Lhasa spread before her. The roar faded. Deceleration ended. The two little ships raced over the rooftops toward their target at two hundred kph. Katja looked off to her left, and saw *Rapier* pulling through a broad, fast turn, top, bottom, and tail turrets still firing at the city square. It was a total diversion to keep the Cerberan defenses focused on the square. Katja hoped it would work.

The true strike zone was a series of residential buildings on the outskirts of town. The strike pods covered the distance from the square in ninety seconds. Katja heard rifles come out, and safeties click off. She looked down at the streets and saw hundreds of people running amidst recklessly driven trucks. What had been rage a few hours ago now seemed turned to panic under *Kristiansand*'s relentless bombardment.

Katja felt her lip curl in a snarl.

Smash the motherfuckers.

The pods landed hard on the roof of the designated building, blasting the sentries with their thrusters. As the hatch opened and her troopers disembarked, the *tock-boom* of suppressing fire told Katja that the landing zone was not yet secure. A second later, she was out of the pod.

"Mother, Alpha-One. Touchdown, ops red."

Pause. "*Mother, roger.*" Thomas did not sound calm.

The splattered remains of several terrorists colored the flat surface. Alpha Team and Bravo Team fanned out to secure the surrounding area, including adjoining buildings. No more shots were fired. Katja activated her quantum-field vision and looked down through the roof. Clear below. Sentries at the stairwell.

But Astral troopers in armored suits didn't need stairs.

She gestured to Chang. *I see. Four. Down one floor. There. Take.*

Bravo Team advanced on the stairs, firing their explosive rounds directly into the roof of the building. The multiple blasts mixed with screams from below. Bravo Team, led by Chang, jumped down the hole and started clearing the third story.

"*Alpha-One, Bravo-One,*" Chang said. "*Clear for descent.*"

Katja suddenly remembered that, in her armored spacesuit, their voices couldn't be heard from the outside. Her hand gestures had been pure reflex.

"Alpha-One," she replied, leading her team down the hole, landing heavily in her suit. She still had her helmet locked down—very handy in smoke and flame—but her audio sensors let her hear what was occurring around her. The crackle of burnt plastic and metal filled the stairwell. Off to the side a loud *thump* told her Bravo Team was moving through the third story of apartments. Katja focused her quantum viewer down the next floor.

It was clear.

"Bravo-One, Alpha-One—descending to two in the clear."

"*Bravo-One.*"

Katja led the way down the stairs and peered over her rifle at the stairwell. Quantum-flux revealed no one beyond the walls, so she moved to lead them through the door, but Hernandez put a firm hand on her armored shoulder.

She frowned, and nodded. The rest of her team took the lead. Alpha-Two and Alpha-Four burst through the door and thundered down the corridor, returning from their sweep just as Bravo Team came down the stairs.

She quantum-scanned the first floor. It was crowded with people. A group hunched ready near the stairwell, likely waiting to ambush any intruders who came that way. A second, larger group was farther off to the side, and vague in the flux—most likely the hostages and their captors. Unfortunately the hostages were wearing dress uniforms, which lacked the quantum signature patches that would confirm their identities.

"Alpha-One, Alpha-Five. Suspect activity on the streets outside your building."

Katja paused. "Alpha-One, roger. Is the threat imminent?"

"Negative, but growing."

Instead of asking for more detail, she chose to focus on the immediate task—retrieve the hostages. She addressed her assembled troopers.

"Bravo Team will strike first to draw their attention and take out the group at the stairs. Then Alpha Team will drop into the middle of the first floor—our objective is the hostages."

Alpha Team thumped down the corridor to the midway point. Katja heard the explosions behind them as Bravo Team opened fire on the floor above their targets. There was a lot of shooting and shouting at that end of the building, and quantum revealed a flurry of activity below her, as more terrorists went to help in the defense of the stairs.

Katja and her team lined up their weapons and fired at the floor. Carefully placed explosive rounds struck the hard plastic and detonated in a storm of fire and smoke. Charred particles bounced harmlessly off her suit and mask, and she leaned in to look through the gap in the floor. There was room to jump.

She gestured emphatically. *"Go!"*

Alpha-Two and Alpha-Four dropped through the hole, and the thunder of gunfire echoed up. Katja and Hernandez were right behind.

The servos cushioned her fall, but she still winced as she hit the floor. Bullets thudded into her chest armor, and she fired off three rounds into the violent fray.

Already the entire floor was choked with dust and smoke. Katja used her quantum-flux to see through the haze, and spotted a small figure in an attack position. She fired, and saw the figure disintegrate as the round impacted flesh and exploded.

"This is Alpha-Two," Assad said in a cool voice. *"Tally-ho hostages, north end."*

Katja and Hernandez turned together and ran toward the north end of the building, their suits protecting them from the horror of battle. Through the chaos, they saw Assad and

Jackson gathering up the hostages.

Katja did a quick survey. Five hostages. All wounded. Two critically. But alive. She even took an extra moment to survey the injuries on Jack, Breeze's boy-toy. His face was badly bruised and his nose was broken, but his limbs were intact. Based on the footage alone Katja guessed that he had internal injuries. He was pale under the caked blood, but breathing.

He stared up at her with bleary eyes.

"Hey, you're Astral Corps..."

She nodded. "And you're a pilot. Can you stand?"

He winced as he shuffled onto his knees.

"I think so."

Katja put an armored arm around his torso and lifted him gently to his feet. He winced, and leaned heavily on her.

"All units, Alpha-One. RV north end for hostage extraction. Pods, report to street level. Bravo-One, pilots."

"Bravo-One."

"Alpha-Five."

"Bravo-Five."

Switch freqs. "Mother, Alpha-One. Break away."

"Mother, roger. We're already en route—we have reports of armed insurgents closing your position."

Bravo Team thundered through the broken walls, firing back as they came. Alpha Team broke out a pair of stretchers and loaded up Jack and the other badly injured hostage, a woman in her late thirties. The remaining hostages were assigned to carry the stretchers.

"Alpha-One, Alpha-Five." It was Cohen's voice. *"There are hostiles in the streets, closing fast."*

"Alpha-One." She pointed at the nearest wall. "Make a door!"

Troopers fired. The wall exploded outward. The heavy beams holding the second floor buckled dangerously.

"Move!"

With Bravo Team in the lead, the strike team burst out onto the street, fanning out in a circular pattern around the strike pods as they touched down.

Locals were fleeing in all directions. A truck swerved to avoid running into pedestrians and crashed into a building half a block away. Through the chaos, Katja heard the distinct sound of rifle fire.

"*Bravo-One—sniper!*"

Troopers opened fire in all directions. Explosions tore through the pre-fab structures. Dust and debris choked the street.

Katja hustled the hostages toward the pods.

"Cease fire! Find your targets!"

The hostages started loading up into the strike pods, but the Fleet crewmen weren't as efficient as troopers, they were injured and they were carrying stretchers. It took longer than it should, and there was more hostile fire inbound. Katja ran through the smoke to where her troopers had formed a perimeter.

Beyond them, dim figures ran in the street.

Jackson fired several rounds. Screams echoed off of the buildings.

"Cease fire!" Katja commanded. "Target hostiles only!" She crouched as bullets whizzed by. Quantum-flux range was too limited. She switched to infrared. Dozens of warm bodies moved in frantic motion through the chaos. Mostly away from them.

But some weren't running. She zeroed in on the cool, practiced movements of several figures on the third floor of the building to her right. They carried weapons, which weren't raised. One appeared to be speaking into a radio.

"Alpha-One—tally-ho forward spotter. Building right, third floor!" She loosed three rounds into the structure. The infrared images of the enemy were lost in the ensuing explosions. They disappeared from sight.

"*Alpha-One, Mother. Report of heavies inbound from the south. Get airborne!*"

Katja hesitated. Neither team could go until the hostages were loaded.

"All units, Alpha-One. Heavies from the south. Form a barrier. On me!"

The streets were crowded with civilians, some throwing rocks but the others warily holding their distance as the entire strike team formed up in a battle line south of the pods. The dust was swirling, but clearing.

The first indication she had of the threat was a glint of metal around the corner to her left. Then a tall, silvery machine rolled into view on its armored tracks, a repeating cannon blasting to life from its humanoid shoulder. Katja gasped as she was knocked backward by the impact of heavy slugs. She stumbled to one knee and swung around to fire on fully automatic.

Her troopers joined her barrage, and within seconds the attacking robot slumped forward, its limb-weapons shattered. A Centauri anti-personnel robot.

Katja switched back to IR and saw five more robots rumbling forward, marked by their power sources, still blocked by the building. She rose to her feet, unable to stop herself from shuffling backward three steps. Centauri APRs. On Cerberus.

"Bravo loaded!"

She barely registered Alayan's voice, her attention riveted on the approach of the Centauri war machines. She had been lucky with the first one—it hadn't had the chance to fire its rockets. But her troopers stood no chance against five such opponents.

Then it sank in—Bravo's hostages were loaded.

"Bravo Team, break away!"

Chang and his troopers backed up, still facing the threat as they climbed the ramp into their ship. Good troopers never fled, they only withdrew.

"Stand by for APR attack. Target weapon pods—use grenades!"

Three men stood with her, rifles raised. The five APRs were still around the corner, but coming. Ten seconds, at most. She dared not look back. The distant crowd of civilians was inching closer as well, shouting and waving their fists.

"Alpha-One, Mother. Report your status!"

"Bravo Team breaking away. Alpha Team still loading. We are engaging Centauri Alpha-Papa-Romeos at the drop zone. Request immediate assistance!"

"Mother, roger!"

As Katja saw the first of the APRs come around the corner, she prayed for the swift, dark form of *Rapier* to come roaring overhead, cannons blazing.

Rapier did not come, but Thomas didn't let her down.

The air burned as meteors struck down from on high. Katja grunted and fell as the ground heaved beneath her. Orange fire filled her vision. Her external audio screamed and went dead.

She rolled over onto her belly, pointing her rifle toward the threat. But twisted heaps of molten metal were all that remained of the Centauri APRs. Crumbling heaps of rubble had replaced the corners of the buildings. Devastation reigned for a hundred meters in all directions from the blast.

Katja and her troopers had been protected by their armored suits, but not so the civilians who had been approaching the scene. Dozens of burned and blackened bodies littered the street. Those who could were fleeing. Those who couldn't simply screamed in agony.

"Alpha-One, Mother. Report your status!"

Katja stared in horror at the carnage.

"This is Alpha-One... drop zone clear. Threat neutralized."

"Roger. I'll pass your compliments to Kristiansand!" There was a triumphant quality to Thomas's voice.

Hernandez came up beside her. "What the fuck...?"

"Orbital bombardment," Katja heard herself say, dimly aware that Hernandez was helping her to her feet. "*Kristiansand* looking out for us."

"Alpha loaded!"

Katja barely heard Cohen's scream over the radio. The entire length of the street was strewn with the bloody remains of blasted bodies. The last of the mob were fleeing in the distance, still easy targets if *Kristiansand* wished to follow up her attack.

Katja tore her eyes from the scene.

"Alpha Team, break away."

Assad and Jackson moved on her order. Hernandez waited for her to follow. They climbed into the strike pod and hung on as Cohen lifted off to rendezvous with *Rapier*.

Katja pushed past her troopers and the hostages as they crowded together in the little ship. She sat down in her seat and strapped in.

"Mother, Alpha-One... mission accomplished."

20

Rapier and *Kristiansand* had to run more than a million kilometers before the Cerberans finally gave up the chase.

Thomas leaned back in his seat, breathing deeply. He scanned his display one more time, just to assure himself that there were no more threats. The scope was clear. He exhaled again, his mind still too wired to properly take in what they had just done. With a single destroyer and a single FAC, they had taken on the most powerful hostile force in Sirius, and won.

And his ship had made the rescue.

"Hot damn, Cox'n," he said, "if you were any better-looking I'd kiss you."

Chief Tamma and Breeze both burst out laughing, the tension on the bridge easing. The last hour had strained the three of them to their limits as they conducted one of the craziest high-speed entries Thomas had ever seen, punched their way through the Cerberan ground defenses, and then taken fire for an eternity while Katja and her troops snatched the hostages. *Rapier* was pounded all to hell, but she was still flying.

He opened the inter-ship comms.

"*Kristiansand, Rapier.* My compliments on a fine bit of cover. We couldn't have done it without you."

"*Well done,* Rapier," Commander Avernell replied. "*Thank you for rescuing my people.*"

Thomas checked the external view, and saw that his strike pods were disengaging from *Kristiansand*'s airlocks. The hostages had been held aboard the pods during the escape, and had only been transferred once the battle was over.

"Truly, my pleasure, ma'am."

"Stay in formation. We're plotting a course for Laika to RV with the fleet, point-zero-five-c. I'll call in the report."

"Yes, ma'am."

The admiral would be waiting to hear if their gambit had succeeded. Thomas was happy to let Avernell tell the tale. He wouldn't want to be seen as boasting.

"Captain, Pilot," Tamma said. "Pods are moving to dock."

"Very good."

Thomas was tempted to go aft to welcome his troopers home and congratulate each one of them on a fine job. But he knew that his place was the bridge—it wouldn't be seemly to go running off through the ship with a big grin on his face. Instead, he sat quietly in his seat and practiced his image as the serene commander.

"NavO, secure from battle stations."

"Yes, sir." Breeze activated the ship-wide circuit. "Secure battle stations." She flipped off the circuit, pausing in thought. "Damn. Whose watch is it, anyway?"

Tamma raised his hand. "Mine, I'm afraid. I have the conn."

Breeze activated the circuit again. "Charlie watch, close up." Then she unstrapped herself and climbed out of her spacesuit. She struggled slightly, and Thomas noticed that her hands were shaking. Her coveralls were soaked with sweat, but clinging to her figure in a way that highlighted the effects of zero-g. He forced himself to look away and think of Soma.

Breeze pulled herself past her own seat, spacesuit in tow. She looked quite pale.

"You okay, NavO?" he asked.

She rested a hand on his shoulder as she floated past, her expression instantly turning to one of casual good humor.

"Yeah," she replied. "Thanks, boys, it was fun. Now I really need a shower."

Tamma grinned over his shoulder.

Thomas did his best to roll his eyes.

Tamma looked back at his console. "Both pods are locked into place, Captain."

"Very good."

There was a long moment of quiet on the bridge. Thomas knew he should start drafting the inevitable report he would have to submit, but all he could come up with was, *We did it, dammit!* He suspected High Command would want something a bit more substantial than that.

A reflection in the bridge windows caught Thomas's attention. In the reflection he saw the tiny, armored figure of his strike officer as she came through the hatch.

His face split into a grin. "OpsO! When we get back to *Normandy* I'm taking your whole team drinking!" He resisted the urge to get up and give her a hug, armor or no armor.

His good humor faded, though, as soon as he saw her face.

Katja moved slowly and carefully, the quiet whirrs of her suit accenting her every move. Her helmet and rifle were strapped to her waist, and she awkwardly hooked them both to her seat before meeting his gaze. Her blonde hair was plastered against her scalp, her skin was even paler than normal, and her large, pretty eyes had that vacant look soldiers had known for centuries as the "thousand-yard stare."

"Captain, sir, OpsO," she said quietly. "Strike team embarked, no casualties."

She was looking at him, but right through him.

He'd seen this before. No doubt he'd looked like this himself after his first real combat. It was hard to know how to handle a trooper in shell shock—everyone reacted differently.

"Very good, OpsO," he replied. "I understand five hostages were recovered alive."

"Yes."

"Then the mission was a success."

"Yes."

Tamma looked back, surprise and concern etched across his dark features. Thomas noticed, and subtly waved the cox'n away. Tamma returned his attention to the console.

"OpsO, did something go wrong during the mission?"

She seemed to hesitate. Her lips moved slightly, but no words came out.

"Katja?"

She blinked, and focused on him for the first time. "There were civilian casualties. We were attacked. We had no choice."

Thomas nodded in understanding, trying to offer reassurance without the cumbersome words. She'd seen death—*real* death.

He vaguely heard the comms crackle to life.

"Captain, sir," Tamma said. "Pilot."

He tore his eyes from the haunted gaze of his OpsO. "Captain."

"*Kristiansand* is reporting an inability to communicate with Fleet. They have no readings on EF beacons. Can we confirm?"

Thomas called up his communication status board. In peacetime, every Terran warship radiated a continuous, secure beacon. Undetectable to normal space traffic, it allowed the different ships in the fleet to find one another in the vastness of the void. Before the Cerberan strike, Thomas had noted a large cluster of beacons near Laika, as EF 15 rendezvoused for their exercises.

Now the scope was completely blank.

He had experienced poor communications before, but never over such a short range. Anubis was barely a billion kilometers distant. Could the gas giant's powerful magnetic field be interfering?

He didn't think so.

"Chief, run a diagnostic on our beacon equipment."

"Yes, sir." Tamma's fingers danced over his console. "Could it be because we stopped transmitting for the strike?"

Rapier had gone silent on her beacon before the strike, just in case the Cerberans had got their hands on Terran beacon codes.

"No, it shouldn't make a difference," Thomas said. "We often run silent, but can still receive."

Tamma nodded. "Equipment checks out, sir."

"Hmm." A flurry of scenarios flashed through Thomas's brain— none of them good. Despite what the recruiting posters said, Astral equipment didn't always work perfectly, and daily life in the Fleet involved working around troublesome kit. The beacons, however, never failed. A ship's beacon was its lifeline in case of distress. It was based on old, robust, proven technology, and after twenty years in the AF, Thomas had never heard of one malfunctioning.

For an entire expeditionary force to disappear off the scope...

"What's wrong, sir?" Katja asked.

Thomas looked at her. She had lost her thousand-yard stare and was focused on the situation. It was as if she had just woken up.

"We've lost beacon with EF 15," he said, "and there's no reason why we should have."

"Jamming?"

"Could be."

"By the Cerberans?"

"Unlikely. They don't have that kind of technology. Besides, we're too far out of their range."

"Laikans?"

"Possibly," he acknowledged. "But why?"

Katja had no answer.

Thomas flipped the comms switch. "Engine room, bridge."

"Engine room."

"I need a main engine report. Can we sustain another prolonged, full-power burn?"

"The engines are good, Captain, but that last strike put real strain on the wings. Please tell me you're not planning another atmo run."

"No, Chief. Deep space the whole way."

"Then you're good to go, sir."

"Thank you."

Thomas closed the channel and hailed *Kristiansand*. After several minutes, his central console lit up with the face of Commander Avernell.

"Ma'am, *Rapier* has no joy with comms. I have no beacon readings anywhere in the Anubian region."

Avernell nodded. "We can still detect the beacons out at the jump gate, so this isn't an effect localized on us. Something is masking the EF from our sensors."

"Could it be a solar storm, energizing the Anubian magnetic field?"

"We checked. Solar activity is normal. I think this is jamming."

"My scope doesn't look jammed—just blank."

"Our sensors detect a very low-level disruption covering the entire Anubian system." She paused for emphasis. "Sirians don't have this kind of technology."

Thoughts of mystery merchants and stealth ships flashed across Thomas's brain. A sinister pattern was emerging.

"Centauria."

Avernell nodded. "Can your ship sustain a high-speed burn?"

"Yes, ma'am." He was pleased that he had anticipated her thoughts. "I can be at Laika in ten hours."

"Then both of our ships will proceed at best possible speed to rendezvous with the fleet. I'll be there in about fifteen hours." She paused, then added, "Stay sharp—we're not alone out here."

"Yes, ma'am."

"*Kristiansand* out."

Thomas leaned back in his seat, aware that Katja was watching him. He ignored her for the moment.

"Officer of the Watch, we are detached from *Kristiansand*. Set a course for Laika, point-one-c."

As Tamma obeyed, Thomas activated the ship's intercom.

"This is the captain—sitrep. Well done on the rescue mission. We successfully recovered all five living hostages and lost none of our own. We are en route to rejoin the EF at Laika, but we have lost their beacons. We don't have all the information, but suspect Centauri jamming." He paused, considering how to word his next thought. "Tensions are high, and we don't know what's waiting for us. Therefore, we will remain on alert. One-in-three watches will stay in effect, but all personnel are to remain suited. Relax when you can, but be vigilant on watch. Information will be provided as it becomes available. That is all."

Finally, he turned to Katja.

"You deserve a hot shower, OpsO, and a hot meal. Why don't you take a break for a while?"

Katja nodded curtly and rose, none of her earlier shock apparent.

"I'll check on my team, sir, and ensure that the strike pods are ready for action."

"Very good."

She left the bridge, and Thomas watched her go. Every trooper dealt with shock a different way. Some withdrew, some drank, and some just buried it deep by keeping themselves busy. The busy ones were the ones that worried him most.

His operations officer would have to take care of herself for the moment, however. As Thomas settled back into his seat, he turned his mind to the tactical situation. His fleet was masked by jamming—or worse. Centauri stealth ships were prowling the system.

And, he suddenly realized, his daring rescue had done nothing to ease tensions. Two Terran warships had just attacked a civilian settlement belonging to the most powerful hostile force in Sirius. This force was clearly—if secretly—supported with Centauri weapons and training, and two Terran warships had just laid waste to its capital city.

And he had led the strike.

Thomas looked again at the conspicuous absence of EF beacons on his scope, and felt a chill rise in his chest. He had always wished for the chance to prove himself in war. He suddenly found himself praying that wishes didn't come true.

21

Laika was a far cry from Cerberus. The large, atmospheric moon had been settled by very different people from the individualists who had claimed Cerberus as their own. Peace, order, and good government were its three founding principles, and Katja could tell the difference from more than twenty million kilometers away as *Rapier* was hailed by the Laikan Long-Range Vessel Traffic Management System.

"*Vessel in position zero-nine-zero, one-zero-two, two-seven-six, this is Anubis Control. Please identify yourself.*"

It was Katja's first time on the bridge of a ship entering Anubian space, and she was impressed. Laika was only one of six Anubian moons inhabited by humans, but it took on the responsibility to manage the considerable traffic spread throughout the entire planetary system that swirled around the gas giant. Laika had tracked, tagged, and queried them while Anubis itself was still little more than a bright disk in the distance.

The Cerberans were having a good day if they noticed you in high planetary orbit.

"Anubis Control, this is Terran warship *Rapier*, en route to Laikan orbit."

There was a delay in the response, but not as long as the light minute between *Rapier* and Laika.

"*Terran warship* Rapier, *roger, system traffic is moderate. Reduce your speed to point-zero-five-c. Be advised one convoy* of five cargo ships is outbound for Cerberus, eight million fine off your port bow. They are led by Merchant Vessel Darcy Harrington. Recommend you make passing arrangements."

"Rapier, roger out."

Katja throttled back to conform with Anubian safety speed, checked her 3-D display and confirmed the presence of five contacts moving in formation five million kilometers ahead. At Rapier's speed they would reach their closest proximity in about nine minutes. Her navi-computer calculated the numbers, and recommended a slight change of course to open up the distance.

Her display was already lighting up with more contacts moving between the Anubian moons, and as Rapier rapidly closed the distance, the scope became busier. Katja was competent when it came to open-space operations, but strike training hadn't prepared her for the navigational hornet's nest of a busy planetary system.

She activated the comms circuit. "Captain, sir, Officer of the Watch."

Thomas responded quickly. "Captain."

"We're entering the Anubian system. I've checked in with long-range VTMS and traffic is getting heavier. Request you come to the bridge."

"On my way."

Moments later, the hatch swung open and Thomas appeared. He eased his suited form into the seat next to Katja and brought up his own display. Katja quickly explained the traffic situation, pointing out the five-ship convoy ahead. They weren't on a collision course, but they would pass a little closer than most space-farers would like.

Thomas nodded. "Any sign of the EF?"

Katja scanned her display, adjusting her scope to examine Laikan orbital space more closely. It was difficult at this distance to make sense of the mass of contacts, but there did appear to be a large grouping in low orbit. She indicated it to Thomas.

"But still no sign of their beacons," he said, then he activated Rapier's secure comms. "Echo-Foxtrot One-Five, this is Rapier on Fleet Reporting, over."

Silence was the only response. No static, no white noise. He switched channels.

"Echo-Foxtrot One-Five, this is *Rapier* on Command Net, over."

Silence.

"OpsO, try hailing the EF on the warfare circuits."

"Yes, sir." Katja spent a minute attempting to hail the fleet on the various channels used for battle coordination. There was no response and she said as much.

When he didn't respond, she glanced over at him. His expression was focused, his eyes hard.

"We just lost the beacon for the jump gate," he said.

She checked her display. Sure enough, where a moment ago the eternal jump gate beacon had shone, there was nothing but blank scope.

"Directed, local interference?" she offered.

He nodded. "Like someone is trying to cut off Astral Force units in the Anubian system in a way that a casual observer wouldn't notice. It might even escape the attention of the ships themselves."

Katja felt her stomach tighten. "But why?"

"Our entire expeditionary force is assembled in Laikan space, doing routine exercises. It's a rare opportunity for an enemy to strike without word getting back to Terra."

"Terra has no quarrel with Laika, or any of the Anubian colonies. Why would they want to attack?"

Thomas's eyes possessed unusual intensity as he turned to look at her. "Terra—by which I mean us—just openly attacked a major Sirian colony. And guess who was already there to defend them?"

Katja's throat went dry. "Centauria."

"Centauria's military presence on Cerberus has been revealed. Terran military circuits are jammed. And the EF is vulnerable in low orbit around Laika."

Katja felt her emotions slip away as the now familiar, pre-mission clarity took over her mind. "Battle stations?"

"Battle stations."

She pressed the general alarm button. For eight seconds the klaxon sounded throughout the ship. She brought up the damage control panels on her left, watching as the engine room began switching systems over to battle mode. The extra generators were flashed up. Secondary fire-fighting and vacuum-control systems came on line. Hull power-transfer took over from the main busses.

Artificial gravity kicked in at the various locations around the ship where crewmembers needed to be grounded. Katja felt her own weight return as she sank into her seat.

Chief Tamma clambered onto the bridge and sank down into his seat in front of Thomas. Breeze was quick behind him. During the moments that the hatch was open, Katja heard orderly shouts and clatter as the crew headed for their stations.

Tamma took the flight controls from Katja, and Breeze brought up the weapons systems.

Anubis' bright, swirling cloud banks began to loom large ahead, but *Rapier*'s path kept the gas giant to port. The 3-D display clearly showed Laika as it moved in its orbit, and as Katja searched she thought she could just make out the brilliant white disk against the background stars. The disk grew quickly into a recognizable sphere as *Rapier* hurtled toward it at nearly five hundred thousand kilometers each minute.

The ships of the EF were still much too small to see from this distance, but then Katja found that she could see them on her display. She stared for a moment at the familiar blue icons of Terran ships, clustered very close in low Laikan orbit.

"Captain…" she said, "I can see the EF's beacons on my display."

Thomas immediately activated the comms. "*Normandy*, this is *Rapier* on Command Net—radio check, over."

A voice came back immediately, with no sense of alarm.

"Rapier, *this is* Normandy, *roger, over.*"

"This is *Rapier*, roger. Request *Normandy* actual this circuit, over."

Katja checked on the status of the Expeditionary Force. They were conducting an underway replenishment in low orbit. The supply ships, hemmed in on all four sides by warships in tight formation, were transferring stores through flexible tubes. The other warships were spread out in a standard picket defense, ready to ward off anyone foolhardy enough to try and cause trouble during this vulnerable but essential fleet evolution. The low orbit provided the cover of a deep gravity well to further render stealth attacks extremely difficult.

"Rapier, *this is* Normandy. *Actual, over.*" Captain Chandler himself was now on the line.

Thomas responded. "This is *Rapier*, urgent message. Terran circuits in the Anubian system are being jammed. We have not held EF beacons since Cerberus—assess you are shining only locally. I suspect hostile action is imminent. Over."

There was a pause. When Chandler spoke his voice was slow and careful.

"*Roger... We have had no indication of jamming. There is no hostile activity to speak of. We have tracked your approach and assume you have just reactivated your beacon—please confirm. Over.*"

Thomas pursed his lips in frustration.

"*Rapier*'s beacon has been shining since Cerberus. Request that you check for the beacons of *Kristiansand* and the jump gate. Both are beyond the jamming radius. Over."

"*Wilco.*" A pause, then, "*Report on the Cerberus operation, over.*" Chandler's voice had grown stern.

Thomas kept his voice calm and professional. "Success. Five live hostages recovered and no strike team casualties." He looked ready to add more, but held his tongue. "Over."

"*Very good. Well done on completing your mission. Normandy is engaged in an UNREP and unable to recover you at this time. Stand off and await recovery in two-zero mikes. Over.*"

"*Rapier*, roger, over."

"Normandy *out.*"

Katja listened on the command net as orders were passed for the next group of ships to prepare for UNREP. She didn't know all the details of Fleet replenishment, but she did know that it wasn't an easy maneuver. Eight ships had to clear a tight formation around the supply ships, and eight more had to maneuver in to replace them, one at a time.

"Captain, sir, Pilot," Tamma said. "Fuel is down to fifteen percent. Confirm standard orbital braking to save energy?"

Thomas considered. "Affirmative. We have time before *Normandy* clears."

Laika had grown much larger, and the lights of civilian ships moved in front of the stars. Tamma had adjusted *Rapier*'s course to whip once around the moon before rendezvousing with the Expeditionary Force. This orbital braking would use Laika's gravity to further slow the ship, place her in orbit, and line her up for a meeting with the EF, all with minimal ship's power required.

Katja stole a glance at Thomas. Bold yet prudent, and absolutely unflappable. The memory of a joke he had told in *Normandy*'s star lounge suddenly flashed into her mind, of how she had laughed and felt so good in his company. She pushed it away, but in the same moment hoped that they would have the opportunity for some personal time again, and soon.

Laika's blue, green, and white surface grew to fill half the sky. Tamma rolled the ship so that her topside faced the planet, and Katja took a moment to take in her first good look at a new world. Lights dotted the dark surface, spaced fairly regularly across the major continent. A few lone ones indicated the far-flung, resource-based cities in the far north.

Several moved against the dark backdrop, reminding Katja that there were other ships in the vicinity, and that *Rapier* was in the middle of a carefully controlled maneuver. She glanced at her display, and idly noted that none of the other orbitals posed a threat along *Rapier*'s path.

An interesting formation of ships was visible on the display, ten of them moving in a line abreast like cadets on the parade square. She wondered if it was some kind of survey mission— the Laikans were well known both for their environmental husbandry and their scientific prowess. The line was located less than one hundred kilometers below *Rapier*'s path, moving in the same direction but slower than the fast-attack craft.

Rapier would pass overhead in about thirty seconds. Katja turned her eyes "upward" to look.

There was nothing there but the dark surface.

She looked again at her display, wondering if she had miscalculated the formation's relative bearing. Then she looked back at the night sky.

Still nothing.

A flash of orange light caught her eye. Then a second. Then more. About 100 kilometers away, between her and the planet, Katja saw a rapid succession of orange flickers in the blackness, like tiny flames burning for a split second before snuffing out. They reminded her of nighttime strike exercises back on Earth. Planetary missiles often revealed a burst of flame as they were booster-assisted from their launch pads, before their ramjet engines kicked in.

Tiny, dazzling points of light suddenly burst in the sky, out ahead of where the flames had been. Katja watched, mesmerized, as one by one the mini-stars exploded to life and raced eastward across the distance, pulling away as *Rapier* continued to brake.

"Holy shit!"

"What?" Thomas demanded.

Katja pointed upward at the dazzling points of light that were racing away ahead of *Rapier*.

"What are those?"

Tamma, the seasoned pilot, recognized them first. "Missiles!"

Katja was thrown sideways in her seat as he instinctively jinked the ship hard left and then hard right.

"Hold course," Thomas roared. "They're not aimed at us!"

Katja stared at her display. "They're in an orbital trajectory. Eastbound!" The line of ten ships increased its speed, and began to spread out. "They were launched from that line of ships!"

Thomas barked orders. "Pilot, intercept course on those missiles—flank speed. NavO, take with turrets—fire at will. OpsO, flash report to the EF—enemy sighted!"

Katja ignored the pressure that shoved her back into her seat as *Rapier* accelerated and dove toward the rapidly receding wave of missiles. She forced her hand forward to flick the comms circuit, switching to AAW—anti-attack warfare. She hailed the Expeditionary Force.

"Flash! Multiple vampires inbound, orbital trajectory!" She studied the info on her display. "Archons two-seven-five!" She needed to indicate the direction of the assault, but the EF was still invisible over the horizon. She pursed her lips in helplessness. "From far-side! From far-side! Look west! Look west!"

Even though *Rapier* had accelerated to a dangerous speed, the missile exhausts didn't seem to be growing larger in her vision. Their combined light cast a faint glow across Laika's largest ocean, far below. She watched as the massive form of Anubis rose above the horizon ahead, its swirling cloud formations shining brightly in the impending sunrise.

The AAW circuit burst to life.

"Station calling flash," came a stern voice, *"this is Echo-Whiskey: identify yourself and explain your last transmission."*

"This is *Rapier*, inbound from the west, still below the horizon! There are about forty goddamn missiles ahead of us, headed in your direction. And there are ten enemy warships coming up behind us!"

"Rapier, *this is Echo-Whiskey... roger, out.*"

Katja jumped as *Rapier*'s top and bottom turrets rattled the bulkheads. No longer in the cocoon of her strike pod, she heard loud and clear the angry, rapid-fire discharge of *Rapier*'s close-in weapons. Rounds streaked across her field of view. Two of the mini-suns exploded as Terran slugs tore through their engines and fuel tanks.

Breeze issued orders to the turret gunners to augment her electronic manipulation of the targeting system. More rounds thundered away, but the enemy missiles began maneuvering wildly, even as they advanced toward their targets.

Rapier pressed the attack, pushing beyond safe orbital speed to try and catch the missiles. A growing cone of red began to form around the ship's nose, and then the blinding light of Sirius appeared and obliterated everything else from view. Katja shielded her eyes from the sunrise even as the bridge windows automatically tinted to block the light.

Her 3-D display showed the tactical situation as it unfolded. *Rapier* was running close behind the missiles, and while some had been destroyed, there were still far too many out there. She grunted softly as *Rapier* jinked hard, then Thomas bellowed over the ship-wide broadcast.

"Brace for shock!"

She grabbed both arms of her chair and hung on as the ship jinked again. New missiles flashed past from behind. The brilliant surface of Laika filled her view as the ship dove, then the planet was swept away as they pulled up again.

The hulls of the enemy ships—Centauri, beyond a doubt—gleamed in the sunlight as they emerged into the dawn. Katja's display indicated ten red symbols, but she could only see three through the windows. The middle one was by far the biggest—most likely a battle cruiser—and even as she watched missiles launched from her massive hull. The other ships were smaller, but looked no less threatening. Frigates, she decided. All of them were surrounded in a halo of fast-moving objects—short-ranged, robotic sentries.

Rapier banked hard to port. Katja looked eastward and caught her first glimpse of Expeditionary Force 15 in its entirety. Even to her trooper eye the ships looked too closely packed together, which left them too busy scrambling away from each other to fight. Only the stealth picket destroyers were in a good position, and while they weren't optimized for anti-vessel warfare, they were pouring out rounds to stop the wave of missiles. There were explosions as the EF defenses scored hits.

Then one of the Terran invasion ships imploded.

One of the mighty invasion ships—*Normandy* or one of her sisters, filled with three and a half thousand troopers, an entire regiment of equipment, over a thousand sailors and pilots, and a hundred strike fighters—collapsed from the center and tore herself apart as her mass was sucked inward by a split-second singularity. The ship simply ceased to exist in the blink of an eye.

The stealth ships had entered the battle.

Then the missiles struck. Explosions rippled through the EF's capital ships. Trapped in close quarters at the center of the formation, they struggled to maneuver under the onslaught. Katja stared in horror as one of the battleships, blackened from bow to stern, slid helplessly into the beam of a supply ship. The smaller vessel's starboard hull crumpled against the battleship's armor plating. Locked together, the two vessels began to drift down toward Laika below.

Rapier jinked again as she took fire from the advancing Centauri ships. Katja's damage control board was flashing, and she pushed the horror behind her—remembered her role to keep the captain informed of the health of his ship.

"Structural damage to the port wing," she said. "Power dropping in the port engine!"

Terran star fighters flashed by outside, as both carriers loosed their fighter wings into the melee.

"Pilot, course one-niner-seven mark three-five-zero," Thomas shouted. "Get us out of the crossfire!"

Rapier turned her nose up and strained to climb.

22

apier leveled out, leaning her starboard wing planetside to keep open the firing arcs for all three turrets. Katja leaned forward in her seat to look past Thomas and watch the battle below.

The EF was hemmed in. The big ships that had taken the brunt of the initial missile attack were struggling to limp away. One remaining battleship and four cruisers were forming a defensive semicircle between the main body and the advancing Centauris, exchanging heavy fire with the ten enemy ships. Five Terran destroyers were moving quickly to clear the main body's escape route. Anti-stealth fighters sprinted and drifted in their hunt for the enemy. Star fighters flipped and turned in dogfights with Centauri robotic sentries.

The pair of damaged ships, identified as the battleship *Lepanto* and the supply ship *Partisan*, remained locked together and were burning up in the atmosphere.

A second invasion ship imploded and disappeared.

Anti-stealth craft swarmed an empty spot in space.

The surface of Laika seemed to ripple and bend as the extra-dimensional explosion of a Centauri stealth ship curled spacetime.

"Oh my God," Breeze said.

"Okay, keep it together," Thomas responded. "OpsO, what's our status?"

Katja tore her eyes from the battle to examine her console.

"Damage to the port wing and engine, sixty percent power only from the port side. Minor breaches aft on both decks, but pressure is holding. Hull power-transfer operative. All other systems within limits."

"Very good. NavO, how are the weapons?"

"Four morningstars ready. Top and bottom turrets operational with ammo at sixty-one percent remaining. Tail turret is down!"

"Very good. Pilot, how's she flying?"

"The loss of power in the port engine has made us sluggish, but we can still maneuver and maintain combat speeds. Top escape speed point-zero-seven-c."

"Very good." He activated the ship-wide intercom. "This is the captain, sitrep. We are in orbit around Laika. Centauri forces have just committed a massive sneak attack against Expeditionary Force 15. The battle is still in progress and we will be rejoining momentarily. The ship is in good shape. We have fought well. Continue to man your stations and follow your orders. We are going into harm's way. This is the captain—that is all."

Thomas closed the circuit and looked out again at the battle.

"Team, we are a small ship with limited firepower, and I'm not going to throw our lives away. Once we've expended our morningstars I intend to get us back to *Normandy*. But first we will make a difference in this battle."

Katja examined her 3-D display, trying to figure where best a little FAC could influence events. A direct attack on the Centauri ships? The star fighters and cruisers were better suited for that. Hunting stealth ships? *Rapier* had no stealth-hunting capability. The only thing she was really good for was surface strikes, or boardings...

"*Normandy*'s in trouble," Thomas said suddenly.

Katja stared at her display. One Terran capital ship had drifted away from the others, and was slipping out from behind the EF's battle wall. One of the Centauri frigates had broken away from the main battle and was closing fast. *Normandy* was much larger, but her anti-ship weapons were minimal at best.

"Pilot, intercept course for hostile zero-two-one, flank speed. NavO, prepare four morningstars for attack."

Katja gripped her chair and felt her stomach lurch into her throat as *Rapier* dove into battle once more. Against the brilliant backdrop of Laika, she watched as the main line of Centauri ships continued to push back the EF's defenses. Most of their fire was concentrated on the lone Terran battleship, *Jutland*, and even from this distance Katja could see the severe damage to the giant warship. The enemy battle cruiser in particular seemed to be dealing out tremendous damage.

But *Rapier*'s target was north of the main battle—the single frigate that was closing on the limping *Normandy*. The huge invasion ship had a dozen point-defense weapons, but these were no more powerful or longer-ranged than *Rapier*'s tail turret. For all her might, *Normandy* had nothing to throw against an enemy warship—or so it seemed.

Without thinking, Katja stabbed at her comms switch.

"*Normandy*, *Rapier*. We are inbound to engage hostile zero-two-one. Recommend you launch *Cutlass* and *Sabre* to press the attack, over."

Thomas looked sharply at her. Then nodded his approval.

"*Rapier*, *this is* Normandy," came the response. "*We've requested star fighter support.*"

Katja looked at her display. There were no star fighters breaking away from the melee.

"Roger, but in the meantime you have eight morningstar missiles sitting in the wings of your FACs—use them!"

She heard Thomas snicker, although his expression remained locked on the attack run.

"*Normandy, roger out.*"

The Centauri destroyer opened fire with anti-ship missiles. *Normandy*'s self-defense guns blazed to life, but failed to stop one attacker from slipping through. A small explosion ripped through her port side, adding to the existing damage. The enemy frigate closed to engage with her guns, staying out of range of *Normandy*'s point-defense turrets.

The two ships sailed high over Laika in a deadly dance, the cumbersome invasion ship trying to maneuver away and the nimble frigate easily keeping station while firing away unimpeded.

"Target locked!" Breeze said.

"Salvo-size four—fire!" Thomas said.

From outboard to inboard, port then starboard, *Rapier*'s four missiles burst forth from their wing pods and cut across the sky. The Centauri frigate never saw them coming. They smashed into her topside with devastating effect—Katja actually saw the ship shudder and tip. Moments later *Rapier* dove between her target and *Normandy*, strafing with both remaining turrets as she did.

The frigate returned fire. *Rapier* shook violently. Katja's damage control board lit up with red warning lights.

"Hull breach aft, lower deck! Temperature warnings forward!" To accent her words, a red cone of super-heated air started to engulf the ship's nose.

"Pull up!" Thomas shouted.

Tamma struggled visibly with the controls. *Rapier* creaked as she tried to pull out of her dive. The rumble of the engines rose to a scream as Tamma fought both Laika's gravity and the ship's own momentum. Red air engulfed the bridge windows. They struggled out of their suicidal trajectory, but still headed down into the thickening atmosphere.

Katja stared in horror at her board. "Port wing under severe strain. Structural integrity failing aft, lower deck!"

Tamma was fighting the controls. "We're going down!"

Thomas spoke over the broadcast.

"All hands, brace for emergency landing!"

Katja shook her head. "Negative, sir! We're losing integrity in the port wing and the lower deck. We'll tear apart in re-entry. We can't take the strain!"

"I've lost the port engine," shouted Tamma. "I can't pull us out of the atmosphere. We're going down!"

Thomas was ashen. He flicked the broadcast.

"This is the captain," he said. "Abandon ship, abandon ship! All hands to the strike pods. Abandon ship, abandon ship!"

Katja was too stunned to move.

Breeze was out of her seat and pushing past them, flinging the hatch open. Tamma tapped in some final instructions and followed.

Thomas didn't budge. Katja stared at him.

"Sir, let's go!"

"Get to your strike pod." He looked ahead, his face grim. "That's an order."

She unbuckled and stood. He still didn't move.

"Sir?"

He looked up at her. "OpsO, I have a plan, but I need you to go with the pods."

She felt tears well up from nowhere, but she fought them down.

"Katja, go." His voice was calm but firm.

He reached to close the faceplate of his helmet, but before he could she leaned in and kissed him.

He was surprised, but after a moment kissed her back with passion, holding her armored shoulder with his gloved hand. Around them, the roar of the deepening atmosphere grew louder.

She broke away, and ran aft.

The hexagonal passageway looked the same as always, and ahead Katja could see the last of the crew climbing up into the strike pods. She was pleased to see Chief Tamma, as senior enlisted man, remaining on deck to the end, and noted with irony the absence of Lieutenant Brisebois.

"Get on board!" she ordered Tamma. "Captain's got a plan, and he's staying behind."

Tamma made to protest.

Katja raised her rifle. "We leave now, or we all die. Go!"

Tamma climbed up into the starboard pod.

Katja clambered up through the narrow port hatch. The inside of the pod was jammed with suited bodies, the orange-filtered light from re-entry giving a warm, sunset-like ambiance to the terror-filled space. Cohen was ready at the flight controls. Assad, Jackson, and Hernandez loomed in their armored suits. The ship's cook and one of the engineers supported an active-feed IV bag for an unconscious and badly wounded gunner.

She closed the hatch and sealed it.

"Lift off!"

At Cohen's command the pod punched upward and free from the doomed *Rapier*. The wall of super-heated air smacked the little ship like a fly, and Katja was thrown into her troopers. The armor prevented any permanent damage, and with a groan she pulled herself up, then took her seat next to Cohen.

The strike pod rocketed upward at full thrust, reversing the inherited vectors of *Rapier*'s dive. In the distance, Katja saw the other pod struggling to rise, and she caught a single glimpse of the fireball that was *Rapier*.

And Thomas.

"Trouble ahead," Cohen said.

Katja snapped her mind back into the present. She was now in command, and it was her duty to see *Rapier*'s crew to safety. She looked up, high into the sky, and saw the distant form of *Normandy* lumbering in the near-blackness. The Centauri frigate appeared to have backed off, and Katja caught glimpses of two smaller objects that occasionally flashed in the sunlight. Hopefully that was *Cutlass* and *Sabre*.

The strike pod had a rudimentary 3-D display which gave the relative positions of vessels, and little more. Katja studied it as the pod continued to climb, then strained her eyes to pick out the flashes of battle still raging above them. The Centauri frigates had closed to engage the Terran battle line at point-blank range. She hoped that the friendly ships could give as good as they got in this game, but she saw that the Centauri battle cruiser was hanging back.

On an impulse, she activated the long-range camera she normally used for surveying the strike zone during a drop. Precious moments slipped by as she figured out how best to aim it. The strike pod was clearing the last vestiges of atmosphere by the time she had a good view.

The battle cruiser launched volley after volley of missiles. Even as Katja watched, it fired a salvo, rotated on its axis about thirty degrees, steadied, and fired again. The missiles were targeted like sniper rounds, snaking through the melee and hitting the fleeing Terran capital ships. None of the Terran battle line could engage the battle cruiser, as they were outnumbered nearly two-to-one by the aggressive enemy frigates.

Perhaps *Rapier* had made a difference by averting that single attack, but *Normandy* and the other capital ships didn't stand much hope so long as that battle cruiser was free to launch her pinpoint-guided missiles.

Katja felt her stomach tighten as an idea formed in her mind.

Thomas's last desire had been for *Rapier* to make a difference in this battle. No doubt his daring attack had saved *Normandy*, but that wasn't enough. There was one more thing that could be done.

She opened the strike frequency. "Bravo-One, Alpha-One."

"Bravo-One," Chang replied from the other pod. It was visible to Katja's left, less than a kilometer distant and rising into space in step with her own vehicle.

"Rendezvous with my vessel and prepare to transfer personnel."

"Bravo-One, roger."

She turned to Cohen. "Hold position here and get ready to mate with the other pod."

If Cohen harbored any doubt, it didn't show. "Yes, ma'am."

The strike pod slowed its ascent until it was hovering in extremely low orbit. The artificial gravity produced by the climb faded away. Katja unstrapped and guided herself out of her chair, noting through the windows that the second pod was closing quickly. She heard a few quick words exchanged between the pilots, then felt a thump as the pods mated. The usual locking clicks and hisses indicated a pressure seal.

When the green light came on, Katja opened the hatch. Bravo pod's hatch opened a moment later, revealing Chang's dark face. Behind him, the pod was as crowded as hers.

Katja shouted for all to hear.

"*Rapier*, listen up! We are still in battle, and things are not going well! Centauria might think that we're out of it, but they're wrong! We are going to transfer Bravo Team to Alpha pod, and transfer Alpha's non-trooper personnel to Bravo pod. Bravo pod will then rendezvous with *Normandy* for recovery. Alpha pod is going into harm's way."

"You gotta be shitting me!" someone shouted from Bravo pod.

"This is not open to discussion!" She stuck her head forward to get a better look into Bravo pod. "With the captain gone, I have assumed command, and we are not done yet!" She paused, then added, "If anyone wants to argue, I will shoot them!"

She caught Breeze's eye. The junior lieutenant dropped her gaze and said nothing.

"Let's move, people," Chief Tamma said. "Pantaleyeva, keep good hold of that IV! Smith, help me with Oyenuga!"

Katja pushed herself clear to let the cox'n direct the casualty through the airlock. Chang took hold of the gunner's limp form and pulled him in. Alpha pod's remaining non-troopers dove through the hatch. Chang pulled himself up, followed by the rest of Bravo Team. They crowded their armored bodies tight together in the tiny space.

Katja looked down into the other pod one last time.

"Lieutenant Brisebois, get these people to safety in *Normandy*. We'll try and get back in this pod!" She came up short, considering her next words. "If not, look for us in the wreckage."

Breeze pulled herself closer and spoke quietly. "You're insane. There's no way—"

She pushed Breeze's face back and shut the airlock.

"Cast off!"

23

The pod decoupled and slid away. Once safely clear, Cohen opened the throttles and headed toward the battle. Katja reclaimed her seat and noted with satisfaction that Bravo pod was moving at speed toward *Normandy*.

"Where to, skipper?" Cohen asked.

Chang looming next to her shoulder, Katja pointed at the Centauri battle cruiser. It stood apart from the fiery melee, still lobbing missiles.

"We're going to board that motherfucker and blast it apart from the inside." She motioned downward. "Don't aim directly at it—if we do the defense systems might think we're a threat. Aim below, and we'll come up suddenly at close range."

Cohen dipped the pod.

"Standard entry pattern?" Chang asked.

She nodded. "Alpha Team takes the bridge. Bravo Team takes the engine room. We take those spaces out, that ship is toast."

"Do we have schematics?"

"Just keep shooting until you find what you're looking for."

"Yes, ma'am."

The battle line melee was fifty kilometers overhead. Sparkles and flashes across the massive, looming face of Anubis gave evidence of the dogfights still underway. With the amount of debris littering the battlespace now, Katja hoped that her little pod was too small and too slow for anyone to notice.

"Shut down all non-essential power. Let's pretend we're a piece of trash."

Cohen's fingers flew over her controls. Lights extinguished and ventilation ceased. The 3-D display disappeared, along with most of the instrumentation.

They were flying visually.

The battle cruiser was fat. Although not as long as a Terran capital ship, it was of comparable displacement. Its hull gleamed in the bright sunlight, except for the blackened launch tubes of its dozen missile batteries.

Her plan rested on two key factors. First, she knew enough about Centauri tactics to know that they relied heavily on machinery to fight their battles for them, keeping their robotic weapons at a distance from living personnel. Second, off-planet combat was fought entirely ship-to-ship, not man-to-man. Since this was the first engagement between Terra and Centauria, it had no precedent, and Katja was betting that the enemy wouldn't think to prepare for a boarding.

She turned to her troopers. They looked back at her expectantly.

"The plan is simple," she said. "We enter together, secure the airlock and split into two teams. Alpha Team will take the bridge. Bravo Team will take the engine room. We will move with stealth until we are discovered, as we don't know if their vital spaces have protection systems and we want to get the jump on them. Take out those spaces and get back to the strike pod.

"If we are discovered, shoot anything that moves. This is not a smuggler ship. We are not searching for anything. This is the flagship of an enemy nation who has attacked our fleet. We are at war."

She let that last thought sink in.

"Captain Kane wanted us to make a difference in this battle. And the nine of us will see to it that we do."

The battle cruiser loomed overhead, rotating thirty degrees on a steady, thirty-second interval. Katja assumed that the staggered missile batteries were being rearmed and programmed during the rotation, then steadied for launch as the ship held position. Cohen slowed the strike pod as it came directly underneath the behemoth, and nudged upward on a gentle collision course.

Katja scanned for an airlock. She spotted one, but the battle cruiser rolled again before she could point it out.

"Look sharp," she said to Cohen. "We'll have about thirty seconds to lock on."

"Got it." Cohen surged the strike pod forward and flipped back ninety degrees to point the pod's clamp toward the Centauri hull. They banged down, and held. There was a hiss as the seal was flooded with oxygen.

"Green," Chang said.

"Faceplates down," Katja barked. "From this moment on, we act as if we're in a vacuum."

When the last of them had complied, Chang opened the airlock and Assad climbed through. Within moments he had overridden the Centauri airlock controls, and the hatch opened. He entered, and the rest of the strike team followed.

Katja was last, leaving only the pilot.

"Shut the airlock," she told Cohen. "Hopefully the Centauri damage control teams didn't notice the opening."

Cohen obliged, and the hatch slid shut between them.

"Entry point clear," Assad reported.

Katja moved forward to catch up. There was no gravity, and the passageways were wide and well lit. There was no sign of internal alarm or defenses—as expected, the Centauris were completely focused on the battle outside.

"All units, Alpha-One—touchdown, ops red. Proceed with mission. Bravo-One."

"Bravo-One," Chang replied.

Katja exchanged a glance with him, then turned to follow her troopers. Assad had point, with Jackson behind. Katja followed and Hernandez covered the rear. Moving in zero-g was troublesome, as it required devoting one hand to repeatedly propel along handles and doorframes.

Through Assad's helmet link, Katja saw her first Centauri. He appeared to be of European descent, medium build, dressed in light-gray coveralls, dark boots, and fire-resistant gloves and hood. He was moving swiftly along the corridor, herding two large crates in front of him. Suddenly his eyes widened in shock.

Then his body was splattered down the bulkhead as Assad fired a single round into him.

"Alpha Team, Alpha-One—pick up the pace."

They pulled themselves faster down the passageway, dodging past the abandoned crates and the mangled lower half of the Centauri crewmember.

Moving through the next door, Assad burst into a large room filled with Centauri crewmembers and damage control equipment. Katja saw the shock in their eyes, and switched off the helmet link to focus on her own field of view—just as she heard the *tock-tock-tock* of weapons fire. Jackson joined in seconds later. By the time Katja reached the door, there was nothing to see but blood and body parts spinning madly in zero-g, colliding with one another and bouncing off all four sides of the compartment.

She looked down at her weapon to avoid retching, thankful that her helmet would block the smell. "Secure this space!"

Assad and Jackson pushed through the carnage and took positions next to the exit on the far side. Hernandez hunkered down to guard the way they came. Katja pushed herself over to what appeared to be a damage control board. Within moments a 3-D schematic of the ship floated before her, with various embedded lights and readings reporting the damage that had been inflicted to the vessel. Far too little damage, she noted with growing anger.

That was about to change.

She studied the board to determine their current location— the midships damage control station. Then she identified the location of the bridge. A central access route would get the troopers between decks.

A stray, floating limb bumped her shoulder and she absently smacked it away as she committed the route to memory. She was about to turn away when she noticed that at least one of the missile batteries lay in the path they would follow.

Another lay just four frames forward of the first. She studied a moment longer, and saw that the batteries were positioned in close pairs, spread equally around the ship. They were easily accessible, and stopping them could turn the battle outside.

"Alpha Team—on me."

Assad and Jackson moved through the gore. Hernandez floated up moments later. All three of them were covered in blood, as the liters of free-floating liquid stuck to anything on contact. Katja was sure she looked the same.

She pointed at the 3-D schematic.

"We're here," she said, showing them the route they would follow. "Alpha-Two and Four will take the missile batteries. Alpha-Three and I will take the bridge. Then we'll assess your progress, and join you if needed. Once we're done, we'll return to the pod using one of these access routes. Clear?"

Assad and Jackson looked at each other. Assad shrugged.

"*It's payback time,*" he said.

"Go."

The two big troopers pushed away and vanished through the door. Immediately there was the sound of shots, and she looked up at Hernandez. His expression was one of resignation.

"*You actually think we're going to make it back to the pod?*"

"Well, *I'm* going to," she replied. "And it's your job to keep me alive. Let's move!"

Katja led the way out. Assad and Jackson had left death in their wake, but she didn't follow their route for long. She grabbed the rungs of a ladder and launched herself upward, bringing her rifle to bear as she moved between decks.

As soon as her eyes crossed the threshold of the deck, she registered movement and fired a spread. The explosive rounds smashed into the bulkheads of the space she rose into, as well as a Centauri whose face she never saw. She moved aside as Hernandez joined her.

A quick look around the corner revealed an empty passageway with an open door at the end, and Katja launched herself toward it, rifle up. Suddenly a piercing alarm sounded through her helmet pick-ups, followed by an urgent voice.

"*Intruder alert! Intruders in the engine room! Lock down security one-alpha!*"

Bravo Team had reached their objective.

She was fast approaching the door when a Centauri appeared, but she fired before he even saw her. His body exploded backward into the space beyond. She grabbed another handrail to pick up speed. Panicked shouts echoed from the doorway. A wide-eyed face appeared for a moment, then vanished.

More shouting.

She was almost there.

The flash of rifle fire blinded her, and she grunted as a dozen tiny fists punched against her torso. Hernandez pushed her aside, and fired repeatedly into the dark space. She glanced down at her armor—it was dented but intact. So she raised her rifle and followed him through the door.

Multiple weapons fired from covered positions in the large, gloomy space, dotted with instrument stations. Hernandez was already far to her left, tumbling for cover behind an instrument panel even as he fired. Katja pushed to the right, shooting randomly in the direction of the flashes. Explosions ripped through the room. The shockwave of an explosion slammed her against the bulkhead with jarring force. She swung her rifle far to the right and pulled the trigger repeatedly, hoping that Hernandez was still to her left.

"Alpha-Three, Alpha-One," she shouted between bursts, "can you see me?"

Amidst the thunder she barely heard his reply. *"I'm at your nine o'clock! Get down!"*

Katja tried to duck, but in the zero-g only rolled into a ball. Bullets pinged off her helmet and left her ears ringing. She fired again. The rounds smashed into the deck beneath her feet as the shockwave knocked her upward into the deckhead. A bullet cracked off her faceplate. A tiny, hairline fracture split into her vision.

With sudden clarity, she saw her attackers. Three armored figures hunched on the far side of what she realized must be the bridge. Hernandez fired at them from his covered position below and to the left, but his shots didn't strike home.

Katja gripped the lower barrel of her rifle and launched two grenades. They lobbed down on the enemy and exploded with the power of thirty rounds each. Body parts and strips of machinery flew in all directions.

Then a deathly quiet descended. Katja pushed off from the deckhead and floated down. Hernandez emerged from cover and swept through the remains of the bridge. Twice the size of *Normandy*'s, it had no doubt been a monument to technological prowess.

Now it was scrap.

Katja shut the door behind her and locked it, ensuring calm for a few moments. From one of her combat pouches she retrieved a small tube of sealant and began applying it to the fracture in her faceplate.

"Bravo-One, Alpha-One—bridge secure," she reported. Chang responded after several moments, with little of his usual calm.

"Bravo-One roger! Heavy fire in the engine room! Bravo-Two is down!"

Squad Leader Lu Chen. That was a blow.

"Alpha-One roger. Break. Alpha-Two, Alpha-One—status." Even through the radio Katja could hear the violence in the background.

"Two batteries taken. We're under heavy fire at number three!"

Two batteries, the bridge, and a whole lot of internal damage. Even if it wasn't destroyed, this battle cruiser was out of the fight.

"All units this is Alpha-One. Break away! Break away!"

"Bravo-One roger!"

"This is Alpha-Two—we're pinned down. Over!"

Katja motioned to Hernandez. "This is Alpha-One. We're on the way!"

Katja unlocked the bridge door and threw it open. Hernandez burst through, firing automatically. Unopposed, they pushed their way back down the corridor to the ladder. Hernandez went down head first to clear the deck below. Katja was right behind, feet first, to cover the rear.

The lights went out. Emergency lights flickered on moments later. Hernandez hesitated at the foot of the ladder, unsure which direction to go. Katja pushed forward, motioning for him to follow. Ahead, she could see the charred, crumpled bulkhead of what had been one of the missile batteries. She pushed past, her helmet protecting her from the thick, black smoke that filled most of the passageway. Four frames further on, a similar scene awaited her. There was little smoke, however, and what remained was being pulled ominously toward the outer hull. Uncontained breach. The ship was losing air.

She saw the ladder of the main access route leading down. She stopped and motioned Hernandez to do likewise.

The thick material of the deck reduced the clarity of her quantum-flux view, but she could clearly see four shapes, crouched in combat firing positions, leaning into and out from doorways. The movement of the weapons told Katja that the rounds they were firing were heavy-caliber—very capable of piercing armored spacesuits. The shooters were coordinated to ensure that at least one of them was firing while the others ducked back under cover.

She motioned for Hernandez to follow her back along the passageway from where they came. Peering down, she saw Assad and Jackson, both hunkered inside a damage-control alcove. She moved further back along the passageway, until the quantum-flux revealed the real source of danger to her troopers below. Around a corner and protected by covering fire, the Centauris were quickly assembling the major components of an anti-personnel robot. Katja wasn't sure they had enough grenades to take it down.

She pushed off the deck to place herself flat against the deckhead above. Hernandez did likewise, aiming his underslung grenade launcher at the deck.

"Alpha-Two, Alpha-One—we're taking out the threat astern of your position!"

"*Alpha-Two!*"

Katja and Hernandez fired. Their grenades struck the deck with twin explosions. Particles flew in all directions and a shockwave rippled away both fore and aft. Even before the debris cleared they fired again, this time into the group below.

Hernandez grabbed Katja and threw her backward away from the hole. A heartbeat later rockets swirled out of the smoke and ripped through his armored body. The APR was functional and loose. Katja yanked herself away from the hole, hearing slugs thud into the deckhead behind her feet. She scrambled along the top of the corridor like a spider.

"Alpha-Two—APR! APR! Take the shooters forward of you

with grenades, and get the fuck out!"

Explosions from the main access ladder ahead of her indicated the compliance with her orders. She scrambled along as fast as her arms could pull, ignoring the swiftly moving smoke that flowed up the passageway. She gave a mighty yank, rolled free in the air and activated her quantum-flux.

The four Centauri shooters were right below her. Two were down, two were firing. She launched another grenade at the deck, and watched with satisfaction as they were distracted by the ceiling collapsing around them. More grenades struck them from below, and as Katja watched her two troopers emerged through the quantum haze.

"Alpha-Two, I'm right above you. Blast up through the hole in the deckhead and join me here!"

She moved to the side and watched Assad and Jackson point upward to fire their grenades. Then both their bodies crumpled and jittered as APR rockets tore through them. She gasped in shock, and shut off her quantum-flux.

"Alpha-One, Bravo-One—Bravo Team embarked!" Chang's voice was distant in her ears. *"Request ETA Alpha Team!"*

Smoke billowed up through the hole, and flowed past.

"Alpha-One, Bravo-One—the landing zone is under fire. Request ETA!"

Katja checked her ammo and her suit. She'd lost at least four troopers. That was enough.

"Bravo-One, Alpha-One. Alpha Team is dead. I'm cut off. Break away!"

"What's your position? We'll clear you a path!"

"Four decks and two hundred meters. Don't argue! Break away now!"

There was a pause.

"Bravo-One, roger!"

Katja could hear shouting on the deck below her. There wasn't much time. She looked at the flow of smoke into the missile battery and saw her escape route.

One grenade blasted a new door for her, into the compartment. She surveyed the destroyed equipment and human remains, noting the red flashing air pressure gauges on every bulkhead.

She pushed herself over to the inside of the ship's hull, watching the flow of smoke carefully to find the breach. It took nearly a minute to locate the centimeters-long crack.

Katja peeked out and didn't see the bright surface of Laika, which was good news. If she was going to blast her way out of a spaceship, she did not want to be blasted in the direction of a planetary gravity well.

More shouts caught her attention, and she heard voices moving past in the passageway outside. Bracing herself against a broken support strut, she aimed her rifle at the tiny breach.

She fired two grenades. The hull exploded outward and she was swept up in the torrent of escaping air. Her body slammed against the edge of the hull and spun out of control. She saw stars, and then nothing.

24

Even in zero-g it hurt to move. Every time Jack shifted in his seat he seemed to bump something, which sent shivers of pain through his body.

One glance in the mirror had revealed that he looked even worse than he felt. The meds he was on had been sent over from *Normandy* and were usually reserved for use planetside. Jack didn't know a lot about Astral medicine, but he'd heard rumors that Corps drugs could keep troopers fighting even after they'd lost any two of their four limbs. Looking down at his suited body, he was pleased that limb-loss hadn't been a part of his ordeal.

But he wished that his drugs could dull the pain just a little bit more.

After the Centauri ambush at Laika the EF had gone to wartime standards, which brought an end to such luxuries as light duties or recovery time. Jack was a pilot. Terra needed pilots in this instant war. So Jack was drugged up, kept alert, and put in the cockpit.

He altered course to port, sticking with his standard search pattern, doing a quick check of visual, flight controls, and hunt controls. No telling if any Centauri stealth ships still lurked here in low Laikan orbit, and Terra had learned all too suddenly the danger of underestimating its oldest and largest colony.

The massive orb of Anubis filled half the sky overhead, a crescent of brilliant cloud bands haloing the shadow of the night side. It was dawn on the surface of Laika below, although at Jack's altitude Sirius had risen more than an hour ago.

Ahead to port, Jack glanced briefly at the broken remains of the destroyer *Kiev* hanging at an unnatural angle in her final, decaying orbit. Earlier Hawk flights had already searched the dead ship and salvaged what they could—Jack was glad to have missed that duty. Beyond *Kiev*, half of the cruiser *Admiral Tojo* was slowly tumbling end over end. These two hulks offered visible evidence of Terran losses, but they weren't the only casualties.

The invasion ships *Gallipoli* and *Sicily* had both been destroyed by stealth attacks—*Gallipoli* with the brigadier on board, *Sicily* with the admiral—and nothing remained of either vessel. The carrier *Athena* had met a similar fate before she could break orbit. *Lepanto* and *Partisan* had collided and burned up together in the atmosphere, and *Rapier* had gone down in flames.

Of all the losses, it was the little fast-attack craft that affected him the most. Apparently half the crew had made it out alive, led by Breeze as the only surviving officer. He was relieved to know that she was alive, but he still felt a real pang of loss. *Rapier*'s captain had seemed a real upstanding guy. And Jack clearly remembered seeing the face of the blonde strike officer during his rescue on Cerberus.

Even in the madness of the evacuation Jack could remember as she led the *Kristiansand* survivors out into the street, got them to their escape pods, and then rejoined the battle. His last image was of her disappearing into the dust and smoke, firing her assault rifle.

Jack owed his life to her.

But the time for remorse was later—he still had a job to do. The Centauri forces had scattered as quickly as they had attacked, and the EF was hunkered down in open space above the Anubian ecliptic. They would be moving into deep space soon, but until then pilots like Jack had to search the battlefield for anything of tactical value.

Laikan traffic had been routed elsewhere by the authorities, who were desperately trying to distance themselves as far as possible from the attack. Jack's display revealed the two pairs of star fighters that were maintaining combat patrol around the battlefield, as well as the two Hawks on ASW duty.

There were still echoes in the Bulk of the gravimetric attacks conducted by both sides, and he wondered idly which knuckles had been Terran capital ships, and which had been Centauri stealth ships. There was grim satisfaction in the knowledge that four enemy vessels had been scattered versus only three friendlies, but hull counts didn't always add up to victory. The loss of a carrier was a serious blow, even though some of her star fighters had made it safely to *Artemis* after the battle. The loss of two invasion ships, however—and with them nearly half of the Expeditionary Force's entire brigade—had seriously undermined Terra's ability to wage war in Sirius.

With the admiral and the brigadier dead, lots of people weren't even sure who was in command.

The biggest Centauri hulk loomed ahead, a battle cruiser. Its once-gleaming hull was blackened and charred by multiple impacts, but it was surprisingly intact. Unlike the smashed remains of *Kiev* and *Admiral Tojo*, this enemy ship appeared to have weathered the onslaught with fortitude. There were no gaping holes in the hull, no fatal impacts that had forced its crew to abandon ship. A smaller Centauri combatant had been destroyed in the battle—its debris cloud was fairly easy to track—and he wondered why the bigger ship hadn't suffered the same fate.

Closer to the dead battle cruiser he maneuvered carefully to avoid the thickening debris cloud. Some recognizable pieces belonged to Terran star fighters, but most of the odd scraps here and there were just twisted, tortured hunks of metal and plastic. Jack sighed, and shifted uncomfortably in his seat to reach for his water bulb.

Movement flickered at the edge of his vision. There was an object tumbling slowly through space off the port bow and getting close. The object was dark, but with each rotation one end of it flashed dully in the Sirian sunlight. Curious, he dropped his visor and tapped the visual lock button on the side of his helmet. A red square appeared on the inside of the visor, marking the bearing and relaying the information to the Hawk's computer.

He activated the viewer and zoomed in for a better look.

It was a body, wearing a black, bulky spacesuit. The dull flash was the faceplate catching the sunlight. Jack watched for a moment and wondered idly why the Centauris had such dark suits and such shiny ships.

Then he noticed the assault rifle tethered to the suit's waist.

His eyes went wide.

Jack hauled the stick over to port. Moments later he slowed to match the velocity of the figure, gauging visually as it approached. He tapped at his thrusters, delicately maneuvering while keeping safely clear. Soon the figure was hovering next to the Hawk, still turning slowly end over end.

He looked for any sign of life. Aside from the steady tumble, there was no movement. No lights on the suit indicating functionality, yet it appeared intact. Jack frowned. Technically his mission didn't include casualty retrieval. He looked at the dark suit again, and a single thought struck him:

If it was his body tumbling end over end like that, in a slowly decaying orbit over a foreign world, would he want it left behind?

Closing his faceplate and switching to suit life-support, Jack unstrapped and pushed his way back into the Hawk's cargo area and into the tiny airlock. The routine movement sent waves of pain through his broken body. His breathing was heavy during the twenty seconds required to evacuate the air, then the airlock light switched to red. He tethered himself to the ship and opened the outer door.

As the protective door slid away, Jack's stomach rose up to his throat. Looking out at space from the safety of a cockpit was one thing. Staring out into the abyss, into the infinite nothingness of space—that was something else. He found himself unable to move. Grabbing one of the airlock handles, he stared at the three meters separating him from the tumbling trooper.

It looked like three light years.

His ribs ached from rapid breathing.

Come on, Jack, he told himself. *Just out, and right back in.*

He pulled himself to the threshold, inching out of the safety of his ship. He switched his grip to a handle on his left, and reached back to double-check his tether. Then he leaned his booted toes over the edge. The trooper was only three meters away. All he had to do was push himself out.

Ready… one, two, three!

His limbs refused to respond.

He stared out at the trooper.

He took a deep, shuddering breath, and forced his fingers to push. With the slightest of jerks, he floated free into open space.

He fixed his eyes on the trooper. Reaching out, he managed to grab the assault rifle and pull. His suit collided gently with the black, armored surface, and he wrapped his arms frantically around it. His momentum slowed the tumbling, but started to push them both away from the Hawk.

His breath was quick and shallow, his arms like a vise around his prize. His body felt weak from the exertion, and it seemed as if everything hurt.

There was a sharp jerk at his midsection as his tether reached its full extent. He gasped as he thought he might lose his grip, but his arms held. He and the trooper were held fast to the Hawk.

He did nothing for a moment. Then, with a slow, terrifying movement, he let go of the trooper with one arm and reached back to grab his tether. A single tug, and they were floating back toward the airlock.

His armored prize fit easily through the opening, and only as he gently pushed the trooper to the inside bulkhead did he realize how small the suit was. Grey dust stuck to patches of a dark liquid that was splattered across at least half the surface area. As the door closed and the airlock was pressurized, Jack took a moment to look through the visor, dreading what he might see.

Eyes closed, cheeks pale, it was *Rapier*'s strike officer.

Jack's breath caught in his throat.

She was breathing.

The airlock light switched to green. He opened the inner door and gently pushed her through into the Hawk. Then he opened his faceplate, and reached to open hers. Unlike standard-issue Astral spacesuits, the armored trooper suits didn't have brightly lit displays on their chests. They wouldn't exactly be helpful during a sneak attack.

He carefully unlocked her faceplate—it slid up easily.

Decoupling a glove to free his hand, he reached in gingerly to place the back of his fingers against her cheek. Her skin was cool, but not unnaturally so. He moved his hand to hover before her nose. He felt the gentle warmth of breath against his fingers.

Suddenly her eyes fluttered open. She was dazed for a second, then her gaze locked onto his.

"Hi," he said. "Good to see you alive." The words came out awkwardly through his bruised lips.

She tried to scramble backward, but her movements were clumsy in the zero-g. Jack pushed away, floating backward to give her space.

"It's okay, it's okay," he said. "You're safe."

She bumped into the aft bulkhead, eyes darting in all directions. With a swift motion she hauled in her free-floating assault rifle and brought it to bear.

He threw up his hands. "Whoa, whoa! I'm Astral Force! My name's Jack Mallory! I'm a pilot!"

Her gaze took him in, and she lowered her rifle. He saw the light of recognition ignite her dark eyes. Incredibly, she *laughed*.

"Jack the pilot." Her voice was very soft. "You look like shit, Jack." She looked around again, visibly relaxing. "Where the hell are we?"

He lowered his hands, shaking from the shock of nearly getting shot.

"This is Viking-Two, the Hawk from *Kristiansand*. We're in low-Laika orbit."

She shivered, and her gaze became distant. "The battle?"

"It ended about twenty-four hours ago. I'm just part of the cleanup—I mean, recovery team."

"What happened?"

He motioned her toward the cockpit. "Come have a look. Maybe you can tell me a thing or two."

He pushed forward and strapped back into his seat. She appeared over his left shoulder, anchoring herself with a hand on his seat. Together they looked out at the orbital battlefield, and the Laikan dawn far below.

"The Centauri battle cruiser," she said.

"Yeah, abandoned. Strange, because it's still in one piece. Not like some of the other Centauri ships."

She was silent for a long moment. He looked up at her. She looked very tired.

"What about *Rapier*?" she asked suddenly.

Jack hated to be the messenger.

"Word is she went down," he said. "Burned up over Laika. Sorry. But both her pods were recovered, with about half the crew alive."

"Both pods made it back?" Her expression was unreadable.

"Yeah."

Her pale face sagged, so tiny in the armored helmet. Her dark eyes shone with moisture and she pushed back, out of Jack's view.

He moved his gaze across the visual, his flight controls. and his hunt controls. Everything was nominal. He set the Hawk into motion again, easing to starboard to resume his search pattern. His patrol was due to last another half-hour, but he suspected he should get her back to *Kristiansand*.

He turned his seat, looking back to ask if she was feeling okay.

She was floating in the cargo area, curled up as tightly as her heavy suit would allow. Her gloves were off and her bare hands were clenched together against the bridge of her nose. Her eyes were tightly shut and her face was locked in a grimace, jerking with each silent sob.

He turned away, and activated his comms.

"Longboat, Viking-Two. I have recovered a Terran survivor from the battle, and request permission to return to Mother immediately."

There was the slightest of pauses before the response came.

"Viking-Two, confirm… you have a survivor?"

"That's affirmative." Jack suddenly realized that he couldn't remember her name. "One survivor."

25

Kristiansand's sickbay was bigger than Katja's cabin in *Rapier*, but the curtains around her bunk made her claustrophobic.

She hadn't minded the curtain that hid her from the door to the main passageway while the ship's medic helped her out of her armored suit, sent her sour clothes to be laundered, and gave her an exam. But after a few hours of lying strapped on the tiny bunk, unable to sleep as her mind struggled to process the wild imagery flashing through her brain, she felt trapped.

So she unstrapped herself and pushed up off the bed.

Then she grabbed for a sick bag and heaved painfully. She steadied herself, breathing heavily. Her body throbbed with heat.

Her hand slipped in its own sweat and she reached out to steady herself again. Fleet doctrine required that any artificial gravity be switched off in wartime, but enough time in *Rapier* had made zero-g second nature to her. Her nausea eased, and she moved to collect her clothes. The routine motion helped to focus her thoughts and push away the images.

She was handling it better this time.

The rest of sickbay was empty, the lights dimmed to conserve power, and Katja exited into the main passageway. This was her first time aboard a destroyer, and here too, the lights were duller than the gleaming white she was used to in *Normandy*, although brighter than the shadows of *Rapier*. Likewise, the rectangular-shaped passageway was tighter than *Normandy*'s broad avenues, but less constricted than *Rapier*'s honeycombs.

A few *Kristiansand* crewmembers were moving carefully along the passageway, never straying more than a few centimeters from the security of the continuous railing fixed to the bulkhead. Katja pushed out easily into the corridor, then put up a hand to slow the first sailor she saw. His rank indicated that he was a trooper, or the Fleet equivalent.

"Rating," she said, "where can I find the ship's officers?"

He frowned, barely looking away from his careful, hand-over-hand movement. "How the hell would I know?"

His insolence shocked her, and he was nearly past before she recovered. She braced herself against the deckhead with one hand, and with the other grabbed the material of his coveralls at the shoulder.

"Stop right there, Rating."

He was a fairly big man, and he pulled away as he turned. "Get your hand off me."

She released him, but glared down from her superior height.

"Rating, I'm new on board, because my ship was destroyed. In case the blue coveralls fooled you, let me point out the strike qualification on my chest, and allow me to add that I'm not in a very good fucking mood." She let that sink in, and continued. "I need to speak to your officers. So humor me and tell me which way I need to go to find them."

His expression remained dark, but he pointed back the way he had come. "The wardroom is up that way, starboard side. The bridge is all the way forward... ma'am."

"Thank you. Carry on."

She turned and pushed herself forward with a long, graceful motion, leaving the petulant crewman behind. She'd forgotten how lax discipline was in the Fleet, and felt a sudden constriction in her chest as she remembered the cool professionalism of *Rapier*'s crew.

She suddenly realized how much she wanted to see them again: although not as much as she wanted to see her troopers. Her mind clouded with the visual image of Hernandez being shot to pieces by the Centauri APR, and the quantum-flux image of Assad and Jackson meeting the same fate. Chang had lost at least one of his troopers, and Katja prayed that the others had made it out.

What was she thinking, boarding a Centauri battle cruiser? Her last image of *Rapier*, plummeting downward in a cone of flame and smoke, held her in thrall for a moment. She shook it off, wondering if she was insane. Trying to impress a man who was already dead instead of getting her troops to safety. Acting on instinct instead of thought, her father would say.

The wardroom door was closed. Katja swung down and righted herself, looking for any sort of DO NOT ENTER sign. Seeing none, she slid open the door and floated through.

It was standing room only in the dim light of the officers' mess. Katja barely had room to let the door shut behind her before she was bumping into the crowd. Young faces turned to look at her with surprise—she was facing the handful of subbies who always crowded in at the back of a briefing. Jack the Pilot was among them, and she nodded. He grinned back as best he could through his bruised and oddly misshapen features, and pulled himself aside to make room for her.

She slipped in among the subbies.

A tactical brief was projected in the air at the front of the room, and Katja immediately recognized the orbital battle she had just survived, the opposing lines located in the center and the Terran main body moving slowly away. A female voice that sounded vaguely familiar was narrating the action.

"…At this point *Normandy* is struggling to pull out of the gravity well, having lost three of her eight generators in the missile attack. One of the hostile frigates breaks away from the main battle line to pursue her, but this attack is thwarted by *Rapier* in a diving engagement."

Katja watched as a single blue symbol moved swiftly across the tactical space. The display paused from time to time, manipulated by the speaker.

"The attack is successful. It forces the hostile to draw back and gives *Normandy* time to scramble FACs *Cutlass* and *Sabre*." Admiring murmurs rippled through the collected officers. "Unfortunately, *Rapier* has taken heavy fire from the hostile, so the angle and speed of the dive are such that *Rapier* is unable to pull up. We lose tracking on her at this point."

The brief continued, showing the continual pounding between the two battle lines and the slow escape of the Terran capital ships.

"For reasons we have yet to understand," the speaker continued, "the hostile battle cruiser stops firing and seems to go inactive. Having lost their heavy fire support, the hostile frigates quickly lose their advantage and are beaten back by the Terran battle line. The hostiles withdraw and are not pursued. Command at this point is unsure if there are other threats elsewhere in the system, and wisely decides to keep the battle line close to the main body."

The wardroom lights brightened amidst a flurry of low comments. A new female voice spoke, and all others silenced.

"Thank you, Lieutenant. And you were in *Normandy* during the attack?"

"No, ma'am," the original speaker replied, "I was in *Rapier*."

Breeze. The crowd stirred with new interest, and Katja watched in surprise as she pushed up out of her seat to face her audience.

"That was quite a maneuver you pulled," a man commented. Katja recognized him as Thomas's friend, the XO of *Kristiansand*.

Breeze assumed a look of suitable humility. "Thank you. I wish we could have done it better, but there was no time to think. I wish it was Lieutenant Commander Kane who was standing here giving this brief."

The XO nodded. Breeze held his gaze for an extra moment.

"Why isn't he here?" the other woman asked. "Why did only some of you get off the ship?"

Breeze took a slow breath, looking pained. "We're still trying to piece together the sequence of events—forgive me, ma'am, but at this point I only know what I saw. I think our captain was killed before everyone could get to the escape pods. He stayed on the bridge to make sure we were all clear, and it seems as if we just ran out of time."

Katja's mouth fell open, but before she could find her voice the XO spoke again.

"I understand only about half of you were recovered," he said. "What happened to the rest of the crew?"

"The pods were separated soon after ejection, and by the time both made it to *Normandy* we were only twelve of eighteen. As senior surviving officer, I'll be conducting an investigation—"

"Thirteen, apparently," Katja said, pushing forward slightly to get a clear view. "And I guess I'll take over the investigation."

She had the distinct satisfaction of witnessing something she had never seen before. Breeze was speechless. The intelligence officer's mouth dropped open. Her blue eyes blinked several times.

All of *Kristiansand*'s officers turned and stared at Katja, including the captain and XO.

She nodded to the captain. "Thank you to your pilot, Jack, for bringing me on board, ma'am," she said. "Lieutenant Emmes, *Rapier*'s strike officer."

The captain met her gaze with interest. "Commander Avernell, *Kristiansand*. Welcome aboard, Lieutenant."

"Yes," Katja heard Breeze say quietly. "Thank God you're alive."

"Good to see you made it to safety," Katja replied, turning. Breeze swallowed, but quickly composed herself.

"Likewise. If by a slightly roundabout route."

"Lieutenant Emmes," Avernell said, "I'm curious to know how your strike pod made it to *Normandy* without you." She glanced at her watch. "But that'll have to wait. We have a call with the commodore."

Avernell rose, and the officers instinctively tried to stand to attention. In zero-g it was an amusing show of acrobatics. The captain pushed off for the forward door, her XO in tow.

Katja turned to Jack. "What commodore?"

Jack shrugged. "I dunno."

One of the other subbies leaned in. "Admiral Macbeth was killed in the attack, so the senior surviving ship captain took command of the Expeditionary Force. Naturally, he assumed the rank of commodore."

"Who is it?" Katja asked.

"Captain Chandler of *Normandy*."

"Is the brigadier alive?"

The subbie shook his head. "Colonel Korolev, also *Normandy*, is in command of the brigade."

Katja felt hollow inside as she grasped just how badly the EF had been hit by this attack. *Normandy* was incredibly lucky to have survived—with the entire Levantine Regiment aboard. She thought of her old friend Scott Lahko, and hoped he was still alive.

She motioned Jack in. "How quickly could you fly me back to *Normandy*?"

His expression was blank for a moment. "Uhh, as soon as it fits the opsked, I guess," he said. "Are you in a hurry?"

Before she could answer, Breeze came gliding over through the crowd, her usual smile firmly in place. Katja barely had time to react as she was drawn into a sisterly embrace—held steady, but not too tight. She reflexively placed her hands against Breeze's back, returning the gesture stiffly.

Breeze held her for another moment, then backed off.

"I'm so happy to see you," she said. "We all thought you were dead. You'll have to tell me all about it when we get back to *Normandy*."

"I can tell you all about it right now."

Breeze's smile shifted into one of pained regret. "I can't wait—but I have to sit in on the captain's call with Commodore Chandler. I've been assigned to *Normandy*'s intelligence team for now."

Jack floated up beside them. "Hey, Breeze, good to see you."

Breeze glanced absently at the pilot, then looked back with sudden recognition. "Oh my God, Jack! I barely recognized you."

He tried to smile. "Yeah, my mug's a little ugly right now. But it's nothing good drugs won't cure. You look great, though."

She gave him a radiant smile, and turned back to Katja.

"We'll talk soon," she said. "Gotta go." With that she sidled past and exited the wardroom through the aft door.

Katja floated in place as *Kristiansand*'s officers filed out. She frowned, wondering who was looking after her surviving crew, struggling against a sudden feeling of helplessness. She needed more information, and she wasn't going to get it standing around here.

"Hey, Lieutenant."

She turned and saw Jack beckoning to her. He was floating next to another officer, somewhat older, who also sported pilot wings on his chest. She pushed her way over.

"I asked Stripes when we're planning a run to *Normandy*,"

Jack said, "and he says we're scheduled to fly Breeze back in about thirty minutes. If you're up to it, you can hitch a ride then."

"Thanks," she replied, and she smiled wryly. "It won't take me long to pack—all I brought was my suit and my weapon." She thought for a moment, then added, "Where *is* my weapon?"

Jack's expression went blank, and he looked at Stripes.

The older pilot thought for a moment. "Probably in the small arms locker. I can take you there while Jack gets the bird ready to fly."

He gave Jack a pointed look. The subbie stared blankly back for a moment, then seemed to realize something.

"Right. I have to get the bird ready. See you in the hangar."

26

The next thirty minutes passed quickly as Katja went to one end of *Kristiansand* and back. Her assault rifle had been serviced and stored properly, she was pleased to see, and the sailor who was the weapons custodian seemed to know his stuff.

She earned more than a few glances as she followed Stripes through various passageways with her rifle in hand. After she had donned her armored suit, in sickbay, crewmembers pressed themselves against bulkheads, wide-eyed, as she passed. Eventually she found herself in the hangar and floating up into the Hawk.

Jack was seated in the cockpit, running through his checklist. He noticed her approach and gave her a smile before turning back to his work. She settled into the port-side seat of the pair behind him.

She heard another person enter the craft, and moments later Breeze pulled herself into the starboard seat. She, like Jack, was dressed in a standard Astral spacesuit.

Jack looked back. "Hey Breeze, glad to have you on board."

"Glad to be here," she replied brightly. "I think we're ready to go when you are."

"Just another minute or so."

The cargo door behind them began to close, and Katja felt the slight shift in inertia as the Hawk was towed into the airlock.

She turned to Breeze. "Who survived?"

"Excuse me?"

"From *Rapier*, who survived?"

Breeze seemed surprised at the question. She thought for a moment.

"All of the Fleet crew, although Oyenuga is looking pretty bad. Of the strike team, all of Chang's team except Lu." Her expression changed to sympathy. "None of your team, I'm afraid."

"Not Cohen?"

"Oh, yes—Cohen. Was she on your team?"

Katja fought down the urge to scream. She forced her words out slowly, steadily, and in the most civil tone she could manage.

"Yes," she said. "The strike team took Alpha pod. You were on Bravo pod, piloted by Alayan, who is the Bravo Team pilot. Cohen is the Alpha Team pilot."

"Of course. Sorry, I've had a lot on my mind. Astral Intelligence has been working non-stop trying to figure how and why this attack occurred."

Katja felt the temperature in her suit rising. "And has our crew been reassigned?"

"What? Uhh, I don't know." Breeze shrugged. "Probably."

"I just would have thought that as 'senior surviving officer' you'd be more concerned with seeing to our crew than giving briefings."

Breeze's expression hardened. "Katja, in case you haven't noticed, we're at war. Several thousand people died yesterday, including our captain. We need to find out why we were attacked and whether it will happen again. The crew will just have to sort themselves out."

A hundred things swirled up in Katja's mind, but she kept her mouth tightly shut. There was no point wasting words. Instead she turned toward their pilot.

"Jack, how long to reach *Normandy*?"

The Hawk had lifted free from *Kristiansand*, and the blackness of space filled the forward windows. The stars appeared to shift as the vessel banked to starboard.

"About ten minutes," Jack said. "I've checked in with *Normandy* control and they're squeezing us into their landing pattern, so we have to go a little faster than normal."

"Good," she replied. "Thanks."

For several moments the silence in the Hawk was undercut only by the usual background hum omnipresent on any small spaceship. Katja ignored Breeze, wondering how long it would take for her to ask what had happened after the pods split.

As the silence stretched on, there were no questions.

"Hey, Breeze," Jack said, "are you going to be visiting *Kristiansand* again soon?"

"I don't know—probably not. I'll probably be staying in *Normandy*, with the rest of the Intel team."

He glanced back, again trying to grin through his injuries. "I guess I'll just have to find more reasons to make shuttle trips to *Normandy*, then."

She smiled blankly. "Yeah, I guess so."

Another moment of silence passed.

"So," Jack said, "any theories from Intel on how the Centauris snuck a battle force through the jump gate?"

Breeze shook her head. "Nothing concrete."

"Could they have snuck through by hiding close to a Centauri merchant?"

"No, because we have visual inspection of all ships coming through."

"Maybe they were hidden inside large cargo ships. Are there cargo ships big enough to do that?"

"Maybe." Breeze rubbed her eyes and stretched.

"Or maybe they've built their own jump gate."

"Jack, come on," she said, snapping at him. "One of the fastest ways to make mistakes is to spread crazy rumors that send everybody down the wrong path." She sighed heavily. "Intelligence is working on it, okay?"

"Sure," he said, but her words didn't seem to take any wind out of his sails. "If I can help at all just let me know." He glanced back again. "I do fly ASW, you know."

She forced a smile. "Thanks, Jack. I'll keep it in mind."

Katja had listened with vague interest, but something Jack said caught her attention. "Hey Jack, were you on ASW patrol that day when we boarded the mystery merchant?"

"Damn right I was," he said. "I had a loose track on the stealth ship before it attacked, but that skipper was good.

Thank God he was just trying to scare us."

Katja remembered the otherworldly feeling of the gravi-torpedo, and how she had been yanked sideways through that cargo space by the artificial singularity. Just another reminder of how much the Astral Force seemed to have underestimated the Centauris.

"How did you track the merchant before the boarding?"

"Well, after I spotted it visually, *Kristiansand* took over gravimetrically. It was tough, but we kept track most of the way."

"So could you trace its route back to its origin?"

"Way ahead of you," he replied. "I did a mission the next day where I picked up its gravimetric wake and ran backward." He shrugged. "It doesn't last long, but it gave me enough of a bearing to locate the remnants of their exhaust stream. That ship had come from Kuiper Base Charlie."

Katja nodded. "Just like they told me when we boarded. How long does an exhaust stream stay intact?"

"Depends on how much thrust they're putting out, and how much gravity works to diffuse the stream. Out in deep space like that, it could last for months."

Katja thought hard. "The merchant captain told me that they'd rendezvoused with another ship, and that's how they got their weapons cargo."

"Oh, yeah?"

"Yeah…" Then her heart sank. "But my copy of their flight log was still aboard *Rapier.* Dammit."

Jack glanced back. "Oh, man, that sucks. I bet we could have tracked that ship's trajectory, if we knew where to start. Did you send a backup to Command?"

She shook her head. "We took over tracking duties right after the boarding. We didn't get a chance to upload before…" she stopped, and Jack continued to look at her curiously with his broken, bruised face. "Before the incident on Cerberus."

His lips pursed, but he quickly stretched them into a crooked smile. "Ah. Sorry about that."

She shook her head and glanced away, regretting bringing it up.

"And hey," he said, "I never got the chance to thank you."

She looked back at him. Beneath the injuries his eyes were bright and sincere.

"Seriously," he said. "Thanks for saving my life."

"Well," she said, "thanks for saving mine. I don't know how much longer my suit would have held up."

He grinned back. "I guess we're even." He reached back his gloved hand. Katja shook it as best she could through her armor.

"I gotta ask, though," he said. "What's your first name again?"

"Katja."

"Ohhh, yeah, right." He withdrew his hand. "But I've learned my lesson about strike officers. I won't ever call you that."

She laughed. "Good thinking, Subbie."

"Yeah," Breeze said, "you've really gotta watch those Corps folks."

Her comment fell flat in the silence.

Then the radio squawked, and Jack exchanged quick words with *Normandy* control. He maneuvered the Hawk again.

"Almost there, ladies."

Up ahead, the stars were blotted out by a vast, familiar shape. The invasion ship was still in one piece, but even with her limited view Katja could see evidence of battle scarring on the hull. The Hawk descended toward the long, flat topside, landed on one of the hangar doors, then began to lower into the hangar. Metal bulkheads rolled past as they descended through the airlock system.

Moments later the view opened up, revealing the giant hangar with two rows of strike fighters lined up, noses outward, ready for launch. Feeling the effects of an artificial gravity well, she unstrapped and stepped forward to look over Jack's shoulder. There was a cluster of people near the two fast-attack craft, next to a conspicuously empty area that used to be *Rapier*'s parking spot.

"Bit of a crowd," Jack said.

Breeze joined them. "That's odd."

The Hawk bumped slightly as the platform it had been riding touched down on the deck. A crewman motioned for Jack to roll forward, and indicated an open spot at the near end of one of the fighter lines. Jack steered the little ship as directed, came to a stop without incident, and flicked a switch to open the cargo door.

"Welcome home, ladies."

Breeze pressed a hand against his suited shoulder.

"Thanks, Jack," she said. "I hope you get better soon." She turned and departed before he could reply.

Katja heard him unstrapping himself as she walked down the ramp of the Hawk. The crowd of onlookers was gathered at the far end of the hangar, and seemed to pay no attention to the arrival of the Hawk. Breeze, she could see, was already halfway down the fighter line and headed with purpose for the group, no doubt determined to take credit for something or other.

Katja felt a sudden wave of weariness as she looked around at the familiar hangar, and had no interest in schmoozing with Fleet personnel. The first thing she had to do, she knew, was find out what was happening with *Rapier*'s crew.

Jack limped down the ramp and stopped next to her. "We have gravity."

"Yeah, it's standard for invasion ships, even in wartime. It's so the regiment can keep the right muscles in shape," she explained. "No good invading a planet if you've been floating in zero-g for weeks."

"But these ships show up like small planets in the Bulk."

She understood his point, and nodded—AG meant danger in anti-stealth warfare.

A short warning klaxon interrupted her thoughts. Looking up, she saw the airlock hatch open in the deckhead thirty meters above, to admit another small vessel. At first it was hard to see from her angle, but as the platform lowered she saw that it wasn't another Hawk, or a strike fighter. Then she recognized the familiar nose and jet-black color and realized that it was a fast-attack craft.

She cast a glance down the hangar and confirmed that both of *Normandy*'s FACs were parked in place. So this had to be a ship that had been reassigned to *Normandy*. Maybe one that had escaped *Gallipoli* or *Sicily* before they were destroyed.

Wherever it came from, it had taken a beating. Both forward turrets were mangled, and impact marks punctured the hull. Judging from the sound, only one engine was operating. All four morningstars had been expended, and both strike pods were missing. The port wing seemed to droop slightly. As the platform dropped to the deck and the FAC rolled slowly off, she strained to read the name.

Then she gasped.

RAPIER TFA 09

"Yes!" Sudden joy filled her heart. Through the warped windows of the cockpit she caught a glimpse of a lone figure at the controls and she didn't have to see his face to know who it was.

"Holy shit," she heard Jack say. "I thought she went down!"

"He had a plan," Katja said. "That son of a bitch said he had a plan. I didn't believe him, but he had a fucking plan!"

Rapier had rolled past them and picked up speed for the taxi to the far end of the hangar. Infused with new energy, Katja jogged to catch up. Over the whirring of her suit and the clanking of her footfalls she barely heard the cheer that went up from the gathered crowd. The battered little ship moved into her usual spot, rotated smoothly, and came to rest. The onlookers closed in to block the nose, waving and cheering.

Katja thumped up to them and pressed against the rearmost rank, straining to see over the raised arms. She heard *Rapier*'s lone engine power down, and thought she heard the hiss of the brow ramp opening in the ship's belly.

A moment later, a huge, roaring cheer went up, followed by applause and whistles. Katja strained to see, but in vain. Jack appeared next to her, puffing.

"Is it your captain?"

She tried desperately to catch a glimpse. "I think so!"

Then the crowd was moving, shifting to one side. It rippled toward the nearest set of doors. Katja moved quickly to try and get around them. She managed to get a view of the doors just as a tall, familiar form in a spacesuit passed through, followed closely by someone in another suit.

She looked back at *Rapier*. The dented, slashed and seared hull. The mangled turrets and broken port wing. The vessel that had brought Thomas home.

It was the most beautiful thing she had ever seen.

27

To feel gravity again. That was the icing on the cake.

Thomas took slow, steady breaths as he strode along the bright, warm passageways of *Normandy*, reveling in the strain his legs felt as they propelled him forward. He could tell by the rate at which he was passed by busy crewmembers that he was lacking his usual pace, but after two weeks in zero-g and nearly two days without food, he was thankful he could still stand.

The crowd who had greeted him had been too much. Thank goodness Breeze had been there to get him away. She'd led him to his cabin and told him to rest, but duty had to take precedence. So a shower and change of clothes later, Thomas was dragging himself up into flag country.

The door to the captain's—*commodore's* cabin opened at Thomas's buzz. He stepped through and found himself in a pleasant living area filled with standard-issue furniture and a backdrop of the stars visible through the broad window on the outboard side. A small dining table with four chairs occupied the closest end of the cabin, giving way to a pair of couches and an armchair placed around a high coffee table.

"*Rapier* reporting, sir," he said.

Commodore Chandler was all smiles as he rose from the armchair, strode over, and shook Thomas's hand.

"You look like shit, boy," he said. Then he returned to his chair and stood beside it. "Take a seat." Thomas followed and gratefully sat down, trying not to flop too much.

"When did you last eat?" the commodore continued.

"A while ago, sir. Some time since I last slept."

"Well, none of us have been getting much sleep lately," Chandler said. He pressed a button next to his chair. "Steward, coffee and sandwiches for two, please."

"*Yes, sir*," came the reply.

Chandler sat back. Thomas forced himself to meet the older man's gaze. Even after all these years, he had trouble figuring out what was going on behind those eyes.

"First off, Thomas, I want to congratulate you on a very bold maneuver—one which probably saved this ship. I'm going to be recommending you for commendation."

Maybe it was the fatigue, but Thomas didn't feel moved by the statement. He dropped his gaze to his hands.

"That's not necessary, sir," he said. "Every other ship in the EF took more of a beating than *Rapier*. We were only engaged for a few moments."

"Do you think we give out medals for suffering?"

The harsh tone took Thomas by surprise. He looked up.

"We're soldiers, Thomas," Chandler continued, "and we're *supposed* to take a beating. That's our job. In your 'few moments' you did more than just take some shots—you saved *Normandy* and everyone in her. And it very nearly cost you your own ship."

The steward entered with a tray of coffee and sandwiches cut into quarters. He laid everything out with precision, and poured two cups before retreating once again.

Chandler poured some cream in his coffee.

"And if it had been one of the cruisers who fended off that attack, I wouldn't be recommending any medals. It's a cruiser's job to protect the main body." He sat back and took a sip. "On the other hand, it's not the job of a fast-attack craft. That's what makes your action notable."

Thomas reached absently for a sandwich, and his mind drifted back. All he could picture were the flames enveloping *Rapier*'s cockpit, the awful shuddering as the single surviving engine struggled to pull up, and the ominous creak of straining bulkheads.

Somehow, "heroic" wasn't the word that came to mind.

"Yes, sir," he said.

"How's your ship?"

Thomas shook off the hellish images of the Laikan atmosphere and recalled what had happened afterward. He'd cleared the Laikan gravity well on the night side, pushing the overwrought engine to continue climbing in order to avoid the bottomless pit of Anubis's pull. There had been a terrifying rush of air as the ship's atmosphere leaked out into space, leaving only his suit's internal supply.

He had shut down every system he could in order to keep his one engine going, all the while searching the skies for Centauri craft. Just getting clear of Laikan space had drained most of the reserve power, and by the time he'd exited the Anubian ecliptic his own suit had been running low.

Only the crew cafeteria had remained pressurized, and by opening the hatch wide enough to scramble through, he'd let most of the air escape. Locating an emergency breathing device, he'd switched to a spare suit, getting pressurized again before his blood vessels burst in the vapor-thin air.

Finding the remains of the Expeditionary Force had been a challenge, as it had gone beacon-silent. Twelve hours of fruitless radio searches had drained his battery power to dangerous levels. In the end, he had activated his own beacon in the hope that he would be found. A warning call from one of the EF ships, telling him to douse his beacon, had revealed their location and enabled him to find his way home.

"Thomas?"

He looked up with a start. "Sir?"

"How is your ship?" Chandler said again. He was frowning. Thomas quickly swallowed the last of the sandwich that had found its way into his mouth.

"One engine is functioning at emergency levels," he replied. "No weapons systems. Hull integrity compromised in every compartment. No strike capability. No boarding capability. I recommend that she be grounded for repairs, sir."

Chandler nodded, sipping his coffee.

Thomas helped himself to another sandwich. That gave him a moment to recall Breeze's quick report on the status of the crew.

He was pleasantly surprised that she had taken responsibility in his absence.

"Sir, if my crew can help out elsewhere while the ship is out of action, they're yours."

"I've already attached your XO, Brisebois, to my staff. She's pretty sharp."

Thomas nodded. The fact that Breeze wasn't actually his XO didn't seem worth mentioning. "And I'm sure Lieutenant Emmes will be welcome back in her regiment."

"Yes, once Brisebois finishes the investigation."

He looked up. "What investigation?"

Chandler put down his coffee cup, placed two sandwich quarters on a plate, and leaned back again. "Thomas, what orders did you give when you told your crew to abandon ship?"

"I told them to get to safety," he said, then added, "and that I had a plan to save the ship."

"What kind of plan required you to get rid of your crew?"

More images. The cockpit windows started to warp under the pressure and heat. The engine was already on maximum climb. The ship was pulling up, but not fast enough. There was a double thump as the strike pods jettisoned. He'd shut his faceplate. Then the flames had started to fade, and the ship had gained altitude.

"I knew we couldn't pull out of the dive unless we shed mass. With the crew clear, *Rapier* was light enough to pull out on one engine."

The coffee was cool, but he drained the cup, then bit into another sandwich.

"Thomas, that was brilliant."

The coffee was turning his stomach. He dropped the half-eaten sandwich to his plate.

"My first priority was saving my crew, sir," he said. "I told them to abandon ship. I trusted my officers to choose the best options after that." Then he remembered Chandler's words. "What happened after they left the ship?"

"We're not exactly sure," the commodore replied. "Brisebois has been taking statements from the survivors, but right now it looks like Emmes might have lost it."

"What?" Thomas was too tired to show his shock, but he felt it.

"Apparently, Emmes insisted that the pods rendezvous in low orbit. She forced all the troopers into one pod and the crewmen into the other. Brisebois tried to talk to her, but got hit in the face and threatened." Chandler shook his head. "Brisebois took her pod and headed straight for *Normandy*. We recovered the other one an hour or two later, but with only four people aboard."

"Emmes?"

"She wasn't with them. We thought she was dead, but from what I've been told, one of the Hawks picked her up in space just a few hours ago. Unconscious but alive." He paused, then continued. "I'm a little concerned about this young strike officer of yours. She fucked up that raid on Cerberus, and now she went crazy during a battle."

Thomas rubbed his eyes, struggling to think clearly. "What did her troopers say happened?"

"Brisebois is still questioning them. She says they're pretty messed up, and are still talking about gun battles."

"What did their helmet recorders reveal?"

Chandler paused. Then his expression hardened. "I don't know all the details. I have a war to fight, and I don't have time to watch helmet-cam recordings. The investigation is underway." The tone of his voice indicated that the discussion was at an end.

"Yes, sir."

The door buzzed. Chandler signaled for it to open.

Thomas turned his head to greet the visitor, and struggled to rise as he recognized Colonel Korolev. The acting brigade commander ignored him completely.

"Commodore," Korolev said, "we've learned how the Centauri battle cruiser got knocked out of action."

Thomas felt a hand at his elbow. It was Chandler.

"Mr. Kane," he said, "it's good to have you back. Get some rest."

"Yes, sir," Thomas responded. He knew a dismissal when he heard one. He headed for the door.

Suddenly Korolev seemed to notice him. "Kane of the *Rapier*?"

"Yes, sir."

"You have a remarkable crew. I think you should stay and

watch this." The colonel's eyes bore into his with an intent he couldn't begin to fathom. He held up a tiny recording device.

"What do you have?" Chandler asked.

"The helmet recording of one Sergeant Suleiman Chang."

It was another hour before Thomas finally returned to his cabin, but despite the fatigue he couldn't even think about sleep. As he flopped down in an armchair, his mind was filled with images of savage violence. Not even Commodore Chandler had had much to say, once the recording had completed its run.

Alone in his cabin, Thomas couldn't help but shake his head in wonder. What had apparently been the beginnings of a court-martial investigation was probably going to turn into a Cross of Valor. Nine troopers had boarded—*boarded!*—one of the jewels in the crown of the Centauri fleet.

Sitting in the dim light, Thomas rubbed weary hands over his eyes.

According to Breeze, word was spreading that *Rapier* had saved *Normandy*, and Chandler himself had said as much. In Thomas's opinion, the whole thing was overblown. If the laws of physics had been working slightly differently that day, neither Thomas nor his ship would have survived to tell the tale.

You always wanted to be a hero, he said to himself. *Well, here you go, hero.*

There had been no plan—he'd just wanted to get his crew to safety. It never even occurred to him that ejecting the strike pods might save *Rapier*. With his ship—his command—burning up in atmo, and the EF being decimated above him, he had thought it best to cut his losses.

His last words to Katja had been a bluff, something quick to get her to abandon ship along with everyone else. After twenty years in uniform, he'd learned how to lie convincingly.

He'd almost found his peace, almost been ready to die, when he noticed that *Rapier* was gaining altitude. It had been with wide-eyed disbelief, not cool calculation, that he had checked the readouts. Most of the ship's air had escaped before he implemented damage control. One way or another, he must've been determined to get himself killed that day.

Now he was a hero, because he'd let Chandler—and everyone else—believe that he'd had a cunning plan. He tried to laugh, but the sound was little more than a scoff.

On the forward bulkhead he'd hung his professional certificates—his commission, basic line certificate, anti-vessel warfare qualification, basic strike certificate, fast-attack qualification, command certificate. An impressive list for an officer so young, but all the checks required for promotion.

Next step, command of a destroyer. After that, for a streamer like him, perhaps a battleship. And then into the admiralty, one day to be Fleet Marshal, commanding the entire Astral Force. A meteoric rise through the ranks, yet so little time spent in each position that he really didn't know what the fuck he was doing.

Commander Avernell had advised against the Free Lhasa rescue, and Thomas had gone over her head. Chandler had his own aspirations, and getting promoted in peacetime was such a slow process.

So here they were. Chandler had his field-promotion, and Thomas was a hero.

He let out a weary sigh and looked over at the familiar image, taken on Olympus Mons. Soma, his beloved fiancée—she was part of the plan, too: beauty, poise, an excellent pedigree—she would make a fine Fleet Marshal's consort. Mixed-race marriages were very much in vogue these days. Even better if they spanned two worlds in the Terran system.

Thomas had no illusions, though. Soma had her own agenda. As part of the Jovian elite, she was thrilled to be marrying a rising star in the Astral Force—one from Earth, no less. That would sit well with the nouveaux riches of the outer planets.

He leaned his head back to gaze at the overhead light. No doubt his parents were proud of him. They would have told their friends exaggerated stories about his space adventures every month at the booster clinic. The number of giddy messages he'd received from Mom about the wedding plans reassured him that they approved of the match.

At least *they'd* be happy.

But sitting alone in his dim cabin aboard the invasion ship

Normandy, somewhere in the deep blackness near the star Sirius, Thomas Kane concluded that his entire life was a sham.

He peered over at his mini-fridge, wishing that regulations permitted alcohol in the cabins. He needed a drink, and debated if he had enough energy to walk to the star lounge.

The door buzzer startled him. He blinked heavily, shaking off the mental cobwebs.

"Come in," he said.

The door slid open. Katja peered in. "Hello?"

His attempt to rise melted into a long stretch.

"Hey, OpsO," he said, stifling a yawn. "Come on in." She stepped into the cabin just enough for the door to close behind her.

"Sorry, sir," she said. "I should have known you'd be asleep. I can come back."

He rubbed his eyes and pushed himself up. "No, no, not at all. I wasn't sleeping."

She stared at him for a long moment; he couldn't make out the expression in her dark eyes.

"It's good to see you," she said finally.

A single ray of happiness penetrated his inner gloom, and he felt himself smile.

"Thanks. It's good to see you, too." Her appearance was… strange. She looked tense, and so small and vulnerable. "I just saw the report—about what you did," he said. "It's unbelievable, Katja."

Her expression relaxed, and she stepped forward to lean one hand on the corner of the desk built into the aft bulkhead.

"I don't know what I was thinking," she said. "I just didn't want your sacrifice to be for nothing."

"My sacrifice?"

"Getting us off the ship, and risking yourself to save *Rapier*," she explained. "I don't know if I could have done something like that alone, sir."

He was amazed at the admiration of her expression, and was reminded of those last moments on the bridge—when she had leaned in and kissed him. The moisture of her lips against his had been a surprise.

But a welcome one.

He knew he should tell her—of all people—the truth. Instead

he shrugged, and heard the lie come out of his mouth.

"I was just doing my duty, Katja," he said, and he thought it sounded sincere. "Nothing more."

She inched closer, dropping her gaze. He couldn't remember ever seeing her so unsure of herself. But he liked it. He also liked the way she looked, very trim in her blue jumpsuit.

"I really didn't think I was going to see you again," she said, "the last time we spoke."

"I wasn't sure either."

She seemed at a loss for what to say next. He stepped toward her, running his own fingers along the desk. Under his jumpsuit he was beginning to rise to the occasion.

"I think when we said goodbye," he said, "we didn't get a chance to finish our conversation."

She was very close now, and she looked up at him with dark, beautiful eyes. "Sir, about that..."

"Don't apologize." He reached out and gripped one of her shoulders, sliding his hand down her slim, muscular arm. "It was what got me through the ordeal."

She stepped into him, and he felt her small fingers climb up his back. The heat of her body pressed against his as his hands roamed across her. The jumpsuit dampened sensations just enough to heighten the anticipation.

"Really?" she asked.

He knew his life was already a lie. Cheating on a fiancée who didn't love him seemed rather appropriate.

"Really."

He grabbed her and lifted her onto the desk, kissing her. She responded with surprise, then intensity. As he started to unzip her jumpsuit, he had a sudden thought that it was unprofessional to have sex with his subordinate. But she was hot and willing. And he needed a release.

28

For the first time she could remember, Katja woke up with a smile.

She stared up at the close bulkhead of her sleeping cabin, luxuriating in the feel of gravity pressing the sheets down on her body. Her reach to turn on the lamp turned into a long stretch clear across her rack, fingers and toes extending out as far as they could go.

Upon her return to *Normandy* she had immediately contacted Commander Vici, her troop commander, to let her know she was still alive. Vici had acknowledged, but since Katja still belonged to *Rapier*, she sent no further instructions.

Her next order of business had been to meet with Chief Tamma to ensure the well-being of the crew. Being a pilot, Tamma had been unable to resist sweeping Katja up into a huge hug, but otherwise had been his usual pillar of professionalism. *Rapier*'s surviving crew had been assigned to the *Normandy* manning pool until they received permanent orders. Master Rating Oyenuga was still in sickbay with life-threatening wounds. Squad Leader McKevitt was also in sickbay, but was expected to recover. Next she had reported to her commanding officer.

And promptly had sex with him.

Perhaps not the wisest of moves, but it didn't stop her from smiling this morning. It was great to feel like a woman again, and even better to know that she had the love and respect of a man like Thomas Kane. If *Rapier* was out of commission and they weren't serving together, maybe a relationship would be professionally acceptable.

Jumping out of bed, she switched on some music—some Handel, to match her mood—and climbed into the shower. She sang along with the notes as the hot water caressed her, closing her eyes and remembering the surprise ending to her visit to Thomas's cabin last night.

It had been quite the ending to a very full day.

As she wrapped a towel around herself and walked through into the main cabin, a colder part of her brain whispered to her that she really shouldn't be so happy, considering everything that had gone down in the past few days. But no negativity was going to shake her emotional high.

She hadn't gone to his cabin for that purpose—she had just wanted to tell him how happy she was that he had survived. But things had gotten out of control really fast, and his obvious desire had been flattering. She was content just hearing that he admired her military prowess—that alone would have made the visit glorious—but to learn that he cared for her as much as she did for him...

It had been intense and incredible, but she hadn't stayed the night. Seeing that Thomas needed to sleep, she had decided to return to her own cabin to recharge.

That—she realized, looking at the clock—had been sixteen hours ago. Good thing no one was looking for her. She got some water boiling for tea, and started getting dressed.

Often when she was aboard *Normandy*, she wore the green coveralls of the Corps, just in case anyone was tempted to mistake her for Fleet. But as she reached into her closet she hesitated, then grabbed for the blues. She was still a member of *Rapier*'s crew, and to wear green would be to dishonor that.

She conducted along with the music with one hand and made tea with the other, savoring her last few moments of freedom. She knew that as soon as she sat down at her message console she would have to become Lieutenant Emmes again. So she sipped her tea and listened, eyes closed, as a particular minuet danced to a finish.

Her screen had a long list of messages. Most were old and routine, and she ignored anything that had been sent before the attack. There were several tactical updates from yesterday which gave no useful information, and one sent this morning from Astral Headquarters in Terra itself.

Her mug dropped to the desk, splashing tea.

Centauri forces had invaded Terran space.

All thoughts of Handel or Thomas Kane vanished from her mind. That cold part of her brain grabbed hold and pushed out everything else. This wasn't just an isolated battle—it was war. Terra's oldest colony was in open rebellion.

Suddenly all the sensations flooded back—*Rapier* going down, Hernandez splattered under APR fire, the panicked cries over the radio from Assad and Jackson, the blackness as she was blown out into space. She blinked away the moisture in her eyes and took short, sharp breaths.

There was one other message. From Sergeant Chang. It described briefly the status of the strike team and the fact that they would be servicing their armored suits in the main Corps hangar all afternoon. She glanced at the chronometer. It was mid-afternoon ship time.

Without another thought she was out the door.

Most Fleet people never made it down to the bowels of the ship where the Corps lived. In peacetime everyone Fleet seemed to think the strike-fighter hangar was the center of *Normandy*'s existence, with its shiny spaceships and vast heights. But the real heart of the vessel—its reason for existence—was the massive Corps hangar way down on Fourteen Deck.

Katja showed her ID to the pair of armed troopers at the door and was allowed to enter. She stepped through and cast her gaze wide, drinking in the sight.

The Corps hangar was longer and wider than the Fleet hangar, but not as high. And unlike the clean, orderly lines thirteen decks up, it was filled with a menagerie of dedicated instruments of war. Flush against the outer hull on both sides were the fifty drop ships—the much larger cousins of *Rapier*'s strike pods—

which delivered troops planetside a platoon at a time.

Lined up at the after end in five columns were the one hundred hover tanks of the Levantine's two armored troops. At the forward end of the hangar were the twenty FEVs, or fast engineering vehicles, with their strange assortment of construction and destruction devices extending from all sides. Clustered directly opposite from where she had entered, Katja saw what looked like a bunch of robotic giants standing around in a gaggle. These were the mechanized suits of one of the shock platoons, twice as tall as the largest trooper, designed specifically to smash any initial resistance to the landing, and to terrify the defenders.

Unlike the Centauris who trusted robots to do their fighting for them, the shock platoons were made up of specially selected troopers who, through their giant suits, took on the power of robots.

It was awe-inspiring to look upon the Levantine Regiment's entire arsenal of military hardware in one place, since back on Earth the various troops were scattered around at different bases in the eastern Mediterranean. But it didn't change Katja's desire to remain a member of the humble infantry. With armor to protect her, a helmet to guide her, and a weapon to fight with, she didn't need any fancy machinery.

As she spotted a handful of familiar troopers chatting and working idly on their armored spacesuits, she was reminded that she really only needed one thing—good people to fight alongside.

To no surprise, it was Chang who spotted her first.

"Attention on deck!"

The surviving troopers of *Rapier*'s strike team all stiffened to attention in whatever sitting or crouching position they were in.

Chang. Sakiyama. Cohen. Alayan.

Five troopers, including herself. Where once there had been ten. Fifty percent casualty rate did not a successful mission make. If she ever had the chance to instruct, Katja decided she would make that her mantra.

Chang rose fully, looming over her. His face was unreadable as ever. "Sergeant Chang reporting *Rapier* strike team. Four troopers ready, one in sickbay."

"Very good, Sergeant. Relax... please."

The troopers dropped their stiff poses, but all eyes remained on her. She glanced at each one in turn, feeling the old mask of command slip over her features. They were still in their *Rapier* blue coveralls, she noted.

They were waiting for her to speak, but so many thoughts flooded her brain that it was hard to think of what would be correct. Something inspiring, to be sure. Or at least something authoritative.

"It's good to see you," was what passed her lips. And then, "Well done."

Sakiyama's face broke into a smile, and even Cohen seemed to lighten up. Alayan dropped her gaze.

"How's McKevitt?"

"Her arm was crushed as the engine room started to come down around us," Chang said. "The suit kept all the pieces more or less together, but it's going to be a while before everything can knit. She won't have strength in that arm for months. Her war's over, ma'am."

There was an awful, unasked question hanging over the entire group, she knew, but she dreaded the answer.

Where is the rest of Alpha Team?

Instead, she stalled.

"I don't know if you've heard, but Centauria has invaded Terra." Glances flickered between the troopers, and from their dumbfounded expressions, she guessed they hadn't heard. "Details are sketchy, but apparently the attack on the EF was only part of a larger Centauri assault on all Terran positions. Centauria has seized control of the jump gate in their system, and are fighting to control the jump gates in Terra. For now, we're cut off and in hostile territory. With *Rapier* out of action, I expect we'll be reassigned to regimental posts. If you have any requests, let me know."

Chang frowned slightly. "We're going with you, ma'am."

She wasn't sure she understood. "I'm not sure where I'll be posted yet."

"Doesn't matter, ma'am. Where you go, we go."

None of them were smiling anymore, but all eyes were fixed on her. She felt her cheeks getting hot, fed by a warm glow deep inside her, but she kept her command mask in place.

"Very good," she said as matter-of-factly as she could. "I'll make sure the regiment knows." Then she added, "Thank you."

"If it's all right, ma'am, we have a question for you," Chang said.

Katja steeled herself to reveal the fate of Alpha Team. It would be the first time she had spoken of it aloud. "Go ahead, Sergeant."

"I'm sorry we couldn't get Lu's body out with us. We tried to get to him, but there was too much enemy fire. When McKevitt went down I knew we had to get out while we could." His eyes flicked to Sakiyama. The trooper's expression was supportive. Chang looked back at Katja. "It's tearing us up. I know it's your duty to inform his next of kin, but when you have the chance to visit his family, we'd like to come."

No questions about her missing squad. No one accusing her of leading her team on what by rights had been a suicide mission. Just concern over not getting their fallen comrade out.

She nodded, momentarily unable to hold their gaze.

"Well," she said with effort, "I won't keep you from your duties. As soon as I have orders for you, I'll pass them along. Get some rest while you can."

She turned and started to walk away, keeping her lips pressed tightly together and her face stiff.

Chang moved into step beside her. She didn't look up at him, and for ten paces he said nothing, but merely walked with her.

"Ma'am."

"Sergeant."

"Ma'am, you're good in the shit. But sooner or later you lose people. I'm not going to tell you how to deal with it, but you have to deal with it."

The mask of command was a fabulous tool to hide behind, and Katja felt her emotions shut down once again. She stopped before she got to the doors, and looked up to meet his eyes.

"I was expecting you to ask about Alpha Team."

His own mask was there, and she was grateful for it.

"It's not our place to question," he said. "It's up to you to tell us, ma'am."

She remained silent for a moment, then spoke.

"They were killed by an APR," she said. "They went down fighting. I blasted my way out through the hull and was picked up by one of *Kristiansand*'s Hawks. I'm sorry they didn't make it."

"Me, too. But we fucked up that ship bad. Alpha Team went down doing what they signed up for. They'll be remembered."

"I hear that I was being investigated for misconduct, but now that the helmet recordings have been examined, I've been cleared of any potential charges."

"Good to hear, ma'am."

She nodded. Chang continued to stare at her with his usual, grim expression. She turned to go once again. This time, he didn't follow.

Chang's words meant as much to her as Thomas's had. So far, nobody who mattered had condemned her for attacking the Centauri ship. Maybe her combat instincts weren't so bad after all.

29

Katja hauled herself up two decks' worth of ladders, but despite the skip in her step a deep fatigue quickly drained her reserves. Suddenly thankful that she was in Fleet blue and not expected to be in shape, she headed for the nearest elevator.

A quick lift later, she found herself on Two Deck and heading into the Fleet hangar. After the heavy congestion down below, the two lines of strike fighters looked positively delicate. She strode absently past the pilot toys, intent on the black, wounded shape at the hangar's far end. Even from a distance she could see that *Rapier* wouldn't be flying again any time soon.

One of the FAC spots next to her was currently empty, indicating the continued presence of her sister ships in the fight. Katja wondered if she and her troopers would get assigned to *Sabre* or *Cutlass*—or, worse, split up to fill in the holes among the EF's eight remaining fast-attack craft. Their unique qualification made them very valuable, especially since the EF's re-supply had been severed while a battle raged over control of the Terran jump gates.

Her boots echoed loudly on the hard surface of *Rapier's* hexagonal passageway, unmuffled by the usual hum of shipboard activity. Abandoned pieces of damage-control equipment still littered the passageway. Lighting indicated that there was power on board, but it was being supplied by *Normandy*. As Katja gripped the rungs of the midship's ladder and climbed to the upper deck, she hoped that the ship's main computer could be fired up, or even that it had survived at all.

The upper passageway was clear of debris, and the open hatch to the bridge allowed additional light from the hangar to stream in at the forward end. She considered going to the bridge to conduct her task, but instead decided to access the computer from her cabin. The hard-mount at her desk was more likely to be working than the virtual consoles on the bridge, and if the computer was slow she could pack her stuff while she waited.

The door to her cabin slid open normally, which was a good sign. Inside, the usually tidy space was a junkyard of gear. She immediately noticed the warped metal and visible cracks in the outer hull, and imagined how anything loose would have been pulled toward the openings as the air rushed out. She stepped gingerly over the clothes and effects littering the deck. A quick glance revealed none of them to be hers.

She smiled. The benefit of keeping her gear properly stowed.

The computer activated at her command, and she began a search for the flight log she had copied from the mystery merchant *Astrid*. She barely had the chance to pull her kit bag down out of storage before *Rapier*'s databanks produced the desired file. She inserted a hard crystal and made another copy, just to be sure. That process took the same time as she needed to empty her top drawer into the kit bag.

She composed search criteria for the computer to hunt for *Astrid*'s rendezvous with the other, unknown vessel which had supplied her with the Centauri weapons. That gave her enough time to empty her two remaining drawers and her footlocker. By the time she'd stuffed the last of her gear into the kit bag, the desk console was indicating that it had completed the task.

She sat down and examined the data.

Sure enough, *Astrid* had rendezvoused with another vessel—whose name did not appear in the records—fifteen days before Katja and her troopers had boarded. Moving through the flight log, she backed the sequence up to watch the second ship approach, then backed it up further to see if the ship noticeably changed course.

Bringing up *Rapier*'s own stellar charts, she quickly plotted

Astrid's position at the rendezvous and projected back the path of the second ship. It projected down from the RV position, through the Sirian ecliptic far from any planet or asteroid and off into deep space.

Frustration welling up, she sat back and sighed. One of Breeze's data cubes lay haphazardly on the desk where it had fallen. Katja smacked it away, figuring it might as well join the rest of her junk on the deck. It landed with a loud clunk.

A moment later, the door chimed. She sat up in surprise.

"Come in!"

The door slid open, and Thomas peered in.

She had imagined several times over the past twenty-four hours how she might greet him at their next meeting. She'd pictured them at the star lounge, in his cabin, or even him coming to hers aboard *Normandy*. None of her scenarios had taken place here, aboard *Rapier*. She stared at him for a long moment, feeling her heartbeat increase.

He spoke first. "Oh. Hi!"

He looked terrible, despite his efforts to smile. His entire face seemed to sag, and he leaned against the doorframe with a heaviness she'd never seen in him. He didn't exactly look happy to see her—more like surprised.

Nevertheless, she couldn't stop herself from smiling.

"Hi," she offered. "I hope you got some rest."

He nodded. "I, uh, heard a noise from the passageway—I figured it was either you or Breeze."

"It's just me."

In the awkward silence her cheeriness suddenly sounded misplaced. She cringed inwardly as he looked at her, somehow knowing that things were not going to be as happy as she'd imagined. But his feelings for her had been clear last night, and a part of her was excited for him to speak.

Either way, it was his initiative now.

He stepped completely into the cabin. The door slid shut.

"What brings you aboard?" He glanced around at the cluttered deck. "Clearing out your locker?"

She ignored the growing knot in her stomach and indicated her full kit bag.

"There's my stuff. This is all Breeze's. But I also came to get some data from that mystery merchant we boarded."

He glanced at the computer screen, and rubbed his eyes. "Looking for anything in particular?"

She couldn't believe it. He really wasn't going to say anything. Well, she could play that game, too.

"I was just trying to figure out where the other ship came from that supplied *Astrid* with her weapons cache. Trying to figure out how the Centauris have been sneaking so much stuff past us."

He moved the chair over to better see the screen—almost touching her, and she couldn't help but shuffle her own chair slightly.

"What have you got?"

He was acting like nothing had happened, but she refused to be the one to mention the elephant in the room. No one was ever going to accuse her of being some clingy girl. Her arm touched his shoulder as she pointed at the screen.

"Well, remember that pilot, Jack?"

"Who?"

"That kid Breeze was stringing along at the star lounge, before we went on the last mission."

"Oh, yeah." His eyes closed for a moment. "What about him?"

"Well, he had this idea that maybe the Centauris have snuck everything through a new jump gate that they made themselves."

He frowned. "That's crazy."

"Maybe, but I figure if there is one, then the ship that gave *Astrid* the weapons probably came through it. And because it was in deep space the whole time, its exhaust stream is probably still intact. If we can get a Hawk to track its route back, we might find the secret jump gate."

He turned to look at her. She didn't back away, but let his face be close to hers. His gaze softened.

"Katja... about last night..."

She suddenly realized how much she wanted to kiss him. How much she wanted to slip into his strong arms and lose herself in his warmth.

"Yes?"

His eyes were haunted, and she felt her heart begin to sink.

"Look… last night shouldn't have happened." He dropped his head and sighed. "I'm sorry. I was feeling all messed up and… I made a mistake."

Her stomach clenched. She realized after a moment that her mouth was hanging open. A thousand things to say flashed through her mind.

"What?" she said.

"Katja, I think you're beautiful and smart and I'm sorry that I've busted up our professional relationship. But I'm marrying someone else—this shouldn't have happened."

Her urge to kiss him had turned into an urge to punch him as hard as she could. But she resisted.

"So what am I?" she demanded. "A squeeze toy? You're feeling all messed up, and I'm just a little treat to make you feel better?" She was as angry at herself as she was with him. She knew better than this. It was her own damn fault for having let herself fall for a guy in uniform.

He still hadn't come up with anything worthwhile to say.

The door slid open, and Breeze strode in. "All right, Captain, let's get—" She stopped in her tracks as her eyes fell on Katja. "Hi." Breeze's usual smile slid into place. "I didn't know we were having a staff meeting."

Thomas leaned back in his chair. "Katja and I were just going over some potential intelligence."

"Well, it's a good thing I stopped by then." Breeze sidled over and placed a hand on Katja's shoulder. "I'm so glad that everything was sorted out. I still can't believe what a brave thing you did."

"Yeah, you're one crazy chick, Ops," Thomas said.

She tried to smile, but the whole situation suddenly seemed unreal. Thomas and Breeze were both smiling at her, but neither looked quite themselves. Despite the fact that she had arrived at the cabin first, she somehow felt…

As if she was interrupting something.

"How did you know the captain was in here?" she asked.

Breeze's face displayed nothing but friendly rapport, except for the slight flicker of her eyes up and to the left.

"Interestingly enough, I'd asked him to go over the last few minutes of *Rapier*'s log before we... took the pods and left. We decided it would be best to look at the data directly from *Rapier*'s computer, and our cabin is bigger than his." She glanced around with her most disarming, self-deprecating expression. "Too bad I'm such a poor housekeeper."

"Actually, I think what Ops was showing me is more relevant," Thomas said. "Maybe you should have a look at this."

Katja kept her expression neutral, but obligingly replayed the logs from *Astrid*, explaining her thought processes. Breeze nodded thoughtfully at the suggestion of a secret Centauri jump gate—an idea which she had angrily dismissed when it had been suggested by Jack.

After twenty minutes of discussion, they agreed that the data and Katja's theory should be taken to Astral Intelligence. Less than a minute after that, Thomas said his goodbyes and left the ship, followed shortly thereafter by Breeze—who didn't bother to clean up her crap.

Katja was left to haul her kit bag off *Rapier*, suddenly feeling very tired and wanting to sleep again.

30

B reeze eased down into the chair with a long sigh. She was alone in the small conference room and she allowed herself a little outward moment of frustration.

She still had trouble believing what she was going to do. Good work in the Astral Force should be acknowledged, she knew, but not when it was the result of stupid decisions and dumb luck. Especially when it was Katja's dumb luck.

Breeze honestly couldn't believe how that crazy butch was still alive. She flashed up the screens built into the table next to every seat, and displayed her report summary on each. No point in fighting it—she began composing herself for the ordeal.

The door swished open to allow Katja to enter, and she rose from her chair, her trained smile spreading easily and without conscious effort. Commander Vici was right behind her. Neither looked too friendly, but that had never stopped Breeze before.

"Hi, Katja," she said. "You look great. Totally recovered." Katja gave her an odd look, a cross between suspicion and appreciation.

"Thanks."

Commander Vici sat down. "Is this the final report, Lieutenant?"

Breeze resumed her seat. "The summary is displayed, ma'am. You can access the full report at the top of the page."

The three women sat in silence for a moment, neither of the other two looking at Breeze. She didn't mind too much—talking to these she-apes was about as much fun as sitting through a lecture on the merits of combining your house and life insurance.

Thankfully, it wasn't long before the rest of the attendees arrived, and Breeze gave warm words of welcome in turn to Thomas, Brigade Colonel Korolev, and finally Commodore Chandler. She noticed immediately that there was some sort of weird tension between Thomas and Katja—they didn't greet each other, and while they glanced at each other, neither would meet the other's eye. The men made a few moments of small talk—apparently Thomas's fiancée was Chandler's goddaughter, she noted with interest—then at last she was able to start.

She sat up straight and gave a professional smile. The men all smiled back.

"Sirs, ma'am, it's a great pleasure today to give my final report on the actions of *Rapier*'s strike team after abandoning ship during the Battle of Laika. The summary is before you on your screen, but I think it's no surprise to any of us that Lieutenant Emmes and her team are to be commended for their heroic actions."

She'd been practicing this speech so much for the past day that she could actually say it with enthusiasm that sounded real.

"After ensuring the safety of the Fleet members of *Rapier*, Lieutenant Emmes and her team flew in an unarmed, unarmored spacecraft through heavy fire, snuck on board a Centauri battle cruiser and proceeded to cause so much internal damage that the enemy ship was forced to retreat from the battle. It was eventually abandoned by its surviving crew.

"A careful reconstruction of the overall Battle of Laika has revealed that the withdrawal of the Centauri battle cruiser from the fight turned the tide and gave Expeditionary Force 15 the chance to fend off the Centauri aggression and withdraw with only limited casualties."

She looked around the table, trying to gauge the reactions. Chandler, Korolev, and Vici were all nodding. Thomas kept his eyes down. Katja kept her eyes on Breeze, her expression grim.

"The report recommends that Lieutenant Emmes be nominated for the Star of Courage, and that every member of her strike team who boarded the enemy vessel be nominated for the Medal of Bravery. The pilot of their ship is recommended for the Military Medal."

Katja's eyes widened slightly. She dropped her gaze as her cheeks reddened.

Vici and Korolev exchanged a glance. Chandler leaned forward and glared.

"I thought there was talk about the Terran Cross, and the Star of Courage for her troopers. Did I miss a memo, Lieutenant Brisebois?"

She'd hoped he'd forgotten, actually, but it was nothing a little well-placed referencing couldn't solve. She put on her best look of painful regret.

"Sir, personally I couldn't agree more." She smiled at Katja. "If it was up to me, I'd say the Cross of Valor itself." She brought up the pained expression again. "Unfortunately, when recommendations for medals are made, it's imperative that we keep to the clear standards set in precedent. It's so easy to get emotional when we have the good fortune to witness true heroism, but the Astral Force has a long history of heroism against which each act has to be weighed."

"I suppose you did a thorough comparison, Lieutenant?" Vici asked.

"Yes, ma'am," Breeze replied. "In the full report I've included three examples each of recent winners of the three medals that were considered. Please review them and compare with the actions in this current report. I think you'll find that Lieutenant Emmes is eminently worthy of the Star of Courage."

Vici stared at her screen for a few moments.

"Some of these are twenty years old."

Breeze nodded. "I think it speaks volumes about the prestige these medals hold when you see how rarely they're awarded."

"And this one's from the Army."

"Again, to find relevant examples I had to go outside the Astral Force." That, and she was very curious to see the reaction when Katja read the name of the example she'd dug up.

It was Korolev who noticed first.

"Banner Leader Gunther Friedrich Emmes, Terran Cross." He turned to look at Katja. "Is he related to you, Lieutenant?"

Breeze watched carefully. Katja's eyes narrowed as soon as the Army was mentioned, and the color fled her face when she heard the name.

"He's my father," she said quietly.

Chandler was still frowning. "Well, we'll have to review this. Lieutenant Brisebois, take Lieutenant Emmes outside. We'll call you back in a few minutes."

"Yes, sir." She rose and rounded the table, following Katja out into the flats. It was very quiet, and Katja seemed happy to keep it that way.

"I wondered if that was your father when I was doing the research," Breeze said with a friendly smile. "You never talk very much about him, but he must be your idol."

Katja looked up, dark eyes peering through pale eyebrows, but it was a long moment before she replied.

"He's a very accomplished soldier."

"I'm sure he'll be very proud of you," Breeze said. It was like twisting the knife, and she knew it. "He's a storm banner leader now, isn't he?"

Katja nodded.

"What he must have thought when you joined the Astral Force." But Breeze knew better. She'd only seen Katja drunk twice—once on the fast-attack course and once in the star lounge. Both times the subject of her father had come out—along with his hatred of officers and her choice of career.

She pressed her advantage. "I know the Army has some strange ideas about officers. Isn't it true that they don't have any? Don't they all start as stormtroopers, and go up from there? What did he think about you going officer?"

Katja was turning red. Amazing how easy it was to wind somebody up, given the proper ammunition.

"Anyway, let's hope we can get home soon, so you can tell him face to face what happened."

Katja's lips were tight. "Yeah."

There was another moment of silence. Katja folded her arms and stared at the deck.

"Thomas has certainly been looking tired lately, hasn't he?" Breeze said. "I wonder if he's been sleeping well."

"How the hell would I know?"

That was a stronger reaction than expected. Had she uncovered something? "I was just asking. I know you two sometimes spend off-time together."

Katja reddened again. "What's that supposed to mean?" She sounded more defensive than angry.

Interesting, Breeze thought. "Well, like that time we all met up for drinks at the star lounge." She smiled. "That seems like so long ago now, doesn't it?"

After a moment, Katja replied.

"How's your boyfriend Jack?" she asked.

That caught her off guard. But she quickly regrouped.

"He's a nice kid," she said. "But there's nothing between us. A shame about his injuries, though."

"I guess the last time we saw him was when he gave us a lift back from *Kristiansand*."

"I think you're right."

"After you gave your briefing to a packed house—about the battle. It was impressive how you told the tale." Katja paused, then continued. "Maybe I'll have the chance to write a report concerning your conduct at the Battle of Laika. You know, return the favor."

Suddenly the conversation was taking an uncomfortable turn.

"I'd be honored," Breeze said, "but I really didn't do much."

"I know."

Breeze glanced at the door to the conference room. What was taking them so long?

"I'm just happy," Katja continued, "that you were able to get to safety so quickly. It's horrible to think of you being in danger." She was about as subtle as a bull in a china shop, but annoying enough that Breeze couldn't think of a decent retort.

"At least I made it back with everyone still alive," she said finally. "How many dead did you leave behind?" She cringed at her own lack of style, but her words had the desired effect.

"Fuck you." Katja's fists clenched.

Breeze stepped back out of arm's reach, feeling her composure returning. She forced herself to smile.

"I've told you, honey—you're not my type."

Katja's face wrinkled in disgust as she turned away. Then the door to the conference room finally opened. Thomas beckoned them both to enter. Breeze let Katja lead, not trusting enough to turn her back on an enraged trooper. Once inside, they took their seats. Surprisingly, it was Korolev who spoke.

"Lieutenant Emmes, I'm sorry that you've had to be aware of this discussion. Usually recipients are simply told of their honor, and are left ignorant of any discussions that lie behind it. This was handled poorly."

His eyes never left Katja, but Breeze felt Vici's glare pass over her.

"Since we have no ability to confer with Astral High Command," he continued, "we—the acting commanders of EF 15, together with your commanding officer and your troop commander— have decided to award you the field decoration of the Astral Star. Sergeant Chang is awarded the Star of Courage, the members of your strike team who boarded the enemy vessel are awarded the Medal of Bravery, and your pilot the Military Medal."

He stood. Everyone followed his lead.

"Congratulations, Lieutenant Emmes."

She shook his outstretched hand firmly, but Breeze could see that she was still bothered by their exchange in the passageway. *Good*, she thought. That helped make up for suffering the indignity of watching this self-righteous psychopath get a medal. Behind her smile, Breeze prayed that the EF got back to Terra soon. This military was one fucked-up organization and she wanted out.

31

Jack never thought that he'd prefer zero-g.

As he limped along the seemingly endless passageway of *Normandy*, however, struggling to keep pace with the XO, he thought back with longing to the freedom of *Kristiansand*'s weightlessness. He was trying to avoid the scary trooper-drugs as much as possible, but he made a note to pop some as soon as this briefing was over.

Finally the XO slowed to pass through a large door. Other officers were approaching from various directions. Jack slipped through the door and had a good look around at the briefing room. It was even bigger than *Kristiansand*'s hangar, he reckoned, with rows and rows of seating, all facing a bulkhead with three big screens.

This was his third visit to the giant invasion ship, but he was still impressed by something new each trip.

"Clear a path, Subbie!" Someone pushed past him roughly. Jack stumbled at the impact, looking up in shock.

A Fleet lieutenant glared back at him, but his expression softened as soon as he saw Jack's face.

"Oh, sorry," he said. "Just keep clear of the door."

Jack dutifully stepped aside, wincing as he pressed a hand against the pain in his left shoulder. The push hadn't been hard, but he just couldn't take the hits like he used to. He walked over to the nearest chair, ignoring the growing number of eyes that were watching him. Suddenly feeling like a circus freak, he sat down quickly to turn his face away.

More people entered, and Jack watched idly, wondering if there were any other pilots coming. He noticed *Rapier*'s CO, Kane, and listened absently as he exchanged greetings with the XO. Kane didn't look happy. But then, the only other occasion Jack had met him was at the star lounge, in happier times. Everyone, he noticed, was looking very serious. Some would glance at him, sitting in the front row, but no one met his gaze.

He sighed and looked down absently at his crooked fingers, resisting the urge again to reach up and touch his bumpy cheek.

The noise level in the room suddenly dropped, and Jack noticed a pair of boots stop in front of him. He lifted his head and found himself staring into the eyes of a man in Corps green, probably in his forties. On his epaulettes there was a single star, though Jack didn't recognize the rank. The man met his gaze without any sign of horror or embarrassment, and even seemed a bit curious.

"You've seen some action, my friend."

"Yeah." Jack wasn't sure how to take that.

"You're a pilot. From one of the carriers?"

"No, *Kristiansand*. I fly Hawks."

"Ahhh." This seemed to trigger something. "It's good to see you here. I'm Sasha Korolev."

This was the first friendly person Jack had met in days.

"Jack Mallory. What do you do?"

"I'm the acting brigade commander."

Jack pondered the words for a moment.

Acting... Brigade...

Oh!

"I'm sorry," he said. "Am I in your seat?"

"Yes, but don't trouble yourself."

Nevertheless he struggled awkwardly to push himself up, wondering if he would ever stop being a dumbass.

"Sorry, sir, I didn't know."

A firm hand on his shoulder stopped him from rising. "Mr. Mallory, I insist. Keep your seat. I can see just fine from over there."

Murmurs rippled through the audience as Jack watched

Colonel Korolev find a seat at the end of the row. He glanced back over his shoulder and caught sight of the XO shaking his head. Kane was smiling next to him.

"Ladies and gentlemen!"

The sudden words startled Jack, almost as much as the sudden movement all around him. Everyone was sitting to attention. He stiffened in place as best he could.

To his left, a man entered the briefing room and came striding toward him. This man, Jack noted immediately, had four gold bars on his epaulettes, and even he knew what rank that was.

The captain whose name Jack reckoned he'd be learning really soon stopped in surprise in front of the empty seat next to him. He looked around briefly, and Colonel Korolev gave a thumbs-up from the end of the row.

"Relax," the captain said. He sat down, and everyone in the audience settled in their seats.

"Who are you?" the captain asked him quietly.

"Jack Mallory. I'm a pilot. From *Kristiansand*." The captain merely nodded and turned his attention to the front of the room as a Fleet commander moved to stand before the audience.

"Commodore, Brigade Colonel, ladies and gentlemen. It's been a hundred hours since the Laikan ambush. EF 15 is in a difficult tactical situation."

The commander proceeded to give what Jack assumed was a tactical update, but most of the TLAs went over his head. He recognized the names and projections of the ships that had been lost—two invasion ships, a battleship, a carrier, a cruiser, a destroyer, a stealth ship and a supply ship. The EF was at sixty or seventy percent strength, depending on how you measured it, and was being probed several times a day by Centauri long-range craft.

A full-scale attack was considered likely within the next twenty-four hours.

He examined with interest the giant 3-D display that was projected to the side of the commander, figuring out pretty quickly that the surviving EF ships were moving as a group away from the sun. The display also showed several positions where Centauri ships were suspected, but not confirmed.

There was some discussion between the captain—or commodore, by now—and various senior officers. There had been no direct attacks on the EF by the Centauris since the Laikan ambush, and except for the probes the enemy seemed to have all but disappeared. The goal was to keep the EF in deep space, away from the planetary gravity wells, where it would be easier to track enemy stealth ships. Far from the distortions of massive bodies and away from the crowded space lanes, ASW was clear and simple.

"We now face a decision," the commander concluded. "In the absence of orders from Terra, we need to determine how best to act in our nation's interest. Commodore?"

The commodore—Chandler—rose from his chair and took center stage.

"Ladies and gentlemen, we know that the Centauri attack has been against all Terran forces, not just here in Sirius. We know that the war has been brought to the doorstep of our home system, and even now the Astral Fleet is fighting to regain control of the jump gates in Terra. Our natural instinct is to run home and join the fight. We could move at full speed to the jump gate, punch through, and come out with guns blazing."

This sounded like a good plan to Jack.

"But to do so," Chandler continued, "would be to abandon our interests here in Sirius. There are still significant Centauri forces in this system, and if we head home we will in a single stroke lose all the positions we've established.

"Without the threat of EF 15, what would stop the Centauris from attacking the jump gate here, and seizing control of this system? Without the threat of EF 15, what would stop them from openly joining their warlord puppets and snuffing out the tiny flames of freedom and democracy that have finally taken light, here in Sirius?

"Terra has maintained a permanent military presence in this system for fifteen years, and all of us who are veterans of the Dog Watch know well the sacrifices we've made to protect the free colonists of Sirius from Centauri interference."

Jack had always wondered why Terra was here. Apparently it was to defend democracy.

"And so," Chandler said, his voice rising to fill the room, "we stay here. We fight our enemies here. We defend what we have sworn to defend. Even if we aren't on the front line of the war, we will ensure that Terra's flank is clear."

Chandler nodded to someone at the side of the stage. Jack looked over and found new interest in the briefing as Breeze rose from her seat and moved to a podium, stage right. She looked all business, but Jack was sure she smiled at him just after Chandler had retaken his seat.

"Good morning," she said as she brought up some new pictures on the screens. "Astral Intelligence's top priority is to determine how the Centauri fleet managed to sneak so many warships past our sensors. If they can do it here, who's to say they can't do it in Terra?

"To find answers, we've recommended resuming the line of investigation that led us to the terrorists in Free Lhasa. Our next move is to conduct a strike against a known Centauri base of operations on Cerberus, as indicated on the center screen."

Jack looked with interest at the picture, which showed a farming community with long buildings extending out in a radial pattern from a collection of smaller buildings surrounding a central square.

"This site was investigated several weeks ago, but the strike team aborted the mission before they had concluded a proper investigation. Our information tells us that, despite our earlier incursion, this site is still being used as a major coordination center for Centauri agents. We're going back to capture those agents. Although we expect there to be additional defenses due to the botched earlier strike, we anticipate that a platoon-sized force will be sufficient to accomplish the goal.

"The strike force will consist of Levantine Regiment, Saracens Troop, Second Platoon. It will be augmented by the surviving members of *Rapier*'s strike team, who conducted the initial raid and thus have prior knowledge of the area." She checked her notes. "Lieutenant Lahko will command the mission, with Lieutenant Emmes advising."

Breeze made even an intelligence brief hot. Jack loved having an excuse to stare at her while she talked.

"Intelligence has high hopes that this strike will produce Centauri prisoners who can be properly interrogated. It is considered very likely that they will have the information we seek."

She concluded with a few logistical details, and Jack suddenly realized that she hadn't mentioned his theory about a secret jump gate. If the EF wanted to find out how Centauri ships had snuck into Cerberus, surely that was something to investigate.

Breeze sat down again, and the commander who had spoken at the beginning gave some kind of closing statement. Then the briefing ended.

The room filled with voices as Jack pushed himself up out of his seat. He spotted Breeze chatting with some other officers, and headed in their direction.

"Hey, Breeze," he said as he moved into her conversation circle. "What about the second jump gate?"

Surprise flashed across her face, as well as a darker shade that looked like irritation.

"I'm sorry?" she said.

Jack jerked a thumb back toward the display.

"The jump gate theory, like we talked about. Shouldn't we be sending a ship to investigate?"

Breeze glanced at the officers she had been talking to, then smiled. But it wasn't the smile he was used to seeing.

"Jack, lots of people contribute their theories," she said, an odd tone to her voice. He wasn't sure he liked it. "It's our job in Intelligence to determine which have the highest priority."

"But how else could they sneak—"

She took a step closer, put a hand on his arm, and gave him a look that made him feel warm all over.

"Jack, you're right," she said. "It's a great theory, but we're really short on assets right now, because of the attack. We have to focus on one thing at a time." She looked past him, over his shoulder, then back into his eyes. "Honey, it's great to see you, but I'm really busy. Can we talk another time?"

The words he wanted to hear. *Well, sort of.*

"Sure, I'm not flying back to *Kristiansand* for a few hours. How about the star lounge?"

Her smile really wasn't as nice as he remembered from before.

"Maybe not this time." She gave his arm another squeeze, and then slipped past him. He turned and saw Commodore Chandler complimenting her on a good briefing. She accepted his praise modestly, and made some joke that caused the commodore to laugh, along with the other men gathered around her.

Looking down at his twisted hands, Jack felt a different sort of heat rise up his neck. He stepped clear of the crowd and headed for the door. Apparently this was no place for freaks, no matter how good their ideas. Every step hurt, and he wondered where he might hole up until it was time to go home.

"Hey, Jack!"

The female voice caught his attention. He turned and saw Katja Emmes striding up, her big trooper friend with her—the one from the star lounge. She wasn't exactly smiling, but her expression seemed friendly.

"Hi, ma'am," he said. "Are you recovered from your little space walk?"

"Yeah, thanks," she replied. "How are you feeling?"

He hesitated before answering, wondering if her question was just polite, or a genuine request for info. Considering what he knew of her, he decided on the latter.

"Pretty shitty," he admitted. "I look like a bag full of smashed assholes, and I feel worse than I look. I stole the acting brigade commander's seat, and nobody's listening to me about the secret jump gate theory."

Katja and her friend exchanged a glance.

"Battle has hardened you, young Jack," the big trooper said with great dramatic effect. "Last time we met, we were drinking and whoring and carrying on."

His name was Scott Lahko, Jack remembered.

"With the drugs I'm on, drinking's not smart and whoring's probably impossible."

Both troopers laughed.

"Well," Lahko said, "with a face like that you can be my wingman at the bar anytime."

"Don't feel bad about your theory," Katja said. "I actually did some more research on it, and I think it's worth investigating. I even discussed the evidence with my captain and Breeze." She shrugged.

"I guess busting up Cerberans is more important to them."

The fact that she had taken him seriously made him feel better. He looked past her to the small group still clustered around Breeze and the commodore. The XO and Kane were there, too.

He focused again on the short woman in front of him.

"Thanks," he said. "I guess I'll keep working on it on my own. You guys have to get ready for a mission." He shifted his weight, and winced at the sharp pain in his hip. "And I need to take some drugs."

"Oh, hey!" Katja suddenly reached into one of her pockets and produced a data crystal. "Here's the research I was talking about. I made a copy of *Astrid*'s flight log. I did some calculations on the other ship's trajectory. It didn't seem to lead to anything— but maybe you'll see something I didn't."

"Thanks." He took the crystal with interest. "This should give me a starting point, if nothing else."

"Good luck," she said. "Take care of yourself." He thought she meant it.

Katja walked off, with Lahko right behind her.

Jack studied the tiny, featureless data storage device. His frustration faded away. What did Breeze know anyway—she was just Astral Intelligence. He pocketed the crystal and limped for the door.

If there was a secret jump gate out there, he was going to find it.

32

It had been a long time since she'd worn terrestrial armor. As she followed Scott Lahko across the broad, clear deck at the center of the Corps hangar, Katja enjoyed the easy movement and peripheral vision that her armored spacesuit lacked.

The armor was standard battle gear for the Astral Corps, designed for up to seven days of surface combat. A soft, black one-piece jumpsuit clung to her body to regulate temperature, all but invisible under the hard, rust-colored outer plates—specially color-prepared for each terrain—that linked together to shield against impact while maintaining full flexibility. The neck plates offered protection up to her ears, and would be capped by the helmet she currently carried in her left hand.

Because the mission was only a raid, her gear was light—assault rifle and eight magazines, a spare power pack for the rifle, first aid kit, and minimal rations.

As she walked the dozen small armor plates covering her legs brushed against each other, clicking softly. It was a very different sound from the whirr of her suit. It was the sound of a ground-pounder, the sound of a trooper. If she hadn't had her war-face on, she would have smiled.

The platoon was already formed up in standard order: three ranks of fifteen with the two sergeants in front and the five squad leaders behind. Chang and the other three members of her strike team were formed up in their own rank off to the right.

"Second platoon, atten-*tion*!"

In a single crisp movement, the fifty-six assembled troopers snapped to attention.

Lahko stopped in front of the sergeant who had barked the order and they exchanged quiet words. Katja moved to the end of the ranks.

Lahko stepped back and surveyed his platoon. "At ease."

Everyone relaxed.

"Listen up, troopers. Today we are going in hot. This is not a simulation. Those people on the ground want to kill us. Our mission is clear—find the Centauri agents and bring them back alive. Everyone else, fuck 'em!" He glared over at Katja and her team. "Lieutenant Emmes and *Rapier*'s strike team are along as our guides. They've been here before, and you will listen to what they have to say."

She walked forward so that the platoon could see her clearly, but kept her distance from Lahko. Sometimes she hated the fact that she was so small, especially when a charismatic giant like Scott had just surrendered the stage.

"The target today is a farming complex near Free Lhasa," she said. "It is populated by unarmed civilians, including children. This region does not have a history of terrorism, and we don't expect there to be any martyrs in the crowd."

Her comment drew a few chuckles. She pushed down the sudden memory of the thrown jar, exploding in midair, followed by the unnamed man's torso exploding as her bullet detonated in his chest.

"Intelligence reports that there is no warlord activity in the area, so we can expect an unopposed landing. The regular population is generally compliant," a vision of her rifle butt smashing through the faces of the man and woman, "so any resistance at all should be treated as indication of hostiles.

"Our primary search area is the equipment lock-up at the south end of the central complex, desig building ten, as well as two shacks of unknown purpose in the southeast corner. These shacks have been erected since our last visit, and are considered extremely suspicious.

"Intel reports that this farm is a drop site for Centauri weapons, and that their agents maintain a permanent presence to coordinate with local warlords. We do not know the exact numbers of agents, but we suspect at least three. They are to be taken alive. *Rapier* strike team will lead the search. Second Platoon will provide cover on all sides."

She nodded to Lahko, and resumed her position at the side of the platoon.

Lahko concluded the briefing. "We'll have strike fighter support. Sublieutenant Wei and Fifth Platoon will be on standby. Fleet will do some preliminary bombardment on Cerberan bases a thousand kilometers away from the target to draw attention there. There's no hiding these big ships, but the goal is for us to get in unnoticed.

"You've all seen the maps. You all know your search areas. The plan is simple—we land, we secure the population, we search, we get out." He offered a wolfish grin. "Then, when Intel has their info, we dish out some payback!"

The troopers muttered their agreement. They were hungry for action.

Katja glanced at her "strike team." Chang, Sakiyama, Cohen, and Alayan were stone-faced. If they were hungry for anything, it was vengeance, and she knew the feeling well. There was no real connection between the farm on Cerberus and the deaths of their fellow troopers in orbit over Laika, but everyone was the enemy now. Vengeance in whatever form would be sweet.

The drop ship boasted a very simple design. The stern was a ramped opening wide enough to disgorge a platoon of troopers in seconds. Low, bubble turrets perched on all four top corners of the hull, with weapons to provide covering fire as the ship landed. The interior bay was large enough to hold a tank, and easily seated fifty-some regular infantry.

Katja edged past the troopers as they unfolded aft-facing seats from the deck and strapped themselves in. She followed Lahko into the cockpit, where there were three seats behind the pair of pilots, raised slightly to give a good view. Lahko, as platoon leader, took the central seat. Katja took the port-side spot and secured herself.

Soon the airlock doors were sliding open, and Katja looked out to once again lay eyes upon the red and brown world of Cerberus. As Lahko conducted last-minute checks with Drop Command, she literally watched the world go by, and reviewed once again the sequence of events from her previous raid. She visualized the drop zone, and where their target buildings were located.

This time, she would finish the mission.

The countdown came from Drop Command. Katja leaned back straight in her seat.

"Three... Two... One.

"Drop!"

She was pressed back as the drop ship launched clear of *Normandy*'s hull. There was a moment of free-fall, and then the ship turned its nose down toward the planet. As it accelerated, she listened to the sporadic radio chatter, wishing she had a 3-D display to track the positions of any Cerberan craft. Before going fast-attack, she hadn't cared about "Fleet crap" like ship movements and positioning: like a good trooper, she had cared only for her mission on the ground.

Now, though, she felt blind as she held onto her seat and watched the orange cone build around the drop ship's hull. The ship began to shudder as the cone grew to envelop the forward windows. Visions of *Rapier*'s dive toward Laika filled her mind. Of bulkheads groaning. Of air leaking out. Smoke in passageways. Hernandez being shot to pieces. Her breathing was quick, straining against the g-forces. She moved reflexively to shut her faceplate and suck in concentrated suit oxygen.

But there was no suit.

Something hard banged against her shoulder. Lahko's fist.

"Hey!" he shouted over the roar. "Don't be a girl, Emmes!"

Sudden anger overwhelmed her. She forced deep breaths in and out, like her training had drilled into her. Her lungs loosened and filled with oxygen.

She punched his arm. Hard.

"If you're lucky and make it back," she said, "you'll be my bitch!"

"Now we're talking!" His eyes were hidden behind the darkened visor, but his grin was clear.

The fires of entry faded and the drop ship raced through the sky, dropping steadily on final approach. Katja surveyed the broad landscape with her eyes, then focused in on the strike camera. The farm looked exactly the same—a central complex of buildings surrounded by long greenhouses that extended out like the spokes of a giant wheel.

"Looks quiet," she said.

Lahko nodded. "Maybe Intel was right!"

The view of the farm grew clearer as they approached. Seconds later, they were braking hard over the farm and dropping to the ground.

She unstrapped, released her rifle and rose in a swift, practiced movement. Unlike a strike pod, however, there were more than three troopers to disembark before her, and she came to an abrupt stop next to Lahko at the forward end of the trooper bay. The platoon spilled out before her with impressive efficiency, but even so, she practically strolled down the deck to the stern ramp.

The familiar hot wind brushed against her chin and jaw, and the strange, slightly metallic smell of Cerberan air was familiar. She lifted her rifle and descended to the dusty ground, watching carefully as the platoon spread out in a standard securing pattern. Lahko barked orders over the helmet comms.

The harsh light of Sirius reflected off the dull white buildings with an intensity that made her squint, even behind her visor. Troopers shuffled forward in pairs, checking windows and doorways. Otherwise, there was no movement. No civilians. No one dropping to the ground or staring in shock.

She turned in a slow circle as she walked, looking over her rifle, taking in the complete scene. The farm looked deserted.

Lahko had noticed it, too. "Pretty quiet."

She nodded. "This isn't right. Last time there were a dozen people within sight of this central area. Maybe they had warning, and ran."

"Could be."

Lahko issued a quick update, advising his platoon to expect trouble.

Building seven, the lab, was on her right. From the outside there was no evidence of the violence that had taken place there less than three weeks ago.

Chang and the rest of the strike team appeared in her peripheral. To keep naming simple, Chang, Sakiyama, Alayan, and Cohen had taken the code-names Alpha-Two through Five. For this mission, they were one squad, one team.

She motioned them forward. They advanced in a line on her flank, weapons up. Pairs of troopers guarded the corners of building seven on the right and building thirteen on the left. Seven fell away to reveal two smaller service huts—auxiliary power units. They gleamed silver in the dazzling sunlight, their sheer newness distinguishing them from the rest of the complex. Troopers used them as cover, guarding the approach to building ten.

Building ten was the same dull white as the rest of the complex, a square equipment storage shed taller than the other buildings. A large garage door was visible on the left, no doubt where the farm equipment was wheeled in and out. A door for pedestrian traffic was on the near wall.

Movement caught Katja's eye. Just a swirl of dust in the street. The rough ground growled under her feet as she shuffled forward. The long greenhouses loomed in the background. Katja could see down the straight paths between them, half a kilometer to the open plains. To her right, those two small shacks stood curiously apart from the rest of the complex.

Second Platoon covered her, and she turned her eyes back to the target.

Building ten had probably once been gleaming white, but years of blowing dust had faded the plastic panels. The grooves in the door were caked with grit, but the handles were clear and smooth. Katja paused at arm's length, and signaled for her team to activate their quantum-flux viewers.

The building walls dissolved in the vaporous view of the subatomic, but little emerged in their place. Katja swept her gaze slowly through a hundred degrees. Beyond a single chair she could make out, just inside the doors, there was nothing to see but a vague, swirling mass.

She deactivated her viewer.

Glances passed between her troopers. She hand-signaled that she could see nothing. They each signaled back the same.

The gnawing pull of indecision tightened in her gut. What was it about this farm?

Chang caught her eye from the far end of the line.

Buttonhook. Alpha-Two. Alpha-Five. Question. He was asking, not telling. But he got the point across—they had to enter to find out what was inside.

She delivered her orders via hand signal. She and Sakiyama would lead. The tall, lean trooper shuffled past Cohen to join her at the door. It was his job to keep her alive today.

She tried the latch. Locked. She motioned for him to kick it in.

Sakiyama's big boot collided with the thin barrier and knocked it open with a crash, revealing darkness.

Katja was through, rifle up.

Sunlight flooded in behind her, and her own shadow played tricks with her vision. She leapt to one side to not be silhouetted. Sakiyama was inside a heartbeat later. Dust floated in the broad ray of light from the doorframe, but otherwise nothing moved. They were in a small room with three chairs on one side and lockers on the other. Katja tried her quantum-flux again. It revealed nothing.

She activated her comms, so that Lahko and Drop Command could hear.

"This is Alpha-One," she whispered. "There's some kind of quantum shielding in building ten. We are advancing visually."

She shuffled forward, rifle up to her eye line with barrel lowered for a clear view. She could feel the adrenaline coursing through her, the old excitement she had experienced during training scenarios. But this was even better—this was real. She had proven herself under fire, and her troopers would follow her anywhere. She felt powerful. In control. If only her father could have been watching.

She reached the doorway at the far end of the room and slipped through. In the dim light the walls extended away on both sides, and the ceiling rose out of view. Two meters ahead, a heavy black screen hung down to the floor and obscured all view. She stepped to the left. Sakiyama to the right. A flick of her thumb, and the tiny spotlight on her barrel lit up, directing a narrow but brilliant cone of light forward into the gloom.

The team shuffled in behind her.

Movement flickered in her light beam. She swung the beam side to side carefully. She saw a leg move. There was someone in front of her.

"Alpha-One—contact!"

Armor plates clicked behind her as her troopers reacted.

She raised her beam to shine at the man's face. He was short and sinewy, like so many Cerberans. His hand tried to block the light from his eyes.

"Please," he said softly, "put down your light. I have a lamp we can use."

He held it up for her to see.

"Go ahead," she said.

As he fumbled with it, she saw Sakiyama's beam from behind her settle on a second figure who was crouched against the far wall. Although this was an equipment bay, the thick curtain to their right had reduced the space to a dark corridor. Much too close for comfort.

"This is the Terran Astral Force," she said. "We're not here to harm you. We are here to arrest Centauri agents who have committed crimes against our nation."

"We are just farmers," the first man replied. "We want nothing to do with outside wars. Please don't hurt us."

The lamp flickered on, and the space was filled with soft light.

The man with the lamp looked familiar as he stared openly at Katja with intense eyes. Those eyes were a brilliant blue against his dark, weathered skin, with wisps of white hair haloing his head. But she was the one with the gun.

"Thapa," she said, feeling the rage growing within her as she advanced slowly. "I thought we were friends. You haven't been very nice lately."

Recognition ignited in his eyes.

Dropping the lamp, he screamed and lunged forward. Shadows danced as the lamp bounced when it hit the floor.

Katja pulled the trigger, but the wall above exploded as Thapa's powerful hand knocked her barrel away. His small body crashed into hers. She stumbled backward, gasping as she felt her feet slip out from under her. As she pumped the trigger, explosions all around showered them with twisted material. She smacked against the floor. Thapa's hysterical face filled her vision and she felt continuous thumps against her armor.

Then he was wrenched off her and thrown out of her vision. She saw Sakiyama move past her, shouting commands at the Cerberans.

She struggled to her feet. The abandoned lamp still cast illumination on the scene. Sakiyama pointed his rifle at the two men, both of whom were on their knees with their hands above their heads. Thapa glared with open hatred.

She could barely contain her own fury.

"Alpha-Two, take these prisoners into custody. We'll clear them from the building and continue the search."

"Yes, ma'am."

Chang moved into her vision, dwarfing the two men before him.

"Remember me?" he said to Thapa, before smacking him with an armored backhand.

Thapa's rage seemed undimmed by the blood that trickled from his mouth. Chang hauled him up and slammed him face-first into the wall. He expertly slipped on wrist restraints and threw him back down to the floor.

Katja keyed her comms.

"Sierra-Two, this is Alpha-One. Shots fired, no casualties. Two Cerberan prisoners. We are withdrawing from the building to hand off same."

"*Sierra-Two, roger,*" Lahko said.

The second man was bound, and Chang took ahold of them both. Cohen and Alayan led the withdrawal out through the small room and into the brilliant sunlight.

Katja spotted at least five pairs of troopers covering them, and Lahko approached with a sixth. She turned to Thapa. He looked nothing like the meek farmer she had questioned before. Now all she saw was the murderer from the news footage.

"Thapa, you picked the wrong side," she said. "And because of you a lot of people are going to die."

He met her gaze fearlessly. "Starting with you, whore."

Her fist smashed into his face.

"Listen up!" she shouted for all to hear. "This is the man—

the actual motherfucker—who assaulted and murdered the *Kristiansand* crew!" Lahko came up next to her, and took Thapa's ragged face in his gloved hand.

"This is the guy?"

She nodded.

"We'll take care of him."

He threw Thapa down. The Cerberan stumbled and fell awkwardly. Lahko kicked him in the stomach, almost absently, then nodded toward building ten.

"Must have been waiting for us," he said. "We're gonna bust this scene open." Then he issued orders for four of his troopers to target the garage door with grenades. On his word, four more troopers targeted the pair of new shacks.

Katja said nothing. Lahko's methods were a bit brutish, but she wasn't in command.

"*Sierra-Two, Drop Command. Air hostiles inbound from the south. Strike Cover intercepting.*"

Katja glanced at Lahko. Enemy aircraft inbound. He reflexively glanced skyward, but remained focused.

"Fire!" he commanded.

Simultaneous explosions rocked the east side of building ten and the twin shacks as Second Platoon grenades impacted against the thin materials.

Katja raised her rifle instinctively, trying to keep both dust clouds in her view as the troopers advanced.

Her left peripheral gave the first warning as things went to shit.

33

The first trooper to reach the smashed opening to building ten flew backward in the air, his insides exploding out of his torso. A heartbeat later a trooper near one of the shacks collapsed backward in pieces. Then all eight advancing troopers were blasted apart, and silver machines came bursting into the sunlight through the dust.

Katja was running before she even formed the thought to do so. Heavy slugs punched into her side. Her feet went airborne. Her vision spun as the red horizon tipped ninety degrees and the hard surface reached up to smack her head.

She slid along the ground.

Then she was motionless on her side, explosions and shouting all around her. The gravelly dirt was warm against her cheek. She took a quick breath, coughing on the dust. Her left ribs ached with each cough.

Not daring to lift her head, she strained to take in her limited field of vision. Troopers were shooting on the run. Some were falling. Others were exploding. She could just see the silver glint of an APR past where her own feet were sprawled. It was rolling forward slowly, twin cannons spraying the air over her head with heavy bullets. Shoulder-mounted rocket pods tracked independently and picked off scrambling troopers. Its shining armor was already crumpling under the counterassault of Second Platoon explosive rounds, but Katja could tell by the explosion patterns that the rifle fire was random, panicked. The weak spots weren't being targeted.

She lifted her rifle to aim, otherwise remaining still as the APR loomed closer. She gripped her grenade trigger. At this range, it was hard to miss.

Target the left rocket pod.

Fire. Fire.

Target the right rocket pod.

Fire. Fire.

Explosion in the left peripheral.

Left cannon bearing down.

Roll!

Slugs chewed up the ground she had just occupied. She reared up into a firing position and loosed two grenades at the cannon that was turning to target her. She angled right and engaged the second cannon with two more.

Twisted, blackened appendages jerked uselessly, but the APR continued to roll forward. As it picked up speed, Katja scrambled to her feet and ran for the nearest cover.

Chang and Sakiyama were hunkered down behind the crumbling corner of building seven. They motioned her in behind them.

"Good shooting!" Chang shouted over the roar of battle. "You got a way to get us out of here?"

"Back to the drop ship!" she shouted back.

He shook his head and pointed over her shoulder. She spun around and saw the billowing clouds of black smoke filling the central square. The flames underneath were fueled by the remains of the drop ship.

"First thing they took out," he said. "And we've lost comms with Drop Command."

"Down!" Sakiyama threw himself on both of them.

Katja grunted as she hit the ground again.

The walls above them exploded. Chunks of plastic fell heavily. Katja shielded her face with armored forearms and struggled to breathe in the choking air.

Sakiyama rolled off and opened fire on another APR that was advancing on them from building ten. Grenades smashed into the machine's forward armor, but did little real damage. She struggled to her feet and grabbed him by the shoulders, yanking him down to a crouch.

"Target the weapons systems!"

Each trooper only carried twenty grenades. Katja had used nearly half her stock on her first APR. Sakiyama had pretty much blown his load in a fireworks display.

Chang was pulling himself up, shaking off debris. Katja did a quick visual assessment. The APR had switched targets to attack some troopers on its flank. The one she'd disarmed was rolling forward, still capable of providing target information to its counterparts.

Around the corner at least two other APRs were advancing on unseen troopers on the far side of building seven. One of them had only the blackened remains of a rocket pod on one shoulder. Troopers were taking cover behind every building she could see, firing indiscriminately at the Centauri war machines.

Scott Lahko was visible with one of the groups. All around him, his platoon was getting scattered and pinned down.

She spoke into her helmet mike. "Sierra-Two, Alpha-One."

No response. She repeated the hail.

Chang tapped her. "I can hear you on the circuit."

"He must be on another freq."

She took in the situation again. Lahko's position was closer to her than the armed APR's, and the enemy seemed to be focusing on Terran groups at the south end of the compound. In small groups, the troopers didn't stand a chance.

"Follow me," she said. "Don't shoot at the APR!" Then she sprinted across the road, praying that by not shooting she wouldn't draw the attention of the enemy mechanicals. Her prayer was answered, and she reached the cover of building thirteen without exploding.

Three Second Platoon troopers stared at her as she crouched down beside them.

"Use grenades only," she ordered. "Take care with your shots, and only target the weapons systems. The body armor's too thick."

She left them to it and shuffled back to Lahko. The big man's eyes were hidden by his visor, but the grim line of his mouth was info enough.

"We've got no comms with Drop Command or Strike Cover."

She nodded. "I know, but we still have platoon comms. Get back on the circuit!"

"We need the big guns," he responded. "One volley from orbit would end this battle."

"Scott, we're on our own," she said. "We need to fall back and regroup."

He shook his head and made another fruitless attempt to raise Drop Command.

"Lahko, get your damn troopers back!"

He shoved her away. "I'm in fucking command!"

"And I'm here to tell you what you fucking *need to do*! Pull your troops back to the north end of the square. As a united force, we can pull together enough firepower."

He bit down a retort, his face going deep red.

"All units, Sierra-Two!" She heard him both live and in her helmet comm. "Withdraw to the north end of the compound." He studied his forearm display. "RV north of building eleven."

Katja checked her own readout. The rendezvous point was a hundred and fifty meters north of their current position, at the edge of the central cluster of buildings where the long greenhouses began.

Chang and Sakiyama joined Lahko's troops in lobbing grenades into the battle down the central avenue. Glancing around, she realized that she hadn't seen Alayan or Cohen since the battle began. She grabbed Chang.

"Status!" she shouted above the noise of battle.

"Two APRs visible," he reported, his voice clipped. "They've focused their attention on some troopers pinned down behind building fourteen—they're putting down suppressing fire on both sides of the building, but not advancing. Even when they shoot at us, they still keep one cannon on suppressing fire."

Katja looked at her readout again. She was at the north end of building thirteen. The trapped troopers would be able to make a clean escape up the east side of thirteen, if they could get a break in the fire.

But why weren't the APRs advancing?

It smelled like a trap.

In her helmet she could hear Lahko coordinating with all his squads. Roughly half the surviving platoon was pinned down behind fourteen, and the remainder was taking a pounding as they slowly retreated up the west side of the compound. Lahko ordered intensive fire down on the nearest APR, to try and open an escape route for the troopers trapped behind fourteen.

Katja still didn't like it. She pulled Sakiyama back, and punched Lahko's arm. He glared at her, but gave her his attention.

"We'll cut round the back of this building and cover the withdrawal of the troops from fourteen," she said, and Lahko nodded.

Katja motioned for Sakiyama to follow her. "How many grenades do you have left, Trooper?"

"Two."

She nodded. "You provide covering fire—I'll take out the heavies."

They reached the northeast corner of thirteen. She did a quick quantum-flux check through the corner. Clear. Shutting off the quantum-flux, she peeked quickly around and withdrew. Clear. She motioned them forward.

The east side of building thirteen seemed like another world. There was a thin shadow cast by the building in which they moved, easing the heat. The avenue between buildings was much narrower, and clear of choking dust. The buildings were all intact. And the sounds of battle were distant, leaving what seemed like silence.

She checked her intel. Building thirteen housed the school, the main kitchen and dining hall, and a common room. There were windows and doors along the wall at frequent intervals, making it an easy place for an ambush. Katja activated quantum-flux again and signaled to Sakiyama.

Me, quantum. There. You, visual. There. She would watch the inside of the building, and he would watch the street as they advanced.

The sounds of the heavy suppressing fire grew steadily louder, and soon they could see the tufts of dirt being torn up by the slugs. Helmet comms told them Lahko's diversionary fire was working, and that the northern APR was turning more of its attention to the grenade attacks raining down on it. She waited for a break in the radio traffic to jump in and inform the trapped troopers that she was coming.

She stopped short of the end of the building. Quantum-flux revealed several figures inside, quickly assembling a device with long tubes. The image wasn't clear. She snapped back to regular vision, gesturing to Sakiyama.

I see. Four. There. Take.

They hustled back, then loosed two rounds at the wall. It exploded inward. They charged forward, rifles firing even before they reached the hazy opening.

The inside of the building was choked with debris. There were vague movements through the smoke, and she fired repeatedly. Dozens of miniature explosions created a thunder that overwhelmed the cries of shock and pain.

One man stumbled to his knees in front of her. Quick shot to the chest. There were flashes and cracks of gunfire, and she felt tiny thuds against her torso. Three shots at the flashes. Two booms and the sickening squelch of human impact.

Then she was at the device with the tubes. She pulled off a Cerberan who was slumped over it, bleeding heavily. The device was silver and sickeningly familiar. It was the same missile tubes she'd seen aboard the merchant vessel *Astrid*. The missiles themselves were half-loaded into the tubes, and pointed through the window directly at the pinned-down troopers.

Her jaw clenched. She looked down at the bleeding Cerberan, gasping desperately and trying to raise his hand to stem the flow of blood coming from multiple wounds. But his gaze met hers defiantly.

She shot him in the head.

The missile launcher was activated. Ten more seconds to finish loading and all twenty troopers outside would have been splattered against the wall. That was why the APRs hadn't advanced. All they'd had to do was keep the troopers from escaping while their Cerberan allies lined up the killing shot.

With Sakiyama covering the room, she looked over the control system. It was absurdly easy to use. It had to be, she supposed, if it was intended for illiterate warlord minions. The system was already locked onto the trapped troopers. She peered through the window and saw the northern APR focusing its fire north toward Lahko, but still dedicating one cannon to suppressing fire.

Turning back, she struggled to lift the last of the missiles into their tubes, swung the device to point at the APR, assigned the new target, and pressed the FIRE ALL button.

She clutched at the side of her helmet and ducked down as the missiles launched through the window with a deafening roar and blinding light. There was an immediate detonation outside. Staggering on all fours for a moment, she grabbed her rifle and rose to a crouch to peek through the shattered window.

The APR was a smashed, smoking wreck.

She motioned for Sakiyama to follow her back through their original hole in the wall. She rounded the corner and waved frantically to the troopers.

"Building fourteen," she said over the comms. "You're clear—on me!" Without hesitation the two squads dashed across the open space between buildings. Katja led them back along the deserted avenue.

"Sierra-Two, Alpha-One, building fourteen clear. We are headed for the RV."

34

With a force of twenty or more at her back, Katja moved with confidence. Any movement from the buildings—real or perceived—drew fire from her troopers, and a trail of debris littered their passage on both sides. They skirted the open space of the central square and the smoldering remains of the drop ship.

Lahko and the rest of Second Platoon were already at the rendezvous, the lieutenant barking orders as his troopers kicked in the doors of building eleven—a set of three family residences—and set up for their defense. He assigned Katja's group to guard their flanks, and she gave quick orders to split her troopers into covering pairs.

There was a volley of fire behind her as Lahko's troopers fired on the advancing APRs, taking down one APR at a time. The machines were brutes, designed to inspire fear in their human opponents, but even they couldn't withstand a focused, coordinated attack by disciplined troopers. Without the fear, they just became huge, lumbering targets.

A second volley exploded forth just as Katja heard a scratchy voice on the Drop Command circuit.

"Papa-Two, Papa-Two, this is Drop Command. Over."

"This is Papa-Two," Katja replied immediately, using the general call sign for the entire platoon. "We are under heavy fire from Alpha-Papa-Romeos. Our drop ship is broken—request immediate fire support and pickup."

"This is Drop Command—roger. We are under attack and repositioning. No bombardment available. Strike support is engaged in neutralizing hostile aircraft. Two drop ships are en route your position. Fifth Platoon will cover your withdrawal. Over."

"This is Papa-Two, roger. We will hold position and await retrieval."

A third volley launched forth behind Katja, followed by a series of explosions. Then cheering.

She turned in surprise, and saw Lahko emerge from the blasted building, smiling triumphantly. "Got the bastards!"

She nodded. "Good work. Your flank is clear."

He clapped a hand on her shoulder.

"Good stuff," he said. "Thanks, Big K."

"No worries."

He patted her shoulder again. "I mean it. Thanks."

She looked up at him and smiled. "Welcome to the shit, Lieutenant."

He laughed awkwardly. She could sense his unease, even without seeing his eyes. But, to his credit, he didn't slip in his role as platoon leader.

"Second Platoon, listen up!" he said over the comms. "We've neutralized the immediate threat, but we are still in hostile territory. And we have a mission to complete. Drop ships are en route for pickup. Before then we will search building ten for evidence to take back. And we'll gather our dead."

He gave specific orders to each of his five squads. Alpha Team was tasked to search building ten. Katja was relieved to see all four of her troopers muster on her. They doubled it down the main avenue again, past the burning drop ship and five dead APRs. The buildings were smashed and battered, the air thick with smoke and dust.

At the Astral College Katja had studied several ground engagements from the Dog Watch, and this was exactly what Sirius in those days had looked like. Every world a war zone, every town a battlefield.

Looking at the destruction now, all she felt was anger. Anger at these stupid people for throwing their lives away in pointless wars. Anger at the Centauris for encouraging and arming them.

Anger that a lunatic like Thapa was allowed to thrive in this environment, and destroy any hope for peace. And perhaps most of all, anger that she hadn't recognized him for what he was the first time they'd met, and shot him dead then.

She couldn't wait to be off this fucked-up planet.

Comms indicated the approach of the new drop ships. She and her troopers were just wading into the wreckage of building ten when the ships touched down outside. The first one opened its doors and disgorged the troopers of Fifth Platoon, who immediately spread out in a textbook covering pattern. Sublieutenant Wei was close behind, no doubt eager for his first taste of action. The second ship was empty, except for a medical team who immediately began helping to load the casualties on board.

Katja turned to the innards of building ten, and her mission.

The building had been designed as a storage garage for large Cerberan farming equipment, but it quickly became apparent that it had been altered some time ago. Centauri maintenance equipment lined the high walls. An APR lay in its component parts next to an assembly station. The black curtain that had obscured all this from view still hung, and Katja quickly tested her quantum-flux against it. It was opaque, and a quick glance around the garage revealed that the entire building was somehow clouded with the same obscuring quality.

This wasn't an accidental weapons depot. Centauria had invested serious time and resources here.

"Alpha-One, Alpha-Two!"

Katja looked over at Chang, and noted with interest that he and Sakiyama were holding a man between them. He looked to be of European descent, dressed in simple, light gray coveralls.

She strode over. "Who's this?"

"We found him hiding in this floor compartment," Chang said, gesturing. "He hasn't said much, though."

Katja produced her DNA-testing device and rammed it against his neck. He winced. After a moment she examined the readout, and smiled.

"Alpha-Two, load this Centauri prisoner onto the drop ship."

"Yes, ma'am."

Katja snapped a few still shots of the converted garage. Alayan and Cohen reported moments later that there were no other hidden compartments.

"We got what we came for," she said. "Let's get out of here."

As she emerged into the bright sunlight again, Katja listened on her circuit to a report of the aerial battle to the south. More strike fighters had been deployed to join the fray, and Drop Command was itching for the troopers to get off the ground. She glanced upward, but couldn't see any flashes that revealed the orbital battle.

Lahko began gathering his platoon into the new drop ship. Katja ordered her team to board as well. She passed Sublieutenant Wei.

"Good to see you, Hu," she said. "First time in the dirt?"

He looked around, eager for a target to shoot, for a story to take home to his buddies from strike training.

"Yes, ma'am," he said. "Sorry we missed the action."

She bit down a retort. She would have felt the same when she was a subbie.

His head rose slightly, and she realized he was looking past her. "Is that one of ours?"

Katja turned to look. It took her a moment to realize that he was looking in the air, and she saw a dark shape approaching low over the greenhouses.

She sprang into action.

"Take cover!" she shouted. "Air attack!"

Flashes lit up the wings of the enemy craft as it bore down on the gathering platoons. Katja threw herself into the shelter of building ten as twin lines of slugs came slamming down into the compound. The turrets of the drop ships blazed to life in response.

Sublieutenant Wei stood frozen in place. Then, to her horror, he raised his rifle and started firing at the plane. A single slug punched through his body armor and knocked him flying backward. As the enemy shot past, his body hit the ground in a bloody heap.

Katja scanned the sky for a second attack. Seeing it was clear, she ran for the safety of her drop ship. It was fully loaded, and ready for liftoff. Fifth Platoon, however, were still spread out in a protective circle and fully exposed to another strafing run.

"Sierra-Two, Alpha-One—lift off. I'm going with Papa-Five."

Without even waiting for Lahko's response, she crouched down by Wei's body, tore off his helmet, tore off her own, and slammed his down on her head.

"All units, Sierra-Five," she said over Fifth Platoon's unique circuit. "Withdraw! Withdraw!"

She grabbed Wei by the shoulders and dragged him up the ramp. Troopers came running and helped her lift his body in.

Ignoring the startled expressions, she surveyed the rapidly filling aft compartment. She noticed one of the sergeants and grabbed his arm. "Wei's dead. I'm Lieutenant Emmes, taking command. Tell me when everyone's on board."

To his credit, the sergeant accepted her words with little more than a moment's pause. "Yes, ma'am."

She reached the cockpit and strapped in. Through the windows she saw Lahko's drop ship lift off.

Both platoon sergeants came forward and took their seats on either side of her. The one she'd spoken to reported, "Fifth Platoon aboard. All personnel, plus four supers."

As the drop ship pushed up into the sky, she looked over at the sergeant. "Four supernumeraries?"

He nodded. "Chang, Sakiyama, Alayan, Cohen. Are they with us?"

She smiled. "They're with me."

Her smile hardened to a grimace as the drop ship jinked right. Her stomach hit her throat and she bit down hard as the ship rolled left and dove. Through the windows she saw a not-too-distant explosion.

"We're under fire!" one of the pilots said.

Another explosion shook her seat. Shockwave only.

"Drop Command," she said over the comms. "This is Papa-Five, airborne. We are under fire."

"*Drop Command, roger.*" The voice at the other end of the radio was no longer calm. Katja went cold. The orbital battle must not have been going well.

One pilot was shouting instructions. Both struggled with

their controls. Through the windows, Katja could see a forest of explosions in the air all around them. Anti-aircraft flak. Primitive, but damned effective. Fill the sky with explosions and sooner or later your target flies into one of them.

"All units, Alpha-One," she said on the platoon freq. "We are withdrawing under heavy ground fire. *Normandy* is under attack. Stand by for a rough ride."

It was hard to tell if they were climbing. The drop ship was jinking left and right, and seemed to be diving under explosions a lot. Shockwaves rocked them every few seconds.

A deafening crack assaulted her ears as her seat slammed up into her body. She grunted and shut her eyes at the pain. Her head swam as she was thrown to the left.

She dimly heard one of the pilots screaming.

"Mayday! Mayday! Mayday! Papa-Five hit! We're going down! We're going down!"

She was jolted suddenly, and felt her mind clear. She looked back over her shoulder and saw a huge buckle in the port-side hull. The sergeant next to her was slumped back in his seat. Both pilots were fighting their controls. Through the window, she could see the familiar, hated red of the Cerberan surface getting closer and closer.

"All units," she shouted into the comms. "Stand by for emergency landing in hostile territory!"

All the troopers were by design facing aft in their seats—easier for rapid exit and safer for crash landings. She and her sergeants were facing forward to maintain command appraisal.

The ground was getting close. She reached down and activated the emergency switch on her seat. It swiveled to face aft and locked into place. The sergeant to starboard did the same.

Drop Command freq. "Drop Command, Papa-Five. We're going down! Request immediate retrieval!"

"Drop Command, roger."

Her back was turned to the pilots, but she could hear them shouting.

"Oh my God! Oh my God!"

"Climb, you bitch!"

She leaned back in her chair and grabbed the armrests.

Platoon freq. "All units! Brace for shock!"

The first hit was a glancing blow, and they were airborne again. A second later her seat slammed into her back so hard she saw stars. Her ears filled with a roar. An unseen force pulled her slowly but inexorably starboard. The deck shuddered.

She couldn't say exactly when the drop ship became still. But suddenly she realized that it was.

Katja forced herself to unbuckle and stand. Her legs wobbled but held. To her left, the sergeant was slowly rising. To her right, the forward-facing body hung lifelessly in its straps. She leaned on her seat and looked forward. Both pilots were slumped over their consoles under the cracked windows.

She turned to the surviving sergeant. He was the one to whom she had spoken earlier. "What's your name, Sergeant?"

"Rao, ma'am."

"Sergeant Rao, we're deep in hostile territory. Get the troops ready to defend our position. Check on the ship's turrets. Sergeant Chang can assist you."

"Yes, ma'am."

She leaned over the unmoving sergeant as Rao struggled to slide open the door to the main cabin. She vaguely heard him barking orders as she checked the casualty. It didn't take long to figure out that this sergeant was dead, probably from the flak impact. With a stony heart she examined the pilots as well. They had both died ensuring that their passengers would live. Katja quickly checked their tags and typed their names into her forearm display.

Like Alpha Team over Laika, they would not be forgotten.

The flight consoles had buckled from the impact. The entire drop ship was listing to port. Through the windows, she could see that they were in a field in a narrow valley. She tried the comms. There was no response from Drop Command.

She clambered through the tilted cockpit and into the main cabin. The rear door was already lowered, she saw, and troopers were busy gathering up all the emergency gear.

Chang approached her. "Ma'am, all four turrets are operational and manned. Two heavy fire teams are taking covered positions forward and aft of the ship. Two dead, including Sublieutenant Wei. Three walking wounded. No joy comms with Drop Command."

She jerked her thumb back toward the cockpit. "No comms with the ship systems either. The jamming must be in place again. Three dead up front. This ship can't fly."

No expression clouded his olive features. "Recommend you assess the terrain, ma'am."

She nodded. Together they descended the aft ramp and stepped onto Cerberan soil. Once again she breathed in the harsh, hot air with its odd, metallic tang.

The drop ship had crashed in a long river valley with flat farmland stretching several kilometers either side of the slow-moving waterway. Steep hills rose up in the distance, with terraced farms cutting long steps right to the top. At a glance, Katja guessed that at least a thousand people had seen them land.

An ugly trench ploughed back from the ship, curving slightly away to the right for hundreds of meters through fields of some kind of grain crop. Scraps of metal and twisted polymers littered the trench. A group of troopers were hunkering down in the ditch fifty meters away, taking advantage of the only cover available.

She walked around to the front of the ship, noting the manned turrets above her as she did, and briefly inspected the half-buried nose and the shattered port-side hull just aft of the cockpit. Not that it mattered—the drop ship was wreckage now.

Ahead in the distance, she saw the other group of troopers spreading out in a defensive line in the waist-high grain. With no cover to speak of, they were scattering to minimize the possibility of mass casualties. One trooper was jogging through the field toward her. Beyond, she could see some kind of settlement, about half a kilometer distant.

The approaching trooper revealed himself as Sergeant Rao. He was breathing heavily but seemed otherwise unaffected by his run in full armor.

"Defensive positions in place, ma'am," he reported. "But we're sitting ducks if there's an air attack."

She nodded, feeling very exposed.

"There's at least another five hours until dusk," she said.

"Anywhere we go right now will be seen by all these civilians. But we can't stay here."

"There's more cover in the hills," Chang offered.

Katja pursed her lips as she looked up and down the valley. She was loath to abandon the drop ship, with its technology and the dead inside. She also appreciated the four turrets, which represented the only really heavy firepower the platoon had available. But Rao was right.

They were sitting ducks.

"The turret cannons are easy to remove," she said, thinking out loud. "I've seen it done for maintenance. Chang, check to see if it's viable for us to carry the guns with us, and enough ammo to make them useful.

"Rao," she said, turning, "see if you can booby-trap the drop ship. First, blow up the flight consoles. Then put the dead in the cockpit and trap the door. Once we've taken everything we need out of the ship, trap every entrance to the main cabin."

The sergeants moved off without question.

Standing alone amidst the alien grain, partly shielded from the blinding light by the wreckage of her drop ship, Katja felt the familiar feeling of uncertainty well up in her gut. Two hours ago she had been safely aboard *Normandy*. Now she was commanding a platoon of strangers in the middle of a hostile nation. Was it really best to leave this position? Where would they go? How would the EF find them?

She forced down the uncertainty with a cold slam. There was no time for doubt. Tactically, they had to move or they'd wind up dead or captured. And she knew well what Cerberans did to their prisoners. A quick image of Jack Mallory's face was all the motivation she needed.

35

Thomas instinctively shielded his eyes as explosions blossomed at close range. The projection of space outside the ship was so realistic against *Normandy*'s bridge that he might as well have been looking at the actual battle itself.

Normandy's point defense cannons blazed to life again. Another pair of incoming missiles exploded.

Thomas forced his eyes down to his display, and to the battle he was supposed to be directing. At least twelve hostiles had popped up out of nowhere amidst the orbital traffic. The destroyer *Baghdad* had taken the brunt of the initial attack, and was still struggling to clear to deep space. The cruiser *King Alfred* had plunged into the battle at point blank range, scattering the Cerberan gunboats.

The lone battleship *Jutland* was still twenty thousand kilometers distant, and not in a position to engage. *Artemis* had scrambled her star fighters. The other two cruisers, *Admiral Nelson* and *Admiral Halsey*, were providing close support to the three invasion ships.

His display flashed with new, red symbols. The Centauri frigates had fired another volley from their positions over the Cerberan pole. At that distance none of the EF's weapons could reach them.

"*Halsey*, this is Echo-Victor," he said on the AVW circuit. "Break from close support and take hostiles one-zero to one-two!" It was a risk, stripping the main body of one of its two escorts. But the Centauri weapons were just too dangerous to ignore.

Acknowledging his signal, *Halsey* broke formation and accelerated to flank speed, firing missiles as soon as she was in range. The Centauri frigates turned and disappeared over the Cerberan horizon.

Predictably, several Cerberan gunboats made a charge for the opening in the EF's defensive wall. *Nelson* opened fire, but the little boats were hard to hit.

"Drop Command," he heard Chandler saying from his position nearby, "what's the ground situation?"

The ground battle was being directed from the separate command center known as Drop Command, located in a chamber abaft the bridge. Thomas heard the harried reply.

"Still no comms. Assess ground forces under fire. We are launching the backup platoon and a spare drop ship for retrieval."

"Roger," Chandler replied. "We're pulling back for high orbit."

On one speaker, Thomas could hear the repeated hails from Drop Command as they tried to connect with the troops on the ground. The raid had been progressing well until comms went silent. Moments later Cerberan aircraft had attacked the strike fighters in atmo and the orbital battle had exploded into existence.

On the large 3-D display that formed the centerpiece of the command station, Thomas noted the position of the EF's assets. Six individual stations like his wrapped around the base of the display. Commodore Chandler sat in the seventh seat, raised higher than the others to give him the overall perspective.

Normandy had put a hundred thousand kilometers between herself and Cerberus. She was likely out of range of any planetary weapons, but she was more vulnerable to stealth attack. Not that stealth was Thomas's concern. The EF had other specialists to deal with that threat. His job was to coordinate anti-vessel warfare. For now his life revolved around a pack of Cerberan gunboats and the three Centauri frigates which had turned this entire raid into a debacle.

The gunboats were a nuisance, but they were only dangerous if they came really close. *King Alfred* was still in low orbit trying to hunt them down one by one.

"*Alfred*, this is Echo-Victor. Break off your pursuit and take station as main body close support."

Thomas watched the 3-D display as the blue symbols of missiles sped away from *King Alfred* and impacted with the red hostile of a gunboat. The hostile symbol flashed for several seconds, then disappeared. The cruiser then rose swiftly to move deeper into space. Her weapons engaged the gunboats still trying to get past *Nelson*.

Another hail went out from Drop Command. Thomas's ears pricked as he heard a scratchy, familiar female voice respond.

"*This is Papa-Two. We are under heavy fire from Alpha-Papa-Romeos! Our drop ship is broken—request immediate fire support and pickup!*"

Katja? Where was the platoon leader, Scott Lahko? Thomas listened as Drop Command gave a quick sitrep and she responded.

"*This is Papa-Two, roger. We will hold position and await retrieval.*"

Flashes to the left caught his eye, and he watched as a gunboat raced past *Normandy* at visual range, guns blazing. Bigger tracers chased it as *Nelson* rolled in to attack. The gunboat took several hits and broke apart.

Admiral Halsey had almost disappeared over the horizon in pursuit of the Centauri frigates. Thomas didn't want to lose them, but he didn't want to stretch his forces, either.

"*Halsey*, this is Echo-Victor," he said. "Do you still hold hostiles one-zero to one-two?"

"*This is* Halsey, *negative. They've gone low and silent and are mixing in with orbital traffic. I am dropping to archons one-zero-zero to sweep.*" The cruiser was dropping nearly into the atmosphere to continue the hunt. Thomas knew a thing about going low into atmo during a battle.

"This is Echo-Victor. Negative. Break engage and return to main body close support." A long pause preceded the sullen acknowledgement. *Halsey* turned and began to climb.

The battleship *Jutland* was nearly in range, Thomas noted. With the EF's massed firepower they'd be able to close Cerberus again and recover the troopers. The drop ships would be vulnerable crossing a hundred thousand kilometers of open space. The troopers were already in the air, so he vectored a squadron of star fighters to guard the extraction corridor over the strike target.

"*This is Papa-Two,*" he heard, "*atmo free and climbing.*"

That sounded like Lahko. So at least Katja and her strike team were clear. He felt himself relax slightly. The last of the gunboats were running for cover and there was no sign of returning Centauri frigates.

"*Mayday! Mayday! Mayday! Papa-Five hit! We're going down! We're going down!*"

The panicked call got everyone's attention. Thomas quickly scanned his display. Had the gunboats attacked the second drop ship? Katja and the first drop ship were safely clear and under fighter escort, but the second drop ship had never even cleared atmo.

A new voice crackled over the radio from the doomed drop ship.

"*Drop Command, Papa-Five! We're going down! Request immediate retrieval!*"

Thomas's eyes snapped to the console. He knew that voice only too well. What was she doing on the wrong ship? He looked up at Chandler. The commodore was grim, though apparently unmoved by Katja's final call.

"Sir," he said, "the extraction corridor is clear. Recommend we move in for a full bombardment while we retrieve Fifth Platoon."

From across the console, the operations officer stabbed a finger at Thomas. "That's not your call, Lieutenant. Keep your eye on those gunboats and those frigates!"

Chandler didn't look at him, or acknowledge the exchange.

"*Fleet, Drop Command,*" a strong female voice said, "*request full cover for a retrieval of Papa-Five.*"

Chandler keyed his circuit. "Negative, Drop Command."

"*Fleet, Drop Command, we assess that the drop ship landed and that there may be survivors.*"

"Orbital defenses are too strong to risk another closure. Request denied."

Thomas squeezed his console and bit his lip. There were troopers on the ground! With a full force of fighting ships to provide cover, what threat could possibly be too much?

Over his shoulder he could still see the red disk of Cerberus, clear among the stars. A small cluster of blue symbols was visible along almost the same bearing—the lone surviving drop ship and its star fighter escort.

A Corps officer suddenly appeared at Thomas's side. He glanced up and recognized her as Commander Vici, commander of the Saracens and thus of both platoons that had dropped. Her sharp features were taut and her eyes burned past Thomas toward his boss.

"Commodore, Drop Command," she declared loudly.

Everyone around the command console looked up in surprise. Usually communications between the two command centers were over the circuit.

Chandler looked up from his discussion with the ASW controller. His expression was cold. "Yes, Drop Command?"

"Sir, Drop Command formally requests the EF to close Cerberus once again. We still have a platoon planetside."

"The drop ship was shot down in heavy fire," Chandler said. "I am not going to risk this entire force to try and recover some bodies."

"I say again, sir, we think they may have been able to land." She wasn't actually shouting, but her voice filled the entire bridge. "That means we have fifty troopers—possibly with wounded among them—stranded on Cerberus."

"We have no proof that anyone's alive."

"Then we need to get in for a look," she pressed. "Sir, all I ask—"

Chandler slammed his fist down on the armrest.

"The answer's *no*! I'm sorry, Commander! That's it!"

Thomas could see Vici's jaw clench tight as her entire face went red. She stared in impotent rage for a moment.

"Yes, sir."

She turned away. Thomas ignored the curse she muttered not quite under her breath. Chandler looked pointedly at the 3-D display for a moment, his lips a thin line.

"Controllers, report your status," he said.

"AAW condition white," the commander on Thomas's left

reported. "No hostiles inbound."

"ASW condition white," the lieutenant on Chandler's other side said. "No stealth contacts."

There was a pause, until Thomas realized that everyone was waiting for him. He glanced quickly at his display to confirm his status.

"AVW condition white," he said. "No hostile vessels within range."

Chandler took in the tactical situation for a moment longer. Then he addressed the operations officer seated at the display.

"Commander Erikson, secure from battle stations," he said. "Inform the EF."

"Yes, sir."

The message went out on the Command Net circuit. A few moments later *Normandy*'s internal loudspeakers stood the ship down from battle stations, and reverted to the wartime one-in-two rotation, where half the crew was on watch at any time.

Thomas relaxed in his seat, watching as the symbol that represented the returning drop ship merged with *Normandy*'s own, and disappeared. Out of three that had launched, one drop ship had made it out. More than a hundred personnel had left *Normandy*, and thirty were returning. Thomas could understand why Commander Vici wanted to go back.

The AAW controller beside him got out of his seat and stretched. He tapped Thomas on the shoulder.

"Good work, Lieutenant," he said. "Was that your first time controlling?"

"First time for real," he replied. Everyone now seemed to ignore his appointment to Lieutenant Commander, even though he wore the star above his two bars. He was technically still the commanding officer of a fast-attack craft, but his ship was permanently grounded and held together pretty much by gun tape. He figured it was courtesy to an old student that had stayed Chandler's hand in permanently reassigning him and thus removing the honorific. If the rest of the staff wanted to ignore it, who was he to argue?

Especially after a performance like that, kind words from the AAW controller aside. Perhaps a qualified AVW controller—and not a hastily reassigned FAC skipper—would have made better use of their assets in fending off the attack.

The current command staff was a real patchwork. The AAW controller, the commander who had just spoken to him, had been the XO of the battleship *Lepanto*, which had burned up over Laika still locked together with one of the supply ships. The ASW controller was from the destroyer *Kiev*—a grizzled old lieutenant who had probably long since given up on promotion and had been coasting to retirement. He knew his stuff, though.

The only one with actual EF command team experience was the operations officer, Commander Erikson. He'd been part of the admiral's staff and had been lucky enough to have been aboard *Jutland* assessing UNREP techniques when the battle over Laika had begun.

Chandler's new chief of intelligence—easily the most junior member of the team—seemed to have gained the commodore's complete trust and attention, however. Thomas was just pulling himself up out of his seat when he noticed Breeze enter the bridge. She crossed straight over to the commodore, her eyes alight with excitement. Thomas stood in place behind his chair and listened as she quickly briefed Chandler on the fact that the drop ship had returned with a Centauri prisoner.

"Sir," she said, "thank you so much for authorizing this mission. The sacrifices made by our troops to capture this spy will give us the information we need to turn the war around."

Chandler brightened considerably, his surly frown vanishing at her words. Thomas turned away, trying to shake off the bitterness. But watching Breeze, he felt like he was seeing her with new clarity. She had been so supportive after the orbital battle, he'd even wondered if what he'd first taken to be innocent flirting was actually a come-on.

But as he stood back and watched her interact with men in power, he saw the same behavior playing out, again and again. Sean Duncan thought that Breeze must be easy, but Thomas disagreed—she was way too smart for that. She was dangerous, and he was lucky things hadn't gone any further between them. He could barely stand to think about it, but he'd suggested to Breeze they meet in her cabin in *Rapier* to go over some data, intending fully to see if he could get her out of her coveralls. Katja's unexpected presence had saved him, one way or the other.

He shook his head and stepped away from the command console, staring out at the projection of the stars. He'd done enough lately that he wasn't proud of—no need to ruminate on things that he hadn't done. Better to focus on what he could do to redeem himself.

Being placed on the EF command staff had been an unexpected honor, but being the AVW controller was a role for which Thomas had no formal training, and he wasn't entirely convinced that he was the man for the job. Still, with *Rapier* grounded this was his opportunity to shine—a second chance to not screw things up.

He licked his lips, anticipating the taste of whiskey when his watch was over. He'd intended to talk to Katja after this mission, but now... a cold pit formed in his stomach.

He stepped back over to the command console and assured himself that the AVW picture was clear. He let Commander Erikson know that he was leaving, then made his way quickly to the aft end of the bridge and through into Drop Command.

Drop Command was much smaller than the bridge, with several large 3-D displays dominating the space. One showed the ground picture, another the atmo picture, and a third the orbital picture. Two rows of consoles would be manned during a full drop, but today only a quarter of the stations had dedicated bodies. And those bodies were still focused on their work, in stark contrast to the relaxed afterglow on the bridge.

He spotted Commander Vici immediately, speaking earnestly with Brigade Colonel Korolev. Thomas held back, not daring to interrupt two senior Corps officers. The conversation lasted another minute or so, and seemed to end to the satisfaction of both.

Korolev nodded politely to Thomas as he passed him en route to the bridge. "Mr. Kane."

"Sir." He was impressed that Korolev remembered his name.

Vici was momentarily unoccupied and Thomas grabbed the opportunity.

"Excuse me, ma'am. Do we have a confirmed list of survivors on the returned drop ship?"

She glared at him, more in surprise than anger, he thought.

"All of Second Platoon are out, although some of them are in pieces," she said. "I don't yet have the names of the casualties."

"What about *Rapier*'s strike team?" he pressed. "They were with Second Platoon."

Her anger was growing again, he could see. Her voice turned to ice. "Is there any particular reason the commodore is requesting such specific information? If not, then get out of my face."

Petty politics were really starting to piss him off. "I'm *Rapier*'s CO, ma'am. Are my people on board that damned drop ship?"

Vici's glare softened. Her eyes suddenly revealed a glimpse of respect, even sympathy.

"No," she said quietly. "I think they were in the ship that crash landed."

Thomas looked immediately to the boards, his heart sinking. "Do we know where?"

"Not exactly." She stepped forward to point at the ground display. "We lost tracking on them right about here. This region is a known stronghold for the Free Lhasan warlords—it's where one of their biggest armies is based."

He felt sick. "Oh my God…"

Vici glared at him again. "Wipe your tears away, skipper. We might have a plan."

"What?"

She nodded past him. He looked back toward the bridge door just as Korolev, Breeze, and Chandler entered Drop Command.

"Colonel Korolev tells me we have special assets on the ground that might be able to help," she said, but didn't offer any additional details.

Korolev glanced at Thomas and Vici, but he was clearly focused on Breeze.

"Last contact with the drop ship was here," he said, pointing at the display. "There are two assets with lift capability based out of New Ngari."

Breeze nodded. "They pose as independent merchants. Low key and enough capacity to get the troopers out."

"Make it happen," Korolev said without seeking permission from the commodore.

A curious look passed between Chandler and Korolev, then the commodore turned and left without ceremony. Korolev and Vici both moved away.

Thomas took one last look around Drop Command, then returned to the bridge. That whiskey was going to taste particularly good this evening.

36

Katja dove to the ground as another shell wailed down.
It struck behind her position with bone-jarring impact. Dirt and rock rained down on her battered armor. She was up again in a heartbeat, crouching behind the pair of boulders that were her only cover. Sakiyama was at her side, blindly firing over the rocks. Among the cracks in the hillside troopers picked themselves up and took their positions again.

But there was no movement where the mortar had hit. She didn't dare order anyone to leave cover to check on wounded—the snipers at the top of the hill had proven their deadly accuracy.

Once again she lifted a spare helmet just over the lip of the rock, ignoring the ache in her ribs. Her own helmet was linked to its camera, and that gave her a quick view of the battlefield. Shots cracked from above and below but none struck home this time. The camera was exposed for less than five seconds, but that was enough to paint the grim picture in the gray morning light.

APRs had advanced as far up the hill as they could before the ground became impassable for them. Cerberan soldiers were massing behind this mechanized line, trying to work up the courage to advance on her platoon. More APRs held the ridgeline behind her, unable to approach but blocking any escape. Enemy bodies littered the rocky slope from two previous attempts to overrun the Terran position.

At least three aircraft circled overhead.

It was dawn. They'd been trapped in this broken collection of boulders and fissures for twelve hours, taking casualties and bleeding ammunition in the hot, black air. Darkness had given her high-tech troopers the advantage. The dazzling light of the Dog Star would soon bring that to an end.

"Air attack! Look east!" The shout came over the platoon circuit.

Katja crouched lower, raising her eyes skyward. One of the aircraft had cut down and was in a shallow dive on their position. Dazzling points of light fired along its wings. Seconds later, high-velocity rounds struck the position, punching through solid rock and trooper armor. There were screams heard over the roar of the aircraft as it flashed overhead.

Before she could even speak, another strafing run riddled the position. Chunks of rock smacked against her armor. She covered her face with her arms. A quick glance up revealed a third aircraft lining up for an attack run.

"Tango-Two, this is Sierra-Five," she said into her comms. "Do we still have ammo for the cannon?"

"About a hundred rounds," Chang replied from thirty meters away.

"Take air hostile to the east."

"Roger."

The third aircraft steadied on course, coming closer, lining up its target. Katja heard the welcome *thud-thud-thud* of the last remaining turret cannon, being manually aimed and belt-fed. For a long moment the aircraft grew larger and larger. A pair of sparks danced off its underbelly.

It wobbled and veered off to the north trailing smoke.

Cheers went up from the troopers, but they were immediately drowned out by a chorus of wails as enemy mortars began to rain down again. Katja curled into a ball and endured the onslaught. She tried to recall how many clips of ammo she had left, and how many grenades.

Her medical kit had already been used up on other casualties, and her rations were long gone—the plan had been for a lightning raid, and so the troopers had packed light. They hadn't even taken the doctrinal combat cocktail of pre-invasion drugs.

As another barrage of mortars struck, Katja thought to herself that a healthy dose of "valor valium" would do a lot to keep her head clear.

Unfortunately, all she had was her wits.

"Tango-One, Tango-Two," she said, "this is Sierra-Five—stock check!"

"*Tango-One.*"

"*Tango-Two.*"

Her sergeants switched to sub-platoon freqs, designated to minimize chatter on the main channel. They spoke to their squad leaders, who in turn took stock of casualties, weapons, and ammo within their five-trooper squads. The entire reporting process took less than fifteen seconds.

Of fifty-seven troopers who had started the day, twenty-two were still in the fight. Fifteen more were alive, but no good for combat. There was one cannon left with about seventy rounds remaining. Each trooper had on average about three hundred rounds and five grenades. If a serious head-to-head fight began, Katja figured it would last about five minutes.

As it was, taking the occasional potshot from the rocks and slowly getting picked off by the Cerberans, they could be stuck here all day. Until every one of them was dead.

She tried to hail Drop Command. It was her new nervous habit.

No response.

She lifted the spare helmet again for a quick look. APRs above and below, with a hundred or two Cerberan warriors lining up for their next assault. Two aircraft still circling.

And one man moving up the slope, just past the line of APRs. He was armed, but his rifle was slung over his back. He held some sort of speaking device in his hand, and gestured.

All firing stopped.

Sakiyama looked at her questioningly. She tapped the helmet in her hand. He made his own connection and watched along with her.

The man on the slope spoke, his voice hugely amplified by the device in his hand.

"Criminals of Terra. You are surrounded and outnumbered. We, the people of Free Lhasa, are peace-loving and wish no more bloodshed. We will give you this chance to surrender. After that, you will die."

Sakiyama suddenly raised his head. "Fuck you, dog-man!"

From among the rocks, other troopers hurled similar responses.

Katja smiled grimly. She welcomed another Cerberan assault on their position. If she was going down, then a few hundred Cerberans were going with her.

The man on the slope continued. "Your courage is admirable, but there is something you do not know. Let me show you our other weapon."

Katja tensed. A new sound filled the air—like the mortars, but much deeper in pitch. It grew louder and louder, and ended abruptly with the roar of an explosion barely two hundred meters west. Columns of fire leapt into the air, throwing tons of hillside with them.

Katja fell to all fours on the shaking ground as the blast wave hit her, then watched in horror as the masses of rock and dirt crashed down across the landscape. Her troopers were barely out of the splash zone.

In fact, they were *precisely* out of it. This was accuracy she had only ever seen in highly regulated war games back home. A new fear twisted her insides.

"We have perfected the use of this weapon," the voice continued. "We will not hesitate to use it against you. You have one chance to surrender. The next volley has already been targeted on your position."

The voice was so calm and rational—so unlike the terrorist lunatics she'd come to expect. Perhaps she wouldn't be signing their death warrants by surrendering. She certainly was by staying put.

No one shouted out any more catcalls, she noticed. Sakiyama was staring at her. The rest of the platoon was waiting for her instructions. She sighed.

So much for her first wartime command. Her father was going to be very displeased with her.

"All units, this is Sierra-Five... This is Lieutenant Emmes. Gather the wounded. We all move down the hill together, rifles slung over our backs. Make no sudden movements. This is not a trick. We are surrendering." She paused, and then added, "I will not throw our lives away. Sergeant Rao, over."

"*This is Sergeant Rao, roger. Fifth Platoon, gather the wounded and prepare to disengage.*"

For a long moment, no one moved. She was afraid to stand up and expose herself to fire, and suddenly realized that everyone else felt the same. Another opportunity to lead by example.

She stood up straight, her eyes just barely clearing the top of the boulder. Sakiyama's eyes followed her. A line of APRs and two hundred Cerberans also watched her. After slinging her rifle over her back, she hauled herself up the rocks so that she was standing on the boulder, an easy target.

"Do you surrender?" the man with the amplified voice asked.

Her hands were shaking slightly, her gut tensed for the bullets she feared would rip through her at any moment. Her left side was burning from what she suspected were broken ribs, and painful shivers rippled up her body. But still she reached up, unhooked her helmet and lifted it off her head. The breeze was cool against her sweat-plastered hair.

"We surrender!" Her voice sounded frightened and girlish, even to her own ears.

Sakiyama stood up below her position and removed his helmet. Chang and his fire team did the same. Rao followed suit, and so did other troopers scattered around the rocks.

A huge cheer erupted from the Cerberans massed behind the impassive APRs. The machines seemed to recognize the moment in their own way by lifting the barrels of their guns to point them skyward.

It took several minutes to figure out how to carry the worst of the wounded, and many more for the troopers to actually make their way down the rocky slope. Katja was careful to give the bodies of the fallen Cerberans a wide berth, all the while watching for any sudden movements from the enemy. The human fighters milled about and talked among themselves, but did not make any threatening gestures.

The APRs stood immobile.

By the time Katja reached the APR line, Sirius had risen over the eastern horizon and the entire landscape was awash in the brilliant pink light of a Cerberan morning. The man with the voice stood with a small group of men slightly apart from the others, watching her intently.

He stepped forward to greet her. "I am Major Xu."

He was not much taller than Katja, and his dark, sinewy features made him otherwise unremarkable. Remembering her POW etiquette, Katja saluted him.

"Lieutenant Emmes," she said. "Service number Charlie-eight-two-three-three-zero-eight-eight-six."

He did not look impressed, but he did return her salute. "Your men will put down their weapons and helmets. They will remove all ammunition and tactical devices."

"Yes," she agreed. Then, "Some of my troopers require medical attention."

"When the medics have finished tending our own soldiers, they will consider looking at yours." Then he peered at her grimly. "I have already given you orders."

She slowly lifted her rifle off her shoulder and with great exaggeration placed it on the ground between them. As her troopers began to follow her lead, she unclipped her remaining spare ammo, unstrapped her forearm console, and placed it all in her helmet, which she set on the ground.

She heard the quiet rush of fusion engines overhead, and saw a Cerberan dhow descending to land on the clear ground behind the APR line. Hardly a military vessel, it bore across its ovoid surface scars from decades of surface-to-orbit travel. A cargo door hissed open and several more Cerberans emerged.

Major Xu watched her, his expression impassive. She wondered if it bothered him that his enemies had been commanded by a woman. At least he'd have the satisfaction of having bested her. All around him, Cerberan soldiers were talking—most likely about her. More than a few laughs erupted.

Angry shouting suddenly silenced all merriment. Katja stepped forward to look, being careful not to appear aggressive. She saw three Cerberan rifles pointed at Alayan and Chang.

"Major," she said, "let me sort this out."

He nodded.

She moved out into the line of clear ground between her troopers and the enemy soldiers. Agitation was spreading through the ranks on both sides, she could see, and she stepped it up to a jog.

"What's going on here?"

Rifles snapped over at her. They seemed to forget that she was still in full armor, and she stared them down with her best glare.

"Ma'am," Chang said, "these guys seemed to think that Trooper Alayan was here for their pleasure. She disagreed."

Alayan was still in a fighting stance, her large brown eyes burning with anger. Katja could see how her smooth, Bedouin features might catch the eye of the locals, especially now that she was a prisoner. The three soldiers with their rifles up looked furious, and one was sporting a fat, bloody lip. The rest just looked amused.

"Troopers," she said, "take two steps back."

They did so. Even the small amount of extra space seemed to ease the tension.

Rifles lowered.

She heard a crunching in the rocky surface, turned, and saw Major Xu walking up behind her.

"Major, I respectfully ask that you make certain your soldiers understand the correct treatment of prisoners," she said. "We are unarmed now, and at your mercy."

"Yes, you are," he replied. "I will ensure that you are not harmed so long as you are here, but once you leave, I have nothing to say about it." His English was surprisingly good for a native, but she wasn't sure she caught his entire meaning.

"Once we leave. Are we going somewhere?"

He pointed at the orbital dhow sitting on the ground beyond the soldiers. "You are being taken to Free Lhasa, to answer for Terra's crimes. I doubt very much you will have any assurances then."

Four Cerberans walked up the line behind Xu. Two of them were dressed in filthy coveralls and two were in white lab coats. One of them was well dressed under the lab coat—sensible, good quality shirt and trousers—and he was limping noticeably.

"Gather your soldiers into an orderly grouping," Major Xu said. "You will be handcuffed and loaded onto that ship."

Katja glanced at Chang. "Three ranks. Help the wounded."

He turned and gave quiet orders, and the troopers formed up in a grouping. She took the moment to study the four newcomers. Or tried to, except the one with the limp hobbled right up to her, his dark, twisted face only too familiar.

"Hello again, whore," Thapa said.

37

Thapa's hand lashed out, smacking Katja so hard she staggered backward.

"Finally you show your face," he said. "I see now why you are so stupid—you are too young."

Katja couldn't hide her shock.

Thapa turned to Major Xu.

"Major, your victory here today is a victory for Free Lhasa. At last we have captured the criminals who have twice struck from the sky to murder and pillage my home." He pointed a finger in Katja's face. "This is the woman—the actual villain—who beat and killed my family."

Xu looked sharply at her. "This is the actual soldier?"

"I know her too well. She is the one who gave me this limp."

One of the Cerberans with the filthy coveralls stepped in front of her. "Let her be saved for the public. Keep your honorable reputation, Major."

Rough hands grabbed her arms and twisted them back behind her. The sharp click accompanied the tight grip of manacles. She was forced to start walking just as the force of the blow began to clear from her head.

Thapa took pace beside her as she and the rest of the platoon were marched toward the waiting dhow.

"Your arrogance is your undoing, whore," he said. "You should never have come back. Do you think we are a simple people? Do you think you can frighten us with your bombs from above? We are Free Lhasa, and we will never bend the knee again."

They reached the ramp and slowly climbed up. The interior of the dhow was poorly lit and all the bulkheads in the main cargo area were blackened and sooty. The troopers were made to sit in a circle, facing inward at the wounded who were laid straight on the filthy deck.

Katja saw three soldiers come on board with them, weapons trained casually at her troopers. Thapa and his lab-coated companion remained at the cargo door opening. Thapa turned and began speaking to the Cerberan troops outside. He used the local dialect, and his words were lost on her, but she could guess their meaning. This new megalomania was quite a change from the sullen, frightened farmer she'd first met.

The other two Cerberans in the dhow—Katja speculated that they were the pilots—left the cargo hold and disappeared into the unseen forward compartment. Moments later the soft hum of the engines trembled through the decks.

She heard cheering from the Cerberan soldiers outside, and the sound made her jaw clench. Suddenly she regretted her decision to surrender. It may have saved the lives of her troopers, but the gall at having lost to these savages was almost too much.

Thapa and his companion stepped back from the opening as the cargo door began to close. One of the pilots reemerged from the forward compartment. He had donned a long, thick coat over his coveralls and was carrying several more on one arm.

The pilot handed the coats over to the three soldiers and to Thapa and his companion, explaining quite loudly in English that things were going to get cold as they gained altitude. He had the look of a middle-aged man by Terran standards, which on Cerberus probably meant he was younger than Katja. He had a simple, humble manner about him, and seemed quite in awe of the soldiers.

He treated Thapa like a VIP.

But when he looked over at Katja she saw, just for a second, a calculating glint in his eye. The way he assessed the cargo space with three quick glances reminded Katja of the way Commander Vici sized up tactical situations during exercises back home.

Thapa knelt down beside where she sat cross-legged, arms still bound behind her. "Are you ready to be humiliated, whore?"

She said nothing, but could feel her cheeks burning.

"Your soldiers will be dragged through the streets," he continued, "but I'm going to make sure there's a special fate reserved for you. The Whore of Terra, I think." His callused fingers slid roughly through her matted hair. "As repulsive as I find you personally, I'm sure our brave soldiers will find you delicious."

Movement from the far side of the circle caught her eye. Chang was struggling to his feet.

"Hey! Little dark guy. Remember me?"

She gave him a sharp look, willing him to sit down again. He ignored her and grinned at Thapa. It was the first time she'd ever seen such an expression on his face. It was disturbing.

"I'd say pick on someone your own size," Chang said, "but she's already bigger than you. So if you want to be the big man, why don't you try me?"

Thapa didn't move. "Oh, I remember you, monkey. You'll get your share soon enough."

Chang scoffed. "But not from you, obviously. You're only good for threatening helpless women." He looked around at the other Cerberans. "I'm the commander of these troopers, and your boss won't even deal with me. He's too busy flirting with my assistant."

The blank faces on the soldiers told Katja that they didn't speak English. Chang seemed to realize the same thing. He caught the eye of the pilot.

"Hey, flyboy. You speak English?"

The pilot, who up until now had been watching the proceedings with great interest, suddenly twitched. "Me?"

"Yeah, you," Chang said. "Tell these soldiers how your boss, Thapa, doesn't even have the courage to address me. He spends all his time flirting with that little girl."

The pilot nodded, and spoke in the local dialect. Without understanding a word, Katja guessed that he hadn't translated what Chang had said. An entire conversation played out between the soldiers, the pilot, and Thapa that included glances toward her and Alayan. There was a growing gleam in the soldiers' eyes that she knew well enough from years of watching drunken troopers trying to score in nightclubs and at parties. A combination of fear, rage, and revulsion shivered up from her gut.

This wasn't going to be nice.

Hands grabbed her shoulders and threw her forward into the center of the circle. Her face smacked against the filthy deck, the impact ringing in her ears. Stars flashed before her eyes as she was hauled up onto her knees.

Her vision cleared to reveal one soldier, his rifle now slung over his shoulder, stepping up in front of her. Beyond, a second soldier had his rifle pointed at Chang's head, and the third had targeted one of the other Five Platoon troopers. She saw the Cerberan pilot moving in her peripheral, no doubt trying to get a good view of what was about to happen.

Her troopers shifted anxiously in their seated positions. Then she heard Thapa's voice behind her.

"And so it begins, whore. Pleasure these soldiers, or your troopers will die."

The soldier in front of her began to unbutton his trousers. The stench this close to him was almost overwhelming. Every inch of her body burned with rage.

"Fuck you."

"Yes, yes, in good time." Thapa's mockery was crushing. "But it would take too long to get your armor off."

The soldier exposed himself before her face. She averted her eyes in disgust, and noticed that the other soldiers were watching in anticipation.

The pilot, however, was watching the soldiers.

"Do it," Thapa said, "or your troopers die."

She looked at the pilot. He was fiddling with his fingers in anticipation, his eyes still darting between her and the soldiers. He stared at her for a second. And his fiddling fingers made a series of short, sharp gestures.

Three targets. I take. You lead.

She looked down, hiding her shock. No time for thought. Instinct. Breathing deeply, she raised her eyes to the wretch standing over her.

She bowed her head as if to start...

...and then head-butted her target with all her strength.

There was a second of commotion, then three shots rang out in rapid succession. She rolled back and up onto her feet. All three Cerberan soldiers were falling to the deck. The pilot had a small pistol out and had it trained on someone behind her. He shouted something in the local dialect. She turned swiftly, covering her blind spots, and saw both Thapa and the other lab-coat raising their hands in shock.

From the forward compartment, the second pilot burst in with weapon drawn. He assessed for a moment, then motioned Thapa and the other lab-coat to drop to their knees in one corner of the cargo bay.

Katja turned to look back at the first pilot. He had already retrieved keys from one of the dead soldiers and was un-cuffing Chang.

The big sergeant nodded to him. "Hello, Ali."

"Good to see you, Suleiman."

The pilot, Ali, then approached Katja. "I'm so sorry it came to that, Lieutenant," he said as he removed her manacles. "I had to find a way to get them distracted, and in that quick conversation this was the idea these filthy bastards came up with."

She winced as she brought her arms forward and flexed them. The three Cerberan soldiers were dead by a single shot each. Whoever Ali was, he was no merchant pilot.

He seemed to read her thoughts.

"Warrant Ali al-Jamil, Astral Intelligence." He held out a hand.

She shook it. "Lieutenant Katja Emmes, Levantine Regiment. How did you know we were here?"

He laughed. "Everybody in Free Lhasa knows you're here. Your little battle has raised quite the cultural fury. But we also had orders. Lieutenant Brisebois sends her regards."

That was unexpected.

There was probably something appropriate for her to say, but words escaped her. Instead, she nodded and looked away to see that Chang and another trooper were busy freeing the rest of the platoon.

Soon the three dead soldiers were being manhandled out of the way. A shiver went up through her body and she felt her lip tremble. She pressed her mouth shut and looked over to where Thapa and his companion were kneeling on the deck with their hands on their heads.

The rage returned. "What about them?"

Al-Jamil shrugged. "Thapa's known to us, but I'd hardly call him a key intelligence target. He's been the local commissar for years, serving his warlord, but beyond ratting out dissidents and housing soldiers he hasn't been much of a player. The first time he attracted our attention was when the Centauris set up shop on his farm."

"With all these speeches, he seems to think he's pretty important."

"Yeah, he's always been a bully and a windbag. That strike against his farm a few weeks ago really flared things up though. When you get back to your ship, you might want to tell whoever beat up and shot those locals during the raid to go easy next time."

Katja felt her stomach tighten. "Why? What difference did that make?"

"Thapa sort of snapped after that, and took his case to the warlord council. They used those attacks as an excuse to kidnap our people from that Hawk. Notice the ritual retribution? Two killed, two beaten to a pulp."

Katja thought of Jack's fresh young face smashed and disfigured. She felt sick.

"Although it was the rescue that really turned things nasty," al-Jamil added.

"How so?"

"It was considered an open act of aggression against Cerberus. They declared war on us that day, and Centauria apparently decided to honor their treaty with Cerberus."

She didn't follow. "How can Centauria have a treaty with a bunch of warlords?"

He shrugged. "It seems to make sense to them."

Several troopers stood guard over the two prisoners, and the second pilot returned forward.

"We're breaking off our route to Free Lhasa," al-Jamil said, "and making a run for deep space. Hopefully an escort from your fleet will meet us before the Cerberans figure out that we're gone."

"So we're taking them with us to *Normandy*?" Katja tried to stay angry as she stared at Thapa, but her churning stomach was sapping her will.

"I guess so. Dipu and I certainly can't go back." He scratched his stubbly chin. "It's been a while since I've worn a uniform."

"And you know Sergeant Chang?"

He nodded, but his expression went neutral. "We've worked together."

They stood in silence for a moment.

"Lieutenant, like I said, Thapa and that other guy from his farm aren't really of any intelligence value. Once we get to your ship they'll be prisoners of war." He gave her a cold, almost disinterested stare. "But if they don't survive the trip..."

He handed her his pistol.

"Your call."

He left her and disappeared into the forward compartment.

She stood in the center of the filthy, blackened cargo bay with the pistol in her hand. All around her, the wounded troopers who had been carried off the hillside lay in various states of consciousness. Three dead enemy soldiers lay piled against the aft bulkhead.

Below her lay hundreds of dead Cerberans both on that hillside and in the ruins of Free Lhasa. High above her, orbiting the distant moon of Laika, was a new, orbital graveyard for thousands of Terrans and Centauris. Countless more had no doubt died in other star systems as this war spread.

Did it all really come down to her and Thapa?

She looked over at the man, on his knees but unbroken. Even against the might of Terra he stood proud, just as his nation would as this war ground on. As a people they were strong, as an enemy they were dangerous.

She looked at the weapon in her hand. Small, with impact-only rounds. But effective.

What would her father think of her? All her life he had preached the nobility of the warrior profession, had raised his children to appreciate the supremacy of their culture and the importance of protecting not only their own world, but the worlds of the colonies.

Protecting them from whom? Even after centuries of space exploration, humanity had found no other intelligent life in the galaxy. The colonization of the eight new star systems had been peaceful and cooperative. It was only after the Silent Century, when Terra had reconnected with the colonies, that problems had started. So from whom was Terra protecting the colonies? The colonists?

Katja stepped closer to the prisoners, seeing them in a new light. Perhaps they weren't rebels. Perhaps they just wanted the freedom to live their lives.

She shook her head. She knew exactly what her father would think. The role of the warrior was not to question, but to obey. She had always hated him for that. It was one of the reasons she'd joined the Astral Force instead of the Army—the Astral Force still had an officer class. In the Army everyone started as a stormtrooper and worked their way up, always through loyalty and obedience. She could never have done it.

She needed to be able to think for herself.

And standing in the cargo bay of the dhow, surrounded by her troopers and facing the prisoners, Katja Emmes thought for herself.

Maybe this war was Terra's fault. And more than that, maybe it was *her* fault. But like it or not, she was in a war. And harboring doubts or developing sympathy would serve neither her nor those under her command.

She recalled the footage of *Kristiansand*'s crewmember being dragged around the square in Free Lhasa. She thought hard about the brutal beatings and murder of the hostages. She remembered Jack Mallory's broken face and hands and the souring of his youthful spirit.

These bastards had intended to rape and humiliate her.

The rage burned up within her again, fueling her. She was a soldier at war. This was her reality now.

The troopers stepped aside as she approached the prisoners.

Thapa glared up at her. "We will never surrender, whore!"

She pointed the weapon at the other prisoner and pulled

the trigger. The pistol jerked slightly as the bullet released and punched through the target's forehead.

Thapa's eyes went wide in shock, but he didn't back down. "One day…"

She pointed the weapon at his groin, but a moment of uncertainty struck her. He had planned to have her raped to death, she reminded herself.

The rage enveloped her, gave her strength.

She pulled the trigger.

His gargled scream echoed off the bulkheads. She let the target live in agony for several more seconds, then shut him up with a shot to the head.

She looked around at her troopers. "We are at war. Anyone who isn't with us is against us."

The rage faded to a warm, soothing anger. She left the troopers to deal with the bodies and went forward to confirm their safe passage back to *Normandy*.

38

Jack hadn't actually done the math, but he was pretty sure he was spending more time in his cockpit than he was in his rack.

All those preachy regulations about how pilots were required to have eight hours of uninterrupted sleep between flights. Those had been tossed out the airlock now that it was wartime, and his pain meds had been augmented with more of those crazy trooper-drugs. These kinds of amphetamines would be gold-standard on the black market.

He scanned the visual, his flight controls and hunt controls. He was deep into his patrol, and he'd lost all sense of time. *Kristiansand* was on long-range ASW picket, and his Hawk was perched out at the limits of its range, trying to extend the Expeditionary Force's anti-stealth sensors as far as possible.

The hunt controls began to process the readings from the last line of barbells he'd sown. Tied in with the two previous groups, some bearing lines from *Kristiansand*, and the data passed on from an earlier patrol, Jack was beginning to build a real picture. At least one Centauri stealth ship had been trailing the EF for days, but it hadn't been able to get close enough to get in a shot at the heavies.

Two of the six new barbells were indicating some kind of gravimetric irregularity. Way out in deep space—halfway between Sirius and the jump gate, and clear of the busy traffic of the ecliptic—the spacetime picture was far less cluttered and even the tiniest disturbances were detectable. He studied the hunt controls further, and input bearing lines from the barbells of interest.

Two more red lines appeared in his 3-D display. They joined five other bearing lines already in place. Doctrine stipulated that at least eight passive bearing lines match before he could prosecute a contact. He had seven, all pointing more or less at the same region of space.

He rubbed his hands slowly across his face and tried to think in four dimensions. How far into the Bulk was this stealth ship hiding? How was it going to try and sneak past the picket?

All he could come up with was that he'd forgotten to shave this morning.

Doctrine demanded eight bearing lines. But doctrine also said he was owed eight hours of uninterrupted sleep. He input the command to name his near-crossfix of bearings as a datum.

"Longboat, Viking-Two," he said. "New datum one-six, request permission to investigate."

There was a pause, then Lieutenant Makatiani's voice.

"Viking-Two, Longboat—affirmative."

Jack turned his Hawk to point right at his crossfix—now upgraded to a datum—and pushed the throttles forward, thankful that *Kristiansand* shared his loose interpretation of doctrine. If the ASW team was feeling anything like Jack, they were anxious to score a kill.

This was only his first war, but Jack was pretty sure things weren't going well. In this morning's pre-mission brief he'd learned that the ships guarding the jump gate back to Terra had been surprised by a Centauri attack through the gate itself, and had been destroyed.

EF 15 was completely cut off and being harried at every step. One of their priceless stealth ships had been hunted down and destroyed, and *King Alfred* had taken serious damage fighting off an orbital attack. Every day, attacks were getting through and causing trouble.

Kristiansand herself was showing scars from her engagement with a lone Centauri frigate. The two ships had exchanged missile volleys at long range before the enemy finally retreated. The indecisiveness of the outcome had only added to the frustration among the crew.

His high-speed run lasted seven minutes and took him to within a thousand kilometers of the datum. If his analysis was right, the stealth ship should be close enough for him to spit at. Getting close to a stealth ship was generally considered suicide, but Jack figured he was pretty safe in his Hawk. His ship was so small it was almost impossible to detect, and no stealth captain would want to waste a gravi-torpedo or give away his position. No, the enemy would prefer to sneak past in order to reach the invasion ships and the carrier.

Well, he thought as he slowed up and waited for his hunt controls to clear, *that isn't going to happen today.*

"Longboat, Viking-Two," he said. "Deploying big dipper."

"Longboat, roger."

With practiced ease he deployed his dipper into the Bulk, and set his initial search depth at twelve peets, below the weakbrane. Within seconds he was studying the gravimetric picture.

Against the background curvature of Sirius and its white dwarf companion, the EF capital ships stood out like beacons in the darkness as their artificial gravity dug holes in spacetime like a cluster of planetoids. Jack shook his head and sighed in frustration.

From his briefing he knew that the EF main body was over ten million kilometers away—no spaceship should be detectable at that range. Were they trying to draw the attention of every enemy stealth ship in the system? Or was keeping their AG activated some clever ruse to lure in the Centauris?

Cynicism wouldn't help him find stealth ships, he reminded himself. Ignoring the EF's spacetime curvature, he looked for other disturbances.

Jack noticed the distinct bending of space to starboard, just as the warning light began to flash. He held the reading for a moment, then it faded. He frowned.

Gravimetric curvature wasn't supposed to fade away.

Weakbrane! In a flash of insight he saw the picture from the enemy point of view. The stealth ship suspected it was being prosecuted, and was moving in the Bulk, coming up to put the weakbrane and its distorting qualities between itself and Jack's sensors.

Sure enough, as the sensor passed through the weakbrane, the curvature to starboard returned.

"Longboat, Viking-Two," he reported. "Fishing true, two-seven mark one-six. Request active!" He had the bastard by bearing, but he needed a range before he could fire.

"This is Longboat—affirmative. Go active and take when ready."

With the big dipper steady at five peets, Jack released an active graviton pulse. In a microsecond burst, a wave of gravitons projected forth from his big dipper, in effect making the sensor appear as a massive object in the Bulk. If there were no other nearby objects, the gravitons would disperse without incident. But if their path was bent by a nearby mass... all Jack needed was the time differential to get a range to target.

His hunt controls and 3-D display flashed to light. Gravitons were bending heavily to starboard at ninety kilometers. New symbology automatically designated the disturbance as a hostile stealth ship, number one.

He hauled to starboard and released the safeties on his weapons.

"This is Viking-Two. Hook shadow zero-one. Taking with torpedo!"

Jack toggled the firing key. There was a bang against the hull as the weapon rocketed clear. He saw the fire of its propulsion system kick in. Then it shrank to nothingness as it phased into the fourth dimension.

"Torpedo in the Bulk!"

On his hunt display he saw the knuckle in spacetime deepen as the stealth ship increased speed. It was so close that the bearing began to change visibly, even as he watched. The torpedo was firing graviton waves every microsecond to update its target's position, making so much spacetime noise that even the EF capital ships faded on his screen. But its data was automatically relayed back to the Hawk, and Jack watched as the stealth ship retreated at full speed, descending into the Bulk as it did.

Huge troughs in spacetime clouded the chase as the stealth

ship dropped gravimetric decoys, known colloquially as "bowling balls," to distract the torpedo. Jack rapidly designated the real target in his display, sending updates to the weapon. But it was all too fast. He couldn't tell one trough from another.

Hopefully the torpedo could.

Sixty seconds went by without a detonation.

"Dammit!" He slammed his fist down on the controls. He swung his eyes through the visual, flight controls, hunt controls. The brane his Hawk sat in looked quiet. The Bulk was a gravimetric mountain range.

The stealth ship was gone.

"Viking-Two, Longboat—assess shadow zero-one below the weakbrane."

Then an updated bearing line from *Kristiansand* showed the knuckle of the stealth ship deep in the Bulk. He stabbed at his controls to send the big dipper in pursuit. At fourteen peets he paused the sensor and conducted an immediate active graviton pulse.

There she was. Nearly one thousand kilometers away and thirteen peets in.

Stick and throttle moved together as he started another attack run. Torpedo Two locked onto the target. He fired. Another weapon flashed forward into space and into the fourth dimension.

The torpedo started pulsing as soon as it dropped below the weakbrane, but only every ten microseconds. This far into the Bulk, gravity was much stronger, and throwing gravitons around like confetti was extremely dangerous. The stealth ship seemed to grow larger as it accelerated away again, but the torpedo was just too fast. A pair of bowling balls rolled into the Bulk to cloud the picture, but Jack easily kept tracking on the real target and guided his weapon past the decoys.

He prepared his third torpedo for a shallow firing solution in case the stealth ship tried to escape through the weakbrane again. The Hawk was chasing at full speed, and closed half the distance to the target before the torpedo struck. The hunt controls gave evidence of the impact, the gravimetric strike tearing a hole so massive that it showed as the deepest purple.

In visual, Jack saw the stars ripple before him.

Then he gasped as some unseen force yanked him forward. For a second it felt like the g-forces in a hard turn, and he instinctively switched to heavy-gee breathing. His vision went red at the edges and he grabbed to hang onto his seat.

The pressure eased, and Jack did a quick check of the visual, the flight controls, and hunt controls. The star field had returned to normal. There were no contacts on the brane. The spacetime disturbance that had once been a Centauri stealth ship was flattening out. He activated a routine sensor sweep, checking for matter on the brane just in case the stealth ship had released message buoys or escape pods. Nothing.

"Longboat, Viking-Two—shadow zero-one destroyed."

He was sure he could hear cheering in the background when Makatiani responded. "*Viking-Two, Longboat, roger. Bravo-zulu.*"

He sat back in his seat and wiped the sweat from his eyes. Ahh, the coveted bravo-zulu. A traditional phrase from days of flag communication between sailing ships—perhaps the highest form of congratulations a line officer was capable of uttering. Jack had seen the other subbies blush with pleasure upon receiving one. And, he had to admit, it felt pretty good.

His eyes came to rest on the hunt controls again. The curvature of spacetime was still bent from the torpedo detonation. Doctrine stated that it was safe to fire gravi-torpedoes all the way to sixteen peets before the singularity became permanent, but for a few moments that last blast had looked pretty close to becoming a black hole.

He began retrieving the big dipper and wondered idly what was supposed to happen next. In an exercise, the successful prosecution of the contact was followed by a debrief, a landing, and a shower. But as this was his first actual kill…

Things suddenly seemed kind of anticlimactic.

He checked the results of the routine matter sweep, wondering if Centauri secrets had been ejected from the stealth ship at the last second, to sneak their way back to the brane and await retrieval. The sweep revealed no obvious objects in space, but what it did reveal froze Jack in his seat.

A thin, perfectly straight line of slowly diffusing particles passed within two thousand kilometers of the Hawk and extended away in both directions, stretching to infinity. It was the old exhaust trail of a ship.

Jack pulled out the data crystal Katja Emmes had given him, and transferred the data to the Hawk's computer. He'd been studying her findings in his off time, and his current mission placed him more or less in the same part of space that should have been traversed by the mystery ship—the one that had delivered Centauri weapons to *Astrid*.

He overlaid Katja's extrapolation of the mystery ship's trajectory on his own 3-D display. The two lines formed nearly an exact match.

A signal from his console indicated that the big dipper had been retrieved. He glanced at his hunt controls and saw that the scope was clear. Without hesitation he turned the Hawk to follow the trail as it led down toward the ecliptic.

"Longboat, Viking-Two. I am patrolling my sector down a bearing of two-six mark one-niner."

With no other ASW activity, he figured he was free to choose whatever direction he wanted to patrol, so long as he remained within his search sector. And now that he'd dispatched the bad guy, he had an even bigger mystery to solve.

39

Jack's fuel lights flashed red as he approached the dark shape of *Kristiansand*.

Like all Terran warships, *Kristiansand* was a dim, charcoal color. Her navigation lights were extinguished and no interior lighting was visible. She was running as silent and as invisible as possible, and if not for her ultra-tight homing beacon Jack would never have found her in the abyss. From a distance her compact form was defined more by the stars she eclipsed than by any distinguishing features Jack could see.

On final approach, however, he spotted the dim red lights of the hangar door, four fifths of the way back on the starboard side. He took station one kilometer off *Kristiansand*'s starboard quarter, matching velocities at this safe distance and locking the vectors into his computer.

Following the trail of exhaust particles had taken him right to the edge of his sector, and nearly out of range for a safe return. It was standard for his patrol time to overlap with the next Hawk in the rotation to ensure that the EF was never without proper ASW coverage, but he hadn't even started back for *Kristiansand* until the Hawk from *Cape Town* had launched. What was normally a fifteen-minute handover had become forty-five minutes.

In fact, Jack had technically been relieved of ASW responsibility for nearly half an hour before he finally saw his mother ship emerge from the darkness. No doubt he'd get a lecture for unnecessarily straining EF assets, but he figured that today of all days—what with him having destroyed a stealth ship and all—he might be shown leniency.

He pushed his little ship forward with thrusters and watched the red outline of the open hangar airlock grow larger. He wasn't aimed directly at it, but just to the side. He trimmed slightly to starboard to ensure a safe separation as he passed *Kristiansand*'s stern, then fired reverse thrusters to kill his relative forward momentum. He eased to a stop directly abeam of the open hangar door, then slowly rotated his craft so that he was facing into the airlock. One more thrust and he floated through into the waiting maw. Magnetic arrestors gently gripped the Hawk and pulled it down to the deck.

As the outer airlock door closed and the space pressurized, he took the time to start shutting down his non-essential systems. He did a quick upload of his new findings to his personal account in *Kristiansand*, then backed up the data on the crystal. As he did so, the inner airlock doors opened and the Hawk was towed into the hangar. He continued to shut down systems and finally unstrapped from his seat.

The aft cargo door began to open, activated by the ground crew outside. He pushed off from his seat and floated back into the main cargo area, expecting to be greeted by his crew chief.

Instead, he was greeted by the smiling face of the XO, Lieutenant Duncan. Behind him was what looked like the entire ground crew. As soon as Jack came into view, the crew started applauding.

He felt a stupid grin spread across his face.

The XO steadied himself against the doorframe and extended his hand. "Nicely done, Jack."

"Thanks, sir. Feels pretty good to wax a bad guy."

"Hey, Sublieutenant Mallory, check this out!" His crew chief had positioned himself forward against the Hawk's hull, just below the cockpit windows. Jack pushed himself out through the cargo door and looked over to see the chief stenciling a hand-sized silhouette of a stealth ship onto the hull.

"That's just our first!" the chief said, amidst fresh applause.

Jack joined in the clapping for a moment, then waved to the group. With only one Hawk left—the other having been destroyed in Free Lhasa—there was plenty of room to spread out, and they were floating almost all the way up to the deckhead.

"Thanks, everybody," he said. "We're an awesome team."

The XO leaned in. "The captain was wondering if you'd dine with her tonight."

New surprise washed over Jack. He didn't think he'd said more than two dozen words to Commander Avernell in his four months on board, and most of those had been "Yes, ma'am." And now she wanted to have dinner with him? He wondered what he'd talk to her about for an hour or more.

Then he remembered the data crystal in his pocket.

"I'd be happy to, sir."

Lieutenant Makatiani was just climbing into his rack when Jack found him, and even with Jack's new credit as a stealth-hunter, he had to convince *Kristiansand*'s anti-stealth warfare director to stay up and listen to his theory.

It took more than half an hour to present all the evidence he had, but by the time he'd finished Makatiani had long forgotten about sleep. The lieutenant had already done several tours in the Sirian system, and was well versed in the local spacetime landscape. He also had the experience to know where to look to find more evidence, and the final piece he was able to add to the puzzle left them both speechless.

He barely had time to race back to Club Sub, shower, and put on fresh coveralls before it was time to present himself at the commanding officer's cabin.

The door slid open at his knock, and he struggled to float through with his hand computer and portable 3-D display projector. The dining table was set for two, just inside the door, and there was a small sitting area with a couple of doors on the forward bulkhead. A thick black sheet had been fastened on the far bulkhead, covering the broad window he knew to be there.

"Good evening, ma'am."

Commander Avernell let loose the hand computer she'd been reading. It floated at an angle above the table. She looked tired, like everyone, and he wondered if her round face hadn't thinned a bit.

She took him in curiously with her large eyes.

"Good evening, Mr. Mallory," she said, peering at the equipment he carried. "I hope you realize that this is purely a social visit."

He fumbled to clamp the disk-like projector to the dining table. "Yes, ma'am. I, uhh, thought you might like to see what my hobby has been lately."

Boy, that came out smooth. He forced himself to smile into the captain's intent gaze.

Her lips curled in what might have been amusement.

"Wonderful," she replied. "Would you like to sit here, or would you prefer the dining table?"

Since he had already clamped the projector, he thought it best not to move it again.

"The table would be good, if that's okay."

Avernell pushed herself forward and floated across the cabin, stopping her movement gracefully by grabbing the back of one of the dining chairs. She hooked herself into the seat and did her best attempt at leaning her elbows on the table. Her face wore the same, carefully neutral expression it always had.

He couldn't hold her gaze, so he looked down at his computer as he hooked himself into the seat facing her and quickly called up his brief.

"I'm impressed that you still have time for a hobby," she said. "Especially one that requires a 3-D display."

As if on cue, the projector blossomed to life. A spherical image one meter in diameter lit up the air between them, revealing the Sirian star system, complete with planets.

As a reference point he had also dropped in the Terran jump gate, right at the top of the display. Other symbols were ready to project, but he had thought very carefully about how to present them.

"Ma'am, when I was with the XO in *Normandy* their top priority was to find out how the Centauri ships were sneaking through the jump gate. I know that lots of people have been putting together theories, but I've been gathering some hard evidence to support my own."

She didn't look too impressed. Jack felt butterflies in his gut.

"I'm sure this won't be new to you," he said apologetically, "but I really want to show you what I've found."

Her expression didn't change, but she nodded. "Go ahead, Mr. Mallory."

Her words gave him a little courage.

"Okay, let me set this up. A few weeks ago, we covered *Rapier* when she boarded that cargo ship *Astrid*. That was here."

On his command, a marker lit up on the 3-D display above the ecliptic. "*Rapier*'s boarding officer got a copy of *Astrid*'s logs, which record the ship's transit from this point, where she rendezvoused with another ship that gave her the weapons cargo."

A line traced back to a second point, much higher above the ecliptic and far from any space lanes.

"Based on *Astrid*'s logs, the other ship approached on a bearing which would backtrack its course along this trajectory." Lieutenant Emmes's extrapolation stretched down across the display. It crossed the ecliptic between planetary orbits, and extended to a point almost as far below Sirius as the jump gate was above.

"Today, on my patrol, I detected an exhaust trail. Based on its diffusion, it's about five weeks old, which would tie in with the mystery ship on a low-energy run to its rendezvous with *Astrid*. I detected the trail here." A point on the long trajectory line lit up.

"With Lieutenant Makatiani's help, I searched through the EF's database and discovered three similar detections from other patrols over the past six weeks."

Three more points lit up, each hitting the extrapolated trajectory. The oldest instance was from six weeks earlier, and was actually south of the ecliptic.

"There's nothing down that path for light years. Or so I thought." He was feeling excited now, spurred on by the fact that the captain hadn't told him to shut up. She was still listening, wearing that same neutral expression.

"Lieutenant Makatiani told me about some unexplained spacetime irregularities that were charted by *Cape Town* when our deployment first started—two months ago, right down around here." His last pre-programmed marker lit up at the southern end of the trajectory path.

"Since they were far away from the Expeditionary Force, any investigation was considered a low priority. But I took *Cape Town*'s readings and compared them to the spacetime signature of the jump gate back to Terra." 3-D graphs appeared in the empty space at the bottom of the display. "We ran an ASW analysis on them.

"Ma'am, they're virtually identical."

He stopped, and watched her reaction. Her eyes rested for a long time on the pair of graphs, then flicked over to his final marker. Finally he couldn't stand the silence.

"Ma'am, I know it sounds crazy, but I think the Centauris have actually built their own jump gate, and have been using it to sneak weapons and even ships into the system."

Then Commander Avernell picked up the handset hard-mounted to the table next to her seat and tapped in a number.

"XO, Captain," she said. "Tell comms to prepare for a data-heavy burst transmission to *Normandy* in about twenty minutes. And come to my cabin." She replaced the handset and looked at him through the 3-D display.

"Mr. Mallory, just before you arrived this evening. I was reading a report in the file concerning a prisoner who was captured on Cerberus. He was a Centauri agent arming the warlords, and we picked him up a couple of days ago. Under interrogation he confessed that he'd arrived through a Centauri-designed jump gate. The problem was, he had no understanding of astro-navigation. Even deconstructing his brain didn't give us any clues as to where this jump gate is. He just didn't know."

The door chimed and opened as the XO floated in.

"But you seem to have added that last piece, Mr. Mallory," she said. "What I want you to do now is go through that presentation again exactly the same way." She tapped a command in her tabletop console. "It'll educate the XO, and we'll be recording for the commodore and his staff."

Jack quickly backtracked his presentation to the start, gathering his thoughts.

"Oh, and by the way…" the captain said. He looked up at her. She smiled. "Nice job on waxing that stealth ship."

Jack grinned. He hoped that the recording for the commodore

didn't include a visual on him. No matter how solid a presentation he had, he figured no one would take it seriously from a pug-faced kid like him. Then he shrugged. Their loss.

40

reeze read the message again, stunned that so few words could carry with them so much meaning.

To: the commanding officer of the surviving Terran forces in Sirius

From: Admiral Yukiko Matsumoto, Commander, 3rd Squadron, Centauri Republican Defense Force

I control Sirian space and have the support of the free citizens of Cerberus, Laika, and the outlying settlements.

Centauria controls the jump gates in all star systems and is massing the assets needed to attack Earth.

If the Terran forces in all star systems surrender peacefully, the invasion of Earth will not occur.

Surrender.

Admiral Matsumoto sends.

Given the current state of affairs, the Centauris were in a good position to make demands. Breeze had personally delivered the message to Chandler, seen with her own eyes his reaction. She'd always known that he was arrogant and ambitious, but underneath that she had always assumed him to have the sense of self-preservation all leaders should possess.

Apparently not.

Breeze did not want to die in space. Whether Chandler's cause was just or not didn't matter in the slightest. Breeze did not want to die in space. Thus, message in hand, she arrived at the cabin of the one person she thought might be able to change his mind.

She knocked, and the door opened a few moments later. The cabin was dark, lit only by a lamp over the desk, and Thomas sat slumped back in his armchair. A glass sat on the table next to him. He looked up with vague interest.

"Evening, Breeze," he said. "What brings you by?"

Not knowing quite how to respond, she just walked in and handed him the printed message. He glanced at it, then sat up straighter and actually *read* it. She looked at the glass next to him.

He lowered the message and stared off into space. "Holy shit."

"It was transmitted about thirty minutes ago," she said. "I just came from the commodore."

Thomas pulled himself up and reached for a bottle that was hidden in the shadows. He tilted it to her with an inquiring glance. Whiskey wasn't her drink, but she found herself nodding. He pulled up another glass and poured a healthy portion.

Then he refilled his own.

"So let me guess," he said, collapsing back into his seat and sipping. "Chandler wants to attack the jump gate."

A ray of hope cracked through the doom in her soul. Her instincts about Thomas were right.

"Yes, in about twelve hours. He wants us to move quickly, before they can consolidate their position."

Thomas snorted. "Everything the Centauris have done has been perfectly planned and executed. They wouldn't even transmit this message unless they were ready for us." He gestured vaguely at the bulkheads. "They probably already have a stealth ship sitting right next to us, with a firing solution already plotted out."

Breeze hadn't thought of that.

She could feel nausea rising. "Thomas, you know I'd never be disloyal to my superior—"

"Oh, yeah..." he replied. "I know that."

She acknowledged his sarcasm with a placating gesture. "Thomas, listen, this is suicide! I think you're right. The Centauris have to expect us to retaliate, so they'll be waiting in an ambush. If we carry out this plan, we will all die."

His eyes narrowed. "Lieutenant Brisebois, you're not talking mutiny are you?"

"Oh, God, no," she said. "Nothing like that! But we have to change his mind."

He smiled behind his glass. "You're new at this," he said. "Once Chandler's made a decision, he doesn't change his mind. Ever. Especially now that he's in command. So you might as well just sit and have a drink with me, Breeze, because it looks like we're all going to die."

But she didn't sit. The nausea mixed with rising terror. And under it all, by far the worst, was a feeling of helplessness to which she was unaccustomed. She crouched in front of him, putting her drink down and placing both hands on his knees.

She wasn't above begging.

"Thomas, please. I don't want to die. Not like this."

He stared at her from his slouch, eyes moving lazily from her face to her hands and back.

"What can we possibly do?" he asked.

"You know Chandler better than anyone, and you have his ear. He always listens when you speak up. You need to convince him that there's a better way."

His face darkened and he looked away. It wasn't the reaction she was anticipating.

"Why don't *you* convince him," he said. "You're the favorite."

She didn't know what to say. Of all the emotions she might have expected from Thomas Kane, jealousy wasn't one of them. She groped for words. To buy time she slipped her hands up his legs just a few centimeters, and squeezed.

"Thomas, I am *not* his favorite." She smiled at him, suddenly knowing the angle she needed to take. "Despite my best efforts.

It has frustrated me no end trying to figure out how to get him to listen to me instead of you... or at least *before* you. I've been watching the interplay among the command staff, and even though you're the junior controller, Chandler always puts the most weight on your opinion."

He gave her a long look.

Her mind raced as she formed her thoughts.

"That's why I came to you now. He'll never let another captain change his mind, because that would show weakness. But he doesn't see you as a threat, or a rival. He sees you as himself."

Oh, brilliant, Breeze.

"He wants you to succeed, because he sees in you all the talent and ambition that he had at your age. You're his protégé. To change his mind on your recommendation wouldn't be a failure to him—it would be a confirmation that he's trained you well."

Thomas was staring at her, but the expression in his eyes went much deeper. She allowed herself a moment of hope. And triumph.

She leaned back slightly, bringing her hands to his knees again.

"Thomas, I envy you. And in the normal world I'd be trying to unseat you." She took a deep breath and stared into his eyes. "But right now I need you. And so does the entire Expeditionary Force."

He nodded. With some effort he leaned forward, bringing his face closer to hers. "I think I might have a good alternative. When is he issuing the orders?"

"He said he was going to assess our current strength, and he wanted some input from Intelligence—wants to know if the Sirian worlds really are allying with Centauria. I told him I'd need at least three hours. So he gave me two. At midnight he's briefing the command staff, and then issuing orders to the entire EF."

He glanced over at the clock. Then back at her with a look she had desperately hoped not to see.

"So we have two hours." His breath was heavy with the booze.

Behind her neutral face she grimaced. What was it with men? Wasn't the admiration of your mentor motivation enough?

"Not much time," she said, and she leaned back slightly, still holding his eyes.

His hands slid up her arms.

So much for "mission accomplished." She prided herself on never having to make good on her innuendo—it was amazing how far flirting could get you—and usually she'd have the option to walk away and leave him approachable at a future date.

But not today. There wasn't time.

She let her hands slip up his legs again.

"Thomas, you naughty man."

He pulled her closer. She came willingly, with just a hint of resistance to heighten the arousal. Behind her sultry eyes, however, she was doing a quick, cold calculation.

What was she giving up? Not much. Some mystique, really.

What was she gaining? Hot, meaningless sex with one of the better-looking men in the ship. The delicious opportunity to "accidentally" let slip to Katja the fact that Thomas was a stallion in bed, regardless of the reality.

And something she could use in the future, when he was married to Chandler's goddaughter.

All in all, not a bad deal.

41

Thomas's head was still foggy as he sat down at the command console. He hadn't drunk that much, but Breeze and her hot body had left him exhausted.

The memory of her was already being overshadowed by the now-familiar self-loathing, and he focused instead on how best to propose his alternative to Chandler's suicide plan. He called up the notes that he had been frantically compiling, grateful for the lucky find that his old friend Sean and *Kristiansand* had uncovered. He knew that he only had one chance at this.

Once Chandler announced the orders, there would be no turning back.

The other members of the senior staff were taking their seats. Korolev and Vici stood grimly behind the seated Fleet officers. Chandler arrived last, as always, and sat down in his chair without ceremony. As was his habit, he intended to discuss his plans with this small group of advisors before moving forward.

"By now you've all read this message from the Centauris," he said. "We don't have a lot of time, but I want to hear your thoughts."

Thomas knew it was a sham. Chandler had already made up his mind. But it was little gestures like this that so endeared the commodore to his subordinates. The operations officer, Commander Erikson, was the first to speak up.

"The key question is," he said, "are the Centauris telling the truth?"

Glances passed around the conference table—tired faces half-lit from below by the personal screens embedded in the tabletop. All around them, the starry backdrop projected on *Normandy*'s bridge gave silent reminder of the absolute isolation they endured.

"There still hasn't been any word from Terra," Breeze said, "and right now I don't trust anything the Sirian news channels say."

"Trust them or don't," Vici responded. "They're pretty unanimous in condemning us and cheering for Centauria. Part of the Centauri message is true, at least. How much, I can't say."

"I don't care about the Sirians," Chandler said. "We don't have the strength to retake control—no offence to the Corps—and frankly, our priorities have shifted. Holding Sirius is meaningless if we don't have access to our home star system."

"What are you suggesting, Commodore?" Korolev asked.

Chandler looked around the table, daring anyone to argue with what he was about to say. Thomas had seen that expression many times before during the Dog Watch.

"Whether this message is true or not, the fact that the Centauris control the jump gate says enough," Chandler said. "Terra is in serious trouble, and we need to open the road back home. We have a tough fight ahead of us, and need to act now—before even more hostiles arrive." He turned to Erikson. "How long for us to reach the jump gate at maximum cruising speed?"

"Ten hours, sir."

"They'll know we're coming, but there won't be time for them to get reinforcements to the gate. We'll smash our way through, and jump back to Terra."

"Sir," the ASW controller said, "at that speed we'll be vulnerable to stealth attack."

"We're vulnerable no matter what. Six hours before we reach the gate, I want the entire EF at battle stations with every Hawk on patrol and every star fighter ready for launch." He looked around the room. "We have one chance at this, so we don't hold anything in reserve. I want the strike fighters launched, as well—they don't have great weapons, but they'll create three hundred more targets to keep the enemy busy."

"That's three hundred dead pilots," Vici said, "guaranteed. And us with no air support."

From his expression, it was clear that Chandler was more than tired of her criticisms.

"You don't need air support in a space battle," he said. "You don't need troopers, either, Commander... so shut up!"

Vici fumed, but held her tongue. Breeze, sitting next to Chandler, leaned forward. She was trying to hide it, but her fear was beginning to show through. Thomas looked around the table. No one looked eager.

Except Chandler.

"Every one of us swore an oath to protect Terra," Chandler said, his voice rising. "That means a lot more than just leaving home for a few months, or working long hours until we're exhausted. It means that we're willing to die." His glare passed over every member of the senior staff. "Understand this—I will take issue with *anyone* who I have to remind of that again."

Thomas had expected this. Recent events had revealed to him a certain predictability in his mentor. Chandler didn't just pay lip service to the ethos of the Astral Force, like so many people did—he genuinely believed it. It had been that certainty that had enabled the young XO to inspire a ship to rise to the occasion during the Dog Watch. It had no doubt been that certainty of belief that had driven Eric Chandler to work so hard, and to rise so fast in the ranks.

But now, Thomas knew, that certainty of belief was clouding the judgment of a senior officer responsible for the lives of thousands of men and women. Perhaps it was just because he knew Chandler so well, but it was no surprise to Thomas that Chandler would choose a suicidal charge. Perhaps, before this war started, he would have chosen the same.

But now no one—not even Colonel Korolev—could overrule the commodore. Their only hope, Thomas realized, was for Chandler to change his own mind. With a little bit of help.

He rolled the dice.

"With all respect, sir," Thomas said, "there may be another way."

The glare focused on him, and Thomas felt like a young subbie again. He searched for his voice.

"Yes, Lieutenant?" the commodore said.

All eyes were on him. He chose his words carefully.

"Sir, it's true that our primary objective now is to defend Terra, and to do that we have to get back. A frontal assault on the enemy position at the jump gate would seriously impede our ability to fight. But there's another route we can take—through the secret Centauri jump gate."

To Thomas's surprise, Chandler had actually listened. Now his expression turned to the disappointment a teacher might reserve for a bright student who has said something profoundly stupid.

"Lieutenant," he said, "that jump gate leads right to Centauria. How is that a better plan?"

"Because they're not expecting it. Sir, the enemy holds the high ground in Sirius. They're waiting for us at the jump gate, and are expecting us to attack. Statistically speaking, we might win the fight, but then we'd be jumping back to Terra in a seriously weakened state, and no good against what might be waiting for us there." He paused for effect. "Based on the tactical ingenuity we've seen so far, frankly I expect the Centauris to whip our asses before we even reach the Terran jump gate."

Chandler looked ready to speak. Thomas knew he would never get another chance, and he pressed on.

"However, the enemy has no idea that we've discovered their secret gate. The number of ships they must have dedicated to the battle over the Terran gates has probably spread them thin, which means their secret gate will be lightly guarded, if at all. And their home star system is probably pretty empty—because most of their ships will be at the front."

No one stopped him, so he kept talking.

"Sir, this is what I recommend," he said. "Douse the artificial gravity on all ships, and go silent. The Centauris will see this, and prepare for a sneak attack on the Terran gate. They'll focus their search for us at that end of the system. Meanwhile, we fade away in the other direction and slip through their secret gate. We get through Centauri space, punch through their defenses at the Terran gate in Centauria—where we'll have the advantage because they'll never expect us to be there—and then jump through to join the real battle for Terra.

"It's the long way round, but they'll never see us coming and we'll join the main battle with substantially greater strength."

Chandler's expression was unreadable. "And what if we're discovered transiting Centauria, Lieutenant? That's a long way to go, through the heart of enemy territory, without being seen."

Thomas had anticipated the question.

"Then our presence will create a huge distraction for Centauria, as they scramble to figure out how the hell a Terran expeditionary force got into the heart of their home system. They'll have to pull back forces from the front. That might give Fleet the chance to seize the initiative and regain control of the jump gates."

He looked around the table, trying to read the faces watching him in the dim light. No one spoke.

"Either way," he concluded, "we'll be of much greater help to Terra, hitting Centauria from behind, than if we walk into their trap and try and fight our way out of Sirius. Respectfully, sir."

All eyes shifted from Thomas to Chandler. The commodore sat back, his gaze focusing out on some distant point. He remained still for a long moment. Then a wry smile curled his lips as he looked at Thomas.

"For a moment there, Mr. Kane, I lost faith in you. But you're as devious as I'd ever hoped. But you didn't think your plan through to its logical conclusion. We'll sneak away and jump to Centauria, as you suggest. But they'll be guarding their side of the Terran jump gate in Centauria, too.

"There's a good chance we'll be detected, so I say let's go right into the lion's den." He sat forward and addressed the assembled staff. "Get the ship captains on the line. We're not sneaking through Centauria—we're invading Centauria."

Thomas tried to speak, but no words came out. All around him, jaws fell open, and glances were exchanged.

Breeze was white.

"Commodore," Korolev said slowly, "I'm afraid I'm having a bit of trouble keeping up with your thinking. If the EF is outclassed here in Sirius, why would we fare any better in the heart of Centauri space?"

Chandler had a gleam in his eye. One which Thomas knew well.

"I'm not saying we'll fare any better. But by taking the fight to Centauria we can make a difference in this war. Kane's right—smashing ourselves against their ships here in Sirius won't help Terra. But if we can hit our enemy where it hurts the most, we can steal the initiative and turn the tide."

Korolev nodded slowly. "And we all die glorious deaths for Terra."

There was no sarcasm in the colonel's tone, but Thomas sensed a subtle lack of conviction.

Chandler appeared to take the words at face value. He nodded curtly, and turned to Erikson. "How long to reach the Centauri gate at maximum stealth speed?"

"With AG disabled, we can make better time," the operations officer said, sounding anything but convinced. "So… forty hours."

"At which point they'll still be waiting for our attack at the Terran gate. They'll spend days trying to locate us in the Sirian system." Chandler smiled. "Spread out the force to maximum dispersion. Stealth is the only thing that matters now."

Thomas listened as Chandler discussed various aspects of stealth warfare with the ASW controller. He caught a wide-eyed glance from Breeze, and an ambiguous look from Colonel Korolev. He dropped his eyes, and tried to shake off the cobwebs in his head.

Breeze had been right—he did know Chandler best. And knowing Chandler, he should have realized that the commodore had one driving motivation, above all others: one thing he sought with single-minded focus.

Glory.

To die in Sirius would have sufficed, since the cause was noble. But to die striking at the heart of the enemy, to save Terra from afar, a lone commander with his rag-tag fleet making the ultimate sacrifice…

Thomas had unwittingly dangled the ultimate prize in front of his mentor, and in doing so, he had condemned them all.

42

The remnants of the EF moved south through the huge Sirian star system, spread out to avoid any unnecessary curvature of spacetime caused by their combined masses.

The five destroyers fanned out in an anti-stealth detection net millions of kilometers across, slowly clearing the path southward and across the Sirian ecliptic. The four stealth ships formed a second line of defense over a smaller area. The three invasion ships and three supply ships formed the main body of the force, with the sole surviving battleship serving as point defense.

The three cruisers and the remaining carrier served as rearguard against brane-based attacks, safe in the knowledge that no stealth ship could catch up to the force without giving its position away.

As they approached the coordinates of the gate, the EF moved into a much tighter formation, lining up in single column so the ships would pass through the gate in rapid succession. *Normandy* was far back in the column, behind all the fighting ships that would pave the way for her and her high-value sisters.

Kristiansand's Hawk managed to pinpoint the exact location of the jump gate, and a detailed ASW sweep revealed it to be unguarded on this side. The Hawk offered to jump through alone, to clear the other side, but direct orders from Commodore Chandler stopped such recklessness. While a Hawk was certainly small enough to avoid detection, the passage of a ship through the gate would stand out like a beacon to anyone in the vicinity.

No, Chandler had decided that the first Terran incursion into Centauri space would be a knockout punch.

The last two days had felt like the longest in Thomas's life. He served his hours on watch as AVW controller, then tried to sleep the rest of the time.

Zero-g in an invasion ship took some getting used to, and many crew members suffered from space sickness during the first twenty-four hours. Thomas even contemplated sleeping in *Rapier*'s broken hulk in the hangar—at least within that little hull, zero-g was familiar. Mostly, though, he just existed from moment to moment, sharing the discomfort and unease of the crew around him.

Word had spread quickly about the plan, but Thomas sensed little enthusiasm for it. Most people didn't even believe that there was a secret jump gate, and assumed the whole exercise was a waste of time. At his most pessimistic, Thomas flipped between wondering if the EF would be able to find it at all and, if they did, what sort of hostile reception they'd encounter.

Navigating around a corner on his way to his battle station, he bumped, literally, into Katja. *Normandy*'s passageways were large and difficult to navigate in zero-g, especially given the sheer number of people trying to get from place to place.

It was the first time he'd seen her since her return from Cerberus.

He steadied her at arm's length with hands on her shoulders. She looked much the same as before, with big dark eyes and short blonde hair. She was wearing the Corps green instead of Fleet blue, he noticed.

"Hey, sorry. You all right?" Despite the awkwardness he felt, he was genuinely pleased to see her.

She pushed off his hands with surprising strength. Her glare was cool, if not angry.

"I've been shot, crash-landed, showered by artillery, and had filthy genitals shoved in my face," she snapped back. "Bumping into you is hardly enough to upset me."

He tried to back away slightly—difficult in zero-g.

"I heard it was rough," he offered. "I'm really glad to see you."

"Well, good," she said as she pushed off the bulkhead to float to the far side of the passageway. "Because I'm not available if you're 'feeling messed up' again. I hear you prefer fucking Breeze now, anyway."

Before he could reply she maneuvered off down the passageway with the stream of people. He wondered how Katja knew about him and Breeze—or, more exactly, why Breeze would compromise herself like that.

As long as Chandler—and by extension Soma—never found out... Still, he felt bad that Katja had been hurt by the whole thing. Poor kid. He wished there was something he could say. But he had more important things to worry about.

He made his way to the bridge and took his usual seat at the command console. Chandler was already there, eyes focused on the central display. He gave a conspiratorial wink to Thomas then turned back to his thoughts. Thomas did a quick survey of the AVW situation, and made his routine report to the operations officer, who gave him a cool stare in response.

Relations with Commander Erikson had taken a recent dive, Thomas had noticed. He'd wondered if this was due to the OpsO's disagreement with the current plan—which everyone now seemed to think of as Thomas's plan. But he was beginning to suspect there was something else at play. Perhaps envy at his easy rapport with the commodore?

Thomas shrugged mentally. It wasn't his fault that Chandler thought highly of him.

Preparations for the passage through the secret jump gate were already underway. *Normandy*, like all the other ships, was going to battle stations in anticipation of a hostile reception.

Through the bridge sphere, he could see the blue symbol of *Artemis* positioned squarely in the middle of the carrier's visible, black hulk that eclipsed the stars. It was rare enough to be able to hold a visual on one of the other capital ships, let alone to see it blacking out a section of the sky five degrees wide. Behind them, *Troy* held station three kilometers astern of *Normandy*.

First to transit through would be the battleship *Jutland*, the mightiest ship in the Expeditionary Force, and the most capable of dealing with any threat on the other side. Right behind would come a cruiser to help against brane-based vessels, and a destroyer to help against enemy stealth ships. Next the EF's stealth ships, then more fighting ships, and ultimately the carrier, the three invasion ships, and the supply ships.

One cruiser and one destroyer were holding back as a rear guard, to avoid leaving the main body vulnerable.

It was a sound plan, but Thomas still felt his stomach tighten as *Jutland* approached the gate. The general murmur on the bridge faded to silence as all eyes watched the long line of ships swiftly approaching the invisible point in spacetime.

Four new blips popped into existence on Thomas's scope—the four Terran stealth ships phasing onto the brane for transit through the gate.

"Sixty seconds to *Jutland* at the gate," Erikson reported.

"Status report," Chandler said.

"AAW condition white," the commander on Thomas's left reported. "No hostiles inbound. Go for jump."

"ASW condition white," the lieutenant on Chandler's other side reported. "No stealth contacts. Go for jump."

Thomas made a final sweep of his sensors.

"AVW condition white, no hostile vessels," he said. "Go for jump."

In theory, the first ships through the gate would assess the situation and jump back if things were too hot. In reality, however, *Jutland* and her escorts would have about twenty seconds to assess and—if required—withdraw before the next ships in the column jumped through. And then the freight train of ships would appear on the other side at the rate of one every two seconds. It was supposed to be an overwhelming show of Terran force. But it had the potential to be a shooting gallery of Terran targets.

It all depended on what was waiting for them on the other side.

Jutland, *Admiral Halsey*, and *Cape Town* closed in on the datum that pinpointed the secret jump gate, then merged with it. Thomas glanced up, and thought he saw a slight ripple in the star field ahead. Then another, and another.

The long line of EF ships continued to close on the gate. Thomas locked his eyes on the 3-D display, waiting for one of the three ships to jump back and warn them all off.

Nothing lit up on the display.

The seconds ticked by. Somebody made a redundant report that there was no change. Everyone else was silent.

The first stealth ship reached the gate. Every two seconds a blip disappeared from Thomas's display, and *Normandy* pushed forward with the column. He just had time to see *Artemis* ripple and shrink out of sight before he gripped his chair and waited for the mind-bending moment of extra-dimensional travel.

Whatever fate awaited them, there was no turning back.

43

Troopers in general were renowned for not sweating the political implications of their actions. But even the most jaded trooper in the surviving regiments of Fifth Brigade paused in consideration at the upcoming mission. This under-strength brigade, with a battered collection of Fleet ships to support it, was going to invade one of the most populous, heavily defended planets in the human sphere—second only to Earth itself.

The officers in charge realized this, and fell back on an age-old method for preventing troopers from thinking too much—constant activity.

The Corps hangar in the bowels of *Normandy* practically writhed with movement. At the after end, rows of hover tanks hummed in position above the deck, their turrets shifting as they engaged simulated targets. Inside the tanks, troopers were embroiled in their second four-hour simulation of the day.

At the forward end of the hangar, engineers conducted quick construction drills, assembling short bridges and fortifications. And in the vast, open center of the hangar, the infantry fought their way through a maze of hastily constructed alleys and three-story buildings.

Katja paced in the observation gondola perched above the deck on the port bulkhead. She was getting used to the magnetic boots that kept her down in the zero-g, but she wasn't used to the churning in her stomach. Some of the other officers had complained in the morning meeting that troopers couldn't effectively train for ground combat in zero-g, even with magnetic boots, and Katja agreed. Movement wasn't as natural, and loose objects still floated.

At least once an exercise some eager trooper would attempt to leap into the fray, only to find himself floating helplessly away from any handhold.

Commander Vici met the complaints with her usual icy disdain for stupidity. The EF was moving into the very heartland of the enemy, and the Centauri foe was nothing like the primitive, disorganized Cerberans. Centauria—like Terra—had a system-wide tracking system, generally used for rogue asteroids, which would easily detect a cluster of artificial gravity wells moving inbound.

At most it would be a matter of hours before the Centauri Space Guard detected them and sounded a red alert. The sheer gravimetric size of a warship would suggest a body the size of a small moon, and would stir the hornet's nest.

Katja knew that their only hope was utter secrecy, and while the zero-g and magnetic boots impeded training, nausea was a price she was willing to pay to avoid being singularized by Centauri stealth ships.

Recalling the invasion ship *Sicily* vanishing in orbit over Laika she looked around the giant hangar in *Normandy*, and realized that size only made them a target. *Sicily* had been an identical twin to *Normandy*, and despite all her strength and thousands of troopers, she had simply ceased to exist in a microsecond burst of gravitons.

Katja shivered. Better to die from a bullet, facing your enemy, than to go like that.

"Ma'am," one of the simulation operators said, "your platoon is approaching the ambush."

Katja chastised herself inwardly for letting her mind wander, and moved to stand behind the sim operators.

The buildings and streets on the hangar deck were real enough, yet all of her troopers on the exercise were wearing their special training helmets which superimposed a photo-realistic landscape, to give the impression of a real Centauri town. It was fully dynamic with projected civilians as well as combatants, along with smoke, dust, and all the other aspects of the fog of war.

When acting as a participant, Katja often found it easy to completely lose herself in the simulation, but as an observer, she found it looked odd to watch her troopers moving through empty corridors linked with plastic barricades.

Commander Vici had told Katja that morning that her platoon was going to have their chain of command tested—Katja was going to be "killed" in the drop ship descent, so that one of her sergeants would have to take over. She hadn't even stepped planetside.

To his credit, Sergeant Rao had taken command quickly and was doing an admirable job of directing the platoon through the early stages of the attack. Katja had actually recommended to Commander Vici that Sergeant Chang be the platoon second-in-command, but Vici felt it best to keep a long-serving member of Fifth Platoon at the top, in part to avoid resentment from the troopers. Thus, Chang was leading the reserve group.

Fifth Platoon had returned to *Normandy* from their disastrous raid on Cerberus with heavy casualties, and the ranks had been filled in by members of the other FAC strike teams. Scott Lahko's Second Platoon had been similarly reinforced. Platoon personnel could be wary of replacements, especially just before a battle, but fast-attack troopers were chosen from the very best, and were generally quite senior.

Fifth Platoon now had two extra sergeants who were serving as squad leaders, and five extra squad leaders who were reduced to grunts, but Katja hoped that the extra experience would overcome any ego issues, especially when the bullets really started flying.

And when people were getting killed, each squad had an experienced member who could take over.

There had never been any real question, upon their return from Cerberus, of whether Katja would remain in command of Fifth Platoon. She hadn't assumed anything, but had simply reported to Commander Vici, fully prepared to relinquish her position. Vici had conducted a thorough debrief and sent Katja on her way. Katja carried on filling in as platoon commander, and waited for new orders—which never came. It might be that everyone was just too busy to worry about whether she was supposed to be commanding Fifth Platoon.

Whatever the reason, she wasn't going to speak up.

On the training ground below, Rao was leading his troops right into the trap. On the sim panel, Katja could see the snipers in the upper windows of the street and the fortified defenders behind the double doors. She frowned, and gripped her belt restlessly. This wasn't going to be pretty.

Just as Fifth Platoon blew open the double doors, the snipers opened fire from above. The leading troopers through the doors were mowed down by the defenders. Shouts echoed up from the training ground over the clatter of scrambling bodies, while in the sim world Fifth Platoon charged aggressively into the guns of the defenders. With overwhelming firepower they took out the defenders inside the building.

Chang's rear guard lobbed grenades into every window in the street, taking out the snipers with deadly—and completely excessive—use of force.

Not good enough. She leaned over to the sim operator. "Sergeant, upgrade the snipers to rocket snipers, here and in the next street. And double the number of APRs."

"Yes, ma'am."

There were thirty units vying for training on this same simulation ground—Levantine Regiment alone had six troops of infantry, and each troop had five platoons. That meant more than fifteen hundred troopers trying to get training on this same simulation ground. Even with each scenario limited to an hour, each platoon got less than one combat training session per day.

Every scenario had to push them to the max.

The platoon regrouped beyond the double doors. Katja listened on the command circuit as Rao gave instructions to watch for snipers.

Good. She nodded to herself.

Chang and the reserves cleared the second story, taking out two of the newly added rocket snipers. That provoked hostile fire from the other snipers across the street, but Chang moved quickly to clear the blast zones and return fire effectively.

The operator glanced up at her. "Would you like me to add some more snipers, ma'am?"

She shook her head. The lesson had been learned.

Behind her, five troopers pulled themselves onto the gondola—the ones who had been killed in the initial ambush. They glanced at her with varying degrees of sheepishness. She motioned for them to spread out and watch the simulation. Even if they couldn't participate, they could still learn.

Below, the platoon advanced cautiously, using proper cover procedures to watch all the windows in the street. Katja glanced at the display to where the APRs were rolling forward. She didn't need to access the helmet cam displays—she knew very well what advancing APRs looked like.

Full data downloads had been delivered to Command, revealing the events from combat on Cerberus. Katja cringed when she envisioned all of the senior officers, and then all of the troopers, examining her every move in combat.

She, too, had reviewed the scenarios in Free Lhasa and Thapa's farm, gone over them minutely, and thought about how she could have done things better. Thomas had once said to her that a strike officer learned or died.

Well, she wasn't dead yet, so hopefully she could still learn.

She had expected pitying stares from the senior platoon leaders, yet those hadn't materialized. In fact, she'd noticed a change in attitude from just about everyone. Scott Lahko was still full of his own bravado, but his gentle needling had been replaced by requests for her tactical advice. The other Saracen officers, all of whom were older and had served longer than she, similarly sought her opinions after each of their platoon exercises.

She supposed it was just that she was the latest officer to see actual combat. Once everyone got over that, and really looked at her success rate, she doubted she would be sought after for advice.

Her first strike on Thapa's farm had been a waste of time and had resulted in civilian casualties. With the second strike on the farm, she had walked into an ambush. Her boarding of the *Astrid* had produced no hard evidence, and provoked a Centauri stealth attack. Her crazy boarding of the Centauri battle cruiser had killed half her strike team.

Her command of Fifth Platoon had led to huge casualties, and surrender. If not for the rescue, she'd now be a human public toilet in the central square of Free Lhasa.

And her one mission that might actually be considered a "success"—the rescue of the hostages—had provoked Centauria to declare war on Terra.

What would her father think? Army and Astral Force didn't talk much, but Storm Banner Leader Emmes knew plenty of well-placed Astral personnel.

As she stood quietly behind the simulation operators, towered over by her "dead" troopers, Katja suddenly fought to suppress tears. Her father was respected in both armed services, and rightfully so. As for her...

Thomas Kane had proved himself a hero by saving his crew and risking his own life to save his ship. That kid, Jack Mallory, had single-handedly destroyed a stealth ship and discovered the Centauri jump gate. Even that slut Breeze had proved her worth by finding the hostages in Free Lhasa, and arranging to rescue Katja.

All Katja had done was get a lot of people killed and start a war.

Not now, she thought, and she shook her head. A few muttered comments from the troopers on the gondola focused her on the display again.

The platoon was advancing down APR lane, moving cautiously, still unaware of the impending threat. She began to regret her decision to increase the number of APRs—slaughtering her platoon would do little to increase experience or morale.

Then she noticed movement to one side as someone in simple coveralls—rather than full training gear—pulled up onto the simulator platform. She immediately recognized Commander Vici and felt her stomach tighten. Her platoon was about to get wiped out, and the troop commander had come along to see it.

Katja turned to face her, hopefully distracting her from the action below. "Lieutenant Emmes and Fifth Platoon on exercise, ma'am."

But Vici looked right past her at the display. The lead squads were just about to discover the APRs.

"I know who you are, Emmes. That looks like a few more APRs than the scenario called for." Vici glanced at her. "Trying to make heroes of your troopers?"

She felt her cheeks flush. "No, ma'am. I... just know how little time we have to train."

Shouts from the training ground saved her from having to continue her explanation. The platoon had spotted the APRs, and vice versa. On the deck below, troopers dove for cover and pointed empty rifles at open air. On the display in front of her, a bloody battle played itself out. The sergeants stayed cool on the circuit, deep voices trying to keep the platoon united in purpose, even as they scattered for cover.

Wild shots filled the virtual air.

Then a single voice barked from the deck, clearly audible over the clatter of armored bodies. It was Trooper Sakiyama, forsaking comms and shouting instructions to everyone near him.

"Use grenades on the weapons pods! The armor's too thick!"

Under his direction, one squad focused their fire on the lead APR's vulnerable points, disabling it in seconds. They then switched target and took down the second APR in a similar fashion. Even as simulated fire rained down on them, and troopers dropped to the deck as casualties, Fifth Platoon picked up on the tactic and began to systematically pick off the lumbering Centauri robots.

Katja felt a smile tug at her lips. The bastards had been paying attention after all. Her eyes fixated on the display, and she almost missed Vici's comment.

"Looks like Sakiyama reviewed his combat log from Cerberus."

"Ma'am?"

"On that raid, he wasted most of his grenades against APR armor, until you set the example for him."

Katja remembered the incident well. She just had trouble believing that Vici grasped it so clearly, having nothing to go on but frantically shifting helmet cams.

"Yes, ma'am."

Vici gave her a hard stare, but there was a subtlety in the look that Katja didn't recognize.

"Emmes, tomorrow the EF is sending a Hawk to recce out Centauria's homeworld. As the Saracens have been designated to lead the first wave, the colonel has asked me to go along as the brigade's eyes. I'd like you to come as my second opinion."

Katja was stunned. Surely the first lieutenant should go, or one of the other troop commanders. But Commander Vici had asked her, and was now waiting for her answer.

"Of course, ma'am. Thank you."

Vici glanced again at the simulation display, where Fifth Platoon was advancing cautiously on the wreckage of the APRs.

"Sergeant, amend the scenario to mimic the Fifth Platoon run," she instructed. "If they can do it, and against those odds, so can everyone else."

The simulation operator made a note. "Yes, ma'am."

She pushed off the console and glided away.

Katja felt her smile growing, but pushed it down under the mask of command. Her father might consider her worthless, and Thomas Kane might use her like a whore, but here among the Saracens—in the Corps—she was appreciated.

44

apier was still too broken to fly. Ever since the decision had been made to invade the Centauri homeworld, all maintenance attention had been focused on *Normandy*'s one hundred strike fighters. The mechanics had been doing their best, but parts had been prioritized for those fast-attack craft that were still operational, pushing *Rapier* even further down the priority list.

And Thomas had other concerns. He'd always thought that his time in command would be the surest way to get ahead, but being a staff officer in Chandler's command team was arguably even better.

As an FAC captain, he was just one of nine. Current circumstances had reduced them to executing routine combat patrols for the Fleet. Even though he had received a Distinguished Conduct Medal for his little maneuver at the Battle of Laika, such duties were all but invisible.

However, as the anti-vessel warfare controller, he had a chance to prove himself in a role that was billeted for a commander. Although it hadn't been his intention to be given the position—not under these circumstances—fortune seemed to be favoring him.

He took his seat at the command console on *Normandy*'s bridge, feeling a new sense of self-confidence in this crowd of mostly senior officers. The other two controllers nodded greetings to him. Commander Erikson gave him a glance bereft of warmth. Colonel Korolev and all five of his troop commanders hovered around the console—a concentration of senior officers that was rare.

Breeze rushed in moments before the scheduled start time, quickly uploading some data. Thomas tried to not watch her movements, but even strapped into his seat he found himself rising to the occasion. He hated himself for it, but his thoughts often wandered back to the memory of their hour together in his cabin. She'd certainly enjoyed it, and he couldn't help but wonder if she might be up for an encore.

He shook his head sharply and forced himself to look away, reminding himself that he was marrying another woman when they got home.

If they got home.

Erikson activated the large, central display, causing representations of Centauria's twin suns to appear, along with the five planets that circled each. A cluster of blue symbols far below the system's ecliptic indicated the position of the Expeditionary Force as it transited slowly and silently toward its target.

That target was the third planet circling the yellow orb of Centauria A—the homeworld of the enemy. All the planets of the Centauri system had been named after minor Roman deities— the last to follow the ancient Earth tradition of naming planets from that pantheon. Some were a bit strange, such as Pax, the goddess of peace, and Spes, the goddess of hope. How poetic, then, that the Centauri homeworld—the first planet settled by humans outside the original solar system—was named for Abeona, the protector of children leaving the home.

Today's briefing was a planning meeting for the Terran invasion of Abeona.

Thomas still harbored serious doubts as to the EF's ability to strike so deep into hostile territory. And to his way of thinking, a surprise attack on civilian targets wasn't the most honorable of actions. He didn't know much about Centauri culture, but from what he'd picked up over the years, he didn't think of them as a particularly warlike people. Outspoken and ambitious, for certain, but hardly aggressive.

Chandler arrived at his usual time, precisely thirty seconds after the briefing was scheduled to start. Thomas still hadn't figured out if it was his intention to allow a few moments grace for latecomers to slip in before him, or if he just wanted to make everyone wait because he could.

He greeted Korolev and took his seat.

Erikson pushed up from his seat and spoke. "Commodore, Brigade Colonel, ladies and gentlemen. The attack on Abeona will proceed on schedule. All units have reported ready for combat, and we remain undetected with forty hours to go.

"We've selected the three largest cities as our primary targets, one brigade assigned to each. They're relatively small—back in Terra, they'd hardly be called 'cities.' Other human settlements also are small, and scattered widely across the surface of the planet. The Centauri obsession with environmentalism has imposed growth restrictions on their settlements.

"This unfortunately denies us a single, high-profile target. However, their environmentalism also means a complete lack of permanent transport infrastructure between the many settlements, which will make it more difficult to transfer reinforcements, and should provide us with at least twelve hours where our forces are fighting only the local defenses. That said, Centauri surface weapons are high-tech and survivable.

"Tomorrow morning I'll be leading a recce mission in a single Hawk, to assess enemy defensive capabilities. This mission will risk exposing our presence, but the information gathered will be invaluable to the operation."

"Will the Hawk have fighter support?" Korolev asked.

"No, sir. She'll be doing a close orbit of Abeona, and will be tracked by the Centauri traffic system. There's no way to hide a fighter flying in close to the planet, and two small vessels in formation would be a dead giveaway. In order to get the Hawk that close she has to go solo."

Thomas nodded to himself. Everyone at the briefing understood the risk, but there was no other choice if they wanted pre-battle intelligence. Visuals at this range—even at the highest possible magnification—revealed only the largest of orbital objects, and nothing on the surface.

"We know that there are three orbital platforms around

Abeona," Erikson continued, "and that they are heavily defended. Intelligence suggests more than a hundred missile batteries on the surface, and at least as many swarms of robotic sentries. The recce tomorrow will aim to confirm or revise these numbers."

"What about warships in the system?" Chandler asked. He suddenly turned his gaze to Thomas. "AVW, what do we know?"

Thomas tried to ignore the glare from Erikson. "We've detected a few weak signals indicating Centauri military activity in the system, but nothing to suggest that their big ships are in the area. If the message we received in Sirius is correct, and the Centauris have attacked Terran forces in every system, then their fleet is spread pretty thin.

"Most likely their gamble is that if they control the Terran-built jump gates, they control all traffic into their system," he continued. "It's the perfect choke point. This would mean they can leave their home system relatively undefended. As a result, we can expect Space Guard cutters and small patrol craft."

"Which can still pack a punch," Erikson said, taking back his briefing. "Many of the Space Guard cutters can be fitted with anti-vessel missiles." He brought up a new set of yellow symbols on the display, indicating the dozens of civilian ships transiting the vicinity of Abeona.

"The first part of our plan will be to disguise the EF ships as civilians en route to the target. As you can see, traffic is fairly dense in the Abeona approaches, so finding suitable identities shouldn't be hard. One of the objectives of tomorrow's recce will be to assess and isolate the best candidates from among these vessels."

"It's easy enough to fit the equipment in the Hawk," Korolev said, "but who's going to conduct this search? No offence, Commander, but stealing vessel identities isn't easy."

Erikson flushed slightly, but nodded. "I'll take along a qualified intelligence operative."

"Breeze, I want you to go," Chandler said. Thomas watched with interest as she went pale but still managed to keep her composure. It was unusual to see her off balance, and for some reason he rather enjoyed it.

"Thank you, sir," she said carefully. "But I think one of the field operatives would be better suited to this."

"I agree, sir," Erikson said.

Chandler nodded. "Then choose your best field operative, Breeze, and bring him along with you." She made to protest, but he spoke over her. "It's important to have an officer's big-picture perspective."

"Of course, sir." Breeze pursed her lips together and nodded.

"I volunteer to go, sir," Thomas said without thinking. "I can back up the OpsO's assessment of the orbital and surface defenses."

"Good, good." Chandler smiled slightly, his gaze taking in both Thomas and Breeze. "This'll be valuable experience for both of you."

Commander Vici spoke up. "We'll want to ensure that we get a good survey of the landing zones, as well as the drop corridors. I'm bringing one of my lieutenants with me, but I assume we won't have a lot of time close to the planet."

Erikson shook his head. "Probably just one parabolic orbit."

He turned to address Chandler, trying his best to hide his new irritation. "Sir, the Hawk's getting pretty full, with all these extra bodies. If the Corps is sending two people, which I fully support, I recommend I take just the field operative to help with EM searches. Including the pilot, that'll be plenty of eyes on scene."

He really doesn't want to share this mission with anyone, Thomas thought, easily noting the tension under the OpsO's professional tone.

Unfortunately for him, he didn't know Eric Chandler very well. Thomas looked at his mentor and, as expected, saw the steel forming in his gaze.

"Perhaps you're right," Chandler replied quietly. "I can see immediately how we can reduce the crew by one. This recce is more for the Corps's benefit than the Fleet's, so Commander Vici will be in charge of the mission. Kane and Brisebois will support her in the Hawk, and you can advise me personally here in *Normandy*."

A surprised silence fell over the command team. Erikson's mouth fell open. Breeze made to speak, then apparently thought better of it.

Thomas knew to keep his head down.

"Very well, sir," Erikson finally said, his face red. "This concludes my brief. Do you have anything to add, sir?"

Chandler took a deep breath. "We've all been talking as if we're in Centauri space. I'd like to remind everyone that we are, in fact, in *Terran* space. Centauria is one of our colonies—the worlds here belong to the Terran Union. The colonists have made an open act of rebellion against us, and thousands of Terrans have died.

"We don't have the firepower to restore order, so we'll do the next best thing—we will *disrupt* order. We'll panic the rebels and punish them. We'll make them understand what the consequences are of turning against their rightful authority." He looked directly at Thomas. "On the recce tomorrow, in addition to your tactical objectives, determine the best targets to make them pay."

Thomas acknowledged the direction, trying to share some of Chandler's unflinching belief in the rightness of their cause. All he could manage was to wish that he'd never opened his mouth, and instead let the Expeditionary Force dash itself against the Centauri force at the jump gate.

45

reeze tried to suppress a yawn as she awkwardly pulled herself along the zero-g guide rope that had been set up along the centerline of the main hangar. The sleepless nights were taking their toll—the zero-g in her cabin was a constant reminder that attack and instant death could come at any moment.

Helplessness wasn't a feeling she liked.

As the largest and most valuable ship in the Expeditionary Force, *Normandy* would be target priority one if she was discovered. But somehow they had decided to create an even *more* likely target. And put Breeze aboard.

The Hawk was parked just off the centerline, engines humming. She paused at the side door, taking a deep breath to calm her heart and settle her stomach. The sooner they were launched and busy, the better. Fixing her expression into one of calm professionalism, she pulled herself into the main compartment.

She had barely steadied herself against the newly installed intelligence console when the pilot appeared, looking from behind his seat in the cockpit. He was young, ugly… and grinning.

"Hey, Breeze! Welcome aboard!"

Her heart sank. Was she doomed to have this puppy nipping at her heels forever?

"Hi, Jack," she offered. Then a sudden thought struck her. "Why are you flying this mission? Doesn't *Normandy* have any Hawks?"

He gave her a quizzical look. "No." Then he grinned again.

"Besides, none of their pilots have the old eagle-eye." He pointed proudly at his misshapen face. "I guess *somebody* thinks I'm doing a good job." He laughed. "Or they want to get rid of me. Can you believe this mission?"

She exhaled deeply, maintaining composure.

"It's going to be…" The first word that came to mind was *suicidal*. "Challenging."

"I'll say. I mean, I've seen the reports. Do you have any idea how tight their planetary defenses are?"

She pushed down her growing anger. "That's what we're going to find out, isn't it?"

"That's the plan."

She turned away and started flashing up the intelligence console, ignoring Jack's humming and the arrival of other crew members.

Warrant al-Jamil floated in beside her, and she looked up. He was remarkably clean-cut and in his regulation blue coveralls was hard to recognize as the "Cerberan trader" who had landed his orbital dhow barely a week ago.

"Morning, Breeze." He gave her a smile.

"Morning, Ali," she said. "Ready to go?"

"Ready as ever." He took over the console with an air of serenity accompanying each smooth gesture. She wondered how a field operative could remain so calm in life and death circumstances. Personally, she preferred the support role—close enough to the action to be included in the credit, but far from any real danger.

The Hawk's cargo door began to close, and she realized it was time for launch. She checked on the location of the nearest spacesuit, ensuring that it was in standby and ready for wear.

Jack was invisible behind his seat, but his voice sounded quietly in the speakers around her.

"We're rolling, folks. I'll be dousing the cabin lights as soon as we airlock. Just a reminder that we are in full stealth mode today—no lights, no emissions. Absolute radio silence."

Breeze looked around the cabin, noting the others who had arrived while she was busy with the console.

Thomas was there, of course—Chandler's pet, and the only officer stupid enough to volunteer. She wondered what fallout there would be from his replacing Commander Erikson on this mission. She'd have to watch the growing rift between Thomas and his new rival.

The Corps was represented by Commander Vici, and she seemed to have a new pet of her own. Surprisingly enough, Katja Emmes hovered close to her boss, studiously ignoring Breeze and, she noted with interest, Thomas. That, too, would be worth watching—at least for a laugh.

She remembered with sweet satisfaction Katja's pale, tight-lipped response after she'd let slip oh-so casually her opinion of Thomas in bed. She was pretty sure it was the closest Katja had yet come to punching her. Let the bitch try. A court martial could be fun, too.

The cabin went dark as the Hawk entered the airlock. After a few moments a faint wash of light spilled in from forward as the ship emerged from *Normandy* into the starlight. A few console lights added their faint glow to the shadowy compartment. Breeze felt a persistent tug aft as they accelerated clear. The tug shifted direction as Jack made a broad turn.

"How long for the inbound run?" Vici asked.

"About six hours," Jack replied. "I have to point us well clear of any Centauri planet or base to avoid getting picked up by their asteroid hunters. Their system also automatically raises an alert on anything going above a certain speed, so I have to throttle back a bit. Low and slow."

"Have you got your passive EM sensors up?" Thomas asked.

There was a pause. "Yep," Jack replied. "I'll be keeping an eye on their sensor sweeps, and a visual for anything close."

Breeze listened absently to the chatter, tuning out as it got more and more technical. Her role was specific. She and Ali were to locate and record the electromagnetic emissions of fifteen civilian ships that were all headed for Abeona. By the time the EF got to within striking distance, each ship would need to be able to identify itself to satisfy the curious authorities. To get that close, the EF ships were going to have to steal identities. It was Breeze's job to identify the victims.

The gentle tug of acceleration faded. Breeze paused for a moment to let her stomach settle, then unstrapped from the bench. She pulled herself aft to hover next to Ali at the console.

"Let's start looking."

Ali nodded, and brought up a dim 3-D display with the Hawk at the center.

"So far I've got five vessels within ten million kilometers," he said. "Three merchants, a tug, and a yacht."

"How many barges does the tug have?"

"Three."

"Good, that'll probably work for the invasion ships."

He nodded again as he adjusted the scale of the display. "We have a lot to choose from."

"Well, start recording them all. We'll probably go with those engaged in the least chatter. They're the easiest to imitate."

She watched and listened to the scattered civilian ships for a while, looking for odd patterns or irregular beacons that might disqualify any as being too hard to imitate. Most of them were running silent, happily radiating their ID beacons as they puttered along toward their destinations.

The Intel console precisely recorded those beacons, ensuring that every nuance was faithfully reproduced before it might be assigned to an EF ship.

The data collection was fully automated, but analysis took a substantial amount of effort. It was going to take hours for them to select enough promising vessels, with backups.

"We're being hailed."

Ali rocketed forward to the cockpit. Breeze was quick in his wake.

"Who is it?" Ali asked Jack.

"Abeona Traffic. Standard hail, our position exactly."

Ali slipped on a headset and brought up the frequency. Breeze grabbed the sole spare and did likewise. A surprisingly clear voice, with a polished Centauri accent, sounded in her ears.

"*Vessel in grid position one-seven-nine mark two-five-zero, this is Abeona Traffic. Please identify yourself.*"

Ali the field agent was ready to respond. "Hey, Traffic, this is *Dream Weaver* on a pleasure cruise over from Big Side. Thought we might come have a look at your pretty planet."

"Dream Weaver, *Traffic, roger. Are you intending to dock with a platform, or land on the planet?*"

"Not this time, Traffic. Just coming for a look."

"*Roger, be advised transit orbital distance is forty thousand kilometers. Enjoy your journey. Abeona Traffic standing by.*"

Ali glanced at Breeze and Jack. "Well, nobody can fault their tracking systems."

"Good thing the EF didn't try the direct approach," Thomas said.

Vici floated forward, making the cockpit rather crowded. "How long before we can see the planet?"

Jack pointed at a very bright, blue-green dot fine off the port bow. "That's her. I can give you magnified visuals on your screen, if you like."

"Maximum mag, please."

Jack tapped a series of commands into his console. Vici retreated to rejoin Katja at their console.

Breeze couldn't pry her eyes away, though. Abeona. The first planet colonized by humans outside of Sol's nurturing warmth. The beginning of a new era. Apparently a near-twin to Earth, the planet when first surveyed three hundred years ago had caused such an uprising of enthusiasm that the first group of ark ships had been built in an amazing five years, and five years after that the colonists had seen exactly what she was seeing now.

The blue-green disk grew larger, and within thirty minutes she could clearly see the three-quarter crescent on the orb. There were other lights in the sky as well, as traffic became denser in the planet's outer gravitational reaches.

Vici appeared beside her again. "What kind of orbital defenses, Lieutenant Kane?"

"The three orbital platforms are active," Thomas replied. "They're equatorial, one-twenty degrees spread in geostationary orbit. From this far south, all three have line of fire on us. The EF will definitely want to approach along the ecliptic."

"What about ships?"

"EM is picking up two, maybe three Space Guard radars, but otherwise nothing obviously military."

"Docked at the stations?"

"Impossible to say at this range. I'll get a better look when we're in closer."

Vici leaned in to Jack. "How close can you get me to the surface without risking a visual ID?"

"Our legal distance is forty thousand klicks, but at that range I'll have to play it by eye, based on other traffic."

"I'll want to take control of your camera."

Jack paused in thought, lips pursed. He scanned his console.

"Did you hear me?" Vici asked.

He nodded. "Yeah, yeah. I'm just trying to figure out how to give you control."

The orb of Abeona grew into a real planet, with brilliant, swirling cloud patterns over a green, brown and blue surface. The night side was pure black, with surprisingly few lights for such an important world. Compared to Earth, which still sagged under its billions of inhabitants, this was a wilderness paradise.

An extremely sophisticated and dangerous wilderness paradise, Breeze reminded herself as Ali fielded another call from Traffic. There were dozens of lights moving slowly across her field of view.

"Getting crowded," she said.

"I'm going to switch on our nav lights," Jack said, "so that we're not doing anything overtly illegal."

"Keep us on a steady course," Thomas said, eyes on his console, "and keep us out of visual range. We're being tracked, but I think it's just civilian."

Breeze pushed back out of the cockpit, suddenly feeling exposed as the shining face of Abeona grew larger. Vici and Katja were focused on their screens, which were zoomed in far enough to make out major geographic features.

"They have auto-defenses here and here," Katja said, pointing, "and a fighter base here."

"It's not pretty," Vici said, "but it's the clearest run and it keeps us under the horizon of their big guns until we're on the ground. Orbital bombardment should pave the road for us, and strike fighter support can take whatever they get into the air."

Breeze pushed forward to hover by Thomas's chair. "How

are the orbital defenses looking?"

He glanced up, then returned to his work. "Strong enough. Besides the three bases, I count maybe five Space Guard ships in the area. Most of them are just for local defense, but Centauris don't build cheap, and a missile still hurts whether it's fired from a battleship or a patrol boat."

"Will they have much chance to see the EF during the approach?"

"Plenty. If we don't get challenged, we go all the way into low orbit for the drop. If we do get challenged, we charge, open fire, and drop on the run."

"Is there a lot that can hit us from the ground?"

He glanced up again. "I'm working on it," he said irritably.

Her stomach churned. Abeona was looming large now, beautiful in the sunlight. Her earlier fascination had faded, though, as she imagined all the weapons that were hidden from her view in plain sight. This was insane.

"Okay, we're approaching perigee," Jack said. "Do you need me to alter north or south?"

"North," Vici said, "as close to forty-five degrees as you can."

Jack leaned his stick to port slightly.

There were ships all over the sky now. Breeze tightened her grip on Jack's chair.

"Can any of those ships see what we are?" she asked.

Jack glanced around. "Can you see what they are?"

She was surprised at the question.

"Neither can I," he said. "And we're *really* small. They can see our nav lights but that's it. If anybody even cares, we look just like any other ship doing its thing."

She wasn't convinced. Both Jack and Ali seemed completely at ease, though, so she held her tongue.

The planet now filled a quarter of the sky. Lights moved below them. Breeze watched and waited for the telltale flash of missiles.

"Okay, that's it," Jack said. "We're past perigee and climbing. Take your last look, folks."

"I need you to turn around and go back for another sweep," Vici said.

"No-can," Jack replied. "I skimmed forty thousand as it is. If we descend any more, we're inside their safe distance."

"Then don't descend. Turn around and do a northwest diagonal cross. We didn't have time to get all the images we need."

Jack paused at his controls, in a pose Breeze was coming to recognize as deep thought. Then he pursed his lips and did nothing.

"Sorry, ma'am, but I can't do that," he said, his voice neutral. "We're stretched for fuel as it is, and I don't have the reserves to do heavy maneuvering. If I turn us around, I'm in effect putting on the brakes, and we'll drop fast into the geostationary zone."

Vici appeared next to Breeze, eyes blazing. "I don't give a rat's ass what zone we're in. My troopers are landing on that planet in twenty-four hours, and I need to see the landscape."

Jack and Thomas exchanged a glance. The tension in the little cockpit was suddenly thick. Breeze knew enough about orbital physics from her fast-attack training to know that Jack was protesting for a good reason.

"Uhh, ma'am…" Thomas began.

Vici stabbed a finger at him. "I don't want to hear it."

"Ma'am," Jack said, still looking forward, "Abeona Traffic cleared us for an observation orbit. If I drop any lower I'm going to cross into the zone where all their satellites and orbiting defenses sit. This is my first time to Centauria, but I know in Terra the local authorities get real upset when strangers drift into that zone."

Vici made to speak, but Jack plunged on.

"Also, even if I *could* turn us around and stay out of the geo-zone, we're still being plotted by Traffic and they're going to get suspicious at our sudden and dramatic change in flight plan. That will cause someone to investigate, and there's an orbital platform not too far from here." He pointed out the windows, to where a large, distant, silvery object was flashing in the sunlight. "If anybody identifies us, we're fucked. And then they'll know the EF is here, and the EF is fucked."

Breeze had never heard Jack swear before.

His words seemed to have an impact. Vici's features relaxed.

"Very well," she said. "We'll go with what we have. Take us back to *Normandy*."

"Yes, ma'am."

The commander returned to the console with Katja. Jack kept his eyes forward, as he had through the entire exchange.

Breeze glanced at Thomas. He gave her a shrug and turned back to his console. She looked back at Jack.

The puppy had teeth after all.

She was impressed.

She watched the surface of the planet slip by beneath her as the Hawk slowly began to pull away. They were on their way back to the EF with their precious information. In twenty-four hours this peaceful, beautiful, unsuspecting world would learn the consequences of picking a fight with Terra.

46

Thomas's display showed the ships of the Expeditionary Force as they moved like shadows through Centauri space, and each one was preparing to strike. As the AVW controller he had issued the orders only hours before, and he couldn't ignore the knot in his stomach as the final minutes ticked away.

Normandy's spherical bridge gave a front-row view. Centauri A was a brilliant, yellow-orange disk low off the bow, so much like Terra's own Sol that it was easy to pretend the ship was making the final approach for home. After months of averting his eyes from the dazzling orb of Sirius, Centauri A was a welcome relief.

Centauri B was a dim, heavy orb high over the stern, larger and redder than its companion but equally capable of supporting life. Thousands of human settlements dotted the worlds orbiting each star.

One such world was growing brighter off the port bow—a dazzling, blue-green point of light. Abeona was their next stop, but first there was an immediate matter to which they had to attend.

Moving against the stars above him was a brightly lit tug and its three barges. It was called the *Starspan Rose*, bound for Orbital Platform Three with a cargo of unrefined iron ore. It looked almost close enough to touch, so close that to Abeona Traffic the radar images practically melded with *Normandy* and her sister ships. If anyone was even looking. The tug and barges all had blinking yellow beacons and floodlights on their hulls, intended to ensure excellent visibility as the cumbersome train approached the busy space lanes.

Behind them, visible only for the occasional stars it eclipsed, was the massive shape of the battleship *Jutland*. She approached her prey in the blind spot astern, like a giant shark in the ink-black sea. A new symbol momentarily lit up on the display, but nothing appeared visually as *Jutland* fired.

The tug imploded, winked out of existence by the torpedo.

Across the 3-D display, spread over six million kilometers, torpedo symbols flashed from EF ships as they singularized their targets. Civilian beacons vanished, then reappeared as the hunters took the identities of their prey. There was a slight acceleration as *Normandy* maneuvered to take station astern of *Jutland*. She was now the first of the three barges.

All around her, the ships of EF 15 took on their assumed roles and continued to close Abeona. Thomas kept watch on the radar emissions from Traffic, waiting for the pinpoint beams of interrogation radar.

There was no change to the weak, steady pulse of the distant surveillance radar. There was no sudden chatter on the Traffic channels. He took a deep breath, trying to loosen the knot. So far, the ruse was working.

Jutland and the three invasion ships formed up as the tug and tow *Starspan Rose*. The carrier *Artemis* became the luxury liner *Nebula*, and the cruisers, destroyers, and supply ships morphed into a variety of cargo ships, yachts, and a cluster of mining vessels returning home. Thomas willfully banished from his mind the hundreds of innocent people who had just died. Their blood would be nothing compared to what was about to come.

"Commodore, Echo-Victor," he said, "deception completed. All units in place, no response from Abeona Traffic."

"Roger. Time to controlled zone?" Chandler sat very still in his raised seat, eyes fixed on the central display.

Thomas quickly manipulated his controls. "*King Alfred* will reach it first, ETA seventeen minutes. *Normandy*'s ETA is thirty-five minutes."

Chandler nodded slowly. "Very well."

The command team was quiet, each controller focused on his display. Around them, *Normandy*'s bridge crew moved like ghosts across the transparent deck.

One circuit crackled with myriad reports of the Levantine Regiment. Thomas recognized the routine drop preparations from his own days as a platoon commander. The troopers would have all formed up for a stirring speech by the colonel, then broken into troops for final instructions from each commander. By this time, the troopers of the first wave were loading into their drop ships.

Katja would be there, floating down the line of her platoon, her large, dark eyes taking in every detail, her voice carried over the rumble of machines, instilling confidence. She was probably afraid—who wouldn't be?—but hiding it behind her polished mask of command.

He wished that he'd made the effort to visit her, to make peace with her so that she could focus on her mission. Those hours in the Hawk had been brutal. She'd been closed and hostile the entire trip.

Thomas refocused on his display. His job was to make sure she could get to the planet, to do hers. He just hoped she'd be all right.

Abeona grew larger. He pinpointed the three separate emissions of the orbital platforms. At this range all three still had line of sight on the invasion ships, but if all went according to plan, two of the stations would be masked behind the planet itself when the drop occurred.

Three of the EF's stealth ships had been sent ahead of the attacking force in absolute emission silence to target the platforms, but maneuvering in the Bulk so close to a massive body like Abeona was a tricky business. No one would know if they'd reached their objectives until the fighting started.

The fourth stealth ship was in close support to the invasion ships, but had gone silent hours ago in preparation for the attack.

There was heavy emission traffic near Abeona, as civilian ships blared away with their beacons, radars, and radios. Through the noise, Thomas was fairly certain he could detect two distinct Space Guard cutters in the vicinity. These ships were small and designed for local operations, but they were heavily armed and maneuverable. With *Jutland* and the cruisers dedicated to providing orbital bombardment for the drop, anti-vessel warfare would fall to the destroyers.

AVW wasn't the forte of these smaller ships. Thomas feared the cutters might have the advantage.

None of the surface batteries were actively scanning, he noted, and there was no obvious sign of surface-based fighters in orbit. His survey in the Hawk had given a good indication of where these threats lay, but there was no way to know if he'd found them all.

Abeona Traffic began to query the EF ships as they entered the controlled zone around the homeworld. Thomas listened carefully to the casual radio chatter, waiting for any hint of trouble. It took twenty minutes for all of the EF ships—each on a unique heading and speed—to enter the controlled zone and be queried. By then Abeona had grown into a visible orb, shining to the left of *Jutland*'s dark bulk.

"Commodore, this is Drop Command. All three ships report first wave ready for drop."

It was Brigade Colonel Korolev, forced to stay behind and coordinate the invasion from orbit. It was a bitter blow to any trooper, Thomas knew, to have to stay behind while his comrades went into battle. And it was a bitterness he shared, especially as the reports came in that the EF's eight serviceable fast-attack craft were ready for the drop.

There was no doctrinal role for FACs in a drop, but with the EF under-strength Chandler had pressed them into service as catchall support vehicles. Capable both in space and in atmo, they helped fill in the ranks of the star fighters and strike fighters, and with their strike pods they were the perfect vehicles for medevacs and quick troop redeployments. Theirs would be a dynamic, dangerous, and pivotal role.

It was the kind of battle experience that would make a FAC captain's career. And Thomas was stuck on *Normandy*'s bridge, a nameless staff officer in the rear echelon.

He still wore the star above his two bars, but hardly anyone addressed him as "lieutenant commander" anymore. *Rapier* sat broken in the hangar—even after weeks of repairs, her hull breaches rendered her incapable of penetrating atmo. And even if Thomas had been able to get her into the orbital battle, who would have crewed her? He and Breeze were both Fleet staff. Katja and the surviving strike team were all loading into the drop ships. Even Chief Tamma had been sent back to the carrier, to pilot a star fighter.

Thomas was the commander of an empty wreck.

"*Echo-Victor,* King Alfred. *I am in visual range of Orbital Platform Three.*"

The knot in his stomach clenched. Radio spoofing was only good if the enemy couldn't actually see you. The EF ships were all now well within the Abeona Traffic controlled zone, and it was only a matter of time before somebody noticed that those mining ships weren't mining ships. That the luxury liner was, in fact, a Terran carrier.

"Roger, *King Alfred.* Alter your course to maintain standoff distance."

The platform was huge, a kilometer in radius and several kilometers long, and it became visible long before a ship the size of *King Alfred*, but that wasn't to say that there weren't telescopic cameras aboard.

Things were going to start happening fast. He sized up the priorities.

"All units, Echo-Victor," he said. "Stand by for final drop orders." He began assigning stations and targets on his internal display, but didn't transmit them yet.

Abeona Traffic made a call to the yacht *Dunsinane*, querying its position. *Cape Town* responded. There was a pause, then another call from Traffic, laced with doubt.

Another minute passed. Abeona was large enough now that Thomas could make out the Great Sea. The EF ships were all slowly converging. At current speed *Jutland* and the invasion ships were eight minutes from the primary drop point. Three minutes until the highest point where the drop ships could conceivably be launched, if necessary.

Abeona Traffic called again, a clear question in the operator's voice.

"Dunsinane, *this is Traffic. Your registration lists you as a thirty-meter yacht… Please confirm, over.*"

Thomas increased the pace of his inputs. *Cape Town* was more than a hundred and twenty meters long—even with her signature-reducing form there was no mistaking her for a yacht at this range. Even as "*Dunsinane*" responded to Traffic, *Cape Town* signalled *Normandy*.

"*Echo-Victor,* Cape Town. *I am being probed by an interrogation radar.*"

On the 3-D display, one of the Space Guard cutters altered course to close *Cape Town*.

The game was up. Thomas sent a quick acknowledgement to *Cape Town* then turned to Chandler. "Commodore, Echo-Victor. *Cape Town* is being probed. Recommend all units take up drop disposition."

Chandler's gaze bore into Thomas. "Echo-Victor, deploy the EF into drop disposition."

Thomas transmitted his orders. There were three landing zones, one for each regiment. *Normandy*, *Troy*, and *Quebec* would all launch simultaneously and use the same upper drop corridor. Surprise was the key, so drop ships and strike fighters would hit atmo together—there would be no strike fighter sweep prior to the first wave.

Jutland would remain on point defense for the invasion ships and provide bombardment for the upper corridor.

Artemis would launch her star fighters to clear the orbital approaches.

The three regiments would split at archons one-zero—low enough to hide below all but local Centauri tracking systems—and slow to supersonic for extreme low-level approach.

Each cruiser was assigned to a specific regiment and would provide bombardment for the lower drop corridor and the landing zone. The destroyers would take the Space Guard cutters—*Baghdad* and *Kristiansand* hostile three-eight, *Cape Town* and *Miami* hostile three-niner. *Goa* would provide close ASW and AVW support to the invasion ships.

The supply ships would blare out with every EM emitter they had, in order to draw Centauri attention and hopefully sow confusion. Then they'd sprint for cover under *Jutland*'s protective sphere. And the stealth ships would do whatever they could, wherever they were.

47

Katja cinched down her straps, preparing for a rough ride.
It was hard to sit comfortably with the full complement of
drop gear strapped to her back.

She checked again that her rifle was secure beside her seat,
and that all her combat equipment was in place. Her armor was
colored a dull, mossy brown, and the black webbing around
her waist blended well. She listened absently to the Fleet chatter
from the pilots' console ahead, surprised at how much she
actually understood after her months on *Rapier*'s bridge.

She recognized Thomas's voice too easily, and felt a pang of
regret for not having made the effort to speak to him before
the battle. She pushed it aside and let herself get angry at the
thought of him and Breeze, cozying up in *Normandy* while she
went into battle.

Fleet pussies.

Chang was already in his seat on her left. Rao entered the
cockpit and wordlessly handed them each a medical injector.
Katja pulled off one glove and stabbed the injector into her wrist.
There was a slight tingle as the combat cocktail rushed into her
system, but otherwise she felt no immediate effect. Experience
had taught her that the effects of the drugs were hard to detect
in the moment, but easy to remember later. If nothing else, she
felt reassured.

"*All units,*" Commander Vici said over the radio, "*prepare for drop.*" They were words she'd heard dozens of times in simulation, but this was the real thing—a hostile drop into the heart of the most powerful enemy Terra could face. Despite the amount of action she'd seen recently, Katja felt her stomach tighten in fear. It didn't help that she was still haunted by Thapa's ghost, and the idea that she was personally responsible for this war.

She felt a jolt as the drop ship rolled forward into its airlock. Faint clunks and hisses suggested depressurization outside the hull, and through the cockpit windows she saw the outer doors slide open. She expected to see the bright surface of Abeona greeting her, but was met instead by a field of stars.

Well, maybe she *was* responsible, in a small way. But then, she was her daddy's girl after all—she was a fucking soldier. Maybe it was the first effects of the combat cocktail, but she felt a cold clarity settle over her troubled heart, and swore to herself that no ghosts were going to get in her way today.

Not Thapa, not Thomas, or Breeze.

Not Father.

She was going to prove to every last one of them that she had what it takes. When this day was done, either she'd be a warrior beyond doubt, or she'd be dead.

A gentle tug toward her left suggested that *Normandy* was accelerating faster than the inertial dampeners could compensate. She saw a distant flash of light through the cockpit windows. A huge, invisible force pulled her forward against her straps, and the dazzling surface of Abeona hove into view.

Her drop ship was fifth on the port side. When the first ships went, hers would be two seconds behind. The Saracens were the first wave, and they were point. Along with the Spartans they would be the very first to hit dirt.

Katja had the landing zone burned into her brain, knew every feature and every obstacle. Her first job was simple—clear the landing zone so that the tanks could get down. There were other objectives, to be sure, but none of them mattered if that landing zone wasn't secure.

Abeona's surface drifted by right to left, the features growing visibly larger. The bright colors faded to blackness as *Normandy* raced eastward over the terminator. The plan was to drop over the night sky. They were close.

"All units, Sierra-Five," she said. "Stand by for drop."

The voice of Drop Command sounded on the cockpit speaker. *"Fifth Brigade: drop now... now... now!"*

Four distant thuds shuddered the hull, then her seat slammed up into her as the drop ship leapt free. She gripped the armrests as they swung hard into a starboard turn, caught a glimpse of *Jutland* and the stream of fiery blasts bursting forth from her bombardment batteries. Her stomach rose into her throat as the drop ship dove and her vision filled with the dark surface far below.

The fires of engine exhausts from a pair of other drop ships moved into view as her pilots tucked into formation for the descent. Off to the far left, she saw the twin burners of one of their escort strike fighters. The pressure against her back said that they were still accelerating. Corps doctrine spoke of sending in the strike fighters first to clear a path for the vulnerable drop ships, but Korolev knew that their only chance against the Abeona defenses was complete surprise and had sent everything all at once. With luck, the first wave of troopers would be on the ground before the Centauris could even get themselves organized.

Being first wave might actually be safer than second or third.

The first glow of super-heated gases formed around the drop ships and strike fighters ahead. Then she felt the frantic vibrations in her seat, and saw the fires begin to form in front of her own ship.

"This is Sierra-Five—into atmo!" She hoped her voice sounded cool and reassuring. Her fingers already ached from gripping the chair so tightly.

Flame enveloped her ship. The pilots struggled to keep on course as they plummeted through the sky like a meteor. She concentrated on her breathing, ignoring the feeling of helplessness that threatened to overwhelm her. The high drop corridor was the most dangerous, with the ship practically blind and still high enough to be an easy target. Their only defense was speed, and faith that the Centauris were caught unawares.

She pursed her lips tight and hung on. The ship lurched violently to starboard. Was that turbulence, or evasive maneuvering? The pilots' voices were lost in the roar. They fought their controls and Katja felt a hard turn to port. Something impacted the starboard side hull. The jolt shook her in her seat. Another long, wrenching turn to port, and the fires outside began to fade.

She had a glimpse of yellow light reflecting off cloud tops, then the world outside plunged into blackness. The ship began to shake constantly, a steady, pounding rhythm.

The darkness lifted as the ship dropped from the clouds and pulled out of its dive. Then she saw the drop ship exhausts ahead, and the scattered, distant lights on the surface. The night sky was lit up with tracers from below, flickering past her view on both sides. Orange bolts flashed down from above. Explosions lit the surface but were instantly astern as the drop ship rocketed forward.

In a moment of sudden clarity, she saw the surface of Abeona laid before her. The ground fire was panicked and uncoordinated. There were no enemy aircraft. She felt a surge of excitement, fueled by aggression. She was actually doing it—she was actually invading the Centauri homeworld. No Terran soldier had ever done something this bold. Not even her father.

Through her clenched jaw, she grinned. Now those motherfuckers were going to learn what the Astral Force could really do.

She keyed her mike, unable to contain her excitement.

"All units, Sierra-Five. Low drop corridor, on final approach: when we land you smash anything that moves. Clear that landing zone!"

The single strike fighter off her port bow loosed a hypersonic missile and banked away. The drop ships dipped and hugged the ground. A low rise on the horizon was lit up by irregular flashes of fire—the landing zone was this side of the rise.

One of the pilots shouted back to her.

"Twenty seconds, Lieutenant!"

The landing zone was a major industrial park just outside Abeona's second city. A valuable target in its own right, it was expected to be lightly defended with lots of open space for drop ships to put down. The low rise to the north provided cover for the regiment to mass before attacking the main objective. The city itself.

Enemy fire was concentrated on the top of the rise. Tracers whipped past the ship as it jinked left and right. Orange blasts struck down from *King Alfred* overhead. Katja was pushed against her straps as the ship decelerated and slammed down for landing.

Quickly she unstrapped, rifle in hand, and stepped aft into the main cabin. The ramp dropped and instantly her troopers were spilling out, firing into the blackness as they went. She reached the edge of the ramp and crouched, rifle raised, to assess.

The air was filled with the thunder of the drop ship's turrets, firing blindly at the distant buildings of the industrial complex. Her troopers hustled outward in an arc, forming their part of the protective ring. There were no flashes of enemy fire. The air was warm and fresh, with a hint of something like honeysuckle.

She jogged down the ramp, felt her boots touch Centauri soil.

"Sierra-Five clear," she reported to the pilots. Immediately the ramp behind her began to rise, and the drop ship lifted off with a roar. All around, other drop ships were already beginning to climb into the sky, turrets blazing.

Distant flashes from the ridge indicated Centauri defenses. Orange meteors rained down at random on the perimeter. A fast, metallic form stomped across her peripheral. She swung her rifle to bear but realized it was one of the Spartans, in towering shock troop armor. The Spartan was joined by four companions and they bounded off into the darkness.

She jogged across the level ground—grass, not pavement—checking her forearm display. Her platoon was just reaching the cover of the nearest buildings, as planned. Their job was to hold the road that led into the industrial park, the main road from the west, until all three waves were safely on the ground.

"*All units, Drop Command,*" a crackly voice said in her headset, "*first wave in the dirt. ETA second wave one-five mikes.*" Katja reached cover under the nearest building—modern, glass, clean lines—and nodded to Chang in the darkness.

"First wave down. Fifteen minutes to wait."

"Fifth Platoon in position," he replied.

She switched to regimental frequency. "Sierra-Zero, Sierra-Five, in position."

"Sierra-Zero, roger." Vici couldn't be more than five hundred meters away, but there was static on the circuit.

Katja did a quick visual survey. She, Chang, and five troopers were hunkered down at the corner of a building. Another squad of five was dug in against the building opposite her, across the street. The last of the drop ships was just lifting off, still firing at the ridgeline to the north. The twenty hover tanks that had come in the first wave were skimming across the ground in pairs to back up the infantry positions.

The sky was dark with broken clouds. Fast-moving lights raced through the pockets of naked stars.

Her forearm display revealed Rao and four more squads guarding the intersection one block west. The remaining four squads were scattered in sniper positions on the second floor of her building and the building opposite. The low, rumbling whirr of two hover tanks moving into position behind her gave added confidence.

There was scattered fire from the ridge, and a few orbital bombardments in response. But they quickly faded into the background as she peered around the corner of the building, activating telescopic night-vision, and surveyed the road before her. The industrial park stretched for four blocks and the road continued into the countryside. There was nothing to see within the limits of her sight.

There was a gentle breeze from the west, cool against her exposed mouth and chin. The road itself was some kind of short, tough vegetation, almost like a golf green. The Centauris had always worked to minimize their ecological footprint, not wanting to repeat the devastation of the Earth.

One of the troopers stood up and looked around the corner over her head. She heard him exhale in frustration.

"Let's go, you bastards," he said.

"Easy, trooper," Chang said. "You'll get your chance."

Faint roars overhead drew everyone's eyes up, but before they could be spotted the unknown craft were already gone.

"Is that the second wave?" the trooper asked.

"No," Katja said, "not yet. Probably our strike fighters."

Static crackled in her headset, the words unintelligible. She checked her watch—about the right time for the second wave to be launching from *Normandy*. Her concern, however, was for the sudden lack of communications with orbit.

"Sierra-Zero, Sierra-Five. Comms fading with Drop Command; assess probable jamming."

"This is Sierra-Zero ... units hold position until ... wave ... assault on ridge ..." Vici's voice was barely readable through the static.

Katja tapped Chang's armored chest.

"We're being jammed—they're coming. I'm moving forward to brief Rao. Hold this position at all costs."

"Yes, ma'am."

"Cover me."

A quick look around the corner, and she slipped out into the road. She paused for a moment, rifle up to her eye line. No threat. She ported the weapon and sprinted along the edge of the building. Her armor plates clacked softly with her rapid steps, her breathing quick and steady.

She reached the end of the building, waving to her troopers on the far side of the intersection. One of them waved back. She peered down the street to the right, then around the corner to her left. Clear. Twenty long strides and she was across, crouching down next to Rao, forced to take a moment to get her breathing under control—too much time in zero-g.

Through gasps she issued her sitrep.

"Comms with Drop Command are jammed, and we're losing local comms as well. Each squad will have to act independently. Your orders are to defend this road and keep the drop zone clear. Hold this ground."

Armor clicked as the troopers shifted in anticipation.

Rao glanced skyward. "How are things in orbit?"

"Not our concern. Let Fleet—" Her words were cut off by an ominous whistling overhead that grew quickly into a roar. The troopers threw themselves flat. Seconds later, the ground shook as a chunk of the road one block north of their position blasted into the air. Another whistling roar, and the road exploded half a block north.

Troopers scrambled away. Katja blocked them.

"Stand your ground! This road is where the enemy is coming from!"

Another artillery shell smashed down, this time into one of the buildings at the intersection. Shrapnel rained down on them as two more explosions rocked the street. Katja stayed on her stomach, shouting at the troopers to hold firm. The barrage increased to a steady pounding, where all she could do was bury her head and hang on.

When the shelling stopped, the intersection was clouded with dust and debris. The artillery strikes had moved east, into the central square of the landing zones. Huge holes were torn out of the grassy street. Katja forced her shaky legs to push up.

"Looks like they shifted targets," someone said. "Giving us a break!"

Katja doubted such a Centauri kindness. The audio in her helmet was overloaded, and she lifted one ear to clear some dirt. As she did, she heard a new noise, one which she knew only too well. She peeped one eye around the corner. And immediately recoiled into a crouch.

The corner of the building above her shattered under the force of the rocket impact, showering the troopers with glass.

"APRs! Set grenades! Fire as one!"

She rolled clear as three troopers took aim through the shattered wall. They fired. Across the intersection, she saw the other squads coordinating their attack. Rockets smashed into them as she watched. Troopers fell and didn't rise. Her squad loosed another volley of grenades. Rockets exploded all around her in response.

She hit the ground hard. Lifting her head, she struggled to rise. Through the holes in the building she saw the flash of a silver hull as the lead APR advanced. She raised her rifle and tried to aim for a weapons pod. Through the wreckage and darkness it was impossible to be precise. She fired two at the center of mass.

The body of the APR exploded backward, limbs spinning off in all directions. Katja stared in shock—her grenades hadn't done that. A second APR just came into view before it was gutted and smashed. Then she heard a familiar, rumbling whirr and saw one of the hover tanks emerge from the eastern end of the intersection.

Its giant rail-gun fired again. She heard another explosion. Rockets struck the armored beast with little effect. It fired again. Crawling forward, Katja peered through the wreckage of her corner and saw three APRs in rapid retreat. The tank sailed over the craters in the road, easily pursuing its quarry.

Lights above caught her eye and she saw the massed drop ships thundering down to deliver the second wave. Artillery pounded the landing zone. A towering column of flame indicated at least one drop ship that wasn't making it back.

Troopers were picking themselves up around her. She looked down the western road again, just barely able to make out the last of the APRs in the distance. The hover tank had advanced another block, firing almost leisurely. She was just taking a deep, calming breath when she saw two dazzling lights erupt in the distant sky down the road. The lights elongated into streaks too fast to follow, striking down on the tank.

It reeled back from the explosive, double impact, turret popping off like a toy. The flaming main body spun slowly before digging into the ground and flipping over.

"Holy shit!" someone said.

Seconds later, a new form emerged from the darkness, flying low over the street. Slim, silver body. Stubby wings with weapons pods. Another pair of blinding streaks launched forth from those pods as it roared overhead. Orange reflections off one of the building windows suggested the death of a second Terran tank.

AAR—an anti-armor robot.

Welcome to the Centauri homeworld.

48

Thomas grabbed his console as the deck shook again. Far below, he could see flames leaping out against the stars where air was escaping from another gash in *Normandy*'s hull. Wiping sweaty palms on his legs he surveyed the battle again.

The third drop wasn't even down and the EF was getting creamed. Surface batteries had popped up in every town and settlement, and with only *Jutland* free to protect the invasion ships, the three behemoths were targets in a shooting gallery. With the third drop now in atmo, *Jutland* had maneuvered beneath her charges to physically shield them from the surface. Even so the pounding was relentless.

Artemis's air wing was fully engaged with planetary sentries, and the carrier itself was faring poorly from the surface fire. The destroyers had managed to dispatch the two attacking Space Guard cutters and were adding their minimal bombardment abilities to the effort of taking out surface batteries.

The three cruisers had all taken position over their respective landing zones, but they were so busy fighting off missile attacks that surface bombardment was less a priority than self-defense. That was bad for the troops on the ground, but no ship could ignore its own protection.

King Alfred, in particular, was getting hammered.

Orbital Platform Three was a scattering cloud of twisted metal shards, thanks to the stealth ship *Asp*. Her sister ship

Sidewinder had made the initial attempt, but the platform's anti-stealth defenses had been unexpectedly effective—*Sidewinder* had ceased to exist in a faint ripple against the stars.

Nor had anyone thought that the huge platforms could move. But even now Thomas could detect the two sister platforms coming over opposite horizons to join the fray. *Asp* had reported tremendous difficulties getting any sort of tracking in this gravimetric landscape, whereas the platforms seemed optimized for the environment.

Thomas stole a glance at the rest of the command team. His AAW counterpart was going nonstop, directing the fighter battle and prioritizing defenses against incoming missiles. The ASW controller was busy making calculations and conversing with other units. The operations officer was giving a charged briefing to Commodore Chandler on the surface and orbital battles. And Thomas...

He stared impotently at his screens. What could he do? Every ship was engaged in close combat. Self-defense would protect them to a degree, but the attacks would eventually wear them down. They couldn't withdraw with three regiments on the ground. The two biggest threats were the inbound orbital platforms, but the entire task force didn't possess enough missiles to destroy those leviathans.

"AVW!" Commander Erikson shouted. "Report your status!"

With a jump he reassessed his threats.

"AVW condition red!" he replied. "We can survive the surface fire and robot sentries, but those orbital platforms will wipe us out." He checked his display. "They'll be in range in fifteen minutes."

The OpsO was red in the face.

"What's your fucking recommendation, Kane?"

Thomas felt his mouth drop open as he scrambled for an answer. Recommendation? Destroy the damn orbital platforms. He didn't know what miracle the OpsO expected him to conjure. Maybe two battleships and a line of cruisers could do it, but not the ragged assets he had at his disposal.

"Torpedoes," Chandler said quietly.

The ASW controller shook his head. "Sir, the stealths can't get close enough. We've already lost *Sidewinder*, and *Asp* is pulling back."

"Then use the Hawks." Chandler stared at the display as he spoke. "Every last one of them."

"The Hawk torpedoes aren't designed for brane attacks. They aren't strong enough to force a gravimetric collapse on something that big."

Chandler glared at him, but the ASW controller stood his ground. The larger torpedoes carried by stealths might have a chance, but Hawk torpedoes against such a large target was like throwing stones at a castle wall.

"Then where are your stealth ships?" Chandler said dangerously.

"*Asp* is withdrawing due to damage. The other two are unlocated."

Thomas guessed that they'd already been destroyed in their attempts to attack the other orbital platforms. But both Chandler and Erikson seemed to have forgotten he was there. He forced himself to speak, before he was dismissed from his own warfare responsibility.

"Ninety Hawks with four torpedoes each—I'll make it happen, sir." *Normandy* shook again. Thomas keyed his mike and began issuing orders.

Then, off in the distance over the dark Abeona landscape, the cruiser *King Alfred* exploded.

49

Katja tucked her head down into her chest and kept running, staggering as the shells struck close behind her. She dimly saw movement ahead of her as troopers sprinted across the open ground for cover.

Bullets whistled past her ears. The darkness ahead coalesced into the tall, spiny forms of trees. An airburst smashed one of the higher trunks. The glowing embers provided a glimmer of illumination as she reached the tree line.

"Saracens clear!" she bellowed.

Thunderous fire erupted all around her as from the cover of the forest the combined platoons of the Saracens opened fire on their pursuers. She slid to the ground, rolling onto her stomach to fire from a prone position. A kilometer's full sprint over broken ground under fire and she still had energy to move—that combat cocktail was magic. Through the flashes of artillery still pounding down, she caught glimpses of the line of APRs advancing across the field.

Those robot bastards were smart, she admitted. The smaller APRs were no match for Terran tanks, and they had disappeared from the battle after the initial assault. The flying AARs had made several devastating sweeps of the landing zone, but the Hoplites and their anti-aircraft battery had managed to hold them off as the second wave deployed. Enemy artillery had made massing of the armor impossible in the landing zone, and the commander of the armored troop Desert Rats had ordered his fifty tanks to begin their push for the city.

Then all hell broke loose.

Without the cover of the Hoplites' anti-aircraft, the Desert Rats were swarmed by AARs on the open road. Without the protection of an armored troop, the infantry guarding the landing zone were attacked by APRs. The third drop descended into a hornet's nest of fire. Katja had no idea how many drop ships had actually delivered their cargo, but the tanks rolled right off their ships and started firing at APRs that had breached the landing zone.

Those tanks forced the APRs to withdraw again, giving the infantry enough time to load their casualties onto the drop ships before abandoning the landing zone. Katja had lost nine—two dead, seven too wounded to continue.

The final wave of armor, the Royal Hussars, rolled out along the road at speed to catch up with the Desert Rats. The infantry ran alongside them as far as possible, then broke across the open fields for the cover of the forest that stretched up the ridge. As soon as the armor rolled out of sight, the APRs attacked again. With no option but to keep running for cover, the infantry were cut down. A pair of strike fighters had made a strafing run to slow the APRs down, but their priority was to protect the tanks, and no further help came.

Where was the damn orbital bombardment? Katja pulled herself up into a crouch and activated her telescopic night-vision. The line of APRs was still advancing, easily a hundred of them. They were holding fire for the moment, letting the artillery bash the Terrans. Artillery was a blunt weapon that caused more fear than damage, but Katja knew her troopers were easy pickings once the APRs closed to engagement range.

The Terran fire was uncoordinated. Bullets exploded to little effect against the APR armor and any grenades fired were falling short.

Her forearm display vibrated with a message. Voice comms were still garbled, but the agile-frequency encryptions of the tactical displays were functioning. She read the quick orders from Vici, and tapped the helmets of the nearest troopers.

"Cease fire!" she shouted over the din. "Cease fire!"

The verbal orders passed quickly down the line and the flashes of rifle fire died out. In the eerie silence Katja examined her forearm display and scrambled through the brush to place herself at the center of her platoon's line. She heard distant voices of other platoon commanders shouting, and bellowed out Vici's orders to her own troops.

"Hold fire until the enemy is within grenade range! We will fire in salvo, one shot each. These are our targets!" She designated four APRs near the center of the line.

Artillery whistled in, impacting somewhere down the line. She crouched down instinctively.

"Stay down!" she shouted. "Hold fire until my command!"

Another airburst blasted through the trees. She tucked her head down as broken branches banged off her helmet and back. Out in the open field, a long line of flashes indicated a coordinated rocket launch by the APRs. She threw herself down. The rockets slammed into the tree line.

Somebody nearby cried out in pain.

"Medic!"

"They've got range on us!"

Another line of flashes lit up the darkness. Another volley of rockets struck down. Katja felt the air blast of the nearest impact. She checked range on her tactical display. The APRs had stopped, just out of grenade range. Her peripheral caught the flash of another rocket launch.

She snarled. *Clever bastards.* As the third attack rained down, she realized what they had to do. Dirt from the blasts was still falling as she climbed to her feet.

"Fifth Platoon! Advance twenty meters! Move!"

She staggered forward past her troopers, rifle raised, as they rose around her. She broke into a run and burst out into the open. In fifteen strides she got within grenade range and slid into a crouch. Her troopers dove for the ground all around her.

She designated the first target, even as the flash of enemy rocket launches lit the darkness.

"Hostile five-five! Fire!"

Forty-three grenades launched. Rockets flashed past overhead and hit the tree line behind. One APR on the line—desig hostile five-five—exploded under the sudden, multiple impacts. Not every grenade hit, but enough did to obliterate the machine. Pieces flew backward from the sudden crater that appeared in the ground.

"Hostile five-six! Fire!"

Another volley of grenades sailed through the air. Another APR was destroyed. With a roar, the massed infantry burst forth from the trees and advanced to Katja's firing line.

"Hostile five-seven! Fire!"

Enemy rockets were inbound, but hit harmlessly behind them. Hundreds of grenades filled the air as the Terrans invented their own, local form of artillery. The line of APRs was decimated in a spectacular series of explosions. Some tried to withdraw, but the coordinated might of the Levantine infantry was too quick, too deadly.

Cheers sounded across the battlefield. They were answered by artillery smashing down.

"Get to the trees!" Katja bellowed.

As the troopers withdrew under cover, Katja received another order from Vici via tactical display. She read it quickly then glanced around at her platoon.

"Rao! Chang! On me." Both sergeants detached themselves from the shadows and hustled over. Artillery hit the trees to the east, too far away to make her flinch. She forwarded tactical details to their displays even as she spoke.

"New orders. Get the casualties to this position for drop ship pickup. Then we take this hill and hold it to cover the armored advance."

The sergeants acknowledged and immediately issued orders to the troops. Stretchers were extended and casualties loaded, even as medics did field dressings. Katja checked her ammo and inspected her armor for any weaknesses.

An airburst exploded above her. She hit dirt hard and hung on as the ground spun through three-sixty degrees. Her hearing was overwhelmed by a single, deafening note, like jamming on a radio. Her vision faded.

Then she shook it off, feeling unusual clarity as she pulled herself to her feet. The sound in her ears faded to a ringing, her vision returned. She felt strong, invigorated. She bared her teeth in a smile. Damn, those drugs worked.

She and the platoon moved quickly through the trees, heading for the RV point. She saw through the branches the fast-moving fires of drop ship exhausts. Four ships were setting down, turrets blazing at the horizon, as she ran out into the open. Two already had their ramps down. Medics waited to load casualties. Her sergeants coordinated the delivery of the wounded—five, including Sakiyama.

Other platoons arrived. She immediately saw the tall figure of Scott Lahko, limping slightly but loudly directing his troops. Her forearm vibrated again. Vici was approaching and wanted her and Lahko. Katja stepped toward the tree line as Lahko issued his last orders and broke away.

Vici emerged from the trees like a wraith. She was walking unnaturally and one arm hung limply at her side. It was clear the drugs were the only thing holding her up. Her eyes were hidden behind her visor, but Katja didn't doubt their intensity.

"Lahko, Gopal's dead. You're first lieutenant now." Her teeth were red with blood as she spoke, but her voice was firm. "That artillery is killing us. I've already sent the Spartans to take down the guns, but they're spread out and it's a lot of ground to cover. We can't wait. Your platoons will take out the Centauri spotters, who we believe are in this village." She indicated it on her display. It was a residential settlement at the top of the ridge. "We blind them, they can't hit us."

She glanced at the drop ships.

"You'll be lifted up the hill, ahead of our advance but behind the tanks. I'll get a couple of Desert Rats to back you up. Take out the spotters and rejoin us on the ridge top."

"What about orbital bombardment?" Lahko asked.

"*King Alfred* was destroyed. We have no cover. I'm trying to get *Jutland* to support us, but she's busy getting tarred up there."

Visions of the Battle of Laika suddenly flooded Katja's mind. She knew well enough what orbital combat was like. Thomas's face flashed before her, and she regretted her earlier scorn for Fleet.

But there was no time to think about the battle in space. There was enough to worry about here on the ground.

50

Jack hoped success on the surface would balance the chaos up here. The captain would know what was happening there, but as a subbie he was just expected to keep his head down and mouth shut.

He locked the second glove of his spacesuit and secured his helmet, faceplate up. The hangar warning lights were flashing as the Hawk moved in from the airlock, but he knew things were about to happen fast. The bird *looked* in one piece, but he immediately noticed the ugly blast marks where anti-missile decoys had fired.

The deck lurched suddenly, causing him to stumble. The captain had reactivated artificial gravity soon after the battle began, but not before there had been several casualties from the wild maneuverings that were too much for the inertial dampeners. Only full AG was capable of keeping everybody more or less on their feet and able to fight.

The inner airlock closed and ground crew moved swiftly to refuel and rearm the Hawk even as it rotated in position. The cargo door opened, and Jack climbed up inside. Right behind him the crew piled into the main compartment and began unbolting the seats and consoles. This Hawk was needed to haul cargo.

"It's like being a fighter pilot again." Stripes lifted himself out of the seat and raised his faceplate. Sweat shone on his brow, but he smiled slightly.

Jack smiled back. "I hear we got it."

Stripes took a deep breath. "Scratch one Centauri orbital platform." He exhaled and added, "And about seventy Hawks."

"Holy shit."

Stripes moved aside and gently pushed him into the seat. Jack automatically strapped himself in and glanced over the controls.

"Seventy Hawks?" He could hardly believe it.

"About that," Stripes said, the smile gone. "Platform defenses got half of us before we could even get into range, and then tagged a few more as we fired and turned away."

Jack couldn't even form the images in his mind. How could so many Hawks be wiped out so quickly? He felt a gloved hand press down on the shoulder of his suit.

"Hey, Jack. Stay focused. I need you to do this for me. Get to *Protector*, bring back those torpedoes. It's just a simple ferry run."

Stripes was calm, his voice giving no hint of the battle raging just outside *Kristiansand*'s hull. Jack glanced up, and forced himself to match that calm. He focused on his controls.

Just a simple ferry run.

"I'm ready."

"Remember, if you get shot at, hit these buttons to release chaff and flares." Stripes leaned in to point at several rarely used controls. "It's not automatic, like in a fighter—you have to do it yourself. Any threat, start jinking in any direction. And get back under *Kristiansand*'s self-defense umbrella as fast as you can."

"Okay."

Stripes slapped his shoulder again. "Piece o' cake, Jack. You'll be back before you know it." Then he turned and headed for the cargo door.

Jack checked his controls and saw that all external links were already disconnected. He closed the cargo doors and glanced out at his crew chief. A thumbs-up cleared him to launch. The hangar alarms flashed anew, and the inner airlock door opened before him.

As the Hawk rolled forward, Jack glanced at the controls for chaff and flares. He'd always wanted to be a fighter pilot, always thought it would be fun. As the airlock depressurized and he tightened his grip on the Hawk's controls, however, he sensed a distinct lack of fun in his situation.

The outer doors opened and he thrusted forward, clearing *Kristiansand*'s hull. He opened his throttles and banked hard to starboard, nosing up to point at the distant cluster of Terran supply ships. The glittering surface of Abeona filled the sky beneath him, but Jack wasted no time sightseeing.

Continuous, random flashes low off his bow indicated the wild dogfight still playing out between Centauri sentries and Terran star fighters. Even as he watched, a star fighter banked hard to pick up a sentry that was breaking away to point at the EF ships. Twin cannon blazed fiery trails at the jinking sentry, catching its body and sending it tumbling out of control.

To port he saw the bombardment batteries of *Jutland* pounding away at surface targets, and smaller, faster bolts of anti-attack guns shooting down incoming enemy missiles. The battleship herself looked like a Yuletide log, orange and red patches burning angrily across her charcoal surface. The three invasion ships loomed high above *Jutland*, their own point-defense guns fending off whatever attacks got through the battleship's shield.

Far beyond, the buckled remains of Orbital Platform One twisted in the sky—the Goliath brought down by ninety Davids and their four torpedoes each. Jack searched for any straggling, injured Hawks. Then he tore his eyes away and pushed the throttles fully open, focusing on his mission.

The three supply ships were in the highest orbit of all, trying to keep clear of the Centauri defenses. *Protector* was the middle of the three and Jack quickly made contact with her landing controller. The big ship held a steady course and speed for his approach, and he lined up the wide hangar door without much trouble. He throttled back the main engines and tapped at his thruster control to glide in. At three hundred meters he put his engines to standby and thrusted back to kill the last of his momentum.

Protector's magnetic clamps grabbed the Hawk and pulled him inside. The supply ship's hangar was huge, and surprisingly empty. As he was taxied in Jack counted the Hawks being serviced, knowing that there should be fifteen on this ship.

He saw three. And one of them had clearly taken heavy damage to its port side. There were racks of torpedoes standing by, and ground crew to load them.

He opened the cargo door while he was still turning in place. As soon as the door hit deck the first of the torpedo racks was wheeled up and locked down in his main compartment. At max carrying capacity a Hawk could haul ten racks of four torpedoes each, and *Protector*'s ground crew crammed in every last rack they could.

The Hawk-torpedo attack against the orbital platform had succeeded, but at such a high cost in casualties that there weren't enough Hawks to make a full attack against Orbital Platform Two, which was even now moving into range. The next attack would employ the few remaining Hawks and all five destroyers. The destroyers had the ability to reload torpedoes, and thus could keep firing even after the Hawks had withdrawn. Hopefully enough weapons would get through before the destroyers themselves were blown to pieces by the orbital platform's huge weapons.

Kristiansand was low on ammo, and Jack was to bring back a full load. Every torpedo counted. If this attack failed, the Expeditionary Force would be fish in a barrel.

Someone shouted from aft that his cargo was loaded. Jack closed the Hawk's door and taxied toward the waiting airlock. His controls jumped as *Protector*'s deck shuddered. The airlock sealed around him and he waited for depressurization in the near darkness.

Everything shook again.

Protector's landing controller shouted over the radio.

"*Viking-Two—emergency evac!*"

Jack hung on as the outer airlock doors flew open and the escaping air hurtled him free into space. He thrusted quickly to regain control and threw open his throttles again. Shimmering blasts of energy flashed by him and struck the supply ship. He cast a terrified glance to port and saw the massive shape of Orbital Platform Two looming near. Energy weapons fired from dozens of batteries up and down its hull, the beams cutting into *Protector* even as Jack sailed free.

He felt a moment of rage, and flicked the safeties of his hull-mounted torpedoes and targeted the platform. On an impulse, he set the implosion level to sixteen peets—the maximum they were rated to—and selected Weapon One. With a bang it launched free and disappeared into the Bulk. It was absurd, he knew, but at least he felt better, like he'd kicked the bully in the shin before running away.

Then he pulled hard to starboard and accelerated to full speed. *Kristiansand* was far below, her dark shape clear against the brilliant planet.

From the visual he scanned his flight controls and hunt controls. His 3-D display was crowded with contacts, and the gravimetric landscape was unreadable. He raised his eyes and flew visual.

He saw them coming fast from the port side, but barely had time even to look before the Centauri sentries opened fire. Rounds flashed past his cockpit. He yanked the stick to starboard. Twin bangs jarred his port side. The Hawk jerked violently, then spun end over end. Jack grunted against the g-forces and fought for control.

The view outside spun madly between Abeona's bright surface and the blackness of space. He pulled back on the stick but could only slow his tumble. He scanned his controls. Aft lower thrusters were blasting at full. He struggled to reach the controls to shut them down.

No response.

New warning lights flashed. The display indicated incoming missiles. Somebody screamed. Then he lunged out to hit the chaff and flare buttons. He heard the rapid *bang-bang-bang* as the decoys fired, and jinked to port.

Nothing hit him, but the Hawk was tumbling in multiple axes. The aft lower thrusters continued to fire on full. He cut power to all maneuvering controls. The thrusters died. He pulled back on his stick and used the main engine power to flatten out his spin.

Within moments he had control again.

Quick check of visual, flight controls, hunt controls. Abeona loomed before him. Fighters and sentries off to port. 3-D revealed *Kristiansand* on his starboard quarter. He yanked back on the stick and turned for home.

Kristiansand was banking hard, firing chaff and flares to avoid the attacking sentries. Several impacts bled smoke and precious air into space. Her self-defense guns fired wildly, filling the sky with rounds. Two sentries exploded as they flew into the virtual wall of bullets. The destroyer came around in another tight turn.

Jack looked up to starboard. Orbital Platform Two seemed farther away now, but a quick survey revealed all the EF ships fleeing east at full speed, trying to stay just out of range of its energy weapons. Farther east, he saw the invasion ships also turning to run, although *Jutland* stood her ground. Even from this distance he could see the damage to the battleship—there was no way it could withstand a toe-to-toe with the orbital platform.

Jack put his eyes back on *Kristiansand*. She needed his torpedoes.

"Longboat, Viking-Two. I am inbound at full speed. Request fully automatic recovery."

"Viking-Two—no-can. Auto-recovery down. Manual approach, port side only."

"Longboat, I have no maneuvering controls. Request emergency recovery."

"Viking-Two, roger. Manual approach."

Son of a bitch. They wanted him to fly his bird right into the hangar. The destroyer was still banking and rolling to avoid sentry fire. He needed her to steady up on a single course for him to vector.

"Roger. Report course and speed for recovery."

A new, female voice came onto the circuit. *"This is Longboat Actual. I'm under attack and I can't steady up for you. But I need those torpedoes, or the whole fleet is going down. Jack, I need you to land your bird and protect your cargo. Over."*

The destroyer was growing larger in his vision, pulling up so hard that he had to yank back his stick to keep her in sight. Commander Avernell was fighting her ship, and she was waiting for him to give her the means to die trying to destroy the orbital platform.

If she wasn't afraid, what gave him the right to be? He located the opening hangar door on *Kristiansand*'s port quarter.

"This is Viking-Two—roger. Inbound for landing. Out."

Alarms flashed on his console. He punched the chaff and flare buttons and jinked hard to starboard. His view shifted to reveal the orbital platform, missiles launching forth. He jinked back to port and released another set of decoys. *Kristiansand* filled his view again. She was rolling, and he lost sight of the hangar door. He touched left to intercept her, hoping for a favorable roll back.

She turned hard to port—his up—and he pulled back on both stick and throttles, cursing. She turned toward him. He banked to starboard and then swung back to port. His flight controls flashed with collision alarms. He saw her bow drawing left, and ignored his controls. This was flying by eye. His nose pointed at her midships as she passed five hundred meters in front of him. He accelerated and swung to port.

The hangar door was visible again—four hundred meters.

Kristiansand banked to starboard. Fouling his approach.

"Shit!" He keyed the circuit. "Longboat, Viking-Two. I need you to hold steady for five seconds. Tell me when you can, and I'll be ready."

"Longboat roger!"

He accelerated and rose up above the destroyer, sighting the hangar door again. She banked slightly to port and fired her self-defense cannons. Something exploded off to Jack's right. He kept his eyes on the door and pressed closer. Three hundred meters. She dove but he followed easily, back in station within seconds.

Two hundred meters.

"Viking-Two! Five seconds! Go!"

He pushed the throttles forward and eased to starboard, turning his nose to port and coming in at an angle. The hangar door loomed on his starboard bow, then his beam. He yanked the stick fully starboard and killed his engines. His view was swallowed by the inside of the airlock.

AG grabbed the Hawk and slammed it down sideways on the deck. The awful screech of metal against metal tore at his ears. He jolted in his seat as his nose hit something hard. Then everything was still. And black.

He blinked as the inner airlock doors opened—up and down, not left to right, he noticed curiously—and light from the hangar flooded in. He felt a strong, continuous pull to the right as the Hawk moved into the open space and he wondered if the ship was doing a long, steady turn. Then, as he saw all the people standing sideways in the hangar, he realized that the Hawk was resting on its starboard side.

Still firmly strapped in his seat, he hadn't moved.

"Sit tight, Jack," a voice said over the circuit, *"we're using the crane to right you."*

He heard several thuds against his hull, then gasped as the Hawk was yanked up and tipped back down on its landing gear. He heard the cargo door open, heard the clatter of boots and equipment as ground crew began to offload the torpedoes.

He sat and stared at his lap for a moment. Then laughed.

51

It was the shortest ride she'd ever had in a drop ship—two minutes up the road. It might have been absurd, except that it had saved her platoon an hour of walking uphill. Tactical repositioning at its best.

Her troopers spilled down the ramp as before, immediately forming a defensive ring around the ship under cover of the turrets. The black sky was clearing, and the landscape was bathed in a dim, red glow as Centauria B rose over the horizon. Katja descended quickly, noting a second drop ship just touching down thirty meters away. It disgorged Scott Lahko's Second Platoon. Her forearm display indicated two friendlies approaching from the east, and she spotted the dark pair of hover tanks just as she heard their familiar, deep whirr.

She rounded the drop ship and scanned the tactical situation. They were on the ridge top, several hundred meters higher than the city that spread out to the north. The water of the round bay reflected the dull red of the rising star, and while there were few lights visible in the city itself, she could just make out the straight boulevards stretching away from the water like spokes, and the broad ring roads connecting them.

A cool, moist wind picked up, and she thought she detected a hint of the sea. On another day she might have thought the view was pretty, but today all she saw were the flashes of combat perhaps a kilometer from her position—probably the Spartan shock troopers taking out one of the artillery positions.

A kilometer or so to her right, she knew, the armored troops were massing on the ridge to commence their attack. And half a kilometer to the left was her target—a collection of large houses and local shops that currently housed the Centauri artillery spotters. The buildings clustered around a single crossroad, spreading about two hundred meters in every direction.

Lahko appeared at her side, his eyes intent on the village.

"Hey, Big K," he said. "What's your strength?"

"Thirty-eight troopers, fully loaded." Her wounded troopers had willingly surrendered their ammunition before being evacuated, giving the survivors all the grenades and magazines they could carry.

"I'm at forty. And we have orbital bombardment standing by."

"Finally."

"All right. We're gonna do this hard and fast. Take your platoon up the right flank. I'll go up the middle with the tanks. Stay low and quiet—let us draw their fire. You pinpoint their location and call *Jutland* for bombardment."

"Roger." She manipulated her forearm display to bring up the Fleet Support circuit. A quick typed message to *Jutland* and an immediate reply from orbit confirmed her connection.

She gathered her platoon and quickly laid out the plan. As she did, a series of massive, orange bolts flashed by overhead, striking down into the Centauri city. She couldn't help but pause for a moment to watch, never having imagined she would think orbital bombardment to be so beautiful. The Fleet was coming through at last.

It was jarring, however, to see the angle of the bolts. Bombardment was always done by a ship directly overhead, and the shots came down nearly vertical. These bolts were streaking through the sky at a forty-five degree angle. She imagined again the violence of the orbital battle. The Fleet had to be getting pummeled, if they were forced to provide support from half a globe away.

Whatever, she decided, pushing the thought away. *Support is support.* She motioned her platoon forward.

They climbed down off the road and made their way carefully

through a field of half-grown grain. Above and to her left, she heard the tanks rev up and move forward. Her platoon advanced several hundred meters in silence, the distant light from Centauria B revealing more features of the village ahead. The houses were very large, with mostly glass sides, probably designed to show off the superb view from this high point over the city.

She activated her infrared, but couldn't see any warm bodies. Yet.

The tanks opened fire without warning. Heavy rounds smashed clear through the first row of houses and exploded in the second. Glass and plastics showered through the street. Lahko's platoon fired blindly with their rifles as they charged forward, tiny explosions riddling the smashed buildings ahead of them.

Katja gave her troops a hand signal, and broke into a run. Staying low and in the fields, she passed the first line of destruction and began surveying the houses deeper in the village. Her first scans on infrared and quantum-flux revealed nothing. She advanced further, rising up out of the field and between the buildings straddling the village's crossroad. Moving cautiously up the side of a low brick building, she tried to listen for enemy movement over the racket of Second Platoon's advance.

Suddenly there was the sound of rockets launching, causing her to duck instinctively. Peeking out into the street, she just saw a pair of APRs exploding backward as the tanks opened fire. She stayed low and surveyed the surrounding buildings. If there were defenders, her target had to be near.

The awful sound of artillery whistled in. She saw explosions in the main street where the Second Platoon was advancing. She ran across the side road and tucked behind another low building—a boutique shop. A flash of silver between the houses forced her to duck and freeze. More APRs were advancing into battle, rockets firing en masse at the Terran attackers.

Katja stayed behind the houses, running through well-groomed back yards as she scanned in infrared and quantum-flux. She paused to check her forearm display, then continued forward. Bullets whistled past her head. She swung her rifle up and unleashed a fully automatic sweep, then dove to the ground and leopard-crawled forward, listening as her troopers returned fire. A quick glance revealed Centauri soldiers—actual human soldiers—running up the hill.

"Targets north! Hostile infantry!"

She reached the end of the houses, finding no sign of the artillery spotters. Amidst the peppering fire of the Centauri rifles, some sort of heavier weapon fired from below, tearing up dirt at her feet.

"Hold this ground," she barked. "Hold this ground!"

Her troopers hunkered down as best they could and returned fire. She ran between the houses and crouched down in the shadows.

The main street was littered with debris as the Centauris and Terrans exchanged heavy fire. She looked down toward the crossroads and saw one of the hover tanks on its side in the middle of the street, smoke billowing from its battered form. The other couldn't be seen.

Some APRs were still up and fighting, advancing slowly on Lahko's troops. Her instinct was to burst out into the street and join the fight, draw some fire to help Second Platoon. But she knew enough about Centauris to guess that they still had more tricks up their sleeves. She couldn't reveal her position until she'd found the artillery spotter.

But that didn't mean that she couldn't help.

She locked onto the slow-moving APR line and sent quick commands through her forearm display to *Jutland*. It was time to bring in the big guns. She confirmed that Lahko's troops were clear of the blast zone, and sent the order.

Seconds later, orange bolts screamed down from heaven. The first obliterated one of the bigger shops at the crossroad. The second smashed into the APRs. Molten metal sprayed across a street-wide crater.

Katja stared in shock for a moment, remembering the orbital bombardment *Kristiansand* had provided in Free Lhasa. It hadn't seemed like that much destruction. She quickly checked her safety ranges to see if battleship batteries had a different radius than a mere destroyer's. But her display offered no info.

Artillery rained down on Second Platoon again, wrenching

Katja's mind back to her task. The spotters were still active, and were protecting their own position now. She needed to take them out. There was so much heat in the street that infrared wasn't effective, so she tried quantum-flux against the line of houses across from her.

Nothing.

In fact, from one house in particular there was *absolutely* nothing. No reading at all. She gasped slightly. Quantum jamming, just like at Thapa's farm. It was the second house from the end, almost directly across the street from her.

She activated her telescopic night-vision and scanned the windows. Sure enough, she caught a glimmer of movement. She punched in the coordinates of the house and sent the order to *Jutland*, even as another salvo of Centauri artillery smashed down on the crossroad.

She watched the quantum-shielded house, feeling awfully exposed even though her display showed her safely outside the blast zone. Just as she spotted the incoming orange flashes from the sky, she wondered if the safety range was affected by the angle of fire.

A blinding flash overwhelmed her vision. She instinctively threw up her arms as a sledgehammer of solid air hit her like a concrete wall. She was dimly aware of floating, and of crashing down onto the ground.

The blinding lights didn't fade, and as she took stock of the warning signals her body was screaming at her she struggled to keep her eyes open. She heard voices, and before she could pull herself up she felt a hand on her arm.

"Easy, Lieutenant."

"Status!" she barked.

"You're fine—just take it easy."

She forced her eyes open, despite the white haze, and dimly focused on the trooper looming before her. She didn't recognize him—perhaps he was one of the medics. He looked back with earnest brown eyes, and it took a moment for Katja to realize, over the continuous thunder of the battle, that she shouldn't be able to see his eyes at all.

"Goddammit, trooper! Put your fucking helmet on!"

His expression didn't flinch, but there was a real edge of fear in his voice.

"Lieutenant, listen to me," he said. "The battle's over. You're safe."

She struggled to rise, but every muscle protested. "No one's safe! Get your head in the game."

He pressed her firmly back down. She struggled against him, trying to look at her forearm display. It was blank.

Things weren't good.

"Help me up, trooper," she insisted. "We have to get tactical comms!" He kept looking at her, but addressed someone else. "I've got a battle-head here! Sedation, now."

The lights were still blinding, but Katja sensed sudden, rapid movement to her left. It was a trap. She slammed her forearm into the man above her, feeling his lungs collapse with the force of her blow. She pushed herself up, but dizziness overcame her and she lost her footing. Two large Centauri soldiers charged down on her. She swung her fists randomly, but hit nothing but air. Suddenly she was pinned, the combined weight of the Centauris bleeding away her strength.

A sharp pain cut into her thigh.

Moments later she felt reality slip away.

When she woke, it was nighttime and she was alone. She lay motionless for a long moment, listening. Shuffling movement indicated people nearby, or possibly the wind through some prefab. She forced herself to relax, breathe deeply, and assess her wounds.

Nothing burned, and she wiggled her fingers and toes to confirm that she was still in one piece. Looking side to side, she saw nothing but shadows and blurry lights.

She tried to pull herself up, but her arms wouldn't respond. She tried again, and realized that her wrists were restrained by some kind of gel ring. Just as she began to try and squeeze her hands through the orange, donut-sized rings, the curtain around her—that's what it was, she suddenly realized—swished aside to admit a woman in medical fatigues.

"Lieutenant Emmes," she said with a slightly apprehensive smile, "how are you feeling?"

"Fine," Katja responded. "Caged."

The medic quickly examined a status board at the foot of her bed—she was on a bed—and nodded. "I'm Master Rating Shin. You're aboard the invasion ship *Normandy*, and it's four days since the battle on Abeona." She looked at Katja strangely. "Do you believe me?"

The question puzzled Katja. "Yes. Why?"

"The last time you were awake, you thought you were still in the battle, and you took a good swipe at one of the other medics."

"Oh."

Shin shrugged. "It happens—common side effect of your combat cocktail. Makes you a good fighter when things go bad, but makes it difficult for you to adjust your reality."

"Is he okay?"

"Wind knocked out of him—he's fine now." Shin touched one of the restraining rings. "Your chemistry is back to normal, so I'm going to trust you enough to take these off. But be aware that *Normandy* doesn't trust you right now, and if you make any sudden moves, you'll be subdued. Nothing personal—it's standard procedure for troopers after battle."

Katja nodded slightly. "I understand." She'd heard of troopers going crazy days after returning from the surface as the combat cocktail worked its way through their system.

Shin removed the rings with practiced ease and stepped back, never taking her eyes off Katja.

"Can I get you anything, Lieutenant?"

"A report from the battle. I was commanding the Saracens' Fifth Platoon."

Shin laughed.

"Is there a problem, Master Rating?"

She shook her head. "Troopers usually ask for food. Officers ask for reports. You guys crack me up every time."

Normally that kind of insubordination would infuriate her, but she just couldn't muster the energy. In fact, she could feel the tension draining away as she truly began to understand where she was. She was safe. She was a veteran of Terra's invasion of Centauria's homeworld. She'd fucking done it and she was still alive.

She had nothing left to prove.

"Indulge me," Katja said. "If any of my troopers are still alive, please ask the most senior one to report to me. And send word to Commander Vici that I'm awake."

"Yes, ma'am."

Shin turned to go. A sudden impulse caused Katja to call after her.

"And Master Rating, please tell Lieutenant Commander Kane of *Rapier* that I'm alive, and would appreciate a visit."

52

Breeze had plucked her first gray hair that morning. Hardly surprising, considering she'd barely slept for days, and had spent most of that time fearing for her life. But it only worsened her mood as she pushed her way along the wide passageway.

She was getting very used to this particular route—from the Intelligence cell to the commodore's cabin—but lately she didn't get the feeling that her hard work was paying off. It was tough to cast herself as the command staff's up-and-coming junior officer when that role was already filled.

Ever since her disastrous attempt to have Thomas talk Chandler out of going into battle, it seemed as if young Mr. Kane could do no wrong in the eyes of his mentor. She still lost sleep over how badly she'd misread that situation.

Nevertheless, she reminded herself as she buzzed at Chandler's door, the past was the past. All she could do now was watch for a new opportunity. But as she saw Chandler's expression, eyes fixed on a slow-motion recording, she knew today wouldn't be the day.

The commodore was still brooding.

"Good morning, sir," she said with a tempered mix of gravity and cheer. "I have the latest intelligence report on the Centauri reaction to the battle."

He glanced at her briefly before turning his eyes back to the 3-D display. He motioned her closer. She studied it, but couldn't make out which point in the combat over Abeona he was studying. The sphere was a mess of red and blue symbols, yet it seemed to mean something to him.

"Shall I just leave it, sir?" she said after what seemed an eternity.

His eyes narrowed, and at that moment one of the blue symbols flashed and disappeared. He froze the recording and looked over at her.

"Give me your summary, Breeze."

For a moment she thought he meant a summary of the readout, then noticed he was looking at her report.

"Terror and panic on every world, sir," she replied. "Local militias are scrambling to build and man surface defenses. Protest groups are marching in the streets. Pundits are questioning the wisdom of sending so many of Centauria's ships out-system, and leaving the planets so exposed. The government is stating again that the attack was repelled, and that the situation is under control, but parliament is a zoo. I expect either the government to fall, or martial law to be declared, probably within the next seventy-two hours. In short, sir, mission accomplished."

Breeze knew better than to smile, but she saw the effect of her words on Chandler. Perhaps there was an opportunity here after all.

His frown morphed into a more thoughtful expression as he nodded. He looked quickly at her report before casting it aside and returning his attention to the frozen recording.

"Thanks, Breeze. It's good to hear that maybe all this was worth it, after all."

The two days of warfare over Abeona had exhausted everyone. When she managed to sleep now, Breeze had nightmares of those first terrifying hours when *Normandy* had been under constant attack. Once the orbital platforms had been destroyed and the EF focused its full power against the surface batteries, the pressure had eased, but Abeona had seemed to have an unlimited supply of missiles and robotic sentries to hurl at them in waves.

Throughout the battle, Chandler had ably filled the role of the confident commander, speaking only when required and wasting no words. Even when losses began to climb, he'd maintained his stern, calm façade.

Then, in the forty-second hour of the invasion, with all three regiments embroiled in vicious battles among the new ruins of Abeona's three largest cities, the Centauris had mounted one final, devastating counteroffensive. The attack had destroyed three ships, including the invasion ship *Quebec*.

Normandy herself had been badly damaged, and there had been a few moments when Breeze had begun looking for the nearest escape pod.

Apparently unfazed by the destruction around him, Chandler had ordered a full withdrawal. Within an hour the regiments had been retrieved and the EF had fled into deep space. As they went, they smashed any last tracking systems on Abeona. As soon as *Normandy* had secured from battle stations, he'd retired to his cabin, and she'd hardly seen him since.

He'd met with the operations officer, she knew, and Colonel Korolev. But otherwise no one had been able to get near to him. And from the bloodshot look in his eyes, she guessed that he'd spent the last twenty-four hours in front of the 3-D display.

"Sir," she said, "our mission was to distract Centauria from the war in Terra. We've done that, without a doubt." She looked at the display. "Such great success unfortunately comes with great cost."

He suddenly turned his full, earnest gaze on her.

"But did it have to, Breeze?"

Her mind raced. Why was he asking her? This entire insane plan had been his idea! She stared at him, at his dark, weary features. What was that pain behind his eyes? Was it anger? At whom? She took a stab at it.

"I don't know, sir, but I'm saddened at how badly the Centauris were able to hit us."

She saw a flicker of emotion deep in his eyes. He glanced back at the frozen image.

"We should have done better at surviving that battle, shouldn't we?" He was unhappy at the number of casualties—that was obvious. And he was looking for someone to blame. Obviously not her, so whom?

"It's so hard to say, sir. An intelligence report before the battle is one thing, but no one can predict how people will react in the heat of the moment."

Come on, come on, she thought. *Who do you think messed it up?*

He frowned again, and didn't bite. "I'm sure everyone did the best they could."

She nodded with an outward show of sympathy, quickly considering her next angle.

"I agree, sir. But with all the replacements we've had these past weeks, sometimes people find themselves in a position beyond their capabilities." Then she hesitated, waiting for his reaction. She could tell that she'd hit a nerve.

He looked at the display again.

"Breeze, you're not a line officer. But let me ask your opinion. In the early stages of the battle, when we were still landing the regiments, what do you think was the single biggest threat to the Expeditionary Force?"

Her heart sank. How could she possibly guess that? She looked at the 3-D display with an air of studiousness, frantically trying to interpret the symbols. She knew that red meant bad, and she noticed a single red symbol that was larger than all the others. She pointed at it.

"At this point in the battle, I think the greatest threat was here." She had no idea what she'd pointed out, but Chandler nodded vigorously.

"Exactly!" he gritted. "The damn orbital platforms. They were chewing us apart! Look at this." He rewound the recording and played the moment where the large blue symbol flashed and disappeared. "When we lost the carrier, we very nearly lost this entire campaign! Why weren't those orbital platforms taken out sooner?"

"I don't know, sir."

"But you're a support officer. I don't expect you to know! Thomas is a damn line officer!"

Thomas? Chandler was angry at *Thomas?* Breeze fought to keep her expression neutral.

"Sir, I'm sure Mr. Kane was doing his best. He's doing a job he isn't qualified for." Her words could be interpreted as a defense, but she knew Chandler didn't take them that way.

"Yeah, that's pretty clear." Chandler sighed and rubbed his

eyes. "I probably shouldn't be saying any of this to you."

"None of us have slept in days, sir." She considered reaching out to stroke his arm, then thought better of it. Chandler was in one of his righteous moods, and wouldn't take kindly to flattery. "I won't remember a thing."

He pressed his palms to his eyes, then slowly rubbed down his unshaven cheeks.

"Erikson nearly tore Thomas's head off, but I kept the peace and kept Thomas in his role for the entire battle." He shook his head. "Makes me wonder if another AVW controller would have seen that counterattack coming sooner. Maybe we'd still have *Quebec*, *Provider*, and *Miami*."

Breeze had done her best to keep tabs on the fortunes of all the command staff replacements who, like her, had been thrown into the spotlight after the Battle of Laika. She'd heard all along that Thomas was quite good in his role as AVW controller, as evidenced by his performance at Cerberus. Erikson was a hardass who Breeze could tell didn't like the special treatment Thomas enjoyed under Chandler. Maybe he was exaggerating Thomas's errors to put him down a peg.

Well, Breeze was happy to join in.

"Maybe, sir. At this point we'll never know. I guess you've been reviewing the AVW decisions made during the battle?" Post-analysis of a combat situation was the surest way to raise questions about someone's competence. With the luxury of time, recordings, and lack of getting shot at, anyone could pick apart the frantic decisions made under fire.

The fact that Chandler was exhausted and stressed would only further cloud his judgment.

"I've done plenty of analysis," he said, indicating the display. "And I'm not impressed at what I see." His expression was actually more sad than angry. It was disappointment in a protégé, she realized. This was a much more emotionally charged issue for Chandler. He was taking it personally.

"Well, I can't really comment there, sir, but I'm sure Mr. Kane did his best. I'd hate for him to be judged unfairly." She made a show of thinking hard, displaying great concern, and then produced an idea. "Sir, perhaps you'd like to review my reports from *Rapier*'s missions during our time in Sirius. If you're having concerns, perhaps those reports will put things in balance."

Hope flashed in his eyes as he nodded. "Yeah, thanks Breeze. I think I'd like to read those."

She smiled, trying hard to contain her delight. Her intelligence reports were separate from Thomas's own mission reports, and in hers she had laid out clearly where she thought Thomas had failed to act appropriately.

Chandler had no idea what he was asking for. From his expression she could see that he really wanted to have his faith restored, and he hoped that her reports would do that. Now that his expectations were suitably raised, her critical review would be all the more damning.

"I'll forward them to you right away, sir—I can see that this is troubling you. I suggest you read them, put your mind to rest, and then try and get some sleep."

He nodded again, and managed a half-smile. "Thanks, Breeze. I appreciate your looking after me."

She donned her most earnest expression. "Sir, the entire EF needs you on your game. This is clearly a distraction, and I want to help you resolve it."

She cringed inwardly at her own blatant sucking up, but Chandler was too tired to notice, and took her words at face value. As she departed his cabin to dig up her *Rapier* reports, she complimented herself on finding an opportunity after all.

Perhaps today wasn't as bad as she'd thought.

53

The door opened soon after Thomas's knock, and he pushed himself through into the commodore's cabin. It looked much as before, with the government-issue furniture and the blackout curtain over the broad window.

Chandler floated in the middle of the cabin, looking up from a report he held in his hand.

The mood among the command team had been strained in the days since the Battle of Abeona, although Thomas couldn't put his finger on why. All he knew was that Commander Erikson had turned into a bastard, and the other controllers kept to themselves.

"You wanted to see me, sir?"

Chandler motioned him closer. "Yeah, Thomas, come on in."

The commodore spent another moment reading the report, nodding to himself as he did. Thomas pushed closer until he floated at a polite distance for conversation, and waited. Finally the commodore looked up again.

"Thomas, with all the survivors we picked up from the destroyed ships after Abeona, I'm going to be making a few staff changes."

"Yes, sir."

"*Miami*'s captain is a seasoned AVW controller, and she brings a wealth of experience to my staff. I also think it's important to keep her fully occupied so that she doesn't obsess over the loss of her ship."

Although he should have expected it, Thomas still felt as if he'd been kicked in the gut. He was losing his position on the command staff.

"She fought *Miami* well, sir," he said evenly. "She has nothing to be ashamed of. I certainly appreciate you giving me the opportunity when *Rapier* was put out of service."

Chandler nodded, but there was something in his eyes Thomas didn't like. There was a strained moment of silence.

"Sir, where am I being posted?"

"Well, this is the thing…" Chandler's tone was hardening. "I need every asset I have in action, and that includes *Rapier*. She still can't do atmo, but she can fly in space and she can carry weapons. That makes her at least as useful as a Hawk or a star fighter."

So he was returning to his command—that wasn't a bad thing.

"Thank you, sir. I'll ensure she's up to the task."

"This is where my doubt begins, Thomas."

"Sir?"

"Frankly, I'm very disappointed with your performance at Abeona. Those orbital platforms were clearly the biggest threat, and you, as AVW controller, pretty much ignored them until they were on top of us. Even then, you couldn't think of a way to fight them. As EF commander, Thomas, I really shouldn't be the one who has to think of tactical solutions."

Thomas felt a cold pit forming in his stomach.

"Sir, I'm sorry if—"

"I've made some time these past few days to take a hard look at your record as *Rapier*'s commander. This is what I see." He counted off the points on his fingers. "You pulled out of your Cerberan farm strike too early. The warlord troops in Free Lhasa wouldn't have responded to that distress call inside of thirty minutes—plenty of time for you to get your strike team back down to search for their target.

"You pulled out of the boarding of *Astrid* too early. That Centauri stealth ship would never have got off a killing shot without your destroyer escort seeing and attacking it.

"You didn't provide proper cover to your strike team in Free Lhasa. If *Kristiansand* hadn't given orbital bombardment, you would have lost half your team on the ground.

"And now, you've dogged it on the repairs to your ship, to the point where she was out of action for the most important battle of this war."

He dropped his hand.

"Honestly, the only thing keeping you in command right now is your heroism at the Battle of Laika. You deserve the medal you got for that, but otherwise you deserve a desk job. For now, though, I don't have any other fast-attack-qualified skippers, so I need to stick you back in command. I think the only reason *Rapier* had any success is due to your officers. That trooper Emmes has the biggest gonads I've ever seen, and Breeze is as sharp as a whip. I'm putting them both back in to support you."

Thomas dropped his eyes and stared unseeing at his feet floating over the deck. Just like that, his career was crumbling before him. Eric Chandler, his mentor and patron, had judged him a failure. Choking under pressure as a ship commander and coming up blank as a staff officer.

He'd been given two chances to shine and apparently he'd blown both of them. Chalk up FAC command and AVW control as two more things Thomas Kane had dabbled in, but really had no fucking idea what he was doing.

"Yes, sir," he said. "Thank you, sir."

"That's all, Thomas."

He retreated without another word. *Normandy*'s wide flats were quiet, but he avoided the gazes of those few he passed. He headed automatically for his cabin, not really knowing what he would do once he reached it. He thought idly that he should probably head up to *Rapier*, go scream at the mechanics to fix her faster, but he just couldn't muster the effort.

Habit moved him to his desk and a quick scan of his messages. Most were routine, but one from a Master Rating Shin in sickbay caught his eye. He scanned the one-liner quickly, and bolted for the door.

Katja wanted to see him.

Sickbay was crowded. Every bed was occupied and gurneys filled every nook and cranny. Thomas was surprised as his feet touched down on the deck under sudden gravity, then recalled that medical spaces often had localized AG for the sake of the medical staff. They moved quietly and efficiently among their patients, individual voices lost in the general din.

He scanned beds and peered past curtains, trying to stay out of the way. Finally he glanced through the crack of one curtain, and felt his heart lift.

Katja was sitting on her bed, cross-legged in pale blue, standard issue pajamas, intently reading a hand-held electronic display. An IV was plugged into her wrist, bandages hid her chin and she had a gel-collar around her neck, but otherwise she appeared in one piece.

He blinked away sudden moisture in his eyes and felt a smile split his lips as he stepped through the curtain. So his career was dead. At least Katja wasn't.

She looked up quickly, then dropped her display on the bed and uncrossed her legs with great effort. She slid bare feet down to the deck and pushed herself up to stand before him. She looked so tiny and delicate, so fragile. He desperately wanted to comfort her, but he forced himself to hold back.

To his surprise, she took a shaky step forward, reached out with both arms and wrapped herself around him, pressing her cheek tightly against his chest. New warmth welled up within him and he carefully put his arms around her. She held him for a long, long moment, taking deep, sighing breaths. He blinked away tears again and hugged her tighter.

She gasped. "Broken ribs!"

He released her. "Sorry."

She stepped back, steadying herself on the bed and carefully climbing back on. He watched her fight through the pain, finally seating herself comfortably against the raised mattress.

"Hi, Thomas. Good to see you still alive."

"Likewise." He tried to think of something witty to say, but her dark, steady gaze kept him earnest. She'd looked at him in many ways in the past, but never quite like this. There was no admiration in her eyes.

"Thanks for sending that message, Katja. I'm really happy that you wanted to see me."

"Well, when they finally untied me, I figured I should practice being nice again. Even to you."

His good mood dimmed. It seemed everybody in his life was determined to have a go at him. In this case, though, he deserved it.

She motioned for him to sit on the end of the bed, then leaned forward to wrap her arms around her knees. When she spoke again her voice was quiet enough that only he could hear.

"I guess I really shouldn't care that you're fucking Breeze, but I do. Even though I don't have any 'claim' to you, it hurts a lot. I really thought that there was something between us, but I've figured out now that I was wrong."

Conflicting emotions battled in his heart as her eyes bore into him. His first impulse was to say something sweet and reassuring, to avoid hurting her any more. But a growing realization finally took hold within him. This woman was a blooded warrior and a brave, natural leader. She didn't look delicate or fragile.

She didn't need his protection.

"That night in my cabin was motivated by lust," he said finally. "I shouldn't have taken advantage of your feelings, especially since I wasn't ready to return them. I'm sorry."

"It's not like I tried to stop it. But I guess at the time it meant more to me than it did to you."

He looked down at the hands in his lap. His emotions were still churning.

"If it matters, it only happened with Breeze once. We're not an item."

"When we first met," she replied, "I thought you were larger than life. Commanding a ship, confident, strong, handsome. I really thought that you were the military ideal. But now I see that you're just a self-serving asshole like everybody else."

He sighed. "Thanks."

She poked his shoulder. He looked up to see her smiling.

"But I've met assholes on every world, and on average you rate pretty well."

He nodded. "But I took something special from you. I regret that."

Genuine good humor welled up from the depths of her eyes.

"Do you think I was a virgin that night?"

Her question stopped him dead. He'd never consciously considered it, but he suddenly realized that yes, he'd thought exactly that.

She lifted one foot and gently kicked him.

"Grow up, Kane. I'm a woman in the Astral Corps. And I'm twenty-nine, not nineteen."

He stared at her, hardly recognizing this vivacious, confident adult sitting before him. Then he burst out laughing, all the tension of the day releasing. On an impulse, he took her cheek and kissed her lips.

She responded for a second, then pushed him back with considerable strength. But the humor hadn't left her eyes.

"That's the last time you ever get to do that," she said. "Save it for Breeze."

He shook his head. "No thanks. She's slobbery."

Katja's laugh echoed through sickbay.

He stood up and stretched. "How are you feeling, by the way? When are you returning to duty?"

She leaned back against the raised mattress and extended her legs out straight. The movement caused her to wince.

"I have nine broken ribs, a few busted organs and a spine they want to keep a close eye on." She sniffed thoughtfully. "I figure I'll be good by this evening."

He smiled again. "Well, as soon as you're ready, I have a seat for you on *Rapier*'s bridge. We're pulling the crew back together and we're going to be assigned to space patrols."

"I have a platoon to command."

"The orders don't come from me. But... I'd rather you come willingly than not. If you want to stay with your troops, tell me and I'll see what I can do."

She thought for a moment, almost as if she was sizing him up. "Well, I've been running a lot lately, carrying heavy equipment and all, and I'm getting kinda tired of it. Maybe growing my ass in a Fleet chair is just the thing."

He felt a new kind of warmth grow inside him. He extended his hand.

"Welcome aboard, OpsO."

"Thank you, sir."

54

"Sir, please stop screwing with the door."

Jack grinned at the medical attendant and pulled himself through one last time. The zero-g of the passageway carried him forward until sickbay's AG grabbed a hold of him and he fell like a stone. His boots thumped down on the deck.

"Sorry," he said. "It's kinda cool."

The attendant sighed and crossed her arms. "Can I help you, sir?"

He nodded, offering up his hand-held display with the medical appointment opened on the screen. "I've just been posted in from *Kristiansand* and I have a flight medical. I'm a pilot."

She ignored his offering and checked her own list. With another glance at him she indicated for him to follow. He enjoyed putting a bounce in his step under the refreshing pull of gravity. His smile faded, though, as he passed bed after bed of mangled troopers, feeling their hard eyes on him. He adopted a suitably serious look as he took the indicated seat next to a bank of steel cabinets.

Normandy's sickbay was as big as a hospital, compared to the closet in *Kristiansand*, but even so it felt cramped in here. Every possible space was occupied by either a patient or equipment, and the general noise was almost as loud as the wardroom during a mess meeting. Nobody paid him much attention, and he spent several minutes simply watching the people around him.

Most of the patients wore pale blue pajamas. Those who weren't had too many things stuck into them or wrapped around them to allow for normal clothes. There was certainly enough chatter, and even a few laughs, but many of the patients sat or lay in silence, gazing intently at personal screens or just staring into space.

"Sublieutenant Mallory?" A doctor approached him.

Jack stood. "That's me."

The doctor quickly examined his file and chatted absently while he conducted a few routine physical tests that Jack knew well. It was nothing too demeaning, and he cooperated without hesitation.

Finally, the doctor reached up and pressed two fingers against Jack's face, repeating the action in several places. He nodded thoughtfully.

"The bone's knit fairly well. It's starting to fuse permanently into place." Jack automatically ran his hand over the unnatural bumps on his face. "Is that a good thing?"

"Yes and no. You're healing, and that's good. But the longer it goes, the harder it'll be for a plastic surgeon to put it back the way it was."

Jack had almost forgotten that there even was a chance to fix his face. The sudden reminder—combined with the doubt that it would ever happen—hurt more than his twisted features ever did. He nodded, sighing.

The doctor patted his shoulder sympathetically. "Otherwise, son, you're fit and ready for duty. What kind of plane do you fly?"

"A Hawk."

"Hm. I didn't think *Normandy* had Hawks."

"You don't. Apparently I'm gonna be learning how to fly a fast-attack craft."

"Well, typical wartime training should give you at least ten minutes of practice time before you go out on your first mission."

Jack forced a smile. "Let's hope so."

The doctor made a few notes on the file and told Jack he was free to go. Jack looked around the busy sickbay. Free to go where? The hangar, he supposed. His pilot instincts always drew him back to the hangar. So he gathered up his hand-held and started for the door.

A firm grip on his sleeve halted him. He turned and came face to face with Katja Emmes. She was dressed in the blue pajamas, one hand on his sleeve and the other hanging onto her rolling IV stand.

"Hey, you're Jack," she said. "You're a pilot."

A real smile split his features. "Why, yes… yes I am. And you look very pretty in pale blue, ma'am."

She scoffed and tugged him to follow her back toward her nearby bed. "Bring your chair, Subbie."

Jack had never considered himself to be a big man, but with him in boots and her barefoot, he felt like he towered over her. Not that he had any illusions about who could kick whose ass, even with an IV in her wrist. He grabbed the chair and followed her across to the tiny, curtained space.

She settled herself, propped up in the bed. "I've been here long enough to be totally bored. But apparently my bones haven't knit yet, so they make me stay longer."

Jack pushed down any thought of knitting bones and resisted the impulse to touch his face. Instead, he placed his chair next to the bed and sat down.

"Well, I'm apparently quite healthy. But for you, ma'am, I got time. Don't they give you reading material or something here?"

She indicated her own hand-held. "I've spent the better part of a day reading the reports from the battle. I've read enough."

Jack hadn't seen any reports, but he wanted to say something intelligent.

"At least we're calling it a victory. We bashed up the homeworld of our enemies and…" He searched for the phrase Avernell had used. "…seized the initiative away from them."

Katja eyed him curiously. "Did you think of that by yourself?"

He couldn't help but smile. "No. I'm just a pilot. I drive the bus."

"Speaking of which, why are you here? In *Normandy*, I mean."

"Well, a pilot's gotta have something to fly, and *Kristiansand*'s all out." He briefly relayed his little adventure to get more torpedoes and its rather sudden and hard conclusion. She looked impressed. He had to admit that he was feeling pretty proud about it, but he didn't want to brag in front of this combat veteran.

"But that's two Hawks I've bashed up on this deployment. My paycheck is going to be small when we get home."

"Two Hawks?"

"Free Lhasa?"

"Oh… right. That one wasn't really your fault, though."

"Tell that to Astral Logistics."

She smiled. He liked her a lot more when she was in pajamas, he decided. Way more relaxed—almost human.

"So are you flying a strike fighter, or one of our adopted star fighters?"

He suppressed the frown that threatened to well up. "Neither. It seems I'm destined to never sit in a fighter cockpit, no matter how much I beg."

"Well, they *are* pretty expensive to replace…" she said.

He tried to laugh, although he knew her words were truer than she thought. He had flown Hawks like fighters, playing star jock in his head while real stuff was happening around him.

"Hey," she said suddenly, "nice job on finding the secret Centauri jump gate. Did my info help you out at all?"

In all the action over the past week or so, he'd totally forgotten about that. Hunting stealths in Sirius seemed like a lifetime ago.

"Oh, yeah!" he said, grinning. "Holy crap was that ever useful. I told my captain where I got the info from—I hope you get some credit."

"Hey, you're the extra-dimensional whiz kid," she countered. "I'm just a jar-head who passed on what I knew."

He'd hardly call himself a whiz kid, but…

"Thanks. It's actually pretty interesting stuff. Like just these past few days, I've been thinking about how we use torpedoes in general. Right now doctrine says we can't detonate one deeper than sixteen peets, but I think that if we changed the way the gravitons were released, we might be able to control it better. You see—"

She held up a hand. "Jack, I'm a jar-head, remember. I have trouble with polysyllabic words. Trust me, the section on multidimensional physics we had to do in Second Year did *not* help my final mark. There was never any danger of me being selected for ASW."

"Actually, I really didn't want ASW either," he admitted. "But I guess Astral Selection knows best."

"But if you hadn't been Jack the Pilot, what then?"

"Jack the Fighter Pilot. What else?"

She sighed thoughtfully. "Honestly, Jack, I haven't met many people who aren't well-suited to their occupation. Like it or not, you do have an aptitude for ASW. As much as we all like to bitch about where Selection puts us, I do think they know what they're doing."

"What did you want to be when you joined?"

"Oh, infantry," she said. "I made sure I met the requirements."

He wasn't sure which was more surprising: that she'd been placed in the occupation she actually wanted or that she'd actually wanted infantry. Suddenly aware that he was surrounded by wounded troopers, he leaned in and lowered his voice.

"With all respect, why?"

Surprisingly, she didn't get angry. Instead, she nodded thoughtfully and dropped her gaze.

"Because of my father."

"Is he a Corps officer, too?"

Her lips curled in a mix of smile and frown. "No. He's career Army. I don't know if you know this, but the Army doesn't have officers. Everybody starts as a stormtrooper, and works their way up from there. These days he's a storm banner leader—kind of the equivalent of a sergeant major."

"So... what did he think of you going Astral Force?"

"He was pissed off, but I think he would've lived with it. When I went officer, though, that pretty much got me kicked out of the family."

"Why did you do it?"

"Because there was no way I was ever going to be subordinate to him."

Her tone had gone hard. Suddenly this was the old Katja Emmes, but he was fascinated and couldn't stop asking questions.

"Why did you join at all? Why not stay a civilian?"

"I could have. Being the child of a veteran, I already had a lot of privileges. Where do you think I went to my first year of university?"

"Not the Astral College?"

She shook her head, a pained, wistful smile dancing across her features. "Canterbury—fine arts."

That he had not expected. "What, *the* Canterbury?"

"Mm-hmm. I was accepted on scholarship for the first year."

"In what? Acting? Painting?"

"Opera."

"Shut up!"

Her smile broadened. "It's true. I was a coloratura soprano. I was planning on doing my thesis performance as the Queen of the Night in Mozart's *Magic Flute*."

Jack sat back, stunned. He stared at this woman in front of him, dressed in blue pajamas leaning up in her hospital bed. He tried to push out his memories of her black, armored spacesuit and imagine her as an opera singer with a huge curly wig and a poufy dress.

"I can see it," he lied politely.

"Well, my father couldn't. He had some pretty clear ideas about what his children were allowed to grow up to be. My older brother is a teacher, so no shortage of prestige there. My younger brother always wanted to go Army, so there were no worries there either. But a daughter in a fine arts school? Utterly unacceptable."

Jack was surprised that she had two siblings—it must have been one of the privileges accorded a veteran.

"He wasn't happy with two out of three?"

"There's four of us, actually. My younger brother and sister are twins."

"Four, wow. But why didn't you stick with opera?"

"There I was, nineteen years old, being told by my father that I was throwing away my life. I couldn't live with that, so I left Canterbury and joined up just to try and please him. But like I said, there was no way I was ever going to be under him again, so I went Astral Force, and went officer."

"And here we are," he said.

A sharp, nasty laugh escaped her lips, followed by a wry smile. "I don't know whether it's the happy drugs," she said, "or just that I've had a lot of time to think these past few days. But I don't really talk about this much—so keep your mouth shut, Subbie." Her expression robbed the words of any real malice.

He grinned. "Just so long as you don't tell anyone how I peed myself when you pointed your gun at me over Laika."

Her laugh came easily again and she relaxed visibly.

"Deal. Now I'm probably keeping you from somewhere. Thanks for chatting with me."

He stood and collected his chair. "Any time. How long till you go back to your troops?"

"Actually, I'm going back to *Rapier*. Looks like we're flying again."

Jack smiled at his own little secret. "Well, take care, ma'am. I'm sure I'll see you again soon."

55

Jack regretted leaving the AG environment of sickbay, but hadn't lost his space legs, so he found his way quickly up to the main hangar. There were still two long lines of strike fighters parked facing outward, ready to deploy. But crowded in were at least three-dozen star fighters, orphaned after the carrier *Artemis* was destroyed by Orbital Platform Two, before the final torpedo attack could be launched.

It had been a devastating blow to the EF's security, and he wondered how many other star fighters had found sanctuary in *Jutland* or the other two invasion ships. *No, wait*—just the other *one* invasion ship. *Quebec* had never left Abeona orbit.

The EF was hurting, and as Jack made his way to the far end of the hangar he saw no more obvious evidence of this than his new plane. *Rapier* was certainly looking better than the last time he'd seen her—both wings were straight, and there were no gaping holes in the hull—but up close he could see the patch-jobs down her once-smooth surface. The port engine was a slightly different color than the rest of the ship, and still had equipment and scaffolding littered around it. Both strike pods were missing, he noticed with sudden relief— he could still remember the hellish ride aboard one of them up from Free Lhasa, and really didn't need another reminder of that day.

"She's coming together," a voice behind him said, "despite

her looks." He turned and saw Lieutenant Commander Kane floating toward him.

"Sir, Jack Mallory reporting for duty. I'm your new pilot."

Thomas slowed his movement by brushing one hand against *Rapier*'s fuselage. He extended his other hand.

"Good to have you aboard, Jack. Lieutenant Duncan tells me you're a hell of a pilot."

Jack shook his hand and grinned. Had the XO really said that?

"I think he just wants to get me away from Hawks because I keep breaking them."

"You're trained in ASW, aren't you?"

"Yep."

"Good. Because *Rapier*'s getting kitted out with the ASW detection gear *Kristiansand* salvaged from your Hawk." He tapped the turret slung under the fuselage. "With these babies we can take on enemy fighters, with our morningstars we can take out enemy ships, and now with your gear and expertise, we can hunt stealths. We're our own little battleship, Jack."

"Cool." Jack was pleased to hear about the ASW gear. It was good to bring something familiar with him. "When's our first mission, sir?"

Kane ran a hand along the patched fuselage. "Day after tomorrow, probably. Still a few things to fix on board, and we need our OpsO to heal a bit more."

"Man, in two days we'll be halfway to the jump gate."

"We're not going to the jump gate."

"What? I thought the plan was to hit Abeona, and then tear off for home."

Kane frowned slightly. "I guess you haven't read today's tactical brief. Yesterday a Centauri squadron jumped through from Terra. This is good news for Terra, because we've forced the enemy to pull back some of its ships from the front line. But it's bad news for us. They're sitting at the jump gate, waiting for us, and we don't have the strength to take them on. It's just like Sirius, only now the EF is even weaker."

Jack didn't like where this conversation was going. "So, what's the plan?"

"There are over a thousand human settlements in Centauria, scattered over the worlds. Most of them don't have any defenses at all. Our mission is to destroy as many of them as possible, to force the Centauri government to surrender, or at least withdraw from Terra."

Now Jack *really* didn't like what he was hearing.

"We're going to slaughter civilians…?"

Sadness flashed in Kane's eyes. "Subbie, we're at war. We're trapped behind enemy lines and for all we know the Centauris have already invaded Earth. Not just Terra—Earth. All we can do from here is make bloody trouble for our enemies, and if that means killing civilians, then yes, that's what we're going to do."

Jack knew better than to argue. This was exactly why he didn't make a habit of reading the tactical briefs posted in the wardroom. Don't look for what you don't want to know.

Better to focus on what he could influence. "Sir, I know we're outgunned these days, and I've been thinking about some of the things that went down at Abeona. Sometime when you have a few minutes, I'd like to bounce some ideas off you about the use of torpedoes against brane targets, based on our engagements with the orbital platforms."

Kane stared at him strangely. Jack felt compelled to explain more.

"It has to do with the behavior of gravitons farther in than sixteen peets. Pretty technical stuff, but if you're interested…"

To his surprise, Kane looked very interested indeed. "I've given those orbital platforms a lot of thought myself lately. Tell me what you got."

On his hand-held display, Jack brought up the consolidated tactical log from the Battle of Abeona and ran the sequence showing the massed Hawk attack on Orbital Platform One.

"The mass torpedo attack worked, but it took hundreds of weapons to pound the target because their graviton pulses are weaker here on the brane, and couldn't do enough damage. Enough to destroy a single ship, for sure, but not a structure as massive as an orbital platform. To really get gravity working for us, we need to go deeper into the Bulk."

"Sure," Kane said, nodding. "The farther into the Bulk we go, the bigger a boom we get. But if the target's on the brane, what good does it do us?"

Jack forwarded the log to the point where his Hawk was ejected from *Protector*.

"I fired a torpedo at Platform Two, but I set it to implode at sixteen peets—as far into the Bulk as our weapons go. The implosion was significant enough to shake up the platform—notice here that it actually stopped firing for a few seconds—but effectively the shot didn't work. Like you say, it was just way too far into the Bulk for the gravitons to grab a target on the brane. But something weird did happen."

He moved aside the tactical log and brought up the hunt control recording from his Hawk. He replayed his torpedo shot and watched as the gravimetric landscape sagged under the implosion, going deep purple, almost black. He paused the recording and pointed at one of the graphs next to the main display. There was a spike at the exact moment of detonation.

"Just for a microsecond, there was a noticeable buildup of dark energy, totally focused on the point of the implosion."

He paused expectantly. Kane stared back blankly.

"Okay, Jack, so there was dark energy. So?"

He quickly brought up some sketches he'd made, as well as some more polished diagrams he'd downloaded from some archived articles he'd dug up.

"So... dark energy doesn't just hang around in pockets. It doesn't even usually exist in a way that we can detect it. We manufacture it to hold the jump gates open, but otherwise you don't see it in nature. Except—" He pointed at his sketches. "—when you get below the Erebos Layer, sixteen peets or so into the Bulk. What I think we're looking at here is a tenebral implosion."

Kane didn't seem to be sharing his excitement. Jack's confidence began to fade and he dropped his gaze to study the sketches again. The diagrams he'd pulled from TacNotes were a lot prettier, and it suddenly occurred to him that he probably wasn't the first person to think of this.

"Jack," Kane said, "I'm not really following you, but I'm not a dimensional physicist. Let me ask you this—are you saying that you have a way to use our existing weapons more effectively?"

His excitement started to rise again. "With a modification to the way the gravitons are pulsed, yes."

"Then let's go to my cabin and write this down. The EF needs all the help it can get."

56

Thomas watched as the lower airlock doors opened in the deckhead of *Normandy*'s hangar, welcoming his little ship once again.

Rapier's new bridge windows were so clear in comparison to the buckled, blackened windows they'd replaced that he almost thought them invisible. Like everything new aboard the fast-attack craft, they only highlighted further the battered disrepair of the ship in general. Much as he enjoyed being in command again, Thomas secretly questioned the wisdom of sending *Rapier* into space.

Not that he would dare mention it, of course. Chandler had somehow convinced himself that Thomas was a coward and a skulker—if *Rapier* had not flown this mission, no doubt Chandler would have found her a new captain.

He shifted in his spacesuit and glanced over at the damage control board displayed on Katja's console to his left. There were far too many red and yellow lights for his comfort, even though he knew none of them indicated critical failures.

The lights of the hangar disappeared as *Rapier* was raised up into the airlock. In the sudden darkness Thomas became acutely aware of the silence that hung over the bridge. Jack would be concentrating on his controls—other than a quick test flight yesterday, this was his first time at the helm.

When they'd boarded, Katja had offered little more than a

polite nod, and her flash-up reports had been brief and unadorned. Breeze had come on board wearing a scowl, speaking only when spoken to. The only life Thomas had seen in either woman had been when Jack had arrived.

Apparently no woman could resist a pilot's charm.

To be fair, Jack was smarter than Thomas had given him credit for. He'd certainly mastered *Rapier*'s controls well enough, and their discussion about modified graviton pulses had strained Thomas's knowledge of extra-dimensional physics. When he drafted his memo on the subject, he'd even called Jack to clarify a few points.

The upper airlock doors opened, and *Rapier* rose up into open space. *Normandy*'s vast topside came into view, large enough to give the illusion of a horizon under a brilliant canopy of stars. The EF was high above the Centauri ecliptic, nearly halfway between the two suns, and the naked stars shone brightly.

Thomas stole a glance at the constellation Cassiopeia, trying to locate the bright star known as Sol only four light years away. He didn't spot it before Jack received clearance from *Normandy* and lifted off.

The big invasion ship fell out of view and Thomas watched idly as Jack cleared to open space to conduct a few routine maneuvers. The ship didn't roll as smoothly as once she had, but he couldn't tell if that was due to the damage or the young pilot. Chief Tamma had flown *Rapier* like an extension of his own body, but Tamma had also been a star fighter pilot by trade. And he had died over Abeona.

Jack had certainly proven that he could fly a plane like he'd stolen it, and Thomas reminded himself that the only way his little ship could function was if he trusted his officers and crew.

"Ship checks out," Jack said. "Where to, skipper?"

Thomas highlighted *Rapier*'s patrol box on his 3-D display and forwarded the update to Jack, clamping down sudden irritation. Chief Tamma wouldn't have needed to ask that question.

"Our mission today is combined picket," he said, suddenly feeling the need to make sure all his officers had their heads in the game. "We know the Centauris have had at least one stealth ship in the area. Once in our patrol box, we'll conduct sprint-and-drift ASW trawling while looking outward for enemy vessels, as well. Pilot is responsible for ASW, Navigator for AAW, and OpsO for AVW. Questions?"

"No, sir," Katja and Jack said, more or less together.

"No, sir," Breeze said.

There was tension all round. None of them were comfortable in their fast-attack roles, especially now that *Rapier*'s mission had changed so dramatically. Thomas was confident that Jack could handle ASW, but he was less sure about Katja and Breeze. Katja at least had a good attitude, which is why he'd given her the more thought-intensive AVW—keeping an eye out for enemy ships trying to sneak toward the EF.

With anti-attack warfare, all Breeze really had to worry about was getting the three turrets to shoot at anything that openly threatened *Rapier*. She was pretty good at self-preservation.

They reached their sector within minutes. Jack aimed for the leading edge, then cut back the engines almost to idle. The ship would drift in space, watching for stealth ships, letting the Expeditionary Force's main body slowly catch up. Several minutes of silence passed on the bridge as Jack examined the Bulk and Katja searched deep space.

"No bearing lines from the Fleet," Jack said finally. "Confirm there's been no contact since the attack yesterday?"

"None," Thomas said. "It's at the point where we think we might have nailed him on the counterstrike."

Jack's response was doubtful. Yesterday, the EF had learned with certainty that the Centauris had at least one stealth ship in the area. The Terran stealth ship *Asp* had conducted a long game of cat-and-mouse with the enemy, and lost. That left the EF with only one remaining stealth ship.

"You don't think so, Jack?" Katja asked.

He shook his head, eyes still forward. "I reviewed the logs this morning. At the depth both stealths were at, nothing would hide from our sensors."

"What does depth have to do with it?"

"The farther into the Bulk you go, the stronger gravity becomes and the more massive everything gets. *Asp* was destroyed at fourteen peets, and the singularity was strong enough to bend radio signals between our ships. The enemy stealth went even farther in after the attack—if we'd got her we'd have known."

"How far in can a Centauri stealth go? Can our torpedoes even get her?"

"I think their newest boats can reach fifteen peets, and our torpedoes are rated for sixteen. Beyond that we start getting into some weird physics. But that's all polysyllabic stuff."

Thomas thought that was a strange thing to say, but Katja seemed amused by it. She made to respond, but cut herself off as a new symbol flashed into existence on the display. Moments later a report came across the AVW circuit from the cruiser *Admiral Nelson*, in the sector several dozen thousand kilometers aft and above *Rapier*.

Unknown contact inbound.

As they watched, another contact appeared. Then a third. In formation, no EM emissions.

"Captain, OpsO," Katja said, "three suspects bearing one-one-five mark one-five-zero, closing. Assess possible Centauri warships."

"Concur," Thomas said. "Battle stations."

The alarm sounded, muffled in his ears as Thomas locked down his faceplate. Throughout *Rapier*, the skeleton crew were bringing the weapons to ready and flashing up all backup systems.

"*Rapier, this is Echo-Victor.*" It was the voice of *Miami*'s former CO, now sitting in Thomas's former seat at *Normandy*'s command console. "*Investigate suspects five-eight through six-zero, weapons free, over.*"

"This is *Rapier*, roger," he said. "Request star fighter cover, over."

"*This is Echo-Victor, confirmed, out.*"

He switched to the internal circuit. "Pilot, come hard right to one-one-five mark one-five-zero, attack speed."

Rapier swung hard to the right and accelerated to her maximum cruising speed. On the 3-D, two blue symbols began to close his position—star fighters. The three suspects accelerated noticeably. Judging from their radar return, they looked like big ships.

"AA weapons free," he said. "OpsO, get the strike camera locked on."

Katja moved quickly to activate the camera. She magnified.

Several shiny objects became clear on the console.

"Looks like Centauri. But I can't tell what kind."

Thomas stared at the monitor, thinking hard. Three big targets. There was no way that many battle cruisers could have snuck up on them—besides, battle cruisers would already have launched missiles at this range. Space Guard cutters? Three of them would be no match for the EF, even in its weakened state. And cutters wouldn't paint so big on the radar.

The star fighters streaked past, easily overtaking the fast-attack craft. The image in the monitor was growing, but not quickly enough. Thomas hated this uncertainty.

"Pilot, flank speed!"

Rapier pushed forward to one tenth the speed of light. Thomas gripped his chair as the entire vessel began to vibrate. The image in the monitor quickly filled the screen and kept growing. Katja zoomed out. Thomas stared at the image. There weren't three big ships—there were many smaller ones, packed in close formation.

Alarms sounded. The ship couldn't sustain this emergency speed for long.

"Pilot, attack speed!"

Jack pulled back. Thomas continued to stare at the image in his monitor, counting up the enemy ships. He opened the AVW circuit.

"Echo-Victor, *Rapier*, suspects now desig hostile. Centauri cutters, ten of them. I say again, one-zero hostiles!"

Echo-Victor's response was lost in the alarms as fast-moving contacts broke away from the cutters. Leading the charge, the star fighters jinked and dodged. One evaded. The other didn't. A visible flash of light through *Rapier*'s bridge windows revealed the kill.

"Hostiles inbound!" Breeze shouted.

"Evasive. AA weapons free!"

Jack pulled hard to port. Then back to starboard. Thomas groaned against the g-forces and vaguely heard the *bang-bang-bang* as decoys launched. The ship heaved over again. Top and bottom turrets thundered to life. Tracers flashed out. Missiles exploded.

Rapier dove hard and dropped below the plane of the battle. Missiles chased. Tail turret joined the fray. All three weapons sprayed a wake of rounds behind the ship. The remaining missiles flew into the maelstrom and were destroyed.

The Centauri cutters spread out in a line abreast, closing the EF at high speed. Thomas saw the second star fighter wink out of existence on his display. More were inbound from the main force, and *Admiral Nelson* was charging forward to engage. The EF main body—the two invasion ships and two supply ships— were moving to distance themselves from the attack, with *Jutland* acting as blocker. The other cruiser, *Admiral Halsey*, was racing from her station on the far side of the Terran ships to join the battle.

Thomas realized that the enemy ships were passing *Rapier* at distance, their attention clearly focused on the EF. A wave of missiles was unleashed en masse, headed for the rapidly approaching *Nelson*. The cruiser returned fire, a stream of missiles launching in rapid succession. From his distance, Thomas couldn't tell which weapons got through on either side.

He and his little ship were now outside the battle, overlooked as the enemy closed to point-blank range with *Nelson*. Thomas felt his teeth grind together. Those cutters were designed for fast interdiction against pirates—they were deadly at close range. *Halsey* was still on the far side of the EF, closing at top speed.

One of the destroyers, *Cape Town*, broke from ASW picket and was moving to help *Nelson*.

Rapier wasn't designed for space battles. Yet she had four morningstar missiles and three self-defense turrets. And now, two torpedoes strapped where the strike pods had once been. He steeled himself for death.

Thomas Kane was not going to be accused of cowardice again.

57

Thomas quickly surveyed the battle. Where could *Rapier* do the most damage?

"Intercept hostile six-seven. Target with morningstars, salvo size four."

Jack swung the ship in the z-axis and pointed toward the Centauri cutter at one end of the battle line. Katja locked on with all of her missiles.

"Target locked, in range," she said.

"Fire!"

Dazzling orbs of yellow light blasted forth in sequence from *Rapier's* wings. They accelerated clear, long tails stretching behind them as they closed on their target. The Centauri cutter, focused on *Nelson*, never had a chance. The missiles smashed through its small hull, tearing it apart in flames that leapt far with the escaping air.

The display revealed a swarm of robotic sentries holding the star fighters at bay, isolating *Nelson* from aid. *Cape Town* tried to charge through the swarm, batteries blazing. *Halsey* was just approaching the main body. *Jutland* launched long-range missiles at the cutters. The other three destroyers closed in for main body defense to free the battleship to engage.

The cutters broke their line, swarming over *Nelson*. The cruiser's defensive weapons fired non-stop, but far too many hits got through. One cutter exploded under a determined counterstrike. Another reeled from *Jutland*'s long-range attacks. But it was too little—*Nelson* was taking too much damage.

"Pilot," Thomas said, "target hostile six-five with torpedo. Close into range."

Jack steered with one hand and activated his weapons with the other.

"Our torpedoes are weak here on the brane. I'll need to fire both to ensure a good singularity."

"Do it!"

The cutters noticed *Rapier* again, and one broke off the attack on *Nelson* to fire. Tracers flashed past the cockpit as *Rapier* banked hard, continuing to close.

"I've got a solution," Jack said. "Coming into range."

"Fire!"

There was a double bang as the torpedoes were ejected from the hull. They accelerated past the ship, slowly shrinking from view as they phased into the Bulk. The Centauri cutter broke off its attack and tried to run, but it had no ASW defenses. Thomas watched as its port side crumpled. A second later its starboard side twisted and wrenched itself apart.

"Holy shit!" Breeze said.

Rapier's turrets opened fire as fast, short-range missiles rocketed toward her.

Jack jinked hard and evaded.

The cockpit lurched violently. Thomas's head slammed back in his helmet against the seat. Alarms screamed.

"Hull breached on upper deck, starboard side," Katja said. "Main cave."

Two of the cutters had broken off from *Nelson* and were closing on *Rapier*. Thomas felt like screaming—but he would not back down. *Nelson* was still surrounded. *Cape Town* was reeling from robot sentry fire. *Halsey* still wasn't in range. *Rapier* was the only distraction.

"Close to point-blank range. Keep them on our beam."

Jack obeyed without question, flying straight into the hail of rounds. *Rapier* shuddered under the onslaught but quickly closed to within the range of her own turrets. Jack swung the ship to port to open the firing arcs of all three weapons.

Nothing happened. No shots fired. Centauri rounds continued to rain down. Thomas stared at Breeze, his AAW officer. She was gripping her console, staring in fear up through the windows at the looming cutters.

Thomas used his command console to designate the two hostiles to the turrets, set to permanent engage. Instantly the rapid-fire thudding of the guns echoed through the hull. He tried to reach out to hit Breeze, but his straps kept him restrained.

"Brisebois!" he shouted. "Man your station!"

The Centauri shots were falling astern. Thomas heard a single bang against the hull, and saw Jack wrench the stick to reverse his turn. The three turrets continued to strafe the lumbering cutters with ease. After Jack's third turn, the enemy retreated from the engagement.

"Damage report!" Thomas said.

"Total depressurization of the main cave," Katja said. "Sealed and contained. Fuel leaking from starboard wing, one percent per minute. Engine room is transferring between tanks to minimize loss. Stress indications in both wing supports. All missiles expended. All torpedoes expended. Turrets at thirty percent ammunition remaining."

Rapier swung low beneath the battle. Thomas surveyed visually and checked his display. *Cape Town* had fought her way through the sentries and had drawn three of the cutters away from *Nelson*. The beleaguered cruiser still battled with three more, and even as Thomas watched she started to break apart, weapons firing defiantly. *Halsey* and fresh star fighters were fast approaching the enemy force.

Then a panicked voice came over the command circuit.

"This is Jutland! *Torpedo! Torpedo! Torp—"*

Static.

Thomas's eyes snapped up toward the Expeditionary Force's main body. The ships were too far away to see, but he caught a faint ripple in the stars. On the 3-D display, the blue symbol for the battleship *Jutland* disappeared.

"Oh my God," Breeze said.

"Conducting graviton search pulse," Jack said. His active ASW search gear sent out a strong, omnidirectional blast of gravitons.

Thomas brought up the ASW circuit and heard other units doing the same. Within seconds, a datum dropped into the display.

The hostile stealth was halfway between the EF main body and the enemy cutters. Rapid commands ordered *Halsey* and *Cape Town* to break off their battle with the cutters and close the datum. *Kristiansand* and *Goa* did likewise from the EF main body. Every Hawk in space moved at full speed to prosecute.

The Centauri cutters turned as one and began fleeing the battle.

"Target moving!" Jack said. His hunt controls gave him more info, but even Thomas could see that the Centauri stealth ship was accelerating, trying to clear the Terran forces descending upon it. The net was closing fast, though.

Suddenly, the ASW circuit erupted with calls of torpedo attack. Jack instinctively fired off a pair of bowling balls, but the attack wasn't against *Rapier*. Thomas looked out and saw both *Halsey* and *Cape Town* maneuvering sharply, flashes of decoys and torpedoes spitting forth from their dark hulls.

Halsey vanished before his eyes.

Seconds later, *Cape Town* followed.

Multiple flashes ahead revealed a pair of Hawks launching torpedoes. Almost before Thomas could refocus, a section of stars warped under the immense curve of gravity in the Bulk as the Terran weapons found their mark.

Thomas scanned the display. The remaining Centauri cutters were already out of missile range and receding fast. He waited a long moment to see if any other stealth threats emerged. The fourth spatial dimension seemed quiet.

"Pilot," he said, "anything on your sensors?"

The young pilot shook his head. "Hard to say for sure in that mess, but I think there was only one attacker."

"OpsO, any threats?"

"Negative. Five hostiles retreating at speed, outside weapons range."

He paused to review his display again, then paid Breeze the courtesy of asking her opinion.

"NavO, any threats?"

"No," she said quietly.

He called down to the engine room for a full damage report.

The situation was serious, but the ship would hold together long enough to get back.

"Pilot, set course for *Normandy*. Cruising speed."

"Sir," Katja said, "before we head home, I recommend we search near *Nelson* for survivors."

"There's no way anybody survived," Breeze said, her voice rising with each word. "Let's get back before someone has to rescue us!"

"The ship broke up slowly," Katja said. "There was time enough that some might have escaped."

Thomas glanced at the damage control board again. They were slowly bleeding fuel, and would start to lose air again if the door to the main cafeteria buckled. They had virtually no weapons and their ability to withstand heavy maneuvering was questionable. His instinct said to get back to safety while he still could. But lately his instincts had been questioned.

"Pilot, set course for *Admiral Nelson*, cruising speed. OpsO, get the camera searching for anything that looks like a spacesuit or an escape pod."

Jack and Katja set about their tasks. Breeze leaned back in her seat and stared straight ahead.

It was nearly three hours before *Rapier* began to lower into *Normandy*'s hangar, two escape pods clinging magnetically to her hull where the drop ships had once nested. The rescue operation was nearly complete, with several Hawks and other fast-attack craft returning home with more than forty *Admiral Nelson* survivors. Many were dressed only in emergency escape suits, and wouldn't have survived more than a few hours.

Thomas was happy to have participated, as it took the sting out of the fact that the EF had just lost its only battleship, both its cruisers, and another destroyer. At this rate, he mused bitterly, *Rapier* herself might be the EF flagship in another week or so.

At least Chandler had finally seen sense and put off the EF's attack on Centauri settlements. With no heavy bombardment capability remaining, any attack would have been pretty pathetic. The commodore seemed to grasp that his new vision of leading a band of buccaneer marauders was destined to get every last one of them killed. In a terse message to the EF, he had ordered all ships to hold position while the rescue operation concluded, then set course for deep space.

Rapier was met by a crowd of medics who escorted the *Nelson* survivors away. Mechanics were standing by to start servicing the ship, and once the escape pods had been lifted clear Thomas saw no need to retain his crew any longer.

It had been an exhausting afternoon.

He floated in his cabin for a while, trying to remember how good it used to feel to be the captain of this vessel. He knew he should be pleased with how the mission had gone today, despite the losses they had incurred, because he and his ship had performed well. Two cutters destroyed and two others chased off—not bad for a thirty-meter raider with a skeleton crew.

Maybe it was the pyrrhic nature of the triumph that robbed him of any elation. Or maybe he just didn't give a damn. If they ever got home—a big if—he was going to find a nice, quiet corner of the solar system to raise a family. Soma had enough money to make things comfortable.

He was surprised by a knock on his door.

"Come in."

It opened and Breeze entered with a hand-held display. Gone was her earlier, stunned expression. Her eyes were as determined as he had ever seen them. He wasn't intimidated in the slightest, however, as he felt the anger well up inside him.

"Thomas," she said, "I want off this ship."

Her arrogance astounded him. "Nothing would make me happier, but unfortunately you're here by the orders of Commodore Chandler himself."

"Yeah, I know. He called me in special to tell me how I was supposed to babysit you."

He clenched his fists as his pulse pounded in his ears. Chandler had actually said that?

She handed him the display.

"On that is the letter of recommendation you're going to send the commodore, telling him how I'm too valuable to be risked on patrol in *Rapier*."

Thomas read the letter with growing incredulity. It praised Breeze's tactical abilities, then went on to say how her greater value as an intelligence officer had been proven time and again during the war. It cited various examples—the uncovering of the hostage location in Free Lhasa, the capture of the Centauri agent at the Cerberan farm, the rescue of the troopers from New Tibetan custody, the pinpointing of critical targets of opportunity for the assault on Abeona—and offered glowing commentary on her general contributions to the EF command staff.

He read and re-read the final paragraph:

In conclusion, while I value her contributions to my ship, I feel that for the greater good of Expeditionary Force 15 and the Astral Force, Lieutenant Brisebois must be transferred back to her staff position. It is my strongest possible recommendation that she be permanently assigned as the EF chief of Intelligence, with the appropriate rank and authority befitting the position.

Thomas Kane
Lt(C)
CO *Rapier*

He stared at her. "You've got to be shitting me."

She stared right back. "No. Sign this letter and deliver it to Chandler. I am *not* going to risk my life in this fucking tin can— not again."

"You're insane," he said. "Why in the worlds do you think I'd do this?"

She shook her head, her expression turning dangerous.

"Your career is over, Thomas. Don't make me destroy your life, as well." Her matter-of-fact tone only added to the surreal nature of her words. He struggled to grasp what she was trying to do.

"Why?"

"How can I ascend if your star continues to shine?"

He couldn't reply. There were no more words to say. She was destroying him for her own advancement.

"Sign the letter," she said, "and nothing else needs be said. You and I can just agree that what happened on deployment stays on deployment."

His anger turned to rage.

"Fuck you."

"Yes, that's exactly what I'm going to tell Chandler you did. Although, I might actually portray it more as a rape. I'll see how the conversation goes. Either way, I doubt the good commodore will long hide the news from his goddaughter or her wealthy family."

He desperately tried to think of a counterstrike.

"But... you're just as involved as I am."

"Yes," she explained patiently, "but I'm not engaged to the daughter of one of Ganymede's richest men." She batted her bright blue eyes. "I'm the victim, Thomas, taken advantage of by an aggressive, egotistical captain." She smiled. "And I'm not quite sure, but I have a sneaky suspicion that if I ask young Katja about her relationship to you, I might uncover some more dirt.

"I'd do it as a public inquiry, of course, so that she'd be duty-bound to tell the truth in front of a tribunal. And I think the media would enjoy hearing about it, too."

Thomas felt sick.

"Sign the letter, Thomas. Then none of this needs to happen."

He stared down at the hand-held, noticing a pen conveniently fastened to it.

"Sign it, and you're rid of me forever. When we get home you can marry sweet Soma and live a life of leisure as a decorated war hero. I'll even get Chandler to recommend you for an honorary promotion upon retirement."

Her honeyed words scraped over him like gravel. He wanted to throttle her, smash his fist into her perfect white teeth. Instead, he picked up the pen and electronically signed the letter. She held all the cards, and he considered himself human enough to want to keep his public dignity.

She took the hand-held, uploaded the file to Thomas's computer and sent it from his address. He watched wordlessly.

Then she gave him a wink and left the cabin. He thought perhaps he should move, but his limbs didn't respond, and he just floated.

He floated in silence. In utter defeat.

58

"Commander Brisebois, briefing in ten minutes."

Breeze nodded to the chief petty officer, and smiled. She did enjoy hearing those words. A quick glance around to make sure no one was looking, and she snuck another peek at her shoulders—at the three gold bars on each. Then she took a long look around at the compartment she stood in, filled with consoles and highly classified equipment. It wasn't Astral Intelligence HQ or anything, but it was hers. She now stood on a par with the commanding officers of destroyers and cruisers. Even Commodore Chandler was really only a captain, just one rank above her.

What once had seemed an almost god-like level of authority was practically within her grasp.

Chandler had seemed so pleased with himself when he promoted her, talking it up like it was his idea. In front of the entire command staff he'd praised her excellent work throughout the war, and said he thought it only right and fitting that she wear the rank of the position she'd been effectively filling so well.

The other commanders on staff had congratulated her warmly, but that lieutenant ASW controller had kept to himself. He probably felt pretty lonely, now that he was the only lieutenant left. Breeze figured he should feel lucky to still be allowed on staff. She was surprised that, with all the destroyed ships recently, there wasn't some spare three-ringer hanging around to take the ASW position.

In all the ships that remained, there were a grand total of twelve commanders, including her. And with only two full captains, that put her pretty close to the top of the pile. Oh sure, the two surviving regiments had their share of senior officers, but the Corps had served its usefulness already—as far as Breeze was concerned, they might as well stay in their bunks.

Nothing was hidden from the Chief Intelligence Officer of an expeditionary force. She'd called up the personnel lists and confirmed that, just a few months shy of her thirty-fourth birthday, she was the youngest commander in the Astral Force. And she hadn't even joined until she was twenty-seven. What was that old navy toast?

A bloody war and a sickly season. This bloody war had served Charity Brisebois very well indeed.

She'd always intended her military career to be short, ending it as a lieutenant. That kind of experience would easily land her a high-profile, middle-management job in big business. But now that she was a commander... starting her business career in upper management looked pretty likely.

More money, better contacts, better chance of marrying right and having her twins before she turned forty. When the kids were old enough for pre-school she'd have to switch back to a more prestigious position—teacher, she figured—before getting into journalism and media to build her public image. And then, politics.

She glanced at her new rank insignia again. What a stroke of luck. She applauded herself for seeing the opening and grabbing it.

Of course, none of this really mattered if she didn't make it through that damn jump gate to get home alive. So for the past three days she'd been driving her team to find a solution to the rather large Centauri battle force that was sitting between her and her future.

The solution, in one of life's sweet ironies, had come from none other than Thomas Kane. One of her warrants brought her a memo Thomas had submitted outlining the interesting implications of Bulk physics and the use of torpedoes. Breeze gave up after three paragraphs but her warrant assured her that the science was sound—at least theoretically.

She'd summoned young Jack Mallory to interpret for her. This had proved prescient, because he was the brains behind the whole idea.

So Thomas was trying to take credit for his subordinate's work. Breeze had to admire him for the attempt.

The chief petty officer approached her again.

"Ma'am?"

She followed him out into the flats, pulling herself along the handholds toward the main briefing room. When they got back to Terra, she decided, she was getting herself posted ashore and never going into zero-g again.

The briefing room looked the same as always, with the three large screens on the wall behind the speaking platform and the central projector for the 3-D display. Her staff had prepared her visuals and her notes were ready on the display screen at the podium. Some of the audience had already arrived, various junior officers she didn't recognize.

Every ship was sending its XO for this briefing, and most of them were lieutenants, but she didn't try to guess who was who. She recognized one of the loud ones as *Kristiansand*'s XO—what was his name, Shane?—but he'd been pretty annoying the last time she'd had a drink with him, and she kept her distance.

When Thomas Kane arrived he went and sat with the man, confirming her instincts. He studiously refused to look at Breeze.

As the other members of the command staff began arriving she found a seat at the end of the front row, close to the podium. Colonel Korolev arrived without ceremony, as always, but everyone floated to attention when the great one finally made his entrance.

Chandler made some opening remarks, then called on the new AVW commander, formerly the CO of *Miami*, to deliver a brief on the orders of battle. These details Breeze already knew.

The Centauris had a battle cruiser and five frigates guarding the jump gate, pretty much the same size force that had attacked the EF over Laika. The EF had three destroyers and a stealth ship guarding the main body of *Normandy*, *Troy*, and the two supply ships. About a hundred star fighters were still serviceable, housed in the four ships of the main body. The hundred or more strike fighters were also being prepped for combat. Add in five surviving fast-attack craft and a handful of Hawks, and it all added up to having their ass kicked.

And then Breeze was invited to the stage to present the plan. She smiled warmly at the AVW controller as they passed— pleasant, name of Karen, post-traumatic struggles at losing her ship, family connections in Terra—and pulled herself in behind the podium. The assembled crowd stared expectantly, and as she looked back she was shocked at how empty the theater seemed. Nevertheless, she put on an expression of suitably grave professionalism and began to speak.

"As Commander Holmes has made clear, the EF is seriously out-matched in a direct confrontation with the enemy force. However, we have science on our side. Through the diligent efforts of our personnel, we have determined how we can use a modified version of our standard torpedo to disrupt and distract the Centauri force."

The large 3-D display activated beside her, configured to give a 4-D representation of space, and Breeze gave her viewers a few moments to adapt their thinking to include the added spatial dimension.

"I'll save you the equations, but very briefly the theory is this: the Bulk extends to infinity in the fourth dimension, but the region we are generally familiar with only extends for sixteen peets. Beyond this, the characteristics of the fundamental forces take a radical shift, perhaps due to the existence of a strongbrane, commonly referred to as the Erebos Layer."

She checked her notes to ensure she'd said that right, then scanned ahead for the next dose of multidimensional physics.

"Beyond the Erebos Layer lies the Chthonian Deep, into which scientists have been able to make only a few direct observations. It is theorized, however, that this region of the Bulk is dense in dark energy which, if properly manipulated, can undergo a..." She checked her notes. "...tenebral implosion and transform into dark matter.

"At this extreme range into the Bulk, the force of gravity starts to increase exponentially and is so strong that objects in the Chthonian Deep can have a direct effect on objects here on the brane. It's theorized that we never see this phenomenon in reality due to the extremely homogenous density of dark energy that far into the Bulk."

She gauged her audience, noting an awful lot of blank stares and one or two approving nods. She didn't even pretend to guess whether the theory was valid or not, but it was solidly backed by the brightest of Astral minds.

"Basically, we're going to drop a modified torpedo right into the center of the Centauri force, seventeen peets in, and yank up some dark energy. The resultant massive object far in the Bulk is going to seriously mess with them. This will give us the chance we need to race past them and jump for Terra."

More nods. Korolev leaned over and said something quietly to Chandler, glancing at Breeze. The commodore nodded and turned his attention back to her presentation.

"Are there any questions?" she asked.

Scattered laughter rippled through the uncertain crowd.

"Who's delivering the torpedo?" someone in the second row asked.

This was the part of the plan Breeze liked the most.

"The modified fast-attack craft *Rapier* is the ideal insertion vehicle. She's well-armed and fast enough to do the insertion, and she's equipped with ASW gear and the ability to fire torpedoes."

And it's pretty likely she'll never make it back. Breeze was willing to have Thomas and Katja both be remembered as heroes, if it gave her the assurance that she'd never have to worry about them stealing her limelight again.

Thomas's expression was grim but determined. His reaction had been her one worry, but it turned out she knew him well after all. He so desperately wanted to regain Chandler's respect that he'd take on whatever suicide mission she thrust at him.

"*Rapier* will launch from *Normandy* six hours prior to our approach on the jump gate," she continued, "displacing herself so that she can attack from a different bearing and seek to avoid detection until she's within torpedo firing range. To help her, every ship in the EF will switch on AG and start radiating as if for battle, hopefully capturing the full attention of the enemy."

"What happens if the magic torpedo doesn't work?" someone else asked.

She knew Chandler wanted to answer this question. Plan B had been his main contribution to the strategy. He was already pushing off from his seat and turning to face the audience. By the time he reached the podium, Breeze had switched the display to tactical.

She half listened as she retook her seat, amused how much Chandler enjoyed the spotlight when he knew what he was talking about. With great dramatic effect he laid out the backup plan, in which the sole remaining stealth ship, *Viper*, would be hiding in the gravimetric signature of *Normandy* and *Troy* until the Centauris got within range. Then she would strike out as only a stealth ship could.

By the end of the briefing, everyone was fired up and ready to go. It never ceased to amaze Breeze how people could convince themselves that charging in to get killed was a good idea. There were a lot of handshakes as farewells were made. She was just about to slip out when she noticed Thomas floating forward to speak to Chandler.

She pushed off her chair to join the conversation.

"…I'm sure you will," Chandler was saying, shaking his hand. "Make me proud." She saw the glimmer of a smile cross Thomas's face, but it faded as soon as he noticed her.

He turned back to Chandler like she wasn't there.

"Just in case something goes wrong, sir, please send my love to Soma. Tell her I'm sorry I couldn't make it to the wedding, but my heart will be there."

Chandler gave a short laugh. "You can tell her yourself, son."

"Yes," Breeze said, stopping her forward momentum with a hand on the commodore's shoulder. "We all know you'll make it, Thomas. That's why the commodore chose *Rapier* for this mission. Not for the ship, but for the captain." Could he tell that she was oh-so-subtly mocking him?

She suspected so.

He looked very tired, and much older. But he forced a smile.

"Well, I'll see you around, sir," he said to Chandler. "Thank you, sir."

Then Thomas rejoined his friend Shane—no, Sean—as they left the briefing room.

"It really was big of him," Chandler commented, "recommending one of his own subordinates for promotion ahead of himself."

"Sir?"

Chandler turned to her. "He recommended you for this promotion. I was already thinking it, but his letter really sealed the deal."

She put on her best look of surprise. "I had no idea!" She took in a fluttery breath and looked to where Thomas had disappeared. "I'm honored. Thank you for telling me, sir. Thomas would never have said anything."

"He's a good man. Let's hope he can pull it off."

"If anyone can, it's Thomas Kane." He was going to be dead within twelve hours, so she didn't mind singing his praises. "Either way he'll be remembered as the hero of the day."

Chandler nodded and moved off.

Breeze looked around for Karen, formerly of *Miami*. The older woman seemed to have taken to her, and it never hurt to have more contacts. Should she lie low, sow business contacts and wait for her term of service to end next year? Or should she stick close to Chandler and ride his coattails?

So much to plan.

59

Katja tried to stretch in her seat. With the shoulder straps, the bulk of her spacesuit, and her sore ribcage it was pretty much impossible. Which of course made her want to do it even more. She shifted slightly, wincing at the pain in her kidneys.

Thomas looked over at her in the near-darkness of *Rapier*'s bridge.

"You're unusually restless, OpsO."

She sighed. "I guess it's all that running I've been doing lately. Sitting here growing my ass isn't as much fun as I thought."

"I'm a master at it," Jack said from his seat in the front row. "It just takes patience."

But Katja's patience was in short supply, five hours into *Rapier*'s flanking maneuver on the Centauri force. With most systems off, and bridge instrumentation down to the lowest possible illumination, there had been little to do but wait as the ship moved gently along her long, curved intercept path.

It had seemed exciting at first. *Rapier* launched under the cover of four star fighters, the planes squawking ident codes and passing routine chatter among themselves to make sure they were visible. Then, a thousand kilometers out from the EF, the fighters had banked dramatically away, making a show of spreading out in pairs for their assigned defensive stations.

At the same time *Rapier* cut her engines and coasted for fifteen minutes. The intention was for any Centauri spotters to focus on the fighters. When there was no sign of detection by the enemy, *Rapier* nudged forward at her minimum cruising speed and opened the bearing between herself and the EF.

After that, absolutely nothing else happened. Internal lighting was shut down and climate control reduced to wintry levels. Air was circulated through every space, but the filters were shut down, so it would remain breathable for twelve hours at the most.

The crew had been reduced to ten—there was no strike team, and Breeze's seat remained conspicuously empty. The rest were scattered throughout the craft, one in each turret and four in the engine room. Two of the engineers were volunteers from *Cutlass*, their skills more useful to this mission than any trooper's. There were no medics, no dedicated damage control teams.

Radio receivers were still operating, but the transmitters were shut down to avoid any possible leakage of signal. Food packs had been issued to all personnel, so the galley was redundant, as were the heads due to the self-contained nature of their spacesuits.

Katja looked again at the display, leaning in to make out the symbols in the dimmed sphere. The Centauri force was holding position, although *Rapier*'s long, elliptical path had brought them considerably closer. The ships were still too far away to see with the naked eye, but Katja needed no imagination to picture their silvery hulls. On the 3-D the EF ships were also visible, closing the Centauris at a leisurely pace. The plan was to fool the enemy into thinking the EF was trying to sneak in close before launching a surprise attack.

And just beyond the enemy position lay the jump gate. The way home. A large, unique symbol marked the location of this beautiful, beautiful thing.

"Pilot," Thomas said, "come left seven degrees and down five."

"Roger."

Jack eased his controls and the stars outside shifted slightly. Thomas had been ordering these minor adjustments every so often for hours.

"Sir, why the minor course changes?" she asked. Thomas frowned thoughtfully at the 3-D display, then glanced over at her.

"Trying to stay off the radar. We don't know exactly how the

Centauris track targets, so I'm doing a bit of everything. We're not aiming at the enemy ships, because just about any military sensor picks up on closing objects.

"I don't want to stay on any one course for too long," he continued, "because if their surveillance gets any hits on us, it'll register a pattern and project where it should see us next. If it spots us there, according to that projection, then we're tagged—not to mention screwed.

"At the same time, we can't make too major a course alteration because there are some sensors that look specifically for changing vectors. Nothing in nature changes direction spontaneously, so an object that's maneuvering is identified as artificial, and likely a threat."

She nodded, and for a moment she felt just a *hint* of her old admiration for him. He was still an asshole, but a talented one.

Earlier in the long flight, he and Jack had discussed options for how best to deliver the torpedo, quickly leaving her behind with their talk of dark energy, dark matter, and different layers in the Bulk. Her role was to operate the missiles and guns against brane-based enemy vessels, so she didn't need to understand. Even so it wasn't her nature to go into a battle armed only with faith.

"Okay," she said, "I admit it. I listened to you eggheads earlier but I still don't get how this torpedo is going to take out an entire Centauri squadron. Give it to me in terms Scott Lahko would understand."

"Big brick fall on ships," Jack suggested.

"We're going to detonate the torpedo way into the Bulk," Thomas added. "At seventeen peets. We need to go deep to get the gravitons working for us."

She'd made it that far in her own thinking—gravity was stronger the farther into the Bulk you went. But something wasn't adding up. "So why wouldn't we just drop torpedoes at seventeen peets for every engagement and cash in on that powerful gravity? Why would we even have missiles and guns?"

Thomas opened his mouth to answer, but then stopped. A puzzled look creased his features and he blinked in thought.

There was a moment of silence on the bridge.

"Because," Jack said, "below the Erebos Layer—below

sixteen peets—we're into the realm of dark energy. There's a theory that a graviton burst in a sea of dark energy will cause the dark matter to collapse together and create a physical, massive object. Even if it's tiny—and it will be due to the limited power of our torpedo—it'll have such gravitational pull that far into the Bulk that the effects will reach all the way to the brane."

"Meaning?"

Jack shrugged. "All the Centauri ships in the area will get knocked around and maybe busted up."

"If nothing else," Thomas said, "it'll scare the hell out of them, distract them, and give us a chance to escape."

Katja nodded. "I can see why the EF chose you guys to conduct this mission. I just hope I'm good enough to keep up."

In the dim light of the display, Thomas gave her a slow, wry look. "Oh, I think Commander Brisebois thinks as highly of you as she does of me. She wouldn't *dream* of letting you sit this one out."

After a moment she caught his meaning, and smoldering anger flared. Not at him, but at the truth behind his words.

"Well, being reminded of that just motivates me even more to succeed—and come back alive. Then I can wipe that smug look off her face. Probably with my fist."

Thomas's expression was lost in the darkness as he leaned back in his chair.

"Breeze is a bit of a bitch," Jack said.

Katja smiled. The boy had become a man.

A warning light flared on each of their consoles. Search radar. She fumbled to call up her EM array screen. Thomas was much faster, and he made his assessment while she was still sizing up the graphs.

"Nothing to worry about yet—just a single sweep. Probably random."

"At this speed," Jack said, "we'll be in firing range in forty-five minutes. But if I light it up, I can have us there in ninety seconds."

"Hold off, Pilot. Steady as she goes." Thomas activated the ship-wide broadcast. "This is the captain—sitrep. We're moving into range where our detection by the enemy fleet is becoming more likely. We will stay at ultra-low power for as long as possible—at most another forty-five minutes—but be ready to switch to full speed attack at a moment's notice. We will waste no time. We get in, we deliver the package, we break for the jump gate. That is all."

The skeleton crew had made sense back in *Normandy*—fewer people, less energy required—but as *Rapier* made another slight turn to further close on the enemy, Katja saw Breeze's hand once again. This had been planned all along as a suicide mission.

Well, fuck her. Katja checked the weapons systems again and watched the movement of the Centauri sentries in their defensive cloud, far off the port bow. The red symbols of the enemy force continued to track slowly toward the center of the 3-D display. After a few minutes another sweep passed over them, but still there was no hostile reaction.

Five minutes after that, the sweep returned, and began to pass over them every few seconds.

"Okay," Thomas said, "we're in sensor range. They're gonna have us within a minute. Pilot, ETA weapon range at flank speed?"

"Sixty seconds."

Thomas drummed his gloved fingers on the armrest, then he reached for his console. A push of a button and a single, burst transmission flashed out from *Rapier*, back to the Expeditionary Force.

Commencing attack.

Ten seconds later, the 3-D display lit up with a barrage of electromagnetic signals as the Terran ships flashed every radar and weapons system they had. All seven ships turned and accelerated toward the Centauri force. Symbols of long-range missiles raced out into the void between the fleets. Star fighters appeared, dotting the region around the EF. They didn't attack the Centauris, though.

That was *Rapier*'s job.

For several long moments they waited for the Centauri ships to take the bait. But the enemy ships stood their ground. At first, only the robotic sentries moved to create a defensive swarm poised between the fleets. Small red symbols separated in waves from one enemy ship: Katja recognized the firing pattern of the battle cruiser.

"We've got to go! The Fleet's going to get pummeled!"

"Pilot, set course for the center of the enemy force, flank speed."

Katja was crushed back into her seat as *Rapier* rocketed forward from a crawl to a full sprint. The Centauri ships on the 3-D display moved quickly, and very soon she began to make out tiny flashes against the stars.

Sensor alarms flashed across her console and 3-D revealed several robotic sentries breaking away from their swarm to intercept. She saw the Terran star fighters suddenly charge the swarm, but *Rapier*'s attackers ignored the move and bore down on their new target.

"AA weapons free!" Thomas said. She designated the incoming sentries and gave all three turrets the green light.

Jack jinked right and left as missiles tried and failed to lock on. Katja groaned with the sharp g-forces—at this speed any vector changes that overwhelmed the inertial dampeners would splatter the humans in their suits.

The sentries flashed past with hardly a chance to fire any shots. They turned more sharply than any human could withstand, and picked up the chase, but *Rapier*'s speed was such that they couldn't close within range.

The silver ships of the Centauri force loomed ahead, multiple flashes revealing their attacks on the EF. The Terran ships were holding off, she saw, and the star fighters had withdrawn from their melee.

Everyone was watching for *Rapier*'s launch.

"Coming into range," Jack said. "Steady... now!"

Thomas slammed his fist down on the armrest.

"Fire!"

Nothing happened. *Rapier* continued to plunge toward the heart of the enemy force.

Jack pressed his launch button again. And a third time. His eyes darted across his console.

"Something's wrong—it didn't fire!"

The top and bottom turrets opened up as another robotic sentry did a high-speed pass. A sharp bang against the hull rocked the bridge. Katja stared up through the windows and saw one of the shining frigates turning toward them, guns flashing.

"Slow to attack speed," Thomas shouted. "Reverse course!"

Rapier banked hard and pointed back out toward deep space—straight into the pursuing sentries. Multiple bangs overhead rang in Katja's ears as the sentries flashed by again.

Jack swore nonstop as he scanned his console, still jinking the ship. She looked at her own readouts. The torpedo wasn't one of her weapons, but she brought up its status with a few quick commands. A red light flashed on the section where the weapon was attached to the hull.

"There's an error with the clamp."

"It won't release," Thomas said, looking at his own board. "We can't launch." *Rapier* shook violently as something exploded just outside the hull. More warning lights flashed. Katja tapped in orders to the turrets, instructing them to fire at will. There was nothing friendly nearby that they might hit.

"We're out of range again," Jack said.

Thomas stared at the 3-D, then gave Katja a long look.

"Reverse course. Steer for the center of the Centauri force."

She stared at him. "What's your plan?"

His face was grim, but settled. "We can't launch the torpedo, but we can still detonate it."

"What, while it's still attached to the ship?"

"Yes."

If Jack heard, he made no sign as he brought *Rapier* around again. Continuous turret fire and warning alarms punctuated the roar of the engines. Thomas gave her a little smile.

"We'll be heroes," he said. "That's something."

Her mind flashed to what her father would think upon hearing the news that his daughter had given her life to save the Expeditionary Force. Would he be proud of her? Would he finally speak well of her?

Probably not, she decided. He'd still find some way to criticize her, and she wouldn't be around to set him straight.

And then she pictured Breeze being the one telling her father about the death, professing great sadness and then smirking as she turned away.

She shook her head.

"No way! I'm not giving that bitch the satisfaction."

She unstrapped from her seat and pushed back toward the door. "I'll release it manually. Just don't get us shot." He didn't stop her, although he didn't really have a chance as she thrust herself toward the airlock door, heaved it open, and pulled it shut behind her.

The honeycomb passageway had only dim, red lighting but it was enough to see by. She pulled herself along the rungs, listening to the thunder of turret fire as she passed their hatches. The ship dove and the bulkhead suddenly slammed up against her, knocking her from her handhold and clear to the far side of the flats. Ignoring the pain in her torso she scrambled aft until she reached the airlocks for the drop ships.

Habit made her slide up into the port-side chamber, but she paused as she saw stars through the tiny window in the airlock's outer door. There was no strike pod waiting beyond—only the great abyss. She released two arm-spans of her suit's tether, hooked on, closed her faceplate, and started the depressurization.

"I'm going external," she said on her suit comms, trying to sound calm.

"*Roger,*" Thomas responded, his voice anything but calm.

By the time the outer doors opened, all she could hear was her own rapid breathing. The view outside was a lightning storm of tracer rounds, missiles, sentries, and ships. She was in the smooth depression of the hull where her strike pod had once nested, the port engine just visible over the lip and the tail turret blasting away barely aft of her, almost close enough to touch.

She grabbed one of the notches in the hull where the pod had once clamped down, and pulled herself forward to peer out of the depression at the main hull. The top turret was twenty meters forward, double barrels tracking aft-to-forward as they fired on a passing sentry.

Enemy tracers struck down from starboard as another sentry strafed the ship. She ducked down, feeling the quick thuds of rounds hitting the hull. Her breathing was loud in her ears.

Not giving herself time to think, she pulled slowly up onto *Rapier*'s black hull, spotting the torpedo mounted on the centerline, less than two meters away. The weapon was dull grey, and secured on a hardpoint three quarters of the way down its body.

She looked down, and kept her eyes on the hull, willfully ignoring the flashes of light reflecting insanely off the smooth, black plates. Within less than a dozen leopard crawls she reached the torpedo hardpoint. A quick examination revealed the obvious source of the problem. Part of the mechanism had sheared. Metal fatigue, she guessed, combined with the extreme cold of the ultra-low power approach and the sudden accelerations of combat.

This wasn't good.

"I'm at the torpedo," she reported. "The clamp has sheared and won't operate. Manual override won't work."

"Can you reach the hardpoint?" Thomas said.

She looked down at the bracket that connected the clamped weapon to the hull.

"Yes."

"Release the hardpoint itself—it's magnetic. The torpedo can launch with the hardpoint still attached."

"Are you sure?"

"Do it!"

The magnetic clamps were simple to operate, and she deactivated the first of the four nearest to her, port-aft. She gasped as the hull slid away beneath her. Her gloved hands swatted at the smooth surface but got no purchase. Suddenly she was free and clear, out of reach as *Rapier* dove away from her.

Her body snapped back as her tether reached its limit. She screamed in pain but managed to keep vague focus on the ship as it continued to dive. She was being dragged along behind, but as *Rapier* dipped her nose Katja drifted down toward the firing arcs of the tail turret. She swore and hauled herself in on the tether until she could grab the open doors of the airlock. The ship heaved again and she hung on for dear life.

"Dammit! Stop maneuvering! You knocked me clear last time!"

"Roger. No promises."

She ignored the burning in her back and pushed off for the lip of the depression. She grabbed it and directed her flight forward over the hull to the hardpoint once again. She switched off the port-forward magnetic lock and climbed over the torpedo to repeat the process twice on the starboard side.

Then she pushed the torpedo with all her strength, and was rewarded to watch it lift slowly off the hull. Suddenly she noticed a thin cable up near the nose that kept it attached to *Rapier*.

"Hardpoint disconnected. But there's still a cable forward."

"That's the control relay. Leave it and get back inside."

Grabbing her tether she pulled herself down into the pod nest and back into the airlock. Just as she started to close the outer doors she risked a glance up at the battle.

The Centauri battle cruiser was in plain view, rolling slowly as it unleashed wave after wave of missiles at the Expeditionary Force. As the doors shut and blocked the view of the mighty ship, she allowed herself a smile. Nothing a few troopers couldn't take down.

"I'm in!"

"Roger!"

As the airlock slowly pressurized, she was thrown against the wall, no doubt as *Rapier* turned back to her attack bearing. Soon the control showed green and she dove down into the honeycomb flats again. She flew forward to the bridge and crashed back down into her seat just as she heard Thomas shout.

"Fire!"

There was no thump of weapon release, but moments later she saw the torpedo pull out ahead of the ship. She watched its fiery exhaust for barely a moment before it shrunk to nothingness and vanished into the Bulk.

"Buckle in," Thomas said. "We're outta here!"

She grabbed her straps and hung on as Jack wrenched his stick over and pushed the throttles forward to flank speed. On the 3-D the blue torpedo symbol cruised toward the center of the red hostiles. She looked for the launch range radius line, but saw nothing. Then she noticed what range scale Thomas had reduced to.

He read her thoughts. "We're a lot closer than we should be."

She clicked her straps and pressed herself back into her chair. Her lower abdomen felt like it was on fire. She turned her eyes to the display. *Rapier* was moving at full speed toward the embattled EF ships, which in turn were trying to flank the

Centauris and get to the jump gate. The Centauris were massed on *Rapier*'s starboard quarter and receding quickly.

The torpedo was just moving into their midst.

There was no flash, no thump. Just a sudden, overwhelming pull that tried to rip Katja from her seat. Outside, the stars dropped below the nose as *Rapier* was pulled off course, high and to starboard. Then the ship started to shudder. She looked up through the windows above, and felt her jaw drop.

The Centauri ships were all moving, converging on a single point in space. And she knew their forms well enough to tell that every one of them was pointed *away* from their direction of travel. She could even see the glow of their engines on full burn as they slowly but surely drifted together. The frigates were moving faster than the battle cruiser, but even as she watched its long hull seemed to grow longer.

Then pieces started to break off its stern and fall away with ever-increasing speed. Within seconds the cruiser was torn apart and sucked down into a growing blackness. The closer frigates went next, while the more distant ones fought a losing battle to break free.

On her display all the red symbols were converging and disappearing. But the point of their convergence wasn't moving farther away from the center—it was slowly getting closer.

Rapier was being pulled in.

Jack knew it too, and pushed his stick forward to point the nose away from the singularity. The view of the stars ahead shifted, but not by much. The shuddering intensified.

"I can't break free!" he shouted.

"We have to reduce mass," Thomas said. He scanned his console, stabbing at the weapons controls.

Katja saw the dazzling flashes of the four morningstar missiles. They burned ahead of *Rapier* for a few seconds and then, from right to left, each was pulled off course and into an ever-increasing dive toward the singularity.

Rapier inched further up in her decaying orbit, but it wasn't enough.

Thomas activated the ship-wide broadcast.

"This is the captain," he said. "Emergency atmosphere

dump!" This was normally a tactic for fighting out-of-control fires. But now, the considerable volume of gas that made up *Rapier*'s air was blasted into space, reducing her mass by a noticeable percentage.

She nosed farther toward freedom.

Thomas typed a command into his console. The ship's projected course extended on the 3-D display. It was a highly curved route, but it slowly cleared the torpedo blast point.

"Steady as she goes, Pilot," he said. "I think we're gonna make it."

The EF ships, well clear of the implosion, were moving at full speed for the jump gate. Katja saw that *Rapier*'s projected path would actually pass wide of the jump gate, and she pointed this out to Thomas.

"I want to make sure we're clear of this thing's gravitational pull," he said. "We can always do an orbit and dive for the jump gate when we've better assessed the situation. Hey, Jack, how long does this tenebral implosion last? Are we talking minutes or hours?"

Jack didn't look back, leaning on his flight stick to keep it on maximum climb.

"I was expecting a few seconds," he admitted. "And I was expecting the Centauris to still be here!"

Thomas glanced at Katja through his faceplate, concern clouding his features. If he expected her to say something, however, she had no idea what. She was just fighting to keep her jaw shut, and her eyes from looking like saucers.

Then she noticed that the symbol for the jump gate was flashing. She was pretty sure jump gate symbols never flashed.

"Hey Jack, don't jump gates use dark energy like our torpedo just did?"

He didn't seem too thrilled by the question. "Uhh, yeah! The gates use dark energy to open up. Why?"

"I'm no expert, but I think our jump gate might be closing down."

Jack checked his hunt controls.

"What the—? That's not right!"

His words didn't fill her with confidence. She noticed that the

EF ships were almost at the gate, neither forming into the usual column for gate passage nor slowing down.

Thomas picked up on it immediately. He activated the ship-to-ship command circuit. "*Normandy*, this is *Rapier*! Confirm status of jump gate!"

The response came several moments later, heavy with Doppler distortion. "*This is* Normandy*! The jump gate is becoming unstable! We're jumping now!*"

Seconds later, the first blue symbol—*Normandy* herself—disappeared. The rest of the fleet followed quickly behind—all except for one. A female voice sounded on the warped circuit.

"*Rapier, this is* Kristiansand. *Estimate forty seconds until jump gate collapse. State your ETA my position.*"

Thomas's fingers flew over his console. The projected course on the 3-D display shifted to intersect the flashing gate symbol.

"Pilot, steer computed course!"

Jack eased his stick to starboard slightly. The projected course wobbled as he struggled to walk the tight rope, fighting between the ship's vector and the singularity's pull.

"*Kristiansand, Rapier.* My ETA thirty seconds."

Katja felt a wave of relief, then realized that at least ten seconds must have passed since *Kristiansand* had sent her signal.

"*Rapier, if you can't make it, abort your attempt and I will stay here with you.*"

Thomas glanced at Katja as he keyed the circuit.

"*Kristiansand*, this is *Rapier*. Thanks, but I have time to spare. Request you make your jump and clear the path for me."

"*Rapier, I assess that you will not make my position before jump gate collapse. Abort your run and regroup with me.*"

Jack grunted as he fought the controls. The projected course altered violently, then steadied back on target.

Fifteen seconds.

"This is *Rapier*, negative. Your readings are false due to gravimetric interference. Jump now and clear a path on the other side." Thomas paused, then added: "Jack Mallory will get me home!"

"Hey," Jack said, "no pressure!"

Kristiansand's charcoal hull was growing visible against the stars, and Katja watched as the destroyer turned away and vanished in a spacetime ripple.

Five seconds.

Jump gates, for all their theoretical majesty and importance to the colonial economy, were actually very hard to spot in real life. Katja grabbed onto her armrests and held her breath. She looked for some kind of marker, some sign that they were about to travel more than four light years in an instant.

She saw a sudden ripple in the starscape.

Then blinding light.

Then nothing.

60

It was only Jack's second time to *Normandy*'s star lounge, yet it seemed very familiar to him. Probably because of all those hours in his rack he'd spent dreaming about meeting Breeze here.

He smiled to himself at that.

"What's so funny, Jack?" Katja asked. She was seated ramrod straight in a back brace, facing him in her own comfy chair, a beer cradled in her hands.

He shrugged and slouched back, dropping his feet on the low table between them and gazing out through the huge window.

"Nothing."

"Jack thinks air is funny," Thomas said from his chair between them, facing directly at the window. "It doesn't take much to get him to smile."

"I guess smiling's pretty easy these days. Gravity abounds, beer is plentiful, and I don't actually have a job to do. Oh, and not being at war anymore sort of lifts my spirits."

"Well, enjoy it while it lasts—it's just a cease-fire."

He looked at Thomas and smiled. "Well, if that cease-fire doesn't hold," he said in his most heroic voice, "don't you worry, because Jack Mallory will get you home!"

Katja snickered behind her beer.

"All right, all right," Thomas said. "Let it go, you guys. I had to say something to get *Kristiansand* out of our way. Avernell thinks you're the best ever."

Jack shrugged modestly, gazing out the window again. "Meh."

His eyes were drawn to the massive form of Astral Base Five looming several kilometers off *Normandy*'s beam—the guardian of the jump gates and Terra's in-your-face presence at this, the nexus of interstellar travel. Although that might be changing, now that the jump gate to Centauria had collapsed and the network of secret Centauri gates had been revealed in all the major systems.

Looking out at the blast marks scarring the base's kilometer-long hull and the wreckage of Terran ships still littering the area, Jack had a feeling an awful lot was about to change.

The Centauri fleet that had besieged Astral Base Five—and held hostage its thousands of people as insurance against a full Terran counterattack—had fled, scattering through the other jump gates to colonies sympathetic to the cause. It seemed that the colonies had been colluding for some time, and had just been waiting for an excuse to lash out at Terra.

But now Terra had a new weapon with which to keep the peace, and the media was already calling it the Dark Bomb. Images of Centauri ships being sucked down and torn apart had been broadcast to all the worlds, presented as if this bomb was a natural product of advanced Terran technology. Its specs had been labeled "ultra-top secret" and spirited away to Astral Intelligence.

Jack doubted he would ever see them again.

His companions looked out over the scene, lost in their own thoughts. None of them had actually spoken about just how close they came to getting smeared across the fourth dimension, but they'd all seen the visuals of the blinding flash, and of *Rapier* breaking apart as she tumbled out of the jump gate dragging a ripple of dark matter behind her.

Thank God they'd all been in spacesuits. The entire EF had mobilized to recover them. Personally, Jack believed that their incredible speed had been what had given them the necessary mass to keep the gate open long enough to squeeze through. But he had no equations to support that hypothesis, and felt no need to conduct further trials.

He took a long pull of his beer and switched his mind to other subjects.

"So do you think we'll go home before they redeploy us?"

"Probably," Thomas said. "Expeditionary Force 15 is going to have to be disbanded, and every ship needs a refit. It'll take time to sort out where to send everybody, so I expect some shore leave all round."

"I'll have my leave request to you today."

Thomas sipped at his own beer. "I suppose you should, before somebody figures out that the ship I command doesn't actually exist anymore." Thomas no longer wore the star of lieutenant commander above his two gold bars—a personal choice on his part.

"The timing couldn't be better for me," Katja said. "My father's birthday is coming up, and I'd hate to miss the annual pilgrimage." She seemed remarkably serene about it. Jack had heard her speak of her family several times since their return to Terra, and each time she had sounded less tense. Not yet enthusiastic, but something more than merely resigned.

Just serene.

"I have to find out if Soma's coming to Earth, or if I'm expected to present myself on Ganymede," Thomas said. "Either way, I'm sure I'm in for quite a parade around the families."

Jack didn't know what he was going to do if they sent him home. Go visit his folks, he supposed. Maybe find a nice girl like Thomas had.

"I need to see a good plastic surgeon," he said without thinking. Thomas and Katja both glanced at him, then quickly averted their eyes. He instantly regretted the comment. He looked around the star lounge for a distraction.

"Hey," he said, "looks like the brass are having a party."

His companions followed his gaze toward the bar and saw a cluster of senior officers gathering to collect from the glasses of wine being poured. There must have been two dozen of them, as well as some civilians. There was general mingling, but he noticed that one officer was standing apart, facing two of the civilians.

"Looks like the commodore has found the media," Thomas said.

"Guess who won't be far behind," Katja offered.

Sure enough, moments later a familiar figure with long, curly black hair separated herself from the crowd and hovered near Chandler. Very quickly the newsmen noticed her and invited her to join the interview. Jack watched in sick fascination as Breeze smiled and chatted for the cameras.

He noticed also the look of cool dismissal Chandler immediately threw at her, and her subtle but quick withdrawal. Jack reveled in an unusual moment of delicious *schadenfreude*. Apparently it *was* possible to resist Charity Brisebois's charms.

He was so engrossed that he almost missed another very familiar female commander walking up to their cluster of comfy chairs.

"I think I see the officers of *Rapier*," she called out, "but maybe gravimetric interference is clouding my judgment."

Thomas leapt to his feet and Jack quickly followed suit. Katja couldn't move so fast, and merely looked up.

"Commander Avernell," Thomas said, shaking her hand warmly. "Thank you again for covering our retreat. And for offering to stay behind with us."

"Think nothing of it, Mr. Kane. I figured our two ships have been through enough together, we could survive being stranded in the heart of the enemy." She smiled. "Plus I know you fast-attack types. You were going for broke no matter what I said. Good thing I gave you my best young pilot."

Thomas stepped aside and gestured grandly to Jack. "The hero of the hour, ma'am."

Jack still had trouble looking his former captain in the eye, even when she was smiling at him. He shook her outstretched hand with a mumbled greeting.

"Mr. Mallory, I know you don't actually belong to my unit anymore, but I'm happy to put in a good word for you. I know the commandant of the fighter school quite well, and the season for the new course start is coming up fast."

Jack felt his heart skip a beat. Fighter school? He tried not to look too stunned as Avernell waited for his response. Over her shoulder he saw Thomas give him the thumbs-up. But then he glanced at Katja and saw her doubtful expression.

For a brief moment he hated her for it, but her look spoke volumes, and he knew she was right.

"Thanks, ma'am, really. But I think I have a bit of an aptitude for ASW—I might stick with it for a while."

Avernell was clearly surprised at the response, but her smile broadened.

"I'll be keeping my eye on you, Mr. Mallory." She excused herself then, muttering about having to go smile for the cameras.

As she left, Jack and his colleagues hunkered down low in their seats to avoid any chance of being dragged into the media spotlight. Once Jack would have loved to be in the news, but he suddenly had no taste for it.

Not that their presence went entirely unnoticed. Several senior officers made their way over to make polite conversation, including that scary, female Corps commander who ignored him completely and even seemed to make Thomas nervous. Katja actually struggled out of her chair to greet this woman—Commander Vici—even though there seemed to be little warmth in their exchange.

Nothing even resembling a compliment passed Vici's lips, but when Katja sat down again after the conversation, she practically glowed. Jack sipped his beer and just figured there was a lot he didn't understand about troopers.

Their drinks were done and they were just working up the energy to leave when Commander Brisebois finally swooped down on them.

"Hey guys," she said with a dazzling smile. "I had no idea you were hiding over here!"

Nobody stood, but Thomas at least turned in his chair toward her.

"Hello, ma'am."

She slapped him playfully on the shoulder. "Oh, Thomas, call me Breeze! I'm still just the same person."

"That's true."

She didn't seem to catch his meaning, and turned her smile on Katja.

"Katja, you look great. I hope you're going to get a long rest now."

When Katja didn't even answer, Breeze turned her full attention to Jack. He had to admit that he still thought she was gorgeous, and he couldn't stop a smile from forming.

"Jack, handsome as ever! We'll have to meet up when we get back to Earth."

Was she serious? He felt a stirring in his loins.

"Uhhh, sure," he said. "When?"

She shook her head, letting out a long sigh.

"So hard to say. I've been just so busy since we got back. The diplomats are all screaming at each other, and I can't produce information fast enough for them. I'm sure you've been busy, too."

Jack shrugged and glanced at the others.

"I've been learning to walk again," Katja said.

"I'm just happy to be breathing," Thomas added.

Their candid statements broke the charm spell, and Jack suddenly saw that Breeze's beautiful smile didn't really touch her eyes. She was a whirlwind in their oasis of calm, and he found the disturbance unwelcome.

"It's good to see you, Breeze," he said, "but we were just going."

The brilliance of her smile faded just for a moment. "Of course. Get some rest. I'll see you around."

And then she was gone.

Thomas leaned forward. "So, where *are* we going, Jack?"

He looked at Thomas, then at Katja, then out toward the stars.

"Home."

ACKNOWLEDGEMENTS

No book is the work of a single person. This tale would never have seen the light of day if not for the following folks: my fellow authors Steven Erikson and Mary Rosenblum, my agent Howard Morhaim, my editors Steve Saffel and Marge Gilkes, my beta-readers Jeela Jones, Craig Piccolo, Erin Stinson, Richard Coles, Brian Jalonen, and my beloved wife, Emma.

"Force, and fraud, are in war the two cardinal virtues."
—Thomas Hobbes, *Leviathan*, 1651

ABOUT THE AUTHOR

Bennett R. Coles served fourteen years as an officer in the Royal Canadian Navy and earned his salt on all classes of ship, from command of a small training ship to warfare director of a powerful combatant to bridge officer of a lumbering supply ship. He toiled as a staff officer in the War on Terror, and served two tours with the United Nations in Syria and Lebanon.

He has maintained an interest in military affairs since his retirement from active service and he makes his home in Victoria, Canada with his wife and family.

GHOSTS OF WAR
Bennett R. Coles

The Astral Force mission to Centauri was a success, and the colonial rebellion was crushed. But victory came at a great cost to the Earth, and those who fought.

Lieutenant Katja Emmes is dealing with post-traumatic stress disorder as the result of her part in the war, and with internal politics that threaten to tear her family apart. Lieutenant Commander Thomas Kane has been given a pivotal mission—one that may prove a valuable stepping-stone, as long as he retains the support of his political patron. And Sublieutenant Jack Mallory has been rebuilt by surgeons, having nearly died in combat.

Kane and Mallory are assigned to the research station that is developing the Dark Bomb, Terra's newest weapon, nicknamed "The Peacemaker." But the greatest threat won't come from outside of the solar system. For a Centauri agent has been planted on Earth, with a mission that will lead to widespread death and destruction. But Kete Obadele watched as his entire family was killed in the assault on Centauri, and he is determined to avenge the deaths that haunt his nightmares.

AVAILABLE 2016

TITANBOOKS.COM

MARCH OF WAR
Bennett R. Coles

The Centauri terrorist was stopped, but not before he caused widespread death and destruction on Earth. This leads to an escalating war between Earth and Centauri.

Lieutenant Jack Mallory is on the front lines, leading a flight of Hawks into the battle zone. His mission is to rescue the demoted Sublieutenant Thomas Kane, whose Astral forces are under heavy fire and in danger of being overrun.

The Astral Force must establish a bridgehead in Centauri territory, where they will place a jump gate in anticipation of a new invasion. Lieutenant Katja Emmes works behind the scenes, to keep the Centauri from learning of the plan before it can be carried out successfully.

AVAILABLE 2017

For more fantastic fiction, author events, exclusive
excerpts, competitions, limited editions and more

VISIT OUR WEBSITE
titanbooks.com

LIKE US ON FACEBOOK
facebook.com/titanbooks

FOLLOW US ON TWITTER
@TitanBooks

EMAIL US
readerfeedback@titanemail.com